AULD FANG SYNE
Twice Bitten: Book Seven

CRYSTAL-RAIN LOVE

Copyright © 2023 Crystal-Rain Love

All rights reserved.

ISBN: 9798373522052

ACKNOWLEDGMENTS

It's been a rough year. Thanks to my readers for having patience after this one had to be pushed back.
Thanks to Greg Bennett for the editing and for the reminders that I can't push myself too hard after getting out of the emergency room. My anxiety and lack of patience tend to make me forget that. ;) Oh, and for letting me make fun of you in my books.
Thanks to Danielle Muething for always doing such an amazing job on narration.
Thanks to Christle Gray for being my rant and rave buddy.
Of course, thanks to Rome Kimbrough for being the inspiration for one of my most-loved characters and not killing me for the things I've done to that character. Tee hee hee…
Thanks to T.L., my writing drill sergeant and bestest work buddy. I wouldn't make it through the day job without my bitchin' and complainin' buddy.
Thank you MANUELA SERRA for such beautiful cover art!

CHAPTER ONE

"They're not balls!"

"They look like balls to me," Daniel said, holding Angel's latest culinary creation up by the small end.

"Ask Danni," Ginger suggested. "She's the testicle expert."

I took my eyes off the couple I'd been watching at the bar to give her a look. The four of us were sitting in a booth at The Midnight Rider. It was late, and the bar wasn't packed, but doing a decent amount of business for the after Christmas season. Mostly singles, subdued and a little depressed. I supposed the end of a year did that to some people. Those who hadn't done the things they'd planned, hadn't achieved the dreams they'd planned to achieve by a specific date. I'd spent many a New Year's Eve scarfing down Ben and Jerry's Cherry Garcia ice cream while lamenting all the resolutions I'd failed to fulfill. This year was going to be different.

I was happy. I was in the best relationship of my life. Not that I'd had many relationships, but Rider was amazing. Caring, sexy, powerful, and working on the whole overprotective, controlling thing. I had great friends like Ginger, Angel, and Daniel. Although I now knew for sure that Daniel was a little in love with me and that kind of sucked because he was the best friend I'd ever had and I never wanted to see him hurt, or worse, be the one to hurt him. Or lose him. I could *not* lose him.

And Angel was my blood donor, there for my dietary needs, as Rider often tried to remind me. But I thought of her more as an adopted little sister, which was nice to have considering my biological sister has been suspended in a coma-like state since she'd tried to kill me in a fit of jealousy after being turned by Rider, which happened at my request after she'd been shot at her wedding. Yeah, it was totally my fault she'd gotten shot since those hunters had been there to kill me and Rider, and I was pretty sure the specific bullets that hit her had been fired at me, but trying to kill me and steal my man as payback was going too far.

But let's get back to the good things I had going on in my life. I had this job. I worked security for Rider. Mostly, I just worked security in the bar, like now. I glanced over at the couple who had caught my attention, but still didn't see anything obvious causing the weird sensation in my gut. I had those now. Ginger called them my Gibbs powers. She had a thing for *NCIS*, ever since she saw Wilmer Valderrama and discovered he was the one man hot enough to break through what she called her lesbian force field.

The job was nice, even though it made zero use of the college degree I'd worked so hard for and still owed money on. Come to think of it, Rider probably paid off what was left of my student loans. I hadn't seen a bill in months and that's just the type of thing he would do. No matter how many times I'd told him not to. The last job I had that made use of my degree wasn't all that great anyway. I mean, I loved the creativity of advertising, and I liked having my own cubicle and the feeling when I won over a new client with my creative talents, but my former boss turned out to be a complete bastard who'd tried to rape me. I'd had to kill him, which was bad because he was just a human. An asshole of a human, but still just a human. Killing humans opens up a whole can of worms and takes more to clean up, so it was generally frowned upon.

My new job lets me kill actual monsters like wererats and demons. And the absolute worst type of monster: pedophiles. Yes, those could be, and often were, humans, but Rider would never frown at the slaying of a pedophile.

Okay, so I was supposed to refrain from actually killing anyone while watching the bar. I was free to crack heads and break limbs, though, so that was fun. Rider allowed me to help in his interrogation room though and I had a tendency to find myself fangs-deep in paranormal clusterfucks fairly regularly and it was kind of an unspoken rule that anything went as long as the bad guys were the only ones to die, however viciously that might occur. I usually go for the testicles. I'm not sure why. I just get mad and oops, there's my blade in some guy's nuts.

Okay, so my life was kind of a shit-show, my friends were a pretty motley crew, my job was kind of bizarre, but I was happy. As happy as a vampire-succubus hybrid still trying to come to terms with both her halves could be. All I knew was I would not be spending New Year's Eve crying into a carton of Ben and Jerry's. Because I still couldn't eat ice cream.

Who was I kidding? My life was shit.

The air shifted in the room, and I knew Rider was near, having returned from a visit to his blood donor, and a little smile curved my mouth because I remembered I'd be spending New Year's Eve with him. My hot, powerful, master vampire boyfriend. Who needs Ben and Jerry's when you have Rider Knight? My life wasn't shit. It was *the* shit.

"What's that slutty smile about?" Ginger narrowed her eyes.

I blinked, snatched out of the beginning of a wicked

fantasy as heat flooded my face. "What? What slutty smile? I don't have a slutty smile." I felt Daniel's gaze on me and turned to see him still holding the chocolate-covered peanut butter treat Angel had made for the crew. The chocolate had started to melt around his fingertips. Looking at the oddly shaped heart, too narrow to really be a heart, and the curved edges too droopy to really fit the idea shape too, I remembered Ginger's previous comment and the argument Daniel and Angel had been having, and cringed.

"I hate to say it, Angel, but those do look like chocolate coated testicles."

Daniel chuckled and set the candy on the edge of the plate holding what was left of the giant triple bacon cheeseburger and fries he'd been working on when Ginger had arrived with Angel in tow, bearing treats.

"They do not! You're just saying that because dragon-breath said it." She gave Daniel a death glare, but the dragon shifter continued wiping his fingers off with a napkin and winked at her, unbothered.

His gaze shifted over to the door and he grinned. "Rome hasn't seen these yet. Let's ask him."

I looked toward the front door where Rome was posted on guard duty for the night and saw him speaking with a man who was about to leave. Once he finished his short conversation with the man and watched him leave, he scanned the bar. His eyebrows drew down in a frown as he noticed us where we sat staring at him, and I was sure he picked up on the mischievous look in Daniel's eyes. He scanned the bar once more and headed straight to us.

"What's up?"

Daniel picked up the chocolate and peanut butter treat and held it toward Rome. "What does this look like to you?"

"My nuts," Rome answered without a moment's hesitation, sending Daniel and Ginger into a fit of laughter.

"You're not holding it the right way," Angel said,

grabbing the treat. She turned it so that the two curved edges were on top, and the part that was supposed to be pointed but wasn't quite there was on the bottom. "Now, what does it look like?"

Rome angled his head to the side as if thoroughly studying the object presented to him and giving it careful thought before answering. "My nuts on a roller coaster."

Daniel choked on the beer he'd just taken a drink of and Ginger's chuckles turned into a full round of laughter, complete with tears.

"You're all jerks," Angel muttered and dropped the unfortunate looking treat into the box she'd brought in to share.

"I'll still eat one," Rome said, reaching for the box.

"Not on your diet, buddy." Daniel grabbed the box and pulled it toward himself, guarding it.

"Man, I've been eating all that crappy health food for—"

"Days," Daniel said, cutting him off. "You've been eating actual decent food for a matter of days and have somehow managed to be bitching about it for months."

"I don't believe that's possible," I said, still listening to the conversation while observing the couple at the bar.

"You'd think it wouldn't be, but believe me, the man has been bitching for months. Or at least he's succeeded in fitting several months' worth of bitching into under a week's worth of days. It's a real talent. Not one I particularly appreciate, but still. It's a talent."

"You're a jackass, Puff. You'd be bitching too if you couldn't eat whatever you wanted. Rider's being too strict with this diet. Eating a burger isn't going to kill me."

"You just had a giant shitberg cut out of your colon," Daniel reminded him.

"Yeah, and now I'm all good. And that was a fluke. You eat burgers and fries and steak and all the things I eat and you don't have any issues."

"I also eat vegetables and drink water," Daniel pointed

out.

"Fine. I'll wash those down with a gallon of water and eat a lima bean for dessert. Hand them over before shit gets ugly."

Daniel laughed.

"What's so funny, scale-ass?"

"Oh, nothing. It's just amusing watching you get so hangry over chocolate covered testicles."

"They're not testicles!" Angel said loud enough to attract the attention of the people in the booth next to ours.

"Laugh away, jackass. I'd eat your nuts right now if they were made of peanut butter and chocolate and I don't care who knows it. This is too much. I need real food."

"I don't think peanut butter and chocolate qualify as real food," Daniel said through a round of laughter, ignoring the curious looks from the people in the booth next to us. "And sorry, bro. My testicles are made of steel and cocaine."

Ginger and I rolled our eyes before looking at the cocky dragon shifter. "Because they're so addictive?" I asked.

"You know it." He swallowed. Hard. "I mean, um, yeah. Because they're so addictive. It's just a joke. I didn't mean to imply that *you* would know that my, uh—"

"We figured," Ginger said, picking up on the sudden awkwardness between us.

"The air over here just got really weird. I don't like weird air," Rome muttered before folding his massive arms over his tree trunk of a chest. "Fine. Keep your stupid chocolate peanut butter testicles to yourself, you testicle Nazi. I'll sweet-talk something out of the—"

It always amused me how Rome's rich brown skin could drop three shades when he got caught, like he'd just gotten caught then by my sexy sire, who was also his boss. Rome swallowed and rolled his eyes to the heavens, where I was sure he directed a prayer before turning around to face the tall man standing behind him in black pants and a deep sapphire button-down shirt that brought out the matching color in his eyes. Eyes that could be just as terrifying as they were intoxicating. Rider's so dark brown it appeared black hair was pulled back into a ponytail at the nape of his neck in his usual style, adding another layer of severity to the unamused expression adorning his handsome face.

"Why are you yelling about chocolate peanut butter testicles in my bar?"

"I wasn't... I mean, Daniel wouldn't share his... his..."

"Daniel wouldn't share his testicles with you?"

"Ah, geez," Daniel groaned and pushed the box toward Angel as Ginger and I bit our bottom lips to keep from laughing out loud. "Technically, they're Angel's testicles."

"The girl has testicles now? And they're covered in chocolate?"

"They're hearts!" Angel grabbed one of the treats out of the box and held it up to show Rider. "Can't you people tell a heart from a pair of balls?"

Rider looked at the treat and shook his head before returning his attention to Rome. "I'm not going to remind you that you're a grown man who should be embarrassed to be whining over candy, but I will remind you that you're on a diet and everyone here knows it. Everyone here reports to me. If you did succeed in sweet-talking someone here into giving you something not approved by me, not only would I kick your ass, but theirs as well. You wouldn't want to be the reason someone here got my foot up their ass, would you?"

"No, boss. Although I'd make an exception for one or two." He speared Daniel with a narrow-eyed look and got a raised middle finger from the dragon shifter in return.

"Children," Rider muttered. "I'm surrounded by overgrown children. No more outside food in my bar."

"Even after Danni regains the ability to eat chocolate

cupcakes?" Daniel asked with a knowing smirk, referencing my memorable reaction to the first chocolate cupcake I'd eaten after turning, thanks to a spell that unfortunately didn't last nearly long enough.

"When Danni regains the ability to eat chocolate cupcakes without getting sick, they'll be added to the menu." Rider grinned as he looked down at me, and I didn't miss the heat that flitted through his eyes. "Then again, it would probably be best if we just kept a private supply upstairs."

"Seriously," Ginger said. "What's the big deal about the way this woman eats a cupcake that you all feel compelled to keep bringing it up?"

"It was like porn," they both answered her, perfectly in sync.

Ginger blinked and refocused on me. "What did you do to that cupcake, girlfriend?"

"Nothing," I said, taking my time to glare at both men, which only seemed to amuse them, before continuing. "I just ate the thing."

"Yeah, but she ate it very enthusiastically," Daniel said, an impish smile tugging at his mouth. "A hell of a lot more enthusiastically than that sad-ass kiss she slapped on you before throwing her guts up."

"Go roast yourself, Daniel. That was not a proper representation of my sexual prowess."

"Sexual prowess?" Daniel laughed until tears formed in the corners of his eyes. "Ah, face it, honey. A cupcake turned her on more than you."

Ginger lunged forward with a growl, but Rider grabbed the back of the collar to her leather jacket before she could make it all the way over the table and effortlessly plucked her out of the booth. "Wait for me in my office," he ordered as he set her on her feet next to him.

"But. He—"

Rider held a hand up, palm side out, directly in front of her face. "You're not in trouble. I have a job for you. Go."

"Yes, sir," she muttered. She made sure to shoot a parting glare Daniel's way and discreetly flipped him off, showing off her newest shade of bright red nail polish before she made her way to Rider's office.

"A solo job?" I studied him, checking for any signs he was holding something back from me, which he often did. I knew he did it for my own protection, but that didn't mean it didn't chafe. He didn't exactly look guilty, but something was off, and he'd taken longer than usual to return from visiting his donor.

"Yes. Ginger often works solo, and from what I can tell right now, she isn't really needed out here." He made a show of looking around the room before returning his gaze to where Daniel and I sat side by side in the booth. "I'm assuming you're both sitting over here because you have the bar well under control and you're not just loafing around on the job."

"Actually, I'm undercover," I said, and gave him my best snooty face. "I'm blending in."

"Hmm. If blending in is your objective, you might not want to sit by people arguing so animatedly about chocolate covered peanut butter ball sacs."

"They're hearts!" Angel said, but quickly averted her gaze and hunkered down in her seat once Rider cut a look her way. As handsome as he was, he was also big and scary, and Angel didn't seem to know how to take him.

"Keep them out of my bar." He looked over at Rome, the big guy still standing close to him. "You're supposed to be on front door duty for the night, right where everyone can keep an eye on you and make sure you don't put anything in your mouth that doesn't belong there."

"Really? This is like being a kid," Rome whined. "Man, I been babysat ever since I got out of the hospital. This is getting—" He shut up as Rider stepped into his personal space, crowding him, with an expression that suggested he didn't give a damn about Rome's complaints. "I'm just sayin'… I don't have to be watched twenty-four hours a day, seven days a week. Man, I can't even wipe my ass in my own apartment without an audience."

Rider turned his head to look at Daniel. "Really? You watch him wipe his ass?"

"No," Daniel replied after swallowing the last big chunk of his burger. "But I do check the bathroom before I leave him alone in there, seeing as how I found a box of Little Debbie's wedged between the back of the toilet tank and the wall. Crafty bastard planned ahead for if he was released with diet restrictions. He also hid candy bars in the vents, but forgot about them and turned on the heat as soon as he got home from being released. Melted every one of them and now he's forced to smell the sweet aroma I still can't get out of the apartment while munching on carrots and bran muffins."

"I hate you, Puff."

Rider sighed and pointed to the door. "Go to your post and think about the things you've done."

Rome walked away like a petulant child to return to his assigned post, muttering to himself all the way. I pitied the fool who got on his bad side coming through the door. A hungry, deprived Rome was not a joy to be around.

Rider watched Rome until the big lug made it to his post, then turned toward me and jerked his head to the side, gesturing for me to get up and follow him. He rested his palm along my lower back once I stood from the booth and fell into step with him, the heat of his body spreading into mine, warm and welcome.

We didn't stop until we reached the hall in the back corner that led to the bathrooms, and I made sure when we did, I angled myself so I could still see the couple I'd been observing at the bar. "What's wrong?"

His eyebrows rose slightly. "What makes you think something is wrong?"

"You pulled Ginger aside for a solo job, you took longer than usual to visit your donor, and now you've pulled me aside to tell me something out of earshot of my donor and bodyguard."

"Maybe I just wanted to get you alone for a moment," he said, his voice deep and low as he lowered his head and pulled me to him before covering my mouth with his own and delving deep inside, teasing me with lips, tongue, and a little fang until we were eventually forced to come up for air. "You won't be going to see Nannette tonight. She's coming here."

"I knew something was wrong."

Rider hefted out a small, mildly annoyed sigh as he straightened. "Just because she's coming here doesn't mean anything's wrong."

"Rider." I leveled a stern look at him. "What's going on? What job do you have for Ginger?"

It took him a moment to respond, as if he were debating whether he should, but we'd both been working on communicating with each other better, so he eventually gave in. "The donor who was on rotation for my next feed was gone when I arrived at her apartment."

"On rotation?"

"I don't drink consecutively from the same donor. I have them on a rotation. Donating blood to me is their job and they're supposed to always be available should I need to drop in or send for them. If something comes up and they need to leave for something while they're next in rotation, they're supposed to call in and notify my team of their whereabouts."

A rotation. Geez. Not for the first time, I caught myself wondering just how many donors Rider had, but didn't dare ask. There were just some pictures I didn't want in my head, and Rider's mouth on other women was right up there at the top. It was bad enough I'd seen him drinking from one's throat shortly after I'd been turned.

"Do you still drink from their throats?" I blurted out the question before I could think better of it.

"No. Not since we've been together. I know you wouldn't like that." He gently stroked the side of my face with his knuckles. "They only give me blood, and only from the wrist now. I've never slept with any of them, not even before I met you. You have no reason to be so bothered by my use of their blood."

"I know." I glanced at the couple at the bar before shoving my hands into the pockets of my jeans and leaned back against the wall. "I don't know why it still bothers me so much. Just the thought of your mouth on some woman's flesh…" I fought down the violent impulse such a thought provoked. "It gets to me. Maybe because when I drink from you, we almost always end up naked and winded."

"That's you and me. And you forget, I've watched you drink straight from Rome and Daniel." He lent a little bit of growl to the latter's name. "Drinking from my donors is no different than when you drink from them. Drinking from them isn't anything sexual. Right?"

"Right," I said, probably a little too fast, and hoped he didn't notice. "You're absolutely right."

And I meant that. He was right. Drinking blood was what we had to do for survival. While I could drink from him, he had to replenish what was taken, and I couldn't ask him to drink only from men. If I couldn't trust him to drink from women without letting things get sexual, I didn't deserve the trust he gave me to drink from men. And he had way more reason not to trust me, thanks to my succubus venom.

I was still working on my insecurity issues and apparently, there was still quite a bit of work to be done. I remembered what had brought up the donors and got back to the point. "So, what does your donor missing her shift or whatever have to do with Ginger?"

"These women have a pretty sweet deal. Free rent and utilities and a nice paycheck, and all they have to do is supply me with blood when needed. It's not the type of gig someone just risks losing because they want to go out and do something."

"You think something bad happened to her?"

He nodded. "It's possible. Some of my donors' pimps were also their dealers. They've all been clean for years now, but addiction is a powerful thing. She could have slipped up or she could have gotten in touch with someone from her past, which breaks our contract, but I still need to make sure she's all right. The same contract that says they're supposed to be available to me when needed also states I'm supposed to keep them safe."

"You take that responsibility very seriously," I said, admiration swelling in my chest despite my previous insecurity.

"Of course. These women provide me with what I need to live and keep the existence of our kind a secret. Or, at least, I hope they do. With Julie unaccountable, it's hard to say what she's done, but I would have never suspected her of betraying me. I've saved quite a few prostitutes in my time, but I haven't turned them all into blood donors. Only the ones who seemed the most serious about doing whatever it took to get free of that life and never return to it, but again… you can never be too sure when you're dealing with someone who struggles with addiction."

I nodded, seeing his point. "So, you're assigning Ginger to track this Julie down?" My stomach grew a little sour as I mentioned the woman's name. Having a name made her a little less faceless blob, more actual person. It was bad enough I had actually seen his donor, Billie. One donor being real to me was more than enough for my tastes. But again, that was my insecurity talking, and I needed to suck it up.

"Yes. After everything you've gone through this month, watching the bar is more than enough work for you. Of course, you could just take a break and relax…"

"I want to work. I'm perfectly fine." My tone was firm. I could understand Rider's concern. It couldn't have been easy for him to watch me smash my head into a mirror and break my own bones while internally fighting with the spirit of the evil old hag who'd gotten into my head after he'd killed her. But I needed to work. "I can't just sit around, Rider, and relaxing isn't even a possibility. If I had nothing to do but sit around, I would never stop worrying about Pacitti or Angel's mom, or my mom, for that matter. Working right now, even if it's just providing security for the bar on boring nights, is what's keeping me sane right now."

"Well, we definitely want to keep you sane." He grinned. "With all the trouble you manage to get into without even trying, having you go a little nutty would be a catastrophe of apocalyptic proportions."

"Hardy har. Hilarious." I fought the smile tugging at my mouth. "I could help Ginger. Daniel would go with us, of course. We make a good team on investigations."

"You do, but not on this investigation. If Julie isn't available because she willingly decided to go AWOL, she's probably gone back to drugs and back to hanging around her old acquaintances. I never give my donors cash. She knows I can track her if she spends anything in the bank account that is monitored by my team so if she wants to be back out there on the street and not be found the minute she makes a purchase, she's going to need to get her hands on some money I can't trace."

"You think she'd go back to her old job?"

"Her old job or her old friends, and eventually those old friends would convince her to go back to work. They won't support her for long without her pulling in some money. I need someone out there who can blend in and find her, if that's what she's doing."

I felt my eyebrows shoot up. "You're going to have Ginger go undercover as a hooker to find your blood donor?"

"If that's what it takes. Ginger will know if going undercover is necessary."

I frowned. "Well, that could be dangerous, couldn't it?

AULD FANG SYNE

She shouldn't be out there alone. I can go undercover with her. Daniel could be our—"

Rider silenced me with a fingertip over my lips. "Danni. You can't even say the word hooker without your lip curling, and I don't think anyone but you even uses the word hooker anymore. No one would believe you were a sex worker due to the way you would be looking down your nose at the other girls, and they definitely wouldn't believe that rainbow-haired goofball was a pimp. I don't think you could talk him into going undercover as a prostitute either."

Something in Rider's tone raised my hackles. "I don't look down my nose at anyone. And if I did, it's not like we're talking about women who work in an office or any other honest type of work."

"Danni, you kill people while working. We both do. It's illegal just as prostitution is, and we can debate all night about the morality of it, but we're all just doing what we have to do to survive, aren't we? No woman ever grew up with the dream of selling her body to avoid starvation or planned on getting so addicted to a substance that she would risk her life every night to do whatever it took to get her next fix. Even if a woman did choose to accept money for sex as her way of paying the bills without being forced or acting out of desperation, is that woman harming you in any way?"

"No," I muttered. "I guess not. It just… it seems gross to me. But that doesn't make me an awful person for not approving of it."

"I didn't say it did and you don't have to approve of it, but maybe you shouldn't be so quick to condemn other women for what they do. You're not awful for thinking the way you do, but you could be an even better version of you if you lost some of that judgmental thinking." He lowered his voice. "There are quite a few people who might think pretty badly of you if they knew what you were capable of. There are people who would label us both as psychotic killers. Monsters. Evil. Do you really want to judge others when they could do the same of you?"

I folded my arms and shook my head. "No. You make a good point."

"Ginger will be fine working this job on her own. One unfamiliar face poking around asking questions about Julie will be less suspicious than a pair, and she knows how to blend in. Also, she's a vampire, so it's not like I'm sending some defenseless, untrained woman out there to get hurt. Pity the idiot who tries to pick her up for the night." He kissed my forehead. "Now. Want to tell me why you keep watching that couple over at the bar?"

I blinked, unaware Rider had picked up on my continuous glancing over that way. "I'm not sure. I just have a feeling they need to be watched."

"They?"

"She," I said, referring to the brunette. There was nothing about her that really stood out. Her hair was an unremarkable shade of brown that fell straight to just below her shoulders. The fuzzy pink sweater she wore did nothing to accentuate any curves she may or may not have had, and it fell past her hips to cover any shape her leggings may have brought attention to. She wore minimal makeup and glasses with very basic frames. "I don't know why, but I just feel like she needs to be watched. Just in case."

"Just in case what?"

I looked at the man with her. He was about five feet, nine inches tall, with an average build. Not a lot of muscle, but not scrawny or weak. His dark hair was buzzed so low I could see scalp, and a diamond sparkled in his left earlobe. His nose was straight and pointed at the tip, his dark eyes almond-shaped and very focused on the woman. Dressed in a dark gray Nike sweatshirt and jeans, he looked like any other average guy who frequented the bar. There was nothing menacing about him. Still… I had the strongest urge to ensure the woman was safe.

"In case she needs someone to watch her back." I shrugged. "I'm not sure what I'm picking up. They both seem human to me."

"Because they both are," Rider said, eyeing the couple for a moment before turning his curious gaze to me. "I'm not getting anything predatory off the man, and she looks like she's enjoying his company."

"I know. That's why I'm just watching. Just in case."

Rider frowned. "Is this another one of those gut feelings you've been having?"

I nodded.

"Damn," he muttered, turning back to look at the couple just as Nannette entered the bar. Seeing her, he turned back toward me. "Nannette's here, so maybe she can help you figure out what's going on. I have to brief Ginger. Do me a favor and don't follow that woman home so you can go toe to toe with another evil Santa Claus."

"What are the odds of that happening again?"

"With you, I'm afraid to think of the odds on things like that." He brushed a quick kiss over my mouth and stepped out of the hallway with me. "Speaking of donors, try to keep yours out of here, especially with outside food that causes disturbances."

"It wasn't that big of a disturbance, and she gets bored."

"It's your job to compensate her with food and shelter, not entertainment," Rider said. "I've told you before that you're too attached to her."

"Hey, you're the one sending Ginger out to track down one of your missing donors. I believe I detected a little concern."

"Yes, because it is my duty to keep my donors safe and I don't take that lightly. I will use all means necessary to locate her and ensure her safety. However, I am not attached to any of my donors. Therefore, if Julie has in fact run off of her own choice and has betrayed me, I won't hesitate to do what needs to be done to rectify that betrayal, nor will I lose any sleep over it." He squeezed my hand before letting go so he could exit the bar through the back door separating the bar from the rest of the building where he lived and where he ran his security business. "Try to stay out of trouble."

"Don't I always?"

Rider rolled his eyes and muttered something that didn't sound very positive under his breath before he disappeared through the back door. I could hear Kutya whining excitedly beyond the door, back from his walk with Hank and ready for a big belly rub that Rider would pretend like he couldn't stand doing, but secretly enjoyed as much as the big pup did.

By the time I started moving across the room toward the booth where I'd left Daniel and Angel, Nannette had just torn herself away from Rome. I was starting to think the big guy had a serious crush on her. She rolled her eyes as she left him, cluing me in that she did not feel the same way.

Daniel stood from the booth just as Nannette and I reached it, and he frowned in the vampire's direction. "I thought Danni was going to see you later at the hospital."

"Change of plans," Nannette said. "I'm seeing her now. Here."

Daniel looked back at Angel before turning his attention back to me. "Do I need to watch the kid while you two go downstairs or—"

"I'm not a kid!"

"It's so annoying when she does that," Daniel breathed the words out so softly they didn't qualify as a whisper.

I looked back over at the couple at the bar, found them exactly as they'd been a moment before. Side by side, close. Talking without any sense of anything being wrong. "We'll stay up here, but we'll go to that booth that just cleared in the back corner. Angel, try not to bring attention to your, uh, chocolate hearts. Rider's being a little grumpy about outside food in here tonight."

"I noticed. What's his deal?"

"I'm really not sure. Just make sure you don't let Rome have any of those. We'll take you home once we're off duty if Ginger can't do it before she starts the assignment Rider just pulled her for. It's almost time for shift change, so either way, you don't have that long to wait around."

"You got chocolate in there?" Nannette said, eying the box on the table in front of Angel.

Angel opened the box to reveal the poorly crafted hearts. The corners of Nannette's mouth twitched, but she didn't say a word as she reached into the box, selected a treat, and took a bite. "Mmm. Thanks."

Nannette was a goddess. Tall, graceful, but lethal. Beautiful with flawless, deep brown skin and warm brown eyes. Her dark hair was shaved down close to her scalp. I'd never be able to pull off such a look, but it fit her perfectly. She had the features for it. Feminine, yet very bold. Any makeup she wore was always with a soft touch and in neutral colors, not that she needed the aid of cosmetics. Her lashes were long and curled, free of mascara, her lips plump and full, the kind women paid money for. She was small-chested like me, but not without curves, which she accentuated in the snug jeans she wore tucked into black leather boots and the matching leather jacket belted at her narrow waist.

Nannette was who I wanted to be when I grew up and got over my issues. Or who I wanted to be like. The woman oozed confidence. She had an air about her that always made me think of her as royalty. She also had an air about her that said she'd kill you in a heartbeat if you looked at her in the wrong tone of face, so I tried really hard not to do that. I used to think she was my enemy, but we'd become pretty close to friends. Not that she'd admit it, but at least she didn't seem to want to smash me under her boot like a bug anymore. At least I was pretty sure she didn't. About eighty-five percent sure.

"If that's all right with you," I quickly added, glancing

back over at the bar. "I'm still technically on duty watching the bar with Daniel, and I wanted to talk to you about something before we start throwing punches."

"That's fine." Nannette took another bite of the chocolate peanut butter treat that I tried really hard not to covet, and nodded her head, gesturing for me to lead the way.

"I'll keep my eye on Angel while doing my walk around," Daniel assured me before stepping away to start his circular route around the room, checking to make sure everyone was behaving.

I led Nannette to the booth in the rear corner of the room, reaching it just as the server finished wiping the table down, and slid into the side facing the front, my back to the wall. I was in the perfect position to watch the couple at the bar.

Nannette slid into the other side of the booth and finished the last bit of Angel's confection before licking the melted chocolate from her fingertips and reached for a napkin. "Mmm. Best tasting ball sac I've had in a while."

I choked out a laugh. "Thank you for not saying that in front of her. They're supposed to be hearts, and she's a little miffed that everyone keeps saying they're testicles."

"She's your donor, correct?"

"Yes."

Nannette gave me a reproachful look.

"Oh, don't you start too. What's so wrong with getting along with my donor? For crying out loud, she's a person, not a blood popsicle."

Nannette raised her hands, palms facing out. "All right. Just as long as you don't get so attached you start to feel bad about drinking from her. You need to stay on top of your blood cocktail, and she's an important part of it."

"I know, and I have been."

"Good. And you might want to store her somewhere safe instead of toting her around with you, given your penchant for finding danger. If something happens to her, there goes your blood source."

Good grief. What was it with her and Rider? Angel was a person, not a juice box. "Thank you for my Christmas gift. I loved it," I said, moving along before my irritation had a chance to grow into a really bad mood. "I'm assuming you spent Christmas with family?"

Nannette actually blushed a little, something I never expected to see. "I volunteered at a food kitchen alongside my descendant. We had a nice conversation. She is a very intelligent, lovely young woman... which I know now thanks to you." She cleared her throat and straightened her posture as she clasped her hands in front of her on the table. "But I am here to work with you today. Rider filled me in on what happened with the krackling. That was a very risky move you pulled, Danni."

"But it worked," I said, fighting the urge to shudder as I remembered purposely calling upon my succubus power and biting into the gross belly of the bat-like thing spewing out of the creature's maw in order to enthrall it. "And now I know I can call my succubus power up at will if I ever need it."

Nannette's eyebrows rose a fraction. "I've been under the impression you've wanted nothing to do with that part of yourself. You've wanted to suppress it."

"I have. Or I did. But is that even possible? I've been fighting against it since I was turned, but that just seems to blow up in my face. And I needed it when we fought the krackling. There was no other way we were going to defeat that monster, so that got me thinking. This side of me could be useful if I could control it."

Nannette nodded slowly. "This is true. Controlling it will take some practice and could be dangerous until you have it mastered. Rider said you had trouble calming the succubus power once you unleashed it."

I grimaced, remembering shoving my tongue down poor Ginger's throat and throwing up right after. "That's what I wanted to talk to you about. I'm hoping you can help me. You've been researching succubi since I was turned, right?"

"Yes." She narrowed her eyes. "In order to better understand your physiology should you have issues stemming from that side, and to know how to treat you medically."

"I was thinking maybe you could develop something. Like those hawthorn oil syringes Rider uses to knock me out. I don't want anything to knock me out, though. I just need something that could help me pull back in my succubus power. If that makes sense."

"I get what you're asking," Nannette said, her brow creased in thought. "I'm not sure what I could develop. I was already looking into a way to suppress the Bloom before Rider and his witch friend figured out a way to do it, and I didn't find anything. Part of the problem is that you're half vampire and things that could potentially weaken the succubus part of you can harm the vampire side as well. Another issue is that there isn't a ton of verified information on succubi. They're not exactly known for seeking medical treatment or revealing their secrets."

"So you've never treated a succubus in the underworld hospital ward?"

Nannette snorted. "We don't treat demons there. They're our enemy. As a hybrid, and one who has given her allegiance to Rider, making him your dominant sire, you get a pass."

My face must have blanched because she reached out to give my hand a friendly pat, which if you had told me would be something she'd do a couple months ago I would have told you that you were out of your mind, but we understood each other better now.

"You're not a true demon, Danni. As a hybrid, you may have traits of the succubus, but you will never be a complete one. You'll never be a complete vampire. You are and will continue to be your own unique entity, which is why treating you isn't all that simple. To my knowledge, there is no one else like you… and I'm not just referring to your penchant to get into clusterfucks of epic proportions."

I resisted the urge to roll my eyes. "So, how do you know what you do know? You knew about the Bloom. I've tried Googling for information on succubi to learn more about this part of me, but I keep getting stuff about anime and role play games, and porn. So much porn."

"Google is often a miss when it comes to finding verifiable information on the paranormal community. Most of our knowledge comes from books and journals written by our own kind. You've seen Rider's collection. You'll find that most vampires of his age have quite the collection. We have a library at the hospital and a database of information that has been scanned in from several texts. Also, there's word of mouth. Just because we don't treat demonic entities in the hospital doesn't mean no one has ever crossed any and … studied them."

I felt the bottom of my stomach hollow out. "By study, are we talking torture and dissection?"

Nannette shrugged. "Some of our information is obtained by hunters, and they don't learn about demons by asking them nicely. I'm sure you're aware Rider had a truce with a family of hunters until that one fool tried to kill you."

I nodded. "I knew they had a pact not to kill each other, but I didn't know they exchanged information."

"Rider would never give any information that would endanger any of us, but if he knew of a vampire nest full of rapists or pedophiles that he could send a group of hunters to instead of carving out time to travel there himself, he'd call it in to the Quimbys."

"And they'd tell him whatever new information they discovered about demons."

"Yes. There was also his brother. Rider didn't fight that man for centuries only to not learn anything about incubi and succubi in the process."

"I guess not." I tapped my fingers on the tabletop and took a moment to check on the woman at the bar. Still talking to the man. Still appearing just fine and dandy. Yet, my gut still insisted I keep my eye on her.

"I can give you my notes from my research. Rider is bound to have some information on succubi in at least one of those books in his office, and I'm sure he wouldn't mind you using the hospital's library if you really want to learn more about your other side."

"It wouldn't be a betrayal?" I asked before I thought enough to censor myself, my heart thumping away.

Nannette frowned and cocked her head to the side as she studied me. "You gave your loyalty to Rider. He wouldn't feel betrayed by you wanting to know more about what you are. It's actually wise that you've come to this decision. The more you know about what you are, the fewer surprises you might run into."

"I suppose, although I'd just be happy to have a quick calming drug." I remembered kissing Ginger. "Wait. I instinctually knew to kiss Ginger when I felt myself losing control over my succubus power. I knew getting that close to someone with estrogen would make the succubus draw back."

"Bet you didn't know it would make you put your head in a toilet." She chuckled.

"No, I didn't, but it worked well enough. What about estrogen? Can't I just carry estrogen pills with me and if I get out of control, I can just pop one?"

Nannette shook her head. "I already thought of that soon after you were turned. Getting close to women or drinking their blood for the estrogen effect has been fine so far, but directly taking estrogen isn't a great idea. We don't know the effect it could have on your body, but I can take a few educated guesses, and none of them are positive."

"Ugh. Then how can I—" I noticed movement out of

the corner of my eye where I'd been watching the woman in my peripheral vision and turned to see her stand as the man who'd been talking with her deposited a few bills on the bar top.

"I gotta go."

"What?"

"I have to follow that woman. Don't ask why because I don't know. I just have to keep my eye on her." I stood from the booth, still watching the woman as she and the man crossed over to the coat rack near the entrance.

"Is this one of those gut things you've been having?" Nannette stood from the booth and awaited my answer.

"Yes, and I really feel it, so don't try to stop me."

"I'm not stopping you," she said. "I'm going with you."

CHAPTER TWO

"I have no idea why I'm compelled to follow her or what might happen," I warned Nannette as we crossed the floor. "We might be walking into a fight."

"Good. It's been a while since I've been in a good fight. Sparring with you has its moments, but I don't really get that warm fuzzy feeling if I don't get to actually crack someone's skull open and watch them bleed."

I turned my head toward her and raised my eyebrows.

"What? I'm a vampire," she said. "It's the nature of the beast. We all need the violence, but we can choose who we inflict it on so we're not monsters."

Very true, I thought, and turned my attention back to the woman just in time to see her slip out the door with the man right behind her, pulling a knit cap on his head. I grabbed my leather bomber jacket off the rack near the door, shoved my arms inside and had just pulled the zipper up when Daniel appeared in front of me.

"Going somewhere?"

"I need to follow that woman who just left."

"Hell," he muttered. "Gut thing?"

"Yup."

"We're on the clock."

"Rome can cover things until our replacements come, or you can stay behind. Nannette's coming with me."

"I go where you go. Period." Daniel moved over to the door and held it open for us before pointing at Angel, where she still sat in the booth watching us curiously and mouthed, "Stay" before turning to Rome. "Keep an eye on her and stay away from her testicles."

"I hate you, Puff."

I grabbed Daniel's North Face coat and tossed it to him before stepping out onto the sidewalk, where the frigid night air slapped me right in the face. "I know you run hot, but as cold as it is, you'll draw attention walking around without that on."

"The man has rainbow hair. He draws attention anyway," Nannette pointed out.

"Rainbow hair isn't as odd as someone walking in this cold in just a T-shirt." I spotted the couple headed toward the parking lot alongside the bar and started after them, careful to keep my distance.

The pair paused by the lot, and we came to a stop, turning toward each other. Daniel took out his cell phone and Nannette and I pretended to look at something he'd brought up on it. Just three friends using a GPS to figure out where we were or checking to see where we could go next at such a late hour. Not suspicious at all.

I watched the pair discreetly and focused my vampiric hearing on their location, and was able to hear them over the wind blowing soft bits of fluffy snow toward us. The woman politely declined the man's offer of a ride home, explaining she lived within walking distance and driving or riding in the snow made her nervous. The man assured her he was a safe driver and pointed out that the snow was light and the roads weren't slick. When she refused again, he earned brownie points by offering to walk her home, refusing to allow her to walk alone at night.

Unless he wanted to walk her home himself so he could hurt her. If so, I would be revoking those brownie points and sending him to meet his maker ahead of schedule. But he still wasn't giving me a predatory vibe, so I gave him the benefit of the doubt as the woman accepted his offer and they started moving again.

After they got a few more feet ahead of us, Daniel put his phone away and we were on the move. I shoved my hands into my coat pockets and wished I'd thought to grab a hat, especially once Nannette removed a black fur-lined cap from her jacket pocket and covered her head with it.

Daniel saw me giving Nannette the jealous stink eye and grinned before he pulled a knit cap out of his coat pocket and handed it to me. "Your ears are turning pink on top."

I thanked him and took the hat. It was black and had Beavis and Butthead on the front, but I was too cold to care about the ridiculous cartoon duo or what the hat might do to my hair. I pulled it on, making sure to tug it down far enough to cover my ears.

"The last time you followed someone out of the bar, you knew she was next on the krackling's hit list. What's the deal with this one?" Daniel asked.

"I don't know. I just have this sense that I need to watch her."

"Is the man triggering it?" Nannette asked, her dark eyes narrowed on the man in question as she flexed her hands, prepping to fight if necessary.

"I'm getting nothing from him. She set off something in my gut the moment I saw her, which was about ten minutes before he approached her. I've watched them all night, and he hasn't done anything questionable so whatever I'm sensing, I don't think he's got anything to do with it even though he would seem the obvious threat, leaving the bar with her and walking her home in the dark."

"So, you do sense that she's in imminent danger?" Daniel said.

I thought about it for a moment and nodded. "Yes. It's

a queasy feeling in my stomach. Something is coming for her."

"Please don't let it be another evil Santa Claus," Daniel said under his breath. "I still can't smell Christmas cookies without wanting to hurl."

"It's not a krackling," I assured him, although I had no clue what was after the woman. I only knew she was in danger. "And you shouldn't have to smell any Christmas cookies for much longer. It's almost New Year's Eve and the world will move on to the next holiday."

"I believe the next big one is Valentine's Day," Nannette said. "Maybe you'll discover and kill an evil Cupid."

"We already killed Cupid, remember?"

Nannette slid a glance my way and shook her head. "Right. I keep forgetting that really happened. It probably doesn't help that I keep picturing you killing a giant diaper-clad cherub with chubby cheeks and dimples when I think about it."

"Picture David Lee Roth on steroids," Daniel suggested. "Far more accurate."

The couple stopped at an intersection ahead and waited for a car to pass before using the crosswalk to reach the other side of the street, continuing down the side street.

"We don't want to spook them by immediately crossing the street and going down the same side street right after them," Nannette said. "Let's fall back a bit more so they don't realize they're being followed."

"I can't lose sight of her." My heart rate increased as I scanned the area. Even at the late hour, downtown Louisville usually had a decent amount of traffic, but the cold temperatures had been keeping people indoors since Christmas, so there weren't many cars on the road and no pedestrians except for the two we were following. And us. I understood Nannette's concern and acknowledged how conspicuous we could appear, but my gut was screaming at me that I couldn't let the woman out of my sight.

"Something is going to happen to her unless I stop it. I have to stay close enough to be able to get to her in time."

Daniel glanced up at the sky. "There's not a lot of people out. I can probably duck in somewhere and shift, and go up to watch them from above, but I'd have to go up pretty far to not be seen and if you're positive something bad is coming for them, I'd rather not leave you." He lowered his gaze as we reached the intersection and started to cross, the light red and the sign indicating it was safe to walk. "Those two haven't looked back once though, so we're probably good. No wonder you sense something bad happening to the woman. Neither of them appear to have the good sense to check their surroundings every once in a while."

Before I could respond, my gut kicked into overdrive. Time seemed to slow, sound and smell ceasing to exist as my head turned on its own to see a pale gray van slowing in the right turn lane. My heart thumped fiercely against my ribcage as that van rolled through the crosswalk directly in front of us and turned down the side street. The driver appeared Caucasian and wore a black knit cap pulled low over his eyes and a black coat and gloves. I couldn't see anyone else in the van, but I could sense them, and I could sense who they were after. I ran.

"Danni!"

Daniel and Nannette called after me as I cleared the crosswalk and my feet punished the snow-dusted sidewalk on the other side. My vampiric speed kicked in as the van slowed to a crawl alongside the oblivious couple and I surged forward down the side street as sound and smell came back. Not that I paid much attention to the scent of fresh snow or the sound of my feet sloshing through the white stuff covering the pavement.

My focus was completely on the van that had just stopped by the couple and the side door of it sliding open.

"Run!" I screamed just as the first masked man jumped out of the van, hands already reaching for the woman, one of them holding a Taser. The second man had his Taser out too, prepared to incapacitate the man who'd offered to walk the woman home to keep her safe. Judging by the slack-jawed look of shock on his face, he'd overestimated his ability to do so. It was good for him that my Gibbs gut had kicked in when it had.

I plowed into the first masked man when the Taser was a hair away from connecting to the woman's exposed neck, knocking him back against the passenger door of the van. I heard something make impact behind me, followed by a groan, and knew my backup had arrived in time to take the second man down.

My guy raised the Taser toward me, and I grabbed his wrist. With a quick twist, I broke the bones, and the Taser dropped to the ground as he screamed in agony.

His broken wrist firmly held in my hand, I twisted his arm behind his back and shoved him against the van just as the driver got out and rounded the front of the vehicle.

He pointed a handgun at us, but didn't have a chance to get a shot off before Nannette appeared in front of him, spinning in midair before she kicked the weapon out of the man's hand and started bashing his head repeatedly into the front of the van.

While the man in my grip struggled to get free, I turned to see Daniel calming the woman while her male friend appeared to hyperventilate next to her. The poor guy was bent over with his hands on his knees, staring at the unconscious man Daniel had knocked out. Well, I wouldn't be getting any answers out of that one or the driver Nannette had just released after the man had given up struggling, knocked unconscious by his head's repeated introductions to the van's hood. That left my guy.

I rammed his head into the passenger side window hard enough to bust out the glass and turned him before slamming him back against the door. I placed my knee against his groin, a threat that needed no words, and gripped his throat tight. I didn't worry about the fact I'd released his arms. With Daniel now at my side and the knowledge of my strength, the man would have to be a complete idiot to make a move.

Daniel must have still thought the guy might risk it because he picked up the man's dropped Taser and held it threateningly.

I removed the man's ski mask, revealing an average Caucasian face with pale gray eyes and a wide nose. I suspected the nose might not have been quite as wide and flat before I'd rammed him face-first into the side of the van. His hair was brown, short, and messy. His forehead was high, showing signs of a receding hairline. I placed him somewhere in his early thirties.

Daniel held the Taser just under the man's swollen left eye, which was already turning shades of black and blue, daring him to do something stupid. "What was your plan, jackass? Rape? Murder? Jehovah's Witness recruitment?"

I gave him a look.

"What? Those fuckers are relentless."

I looked back at the man, who wasn't offering up an answer, and squeezed his throat harder. "He asked you a question. What did you want with the woman?"

The man trembled as he glared at me, as much as he could glare given his swollen eye, and shifted his gaze between me and Daniel. He swallowed hard, focusing on the Taser for a moment before redirecting a look my way that all but screamed, "Fuck you."

I punched him in his soft belly and stepped back when I heard vomit come up, but he swallowed it down.

"My next punch is going to be in your balls, so I highly recommend speaking up."

"And if you don't she's probably going to put a blade in your nut or just rip them both off of you," Daniel warned him. "It's kind of her thing."

"Revolting behavior," the man said, and blood trickled out the side of his mouth. "You condone such vile acts and disrespect from your females?"

"They're not my females, and as free women, they can do whatever the hell they want to do. After that comment, I'm guessing we've caught ourselves an incel, ladies."

"I am not whatever you claim," the man said, dribbling more blood down his chin. "I am a disciple of the prophet Ramson."

"Oh, even better. A cult of religious nuts."

"Who is Ramson?" I asked.

"Ramson is the way. He is the beginning and the end, the alpha and the—"

I squeezed the man's throat until I cut off his ability to speak. "You know what? Forget I asked. Do you know this man?"

The woman was gawking at me when I turned my head to look at her. The man had moved closer to her, and his arm was slung over her shoulders. He held her tucked in against his body as they burrowed deep into their coats to ward off the bitter cold that I couldn't even feel anymore, too jazzed up from the recent exercise. I wondered how many calories violence burned. It certainly got the heart revving and the body temperature up.

She blinked, seeming to just realize I was speaking to her, and gave the man a more thorough once-over before she frowned and shook her head. "I've never seen him before."

"You don't recall seeing him at all, maybe watching you?"

She shook her head again.

I looked at Daniel and picking up on what I wanted, he lowered the Taser and moved over to the man he'd left unconscious on the ground. He tugged off the man's ski mask, revealing another Caucasian man, this one with a shadow of dark facial hair covering his lower face, a sharp nose, and one hell of a pair of lumpy shiners from where Daniel's fist had knocked him out. His hair was graying at the temples, but light brown everywhere else, cut in short curls. And I was pretty sure the bridge of his nose was broken based on the swelling and color.

"What about this guy?" Daniel asked her.

She looked down at the man and shook her head.

"Do you recognize either of them?" I asked the man with her. My gut had said to follow her, but that didn't necessarily mean he hadn't been the intended target. She still would have gotten hurt by them either way, and I didn't really understand how my gut worked.

"No. I've never seen either of them before," the man said.

I looked over at Nannette. She already had her guy hauled back up and spread backward over the hood. She pulled off his ski mask, the movement more of a peeling as the fabric stuck to the bloody, mangled mess of his face, and once the mask was clear of his head, she turned his face toward the couple.

I was pretty sure I winced as hard as the couple, seeing the damage Nannette had delivered to the man. His hair was sandy blond and on the shaggy side, his cheekbones appeared to have been sharp before they'd been broken, and his lips were wide and thin, except for the puffy bottom lip busted in the center. His eyes were swollen shut and his nose was … indescribable.

"Is he dead?" the woman asked.

Nannette placed two fingers along the man's neck, her expression completely blank of emotion as she felt for a pulse. "No. He's just unconscious."

Maybe brain-dead, she said directly in my mind. *Oops.*

I gave my head a subtle shake, not wanting the very human couple to pick up on anything. Even though we'd saved them, I didn't think it likely they'd just let us walk away from a murder and I didn't want to have to hurt them. It would defeat the whole purpose of me saving her. "Do you recognize him?"

I didn't expect her to, given he kind of looked like a Picasso once Nannette had finished with him, but the woman surprised me by nodding. "I've seen him before. I think. It's hard to be certain because his nose wasn't on his cheek when I saw him, but I'm pretty sure he's this weird guy that lives in my building. Who are you people?"

Daniel took a MidKnight Enterprises business card out of an inner coat pocket and passed it to her. "MidKnight Security."

The woman's eyes widened. "You're security at The Midnight Rider. I recognize the hair. You followed me?"

"We just got off work and were headed the same way," I said, seeing no reason to reveal my weird gut powers. "I saw the van slow down and the men jump out with Tasers. I told you to run," I reminded her. "They could have hurt you."

She blushed, as did the man with her. "Yeah... I heard that, but wasn't sure who you were yelling at. Then everything happened so fast. You guys were like ninjas. I don't know what would have happened if you hadn't been here." Her face paled as the man with her grew redder. "I might be dead."

"I wouldn't have let them take you," the man said.

The woman's face said *yeah, right* and I couldn't disagree, but I felt bad for him. I knew how fragile the male ego was, and it had to hurt knowing you'd just stood frozen in the face of fear when you were really trying to make a good impression on a woman you'd just met and were clearly interested in.

"Of course," I said. "I'm sure you would have taken care of them once the surprise wore off, but we're trained to notice things others miss and take action fast. We had the advantage of seeing them first. This is definitely a lesson in being aware of your surroundings though."

"Definitely," the man said, his tone chagrined, although I could see appreciation in his eyes. "I was completely oblivious, so wrapped up in conversation. We're lucky you sprang into action so quickly before anyone got hurt. I guess we need to call the police."

"No, we'll handle that," Daniel quickly said. "It's part

of our job, and you two should get going. Your noses are starting to look like Rudolph's. But, if you could tell us anything else about this man, that would be helpful. We can pass it along to the police."

"Do you know his name?" I asked.

"I don't know him at all," the woman answered. "I just recognize him from my building. He's very quiet and odd. He stares a lot, always frowning and muttering to himself under his breath. He's never even spoken to me before, but he's glared and sneered. I just ignored him, figuring he had some sort of mental problem. I guess I was right. I don't know who his friends are. I've never seen him with anyone else."

Will she be safe now? Daniel asked through our telepathic link as he watched me, waiting for my response.

I stilled myself and took a deep breath, finding a sense of calm as I relaxed and just listened to my body. The instinct that the woman was in danger had lifted. Although there was some residual twistiness in my gut, it was all about the men we'd roughed up. The woman was fine. For now, at least. "I think you'll be all right now," I told the girl, knowing Daniel would take my comment to her as his answer. "We'll take care of these guys and work with the police, but if you don't mind leaving your names and some information with Daniel here, in case the police have more questions."

"Oh, of course," the woman said. "And do you think they'll notify me if they release them? I mean, one of them lives in my building. At least I think he still does. I haven't seen him around in a while."

"I'll call you personally," I assured her. "We'll consider this work-related since it happened after you left The Midnight Rider. We work closely with the police. Since we're the ones pressing charges, they'll share that information with us."

"Oh. Yeah, I guess that's okay. Thank you. For everything. Protecting me and for handling the police. I don't even know your name."

"Danni. This is Daniel, and our friend, Nannette, isn't bar security, but as you can see, she was available to help out."

"Boy, did she help out," the woman said, staring at the mess Nannette had made of her neighbor. "I'm Mandi. Mandi Fittro. This is Shawn …"

"Abel," he said, realizing Mandi had forgotten his last name already. She blushed at her gaffe.

I hid a smile and a wince. The poor guy had failed to be her knight in shining armor and make enough of an impression for her to remember his whole name. I hoped she at least invited him in for a mug of hot cocoa before sending him on his way after he finished walking her home. "Nice to meet you two. Leave your contact information with Daniel and we'll be sure to contact you if we need anything. Or the police will, of course."

My captive chose that moment to try to break free, grabbing my arm with both hands. Before he could break it or whatever else he'd intended to do, my vampiric speed kicked in and I head-butted him hard enough for me to see stars and him to nearly see Jesus before he went lights out.

"Dumbass," I muttered before I tossed him into the back of the van through the sliding door that had remained open since the men had jumped out of it. "Let's pack them in."

Nannette and I both could have just used our vampiric strength to do the job, but we didn't want to show off our freakish strength in front of human witnesses so I walked over to her and grabbed the driver's ankles while she lifted him from under his armpits and we carried him to the side of the van that way.

We'd just finished tossing him in and moved to collect the man left unconscious on the sidewalk when Daniel thanked the intended victims for their cooperation and sent them on their way, reminding them to be more observant while walking at night.

"I got this one," he said, bending to pick up the man he'd knocked out. He effortlessly slung the man over his shoulder and carried him to the van, where he tossed him inside. "I guess we can just take possession of the van to transport them. I'll ride in back in case any of them regain consciousness. There's glass in the passenger seat. We can sweep it out, but there's likely to be tiny shards left after. One of you want to ride in back too?"

"I'll drive," Nannette said. "Are you sure we don't need to follow those two to make sure they make it to her apartment safely?"

I looked up the street where the couple continued their journey to Mandi's building and watched them cross an intersection, doing a better job of watching their surroundings this time. The sense I'd had that Mandi was in danger was completely gone. My gut didn't seem to have any further purpose for her. "No. I don't feel anything when I look at her now. Once we knocked these guys around pretty good, my gut quit sending the alarm that she was in danger. We have their contact information if we need to follow up, but we don't need to watch them anymore tonight. These men were what my gut picked up on. We need to find out why they targeted her and what they intended to do to her."

"And there's no better place to make tight-lipped sacks of shit talk than Rider's interrogation room," Daniel said.

Oh joy, I thought as my stomach took a dip.

"I know that look," Daniel said, grinning. "You're thinking of how you're going to explain to Rider that you just totally left your post before your shift was over, just to go out and collect more trouble that you're now bringing right into his business."

"If I'm in trouble, you're in trouble."

"I'm your bodyguard and my main job is to stay with you, keeping you safe no matter what, so technically, I was still doing my job when I left with you. You left Angel there too. A teenager. In his bar. Unsupervised."

"Rome's watching her."

"Rome's watching that box of candy she's got and trying to figure out how to get his grubby hands on what's inside."

"Let's just get this over with," I said, knowing there was nowhere else to take the men. Getting them to talk might involve a lot of blood and a lot of screaming, two things best done out of sight and earshot of civilians. We were lucky enough the cold temperature was keeping most people indoors and no police had driven past, given our normally busy location downtown and proximity to the police department. "I'm going to have to tell him about the men no matter what, but maybe our replacements arrived before he realized we skipped out."

Where the hell are you two and why did you leave before your replacements arrived to take over your shift? Rider growled through our mind link.

"You just had to say that and jinx us, didn't you?" Daniel shook his head and gestured for me to get into the van.

I shook my head too, adequate words failing me, and climbed in, carefully crawling around the heap of battered men we'd tossed inside. There were no seats in the back, just a couple of sleeping bags, buckets, duct tape, zip ties, rope... Yeah, these men had definitely been up to no good. I moved to the very back of the van and sat in the corner, drawing my knees up to my chest.

Daniel climbed in and slid the door closed just as Nannette got into the driver's seat, closing her door behind her. The van had never been turned off so heat blasted from the vents, and she took a moment to warm her hands while Daniel found a spot to sit.

"It'll be all right," Daniel said. "All teasing aside, Rider will understand."

***

Rider did *not* understand.

"You just left, Danni. You didn't say a word to me about where you were going or why after I specifically told you not to follow someone home and find another ... whatever the hell it is you found this time."

"Actually, you specifically told me not to follow anyone home and find another evil Santa Claus. And I didn't. Clearly, these are all human men. Not one of them is any version of Santa Claus."

Rider's eyes narrowed as he towered over me where we stood in the observation room. "You know what I meant."

"Did I? Because I was pretty sure you meant that you didn't want me to hunt down another krackling, but now I'm getting the feeling that wasn't it."

He glared at me for a tense moment before the anger in his eyes morphed into frustrated defeat and he stepped back with a sigh. He ran his hand down his face, muttering under his breath, something about damn women and the universe's cruel joke on him, before he turned his head toward Daniel, who stood in the corner of the room with his arms folded over his chest, watching us. Nannette stood next to him, watching us just as quietly. "Did you at least make sure they didn't see how they were brought here?"

"They were all unconscious for the trip," Daniel assured him. "Two woke up just as we got them into the hallway down here, and the third didn't wake up until we had them in the interrogation room and the other two were yelling and demanding to be released. At no point did any of them see fangs or wings or glowing eyes."

"Well, at least you did that much before bringing random human men into my building, men who could have just been delivered to their own human police department."

"If you don't care that these men were preying on one of your own customers, fine," I snapped. "The next time my gut tells me one of your customers is in danger, I'll just let her die. Eventually, you won't have any at all to worry about, so it won't even be an issue. Of course, I'll be a despicable monster for ignoring the fact that I could have saved them, but hey, if that's what you want, who am I to complain?"

"Daniel, Nannette, can you wait outside?"

Nannette nodded her head respectfully and moved toward the door. Daniel took a moment longer, assessing me first, checking to see if I was all right. I discreetly nodded my head, barely enough to be considered a movement, and absent-mindedly ran my fingertips over the bracelet he'd given me for Christmas.

Daniel finally joined Nannette at the door and as they both exited the room, closing the door behind them, I released the breath I hadn't been aware I'd been holding.

"One of these days, he's going to try me when I'm in the wrong damn mood for it."

I released a frustrated breath. "Are we going to argue about Daniel now?"

"No." Rider reached out and brushed my hair back from my brow, tucking it behind my ear. "And I don't want you to ignore your gut and let people die when you can help them, but I don't want you to act rash in your attempts to save them either."

"Daniel was with me. So was Nannette."

"Yes, because they followed you. Still, you ran out of here with no idea what you were going to be going up against. There were three of you for three men. Good odds. You got lucky. What if that woman had been hunted by a pack of lycanthropes? What if demons had been after her or someone who works with my brother and would recognize you on sight? I'm not angry that you saved the woman. I'm mad that you didn't take two seconds to tell me so I could make sure someone was available to help immediately if you needed backup or know to check on you if I didn't hear from you within a set amount of time in case you were snatched. Or to get someone in place to watch my damn bar. Just because the bar was calm when you left, doesn't mean something couldn't have happened after the patrons realized the two security guards on duty had just left, and you left your donor here."

"Angel was sitting in a booth minding her own business. She doesn't cause trouble here."

"Angel is a teenager and a recovering addict. Being in this bar isn't good for her and it isn't good for my business. If that girl relapses and sneaks a drink, I could be shut down. I don't think I need to mention the damage a drink could do to her and all her progress."

While I knew Rider had connections everywhere, and he knew witches who could make such trouble go away for the right amount of money, which he seemed to have plenty of, I understood his point. It didn't matter that anyone who tried to shut him down would find themselves in a world of trouble. It was unnecessary trouble he didn't need, and Angel definitely didn't need a relapse.

She was doing so well, I often forgot that Angel hadn't just once been on drugs. Like most addicts, alcohol came into play too. And whether or not she admitted to it, I knew she was under a lot of stress with her mother back in town. Nina Valdez hadn't shown up at my apartment since that night a month ago when Pacitti had first darkened my doorstep, but she'd written Angel a letter. One Angel had read but hadn't shared its contents with me, and I knew she was around, somewhere, ready to pop up when least expected to try to drag Angel down with her.

"I'll keep her out of the bar," I muttered. "I've just been worried about her, what with her mother back in town and the fact she knows where Angel lives now."

"I always have someone in place just outside your door."

"I know, and I know they wouldn't allow anyone to physically harm Angel, but unless you've ordered them to tackle the woman on sight, she can still knock on the door. Just her presence can be a trigger for Angel, and what if she decides she wants to speak with her?"

"What if she does?" Rider said, before biting out a curse. "You are way too attached to that girl."

"What if I am? What's so wrong with treating her like a person with thoughts and feelings instead of like a meal?"

"She is a meal, Danni. Yes, I help my donors, give them a better life than they had before agreeing to give me their blood, and was fully onboard with doing the same for yours, but you're getting too involved with this girl. She is an addict. She could go back to her old ways any moment and an addict back on their drug of choice doesn't give a shit about keeping the secrets of the people who helped them. You need to be prepared for if that happens, because if it does, we can't let her just walk away and expose everything she knows about us."

"Angel would never do that. She's a good person."

"For your sake, I hope that's true and I hope she never relapses." He looked through the newly replaced mirror that allowed us to see into the interrogation room where the three men in black had been deposited without them being able to see or hear us and took a deep breath before returning his gaze to me. "I'm not trying to be an ass, and I genuinely hope your donor is able to lead a good life. I just don't like to see you get hurt, so I can't help being concerned about her. The more attached you are to her, the more you will hurt if she turns on you and that is always, *always* a possibility. You can help her, but you shouldn't let her so deep into your heart."

"I don't work that way, Rider. I can't be as cold as you."

His jaw popped and pain flashed through his eyes, but was gone within a blink.

"I didn't mean that as bad as it sounded. You're not—"

"Yes, I am, and I won't apologize for it. Being cold when needed has kept me alive. It's what enables me to destroy those who betray me before they have enough time to destroy me or hurt the people I'm bound to protect. You could stand to be a little colder yourself. That just wouldn't be you, though, so I have to be cold enough for the both of us."

Being cold had been what allowed him to rip his own brother's heart out to save my life, and the fact he didn't throw that in my face after what I'd said to him made me feel terrible. Rider could kill people who'd been with him for years, and do it without hesitation, but he was far from unfeeling.

"I'm sorry either way. I don't want to insult you or argue with you about this. I can see your point, even though I know in my heart Angel is a good person who needs someone. She needs a family. I can't help but want to be that family."

"I know. That's the way you are and I love it about you, even if it scares me senseless. If anything happened to you, Danni, I would lose everything."

"Nothing's going to happen to me."

He looked back at the new mirror and, from the way his body tensed, I knew he was replaying the memory of me ramming my face into the one he'd replaced. "You should have called the police, let them handle those men. They're human, and there was nothing paranormal about their attack."

"I sensed it was going to happen, Rider. Isn't that paranormal enough? If I sensed it, I was meant to stop it, and if they're part of something bigger, I'm meant to find out and stop that too. They said they were disciples of someone named Ramson. For all we know, they worship Beelzebub and there's a whole lot more of them out there preying on innocent women."

His jaw popped as he watched the men in the other room. "Are you sure you're up for an interrogation so soon after the last one?"

"Trixell is gone for good now. She's not messing with my mind anymore. I'll be fine." I grabbed his hand and squeezed it. "What happened then won't ever happen again."

He stared at me for a moment before pulling me close to him and brushed a kiss over my forehead. "I pray not. I had Ginger drop your donor off at your apartment before she headed out to start looking for Julie. If you're sure you'll be okay in there, go ahead. Just stay focused and stop if you start to feel strange. I'll be right with you."

"I'm fine, Rider. I know you're busy with your missing donor, finding Pacitti, and just your normal day-to-day stuff. You don't have to waste time in this interrogation. I can handle it."

"Maybe I can't handle it," he said with a surprising amount of vulnerability. "I still see you breaking your own bones whenever I look in that room. I need to be in there with you. I need to see you get through an interrogation without hurting yourself. I need to be in there to… to stop you if something goes wrong."

I wrapped my arms around him and rested my head against his chest. "I'm sorry I put you through that. I can't imagine what it must have been like to see me that way."

"You have nothing to apologize for. You didn't put me through anything. That was all Trixell's doing, and you were the one hurt. I'm sorry I didn't stop you from hurting yourself."

"I don't think there was any way you could, and I would never blame you for what happened." As wonderful as it felt to be held in his arms, wrapped in the warmth of his body, I pulled away. "We need to get past this. That evil old hag is truly gone and she can't harm me anymore. You can go into interrogation with me, but you need to let me do my thing. No interruptions."

The corners of his lips twitched. "Remind me who the boss is here again."

I stood on tiptoe and brushed a light kiss on his mouth. "Me."

"That's what I was afraid of. Do me a favor and keep that a secret. I need the others to still fear me."

"You have nothing to worry about there. Now, if we're all good here, I need to go smack these guys around and find out who they're taking orders from."

"After you, Teste Slayer."

CHAPTER THREE

Nannette opted out of the interrogation, choosing to watch from the observation room instead. She often observed me during interrogations, always studying my behavior. I'd long accepted I was the vampire's guinea pig.

Daniel was with us when Rider and I stepped into the interrogation room. The gray-templed man with the five o'clock shadow had been pacing the floor, ranting and raving. He stopped and whirled around to face us once we entered and opened his mouth to unleash what I assumed would be another lengthy tirade about religious persecution and how he had rights.

Before he could get another word of that out, I grabbed his face and shoved him hard enough to send him flying back into a chair. The chair rocked back on its hind legs and toppled over, the man with it.

"Sit down like your buddies and don't speak unless spoken to," I told him.

The man rose to his knees, appearing very much like he was going to be a dumbass and push his luck with me, but a dark look from Daniel had him righting the toppled chair before perching on it.

I didn't let it get to me that the man feared Daniel

more than he feared me. Daniel wasn't some scrawny guy, and he had been the one to knock him out earlier. The man had yet to see me in action. He would learn soon enough that looks could be deceiving, and I was far scarier than I appeared.

The man I'd tussled with sat at the table, his hands clasped awkwardly in prayer due to the broken bones in his wrist as his head bowed over them. The man Nannette had handled had wedged himself into the back corner where he sat on the floor, sobbing and shivering. He'd been given a towel and an ice pack right after they'd been tossed into the room in an attempt to bring his swelling and pain down enough for him to be able to actually answer our questions, but the damage Nannette had delivered would take more than ice to help so I didn't have high hopes of getting anything useful out of him. Both of his eyes were nearly swollen shut, his bottom lip was swollen to twice the size I imagined it originally to be, and dried blood had his blond hair sticking up in hard spikes. And even if he made it out of interrogation, his nose was never going to be the same again.

The interrogation room looked like any other interrogation room you would see on television, except it had a drain in the floor to help with cleanup. A lot of blood got shed in the room, and to my knowledge, no one had ever been brought to interrogation and been allowed to leave breathing. Other than the drain in the floor, it was pretty basic. Gray walls, gray-tiled floor, and a metal table and chairs sat in the center. The walls were bare except for the telltale cracks and stains from interrogations gone wild, and of course, the mirror that allowed whoever was in the observation room to listen and watch without being seen or heard.

I glanced at that mirror, catching my reflection. I saw as well as felt Rider stiffen behind me, ceasing to breathe as he stood against the wall behind me near the closed door. He was watching me check out my reflection too. The last time I'd done so, I'd seen a monster staring back at me. This time, it was just me. Green eyes, fair skin, dark hair, and rosy lips. *It's just me in here*, I assured Rider through our mental link before I got to work.

"Let's start with something simple," I said. "What are your names?"

When the men remained quiet, I released a sigh. Only one of the three bothered to look at me, and that was the one Daniel had knocked out earlier. That one sat glaring at me, defiance oozing out of his pores. I tried to picture myself through his eyes. Only around five feet, four inches tall and roughly one hundred and twenty pounds, most of which was in the butt and thigh area, I knew I didn't strike a very intimidating image, not even while decked out in the black long-sleeved T-shirt boasting the logo for The Midnight Rider over my left breast and black jeans. My attire matched Daniel's and was sort of an unofficial work uniform. It didn't seem to scream kick-ass security guard at the glaring man, however. I was going to have to get rough with that man, but I didn't want to show all my cards so soon.

I turned my attention to the dark-headed man I'd already slammed around a bit earlier. His head was still bowed over his clasped hands and his lips moved, although no sound came out. Normally I would never interrupt anyone while they prayed, but since the man had identified himself as a disciple of Ramson, someone I was sure had ordered him to kidnap that poor woman, I assumed that was who he'd been praying to and I didn't have a lot of respect for the con artist he worshipped or any religion that promoted the abduction of women.

I pulled out the chair across from him and sat in it before leaning forward, my hands clasped together in front of me on the table. I stared at the man so intensely I knew he felt the weight. His left eye twitched, but he kept both closed, focused on his silent worship. I tapped my fingers on the table, my nails on the metal hard to ignore, but he did, other than another twitch. I could twitch too.

I slapped the spit out of his mouth, nearly knocking him out of the chair. "Oops. Had a twitch."

He caught himself before he fell sideways and sputtered, looking at us wide-eyed, or what passed as wide-eyed for the swollen one, as his bearded buddy made to get up from his own seat. Daniel shoved Beardy back with his booted foot, leaving the foot there to encourage the man not to attempt further movement.

"I was praying," the man I'd tussled with said, with a tone implying I should be ashamed of my uncivilized and disrespectful behavior.

"I saw that. You said you were a disciple of Ramson. Is that who you were praying to?"

He swallowed hard before nodding. "I have the right to worship."

"Yeah, and what religion is this, again?"

"I am a disciple of Ramson."

"So you said. What's the religion? It's clearly not Christianity or Judaism."

"We're Disciples of Ramson," Beardy said, grinding the words out from behind clenched teeth. "Like he just told you."

Oh. The lightbulb in my brain clicked on. "That's the name of the religion. Disciples of Ramson?"

"That's what I said."

I fought the urge to ram the guy head-first into the metal table, repeating what I'd done to him earlier, but it was awfully tempting. "Never heard of it, but this Ramson guy seems hella cocky to name a religion after himself."

"Have some resp—"

I slapped the man again. "I stopped you from stun-gunning an innocent woman and tossing her into your murder van, you sick bastard. You don't get to tell me shit about respect. Now answer my question. What is your name?"

"I demand release," he said. "This is religious

persecution. This is—"

I grabbed his right hand and bent the index finger backward until it snapped, then I waited for the worst of his screaming to stop before I spoke. By then, Daniel had leaned toward Beardy, silently warning him not to be a hero. Or maybe he was daring him. Either way, Beardy only glared at me, his jaw clenched tight, but his ass didn't leave his chair.

"That was your right index finger. You have nine other fingers left counting the thumbs. I will go through every single one of them, snapping them like twigs until you cooperate and answer my questions. If you end up being tougher than you look and still refuse after all that, I'll move on to your toes. Then your testicles. But by the time I get to those, I'm going to have to break out my knife and do some digging. Just for my own personal shits and giggles. Now, are you going to be a good boy and answer my questions, or am I going to have to perform a little surgery?"

His eyes bulged as sweat broke out along his brow. "You're evil."

"That's rich coming from the kidnapper with the van full of rope and duct tape." I grabbed his right middle finger and he bit back a scream. From the smell that hit my nose, he'd just released a little urine too. With one hand wrapped firmly around his broken wrist and the other holding the finger securely, I looked him dead in the eyes. "State your full name or lose the bird."

He looked at his friends, only giving the whimpering one in the corner a brief glance given that man's mental state before looking at Beardy for help that wasn't forthcoming. Beardy wasn't going to make any hero moves with Daniel sitting within grabbing distance of him. Then he looked at his finger. He must have been fond of it, because he answered. "Cliff Baker."

"See, now was that so hard?" I gave his finger a little wiggle. "What are your friends' names?"

"Mike and Gary. That's Gary, and Mike is over there in the corner. I don't know their last names, I swear. I don't know much about them at all. We just go to service together and we were assigned this duty."

I narrowed my eyes and studied the man. He was trembling with fear and sweating like a pig, but I didn't sense dishonesty. "What exactly was this duty you were assigned? Kidnapping, obviously, but what after that? What were you supposed to do with the woman after you got her in the van? Why was she chosen?"

"Remember who you serve," Gary said, and Cliff clammed right up.

I looked at the man and sighed. "You interrupted us, Gary, and I don't recall calling on you to speak."

"You don't intimidate me, filthy animal. I am a disciple of Ramson. Untouched. Unstoppable. Put me through your trials and I will walk out free because I am under his protection. The unclean cannot harm me."

"The unclean?" I released Cliff's hand, and the man nearly fainted with relief. My chair scraped over the floor as I pushed it back and stood. Rider remained where he was, watching silently as he leaned back against the wall, and Daniel stayed just as relaxed where he sat. I walked past him slowly, staring at Gary as I neared him and walked just behind him, knowing it would unnerve him for me to be in his blind spot, despite his determination to appear unbothered. "Is that why you attempted to snatch the woman? Was she unclean?"

"Like most of this world's trash, yes. Women no longer know their place and they have neutered many men, but Ramson is here to cleanse the taint of this world's imprint and take us back to the old ways, to the right way. To purity."

Oh geez, this was starting to get really icky. "So, like, what? Only virgins are allowed into whatever version of heaven this Ramson is selling you morons?"

"Watch your tongue, filthy—"

AULD FANG SYNE

I grabbed a handful of Gary's hair, digging my nails into his scalp before I snatched his head backward, forcing him to look at me as I hovered over him, crowding his space. I'd grabbed my switchblade out of my back pocket and flipped it open and now held it so the tip dug into his cheek. "You seem to be under the impression that you can talk to me any way you want or that you have some sort of authority over me. I hate to be the one to tell you, Gary, but it sounds like you and your partners here are in some sort of cult situation. Now, I would be willing to let you go about your dumbass life believing in whatever snake oil salesman you want, except it appears your leader is ordering you to hurt innocent women. That I just can't allow, and I don't give a shit whether you're doing it because you believe in a man who took advantage of your sad, desperate need to belong somewhere, your stupidity, or your boredom. There are consequences and repercussions for abducting women and claiming you did it in the name of religion isn't going to get you out of paying for your crime. Do you understand?"

"You aren't the law," Gary said, ever the stubborn one. "You got no say."

"I realize you guys aren't all that bright given how you honestly believe a holy man would be all right with abducting women, so I'm going to help you out by giving you a piece of advice I highly suggest you listen to." I pressed the pointy tip of my blade deeper into his cheek, drawing blood. "The person with the knife has all the say. Especially when they aren't the law. The law has rules. We don't."

I leaned in closer. "You might want to think about that the next time you call me filthy or any other offensive names you have brewing in that muddled head of yours. I know your type, Gary, and I know you only call women such vile names because you really want one of your own but can't get one. Oh, you blame them, of course. They're dirty. Impure. They've been programmed by the world to think they're better than men, and deep inside, they're just evil. Wrong. But secretly, you still want one. Only, they don't want you because they see you for the scared, insecure little boy you are. It's easier on your ego, though, to blame it on feminism, lack of faith, or, I don't know, whatever political side you root against. Believe whatever you want about that, Gary, but if you keep spewing it out loud, I'm going to have to shut you up and you won't like how."

I released my grip on Gary's hair, shoving his head back into its normal position as I drew back my knife and stepped away. "Now, be quiet unless called upon, Gary. Cliff and I are going to continue our little chat."

Cliff whimpered as I walked behind him, my back to the mirror Nannette watched me through. He'd drawn his hands back the moment I'd left him to deal with Gary and now hid them in his lap under the table.

"Put those hands back on the table, Cliff. Don't make me have to ask twice."

The grown man started breathing heavily, tears gliding down his cheeks as he hesitantly raised his hands. They cleared the table, the right index finger limp and awkward, but he struggled to place them on the table, fear keeping them frozen just above it.

I stepped in close to Cliff's back, smelling the salty scent of sweat and the tang of urine wafting up from him as I ran the dull edge of the blade down his cheek, causing his entire body to break out into a barely controlled shiver. Something deep inside me perked up at the reaction, something cold and cruel, something that loved the power of bending a man to my will, and savored those smells of fear and desperation. Something Selander Ryan had put inside me when he'd torn into my throat that first night at The Midnight Rider. "Do as I said, Cliff, or I'm going to have to put you on the naughty list with Gary."

My voice had gone deeper, so deep I almost didn't recognize it as my own, and I suspected it really wasn't. It was the succubus coming out to play inside me. I knew that part of me was good in a fight, one hell of a persuader, and I wondered how useful it would be at drawing information instead of just blood. I glanced at Gary while Cliff forced himself to lay his hands flat on the table and thought how even that man could be easily broken with a little promise of fulfilling his fantasies.

Don't even think about it.

Rider's hard-edged voice in my head brought my eyes up to meet his gaze. He hadn't moved from his spot against the wall, his arms still folded over his chest, but I knew the easy-going pose was deceptive. He didn't even need the use of his hands to toss around anyone in the room or to stop me from doing anything.

And apparently, he could read me like an open book, sensing the shift in me as my other half raised her hand, volunteering to be called upon. I turned to look in the mirror, and saw my eyes were still green, not the red they shifted into when my succubus side attempted a hostile takeover. Yet, I also noticed Gary and Daniel's eyes were a little glazed over. Gary stared at me in a very uncomfortable manner, but Daniel looked away, and I thought I saw him squirm a little in his seat, a couple of signs some of my succubus power had leaked out without the eye-shift. I really needed to learn how to control my power to lure and manipulate. Being able to target it to a specific person instead of any male in the same room with me would be nice too.

I took a deep breath and stepped away from Cliff to dial back my succubus mojo, and got back on track, reminding myself that Mandi Fittro probably wasn't the only woman this Ramson jackass had sent men after and every minute I wasted was a minute of agony possibly being inflicted on some poor innocent woman who needed my help.

"Who is Ramson?"

"Ramson is the way. He is the beginning and the end,

the alpha and the omega, the light that guides us to the world we must return to. He is the blood that springs eternal to save our souls and cleanse our impurities and weaknesses before blessing us with everlasting life in his vein where we will stand among kings."

I stood blinking at Cliff, who'd recited that little spiel as if in a trance and wondered what went through a person's mind to take them to the point they could believe in someone who spouted something that sounded like utter rubbish. As nonsensical as his spiel had sounded, one word stuck out to me: vein.

Blood.

I flashed back to my last *Buffy the Vampire Slayer* marathon, and a bit of Spike's dialogue that always stood out to me. *"Because it's always got to be blood."*

Blood was power. As a vampire, I understood that completely. Blood was life, which was the reason it was used in so many forms of magic and the one thing my kind needed to ensure immortality. Even Jake Porter, not a vampire, but his own freaky brand of immortal, needed to drink blood.

This Ramson character could have watched the same episode of *Buffy the Vampire Slayer* as I had, and could have latched on to that same bit of Spike wisdom as I had, but I suspected Ramson's cronies spoke of his blood for a far more disturbing reason.

"In his vein is a very interesting thing to say. So, do you drink straight from his vein, or does he pour his blood into a glass for you first?"

"What?" Cliff's lip curled back. "Drink his blood? That's not what we drink."

Cliff's face grew pink as he looked down at his hands, and I knew he'd just realized he'd said too much. Gary's face was more of a red shade and I could just hear the cussing going through his mind.

"Remember our deal, Cliffy. Answer my questions or lose the digits." I grabbed Cliff's hand and squeezed his middle finger again.

The interrogation room disappeared as I felt myself falling. Suddenly weightless, I had no body. I was air, unseen as I observed a large group of people under a white tent in the middle of what looked like a wide open meadow. Mostly women, but a fair share of men as well, all with complete adoration in their eyes as they gazed upon the man in front of them.

He stood at around five feet, nine inches tall, with an average build. His billowy white long-sleeved shirt and loose white cotton pants hid the details of his form, but I sensed strength in what I imagined were lean limbs. He was pale, his skin flawless. His hair was a dark chestnut shade and shoulder length. He let it hang freely in gentle waves, but repeatedly shoved it out of his light brown eyes as he paced back and forth, appearing to address the people who had gathered before him under the tent's protection. His mouth moved, but I heard no sound. Whatever he said, he felt strongly about the words he spoke. From his expression and body movement alone, I sensed his passion.

I sensed another passion as his gaze fell upon one woman after another, but it was not their beauty that captivated him. It was the hunger for the only thing I could hear: their blood pumping through their veins. They were all human. He ... was not.

"Danni!"

I opened my eyes and saw Rider looming above me, far closer than he had been to me a moment ago. I also saw the ceiling over his shoulder and realized I was on the floor, held in his arms. "What happened?"

"You tell me. One moment you were standing on your own two feet, speaking, the next you were completely spaced out, locked on to this jackass's finger, which you broke, by the way."

I registered whimpering and glanced over to see Cliff hunched over his hand, crying. A tilt of my head allowed me to see Daniel holding Gary down in his chair in case the man got any brilliant ideas about attempting to defend his partner. I didn't need to look at Mike. I could hear him moaning in the corner as he'd been doing the entire time he'd been conscious after Nannette's smack-down on him.

"Your body was cemented in place. It took a lot of pulling to break your hold on the guy and once I did, down you went. Are you all right?"

"Yeah. Yeah, I'm fine." I brushed my hair back from my face and was reminded of the man I'd been watching doing the same thing. "I think I just saw him. I think I saw Ramson. I'm pretty sure he's a vampire."

"Yeah, I assumed as much when I heard that bullshit about everlasting life and his vein. Corny as hell, but very vampiric. What do you mean you think you saw him? Like a vision?"

I nodded. "Apparently I don't just have a Gibbs gut. I can see things too."

"Plot twist," Daniel said, earning a perturbed look from Rider before he helped me up.

"Are you sure you're fine now?" Rider asked, still holding onto my biceps to make sure I was steady on my feet before risking letting me go.

"I'm good. I can continue the interrogation."

"All right, but don't touch either of them anymore. Touching him seemed to trigger whatever the hell just happened and until we have Nannette take a look at you, I'm not risking you hurting yourself."

My gut reaction was to argue. If I had the ability to touch people and trigger visions, why not use it? It was one hell of a tool to have at my disposal, but then again, I had no recollection of what had happened to me during that vision and regaining consciousness to find myself on the floor, held in Rider's arms didn't really bode well. For all I knew, I'd fried a few neurons with my little vision trip. I'd never been all that great at science stuff, but I was pretty sure I needed my neurons healthy, intact, and not crispy.

"All right. But you know castration is my best interrogation tactic."

Rider barely suppressed a wince. "Yeah. Believe me, it's never too far from my mind what you can do to a man's testicle. From the looks of these guys, you got in enough violence to satisfy your needs for the night, so there's no reason you have to inflict pain on them. If they need it to encourage talking, Daniel and I can pick up the slack."

"Fine, you two can have all the fun, but for the record, most of the really violent violence was on Nannette's part. She's the one who turned that guy into a weeping, moaning puddle over there."

Rider looked over at the severely battered man in the corner. "Yeah, I recognize her work. Ask what you need to ask, but no touching."

"Yes, sir." I grinned, taking the attitude out of my words, and Rider bit back his own grin before returning to where he'd previously stood against the wall, watching.

"All right, Cliffy. Let's try this again." I tried to remember what I'd been asking him before the vision, but my mind had completely blanked on it, so I moved on. "Tell me about the white tent in the meadow. Where do all of those people there to hang on Ramson's every word come from? Can't say I've seen flyers around town, and this meadow has to be somewhere nearby if he sent you hunting for fresh blood around here."

Cliff's skin paled considerably as the blood drained from his face. "How do you know about the tent?"

"She's guessing, you idiot," Gary snapped. "Use your brain. Don't tell her anything."

"Actually, I'm not guessing at all. I just saw the monster you follow blindly pacing back and forth in that tent while his whole... congregation, I guess, would be the word? While they watched him."

"Ramson is not a monster," Gary said, his words vibrating with barely restrained anger.

"Oh really? Then why was he focusing on the sound of blood rushing through his followers' arteries while preaching or lecturing or whatever it was he was doing when I saw him? While you fools hang on to his every word, he listens to your heartbeats and salivates at the thought of drinking the blood he hears flowing as he riles you up with his lies."

"How dare you!" Gary rose from the chair only to land back in it pretty hard as Daniel shoved him down one-handed.

"Keep getting out of your chair and you're going to give me no choice but to break your legs," Daniel warned him.

"Ramson isn't a monster," Cliff said. "He's here to save us."

"What, exactly, is he saving you from, Cliff?"

"Death," Cliff answered. "I don't know what you saw or how you saw it, but Ramson isn't a con. He doesn't just tell us he will save our souls. He's done it. I've seen it with my own eyes."

"What did you see?" I asked, although I already had a pretty strong suspicion of the signs and wonders a manipulative vampire could fool a group of humans desperate to believe in something into seeing and accepting.

"He cured a young woman with cancer. She had leukemia, and chemo wasn't working anymore. Her doctors gave her six months to live. She went to one of the gatherings and she didn't even have to tell Ramson she was sick. He saw her and he just knew it. He blessed her and cast the cancer out of her body. She's healthier now than she was before she got the cancer. Filled with his holy gift, she went from six months to live to eternal life as long as she praises his name."

"That's because she's a vampire, Cliff. Your miracle-working hero turned her into a vampire."

Cliff's jaw dropped open, and he only stared at me for

a moment before swiveling his head around to look at Gary, who shook his head and snorted.

"You see, Cliff? This is exactly what Ramson told us about. They will call us crazy for our faith, but they are the crazy ones. Stay strong. We've seen the power Ramson has. They can't do anything to us. What are a few broken bones compared to the reward we have in our devotion to Ramson?"

"So let me get this right," I said. "You believe that this Ramson guy, a man you believe to be just a man, can actually rid a woman of cancer with just a blessing, but you think vampires are too far-fetched?"

"Of course we do," Gary answered. "Because we're not idiots, and we never said Ramson was just a man. He is a prophet with the power to heal as he leads us to eternal life in heaven."

"So he says."

"So we've seen. Ramson promised us that those who believe will have everlasting life, and he took a woman's cancer away. I've seen others he has blessed go from sickly to radiating health and vitality after receiving his blessing. He is a conduit of the Lord's power and everything he has shown us can be found in the Bible. I can't say I've ever seen a vampire outside of Hollywood. Because they're not real. Ramson is a prophet, not some fanged creature that can't walk in the daylight."

"I'm pretty sure the only thing biblical about what you've seen of Ramson is the warning of false prophets and Satan appearing in many forms. As for the vampire thing, the movies only got some of it right. Vampires do have fangs, but they retract so they're easy to hide when desired, and vampires don't instantly go up in flames after stepping into the sun. However, mortals aren't aware of this, which makes it easier to hide among you. It makes it easier for a monster like Ramson to fool you."

Gary rolled his eyes. "Who are you freaks? You're not LMPD and it wouldn't matter if you were. We've done nothing wrong. You're the ones who jumped us. Just look at what you did to Mike. You're lucky we don't sue you. In fact, that sounds like a good idea. Let us out of this dump or we're suing you for police brutality. Or vigilante brutality. Whatever the hell you are."

"Dump? That's insulting." I stepped closer to Gary. "And you were caught in the process of trying to abduct a woman. With your weapons literally in your hands."

"You have no proof."

"We don't need proof, Gary. Like you just said, we're not LMPD. We don't work for anyone, which means we have no one to answer to. No one knows you're here and no one will be coming to save you. You made a crucial mistake when you tried to grab that woman and things are not going to end well for any of you. However, there are degrees to just how bad the consequences of your actions will be and how helpful you are to us will determine the degree of your punishment and just how long it will last. You really should be more cooperative."

"I don't even know who the hell you are."

"I'm the last face you're going to see before you die. Now, are you going to answer my questions nicely or am I going to have to start on your fingers? I'm starting to think you're the one I should be questioning. I'll certainly enjoy breaking you more."

A sliver of fear flashed through his eyes before I saw his resolve set in. He sneered at me. "Nice bluff, but I heard pretty boy over there tell you not to touch us."

I kicked him, my foot connecting just under his chin with enough force to send him flying up into the air before he crashed down on the floor. I ignored Daniel's whoop of laughter as I took the few steps necessary to reach Gary's fallen body and planted the sole of my boot in his sternum. "Didn't lay a finger on you."

He opened his mouth to speak and let out a hoarse cough before rubbing his throat. "What do you want?"

"I thought I made that clear. I want to know why you

tried to abduct that woman. Why her specifically, and what were you going to do with her?"

"We were taking her to be saved, like we told you. Ramson cures the unclean, but not all know to come to him. We have to bring some to him."

"What do you mean by unclean? Are you saying the woman you tried to grab tonight was unhealthy or is this some type of puritanical bullshit like all who've had sex out of wedlock are doomed to go straight to hell kind of shit?"

"Any who stray from the Word are unclean. Any who put the values of the world above the values of God are unclean. Any who—"

"Hold up, hold up. All I've heard is Ramson this and Ramson that. Do you worship Ramson, or do you worship God?"

"Ramson is a prophet of the Lord. He performs miracles in His name."

I let out a low whistle. I might not be the most religious person. I hadn't been to church since I was a teenager, other than the one time I'd gone to Rome's church at Auntie Mo's request, but I believed in God and although I'd never be one of those people who could recite a bible verse right off the top of my head and tell you where to find it, I knew enough to know that using God's name to do bad deeds was a one-way ticket straight to Hell. Not that I thought Ramson cared about that. Immortal villains tended to think immortality was a get out of Hell free card, but these fools didn't have the chance to outrun death. If Ramson had intended on turning them, he hadn't done it yet.

"So, when you follow this Ramson guy's orders and do the things he asks of you, you actually believe you're serving God? *The* God?"

"I know I am. The Bible tells us Jesus will return and be known by many names."

"Dude, you're in a cult." I took my foot off the man's chest and lowered myself onto my haunches. When I thought the men were worshiping Ramson of their own free will, I didn't have a lot of compassion for them. They'd made their choice. But if they'd truly been manipulated into thinking they were serving God, I had to at least try to get through to them. "The man you call Ramson is a vampire, not a prophet. He certainly is not Jesus returned to earth. Jesus wouldn't send men out to kidnap women, and that miracle you think he performed was a siring. He turned that woman into a vampire and if he's leading a cult that, from what I could tell from what little I saw, seems to consist of mostly women, I highly doubt he's siring women just to save their lives. He's making slaves."

"I don't know what you think you saw, but no one is enslaved to Ramson. Those who have seen his miracles and heard his promises follow him willingly."

"If that were true, you wouldn't need all that duct tape and rope in your murder van, Gary."

"It's not a murder van. We weren't sent to kill the woman. We were sent to bring her to Ramson to be cleansed. We were offering her eternal life, but you and your meddling friends have sentenced her to a mortal death. We told you not everyone who needs cleansing knows to go to Ramson. Once they're brought to him, once they know him, they stay with him of their own free will."

"How does Ramson know the ones he sends you to collect? How does he choose them?"

"He's a prophet," Gary said, drawing the word out slowly as if I were a little slow catching on. "Prophets see what we can't. They come to him in visions."

"So he just saw the woman you went after tonight in a vision and gave you her name and address and you followed her around until you could abduct her?"

"Invite her, not abduct her."

"You say potato, I say abduction."

Gary's upper lip curled in a snarl before he continued.

"He tells us where to be and gives us a description. We knew to look for the brunette walking downtown with a man at the time we saw her."

"Gary, Gary, Gary, you're forgetting something, dumbfuck." I pointed at the moaning man in the corner. "The woman you went after tonight recognized your buddy from her building. You assholes stalked her."

Gary shot a genuinely surprised look in his partner's direction. "She must have been mistaken. Ramson sent us after her. He told us to look for the brunette walking with a man in that area at that hour."

"That's it? A brunette walking downtown at night, a time of night multiple women would be accompanied by a man and would be walking because they would have been leaving a bar?" I shook my head as I stood back up. "The gullibility in you fools is unbelievable. He sent you after a random woman with a very common hair color. No name? No description of clothing? Not even an eye color? You would have gone after any woman you happened to see walking with a man tonight. You've been abducting random women, and he's been acting as if you've brought him his chosen ones every time just to keep you fooled into believing he's some kind of prophet. He isn't. He's a con man."

"Ramson is a prophet! We test the women first. We know they're the ones before we bring them to him."

"And how do you test them?"

Gary shot a warning look in Cliff's direction before averting his gaze, but not before I saw the panic in it. He'd slipped and said too much and I had a feeling I knew what it was he'd revealed, and it was causing rage to bubble inside me.

"How do you test them, Gary? What do you do to the women?" When he refused to answer, I gave Daniel a look he easily read.

Daniel straightened the chair that had toppled over when I'd kicked Gary out of it, and lifted him by his collar before dumping him unceremoniously back into the seat he'd involuntarily vacated.

"What do you do to the women?" I repeated. "What are the duct tape and rope for?"

"I strongly suggest you answer her," Daniel said in a soft tone. "I've seen that look on her face before. It's usually followed by a castration."

Gary swallowed hard before lifting his eyes to meet my gaze, which must have gone murderous because he swallowed again and nearly choked on his tongue. "You wouldn't understand. You'd try to say it was something else because you don't understand. You haven't seen the truth, so you don't know."

"What do you do to them?"

He shook his head. "I serve and answer to Ramson. I am duty-bound to protect him at all costs, even my life. I know he will protect me as he has protected those he has cured of disease. I do not fear you."

"You will." Ignoring Rider's previous warning not to risk touching either man, I bent forward and gripped Gary's balls through his pants. No instant vision assaulted me. All I received was the sound of Gary's pain-filled shout as I gave his goods a good squeeze. Pain was good, but I needed him to fear me if I had any chance of getting him to reveal his secrets, so I peeled back my upper lip and let my fangs drop from my gum.

Gary's skin paled at least three shades as his eyes grew wide and he let out a blood-curdling scream. He jerked back, trying to jump free of the chair and escape, but I had him firmly by the testicles. I gripped them tighter, feeling them squish as his pain-filled cries grew more desperate. He wrapped both hands around my wrist, trying to dislodge my grip while tears streamed down his face, but despite the pressure he applied and the blood his clipped fingernails drew, I didn't budge, except to twist my wrist, increasing his pain.

"Danni?"

"I'm not having a vision or in any kind of trance," I told Rider, never taking my focus off of the scumbag before me. I could hear Rider clearly, sensed all who remained in the room, but I had tunnel vision. All I saw was the man whose scrotum would never produce another sperm. "I'm just breaking this piece of shit."

"Just checking."

"Dude, tell her what you did to the women," Daniel said. "This shit is painful to watch, and she's not going to stop until you answer her or there's nothing left in your pants but blood and mush."

Gary's horrified eyes stared into mine as he opened his mouth to answer, but he couldn't seem to get any actual words out through his wails of pain. I loosened my grip just enough so he could talk. "What was that?"

"Demon! You're demons!"

"Actually, we're vampires and this one's a dragon. I told you vampires were real and you've been conned by one. Still want to tell me how impossible that is?"

"No." He shook his head, gulping down sobs. "No. Ramson is a prophet. He's a holy man, a savior. He came to save us all."

"He came to hunt you and bleed you. You dipshits are out hunting women for him so he can build up his nest. Funny, he hasn't turned any of you three yet. He probably intends to bleed you dry and leave your rotting corpses behind once you're no longer of any use to him and it's less than you deserve for delivering innocent women to him, women who didn't ask to be turned into what they now are."

"No. Ramson's followers can leave whenever they want. They don't want to. They love him. They are all happy."

"Rider, could I leave you if I wanted to?" I asked, and sensed Rider's anguish roll over me so hard I nearly passed out from the strength of it. *If you were a bad sire like your brother*, I clarified through our mind link, which I also included Daniel in before the protective dragon shifter could get any negative ideas about my relationship with Rider.

"No," Rider answered out loud. The painful emotions that had nearly toppled me just a moment ago had dissipated, but his words were forced. Even in a lie, Rider didn't want to admit what he could really do if he chose to, but he understood why I needed him to say he could keep me against my will. "Not if I didn't want you to leave."

"And would you have to keep me tied up or chained?"

It took him a moment to respond. When he did, his response was low. "No."

"So to all around us, I would appear free. Happy, even. You could make me look adoringly at you and remain by your side with no sort of visible tether whatsoever, even if inside, I hated you and wanted nothing more than to escape?"

Danni... the anguish was back in Rider's voice, along with a bit of warning, as he spoke directly into my mind using the link I'd kept open.

I know where she's going with this, Daniel chimed in to the telepathic conversation. *I'm sure Nannette does too. Forget how you feel about her, what kind of man you really are and answer as if you were the type of soul-sucking leech who conned these men and has been taking women. We have to get this guy talking.*

I felt Rider's relief before he spoke out loud. "Yes. A fledgling is its sire's property from the moment of the turning. With a simple command, I could control you to the point you would devote yourself to me, no matter how you truly felt about me. I could make you look like a woman head over heels in love or a student deeply in awe of her teacher... even if your true desire was to watch me die before escaping to regain the freedom you desperately craved."

Gary gulped, his bug-eyes darting over to Rider. "How?"

Rider released some of his power, allowing his eyes to

glow with golden color before he revealed his fangs. "I made her. She is mine to do whatever I wish with, just like those faithful followers are Ramson's."

Rider drew his power back in, seeming to add a little fresh air to the room that had seemed suffocating when he'd gone all glow-eyed and the energy of his power had crawled over us like an army of ants. I took a deep breath, not just because I'd come out from under the heavy weight of all that power, but because he'd really sold the whole evil, manipulative sire bit. His gaze sought mine and the regret I saw there took away any ounce of trepidation or doubt I may have felt.

I know who you really are, I told him through our link, keeping it between just us this time. *I love you and I trust you.*

He answered with his eyes, the dark blue pools warming in returned love and relief as he dipped his head in acknowledgement, the gesture so subtle Gary wouldn't notice the way the big scary vampire had softened.

"No. You're wrong," Gary said, recapturing my focus. "I serve Ramson. I am faithful to him and he's never... Whatever you freaks are, he's never *turned* me or whatever you think it is he does. He doesn't have fangs or whatever the hell it was that guy just did. We follow him because we believe in him, because we've seen what he... what he..."

"You've seen him cure the sick," I finished for him, noticing the difficulty he was having as he obviously put the pieces together. "Vampirism can cure cancer because when one becomes a vampire, the disease is obliterated. However, the person is no longer human. Turning someone to save their life can be a true gift," I told him, glancing at Rider and smiling softly before I put my blank mask back on and returned my attention to Gary. "But not when it is done to enslave them. I'm sure there are many followers who have not been turned yet and those people follow Ramson of their own free will, but once they try to leave, he will turn them to make them stay. He isn't cleansing anyone. He isn't leading anyone to whatever version of heaven he has sold you. He is using all of you and once he's done and you've been turned, depending on how you handle what you become, you're all more than likely ending up in hell once some hunter or more powerful vampire or other paranormal comes along to kill you. Not even immortals are truly immortal."

"S-sorry," the battered lump of man in the corner cried. "S-so s-sorry. I didn't know."

I moved over to the man and kneeled next to him. His body trembled and fresh tears spilled down his face, but unlike the others he had shed in the room, these seemed to carry an emotion other than fear and the trembling didn't seem to all come from pain. "Mike, is it? How did you test those girls, Mike?"

He looked up at me with his one good eye and his face crumpled as a new onslaught of tears erupted from him, causing him to heave with the weight of his sobs.

"Hey." I reached out purely by reflex and rested my hand on his shoulder. The vision immediately slammed into me. I saw them abducting women over and over, and I saw them testing them to see if they were the right ones, the ones who needed cleansing, and I felt what ran through them, especially Gary. Gary who never felt an ounce of shame because he thought the women deserved what they got. All women did. He'd been denied by so many, looked down upon, but now he had all the power and he took what he wanted and it was okay because he was saving them.

I had to have lost consciousness again because I couldn't remember doing anything during the vision, but I didn't faint because when I came to, covered in blood, I had clearly been in action during the loss of time, and I had kept my word. My face had been the last thing Gary had seen before I'd torn his throat out and ripped the rest of him apart with my bare hands.

CHAPTER FOUR

"Are you mad?"

"Mad about what?" Rider asked. "You killing a rapist? He got less than he deserved. You killed him fast."

I had. Too bad I didn't remember any of it, but my violence needs had been met and I apparently drank from the man while I killed him, so I was topped off pretty well too. All I could remember was the sound of terrified screaming and rancid smells of piss and vomit overtaking the coppery scent of blood as I came out of the vision to see Gary's nearly decapitated head staring up at me from where it rested among the bloody ruin of the rest of his body. It had looked as if a massive beast had torn him apart, but I'd been told I had been his sole attacker.

I remembered the stunned look on Daniel's face and the stony expression on Rider's as he took me by my arm and walked me out of the interrogation room. I remembered the shocked expressions on the faces of the members of Rider's tech team as we passed their area and the way they'd frozen, just staring at me as we passed. The expressions on the other guards' faces we passed were a mixture of respect, curiosity, and wariness. Hank had simply raised his eyebrows once we emerged on the ground floor where he had just brought Kutya in through the attached garage. The dog had whined and his wagging tail immediately stilled, something it rarely did when in my or Rider's presence.

Blood had seemed to run down the shower drain forever before I was able to emerge free of the evidence of my kill and step into the buttery soft blue jeans and warm, gray, Polo Ralph Lauren sweatshirt Rider had set out for me in the bathroom. He hadn't needed a full shower, only a change of clothes to remove the blood that had sprayed on him while I'd torn Gary apart. He'd dressed in blue jeans and a black sweater, and his hair was neatly pulled back into the black band at the nape of his neck.

"You good?" he'd asked after I'd finished drying my hair and met him in the bedroom where he'd waited by the bar.

I'd nodded, unsure how else to answer. I had no recollection of just killing a man, but I was otherwise fine.

"Nannette's gone ahead to the hospital. We'll meet her there."

That was the last he'd spoken to me before we drove to the hospital in his Ferrari, no one coming along with us except for the black SUV trailing behind us. I sensed Daniel's presence inside it along with Juan and another male who I could sense was a vampire, but I didn't recognize him. I didn't know all the guards who worked for Rider, and some of them seemed to rotate in and out from other states he conducted business in.

Now we waited for Nannette in one of the exam rooms underneath the hospital in the section known as the Underworld Hospital Ward, an off-grid facility known only to the paranormal world. At least those Rider would allow to know of it. I sat on the exam table where my blood had been drawn and a physical exam performed not long before, having returned from a trip inside a machine that had scanned my brain. Rider leaned against the wall close to the door Nannette would be returning through with my results, his arms folded over his chest. His body appeared relaxed, but I knew him well enough to know he wasn't even close.

"You haven't really said anything to me since we left The Midnight Rider. I can tell you're not happy about what happened in the interrogation room. I didn't mean to get a vision when I touched Mike. I didn't even think about touching him. I just did it automatically."

"I know, and I'm not mad at you for doing it or what you did to Gary after. I'm just ... worried. The gut thing was a handy tool to have at your disposal, but these visions where you don't know what's going on around you and can even lose consciousness? Those can get you hurt. Anything that can get you hurt scares me."

"I know, and I understand that. I don't like to think of you doing anything that could get you hurt either, but are you sure that's all that's bothering you right now? You don't tend to go quiet for no reason."

He blew out a sigh and raked his long fingers through his hair, his hand getting stuck near the band. He bit out a curse and freed his fingers before smoothing his hair back the best he could with just his hands and looked at me before folding his arms over his chest again. "I sensed your succubus half. We all did. You unleashed enough of it to affect every man in that room. I know what you were thinking when you did it."

"Learning to control that side of me has got to be better than suppressing it until it lashes out on its own."

"Yes, but you can't control it. You were just thinking of using it to get those men to answer your questions and you ended up leaking succubus pheromones into the air. In a room full of men."

"You were there."

"Yes, I was, and you can always depend on me to give my life to keep you safe, but if you'd really unleashed that part of yourself in there tonight, I might have died over something completely preventable. Or your friend may have. Three human men are nothing, but Daniel is a damn shifter. An Imortian shifter at that, one who can breathe fire. And you risked putting me in a situation where I would have to fight him to protect you while we were both feeling the effects of your pheromones. Don't ever do that again unless you want one of us to die."

"But I didn't *do* it. I just…"

"You just thought about using your succubus side to get those men to talk. I know. You were pretty damn tempted and your body reacted. The succubus is part of you. I know that and I can imagine how hard it is for you to keep it under control, but it is a beast just like your vampire half. We have to stay in control of our thirst, our need to kill. Your succubus half is no different. You have to stay in control of its lust. Any small crack in the barrier you've set up and it can break free."

"I wanted those men to tell me about Ramson and why they had tried to snatch Mandi Fittro. I wasn't lusting after them."

"No, you weren't, and I'm not accusing you of that. You desired information pretty strongly, strongly enough to be tempted to use your succubus power on those men to get it, and your succubus side needs very little encouragement."

"Okay, so I screwed up. I didn't know that just *thinking* of using that power would unleash pheromones I didn't even know I had the ability to release like that, but you can't expect me to just keep ignoring an entire half of what I am, keeping it caged until it breaks free and does whatever the hell it wants. If I can't learn how to control it, it will learn how to control me."

"Learning how to control it is fine, but in a controlled way. Tell me first and don't unleash it in a room full of men, especially when a shifter is one of those men."

"I didn't unleash it. The pheromone thing just happened, hence why I need to learn more about succubi so that stuff doesn't keep randomly happening."

The door opened, and Nannette stepped inside, holding a clipboard. She'd put her white lab coat on over her street clothes once she'd arrived at the hospital. She looked up from the clipboard and slid a curious glance back and forth between me and Rider. "Whew. There is some tense air in here," she murmured before closing the door. "So the results of your scans show nothing abnormal going on in your brain and your blood hasn't changed since the last time we drew it. No anemia. Your levels are all well-balanced."

"So what caused her to lose consciousness?" Rider asked. "Is this another issue with her succubus side?"

Nannette set the clipboard down on the counter and walked over to the examination table to stand by me before turning toward Rider. "I think the loss of consciousness was due to the sudden rush of power that would flow through her while receiving a vision. This is a new ability for her and it is a shock to her body. With time, she may adjust to the power surge and be able to maintain consciousness while receiving visions. She didn't faint at all the second time. She just wasn't aware of what she was doing while she killed that loathsome piece of shit, which could be attributed to blind rage, not exactly a new thing for our girl. I've been there myself, as I'm sure you have."

"Yeah." Rider nodded. "But I've never had a vision and I'm thinking these gut feelings she's been having are more than just gut feelings. Where is it coming from?"

Nannette turned to me. "Does anyone in your family have any kind of psychic gift?"

I snorted. "Yeah, right. My family is notoriously ungifted."

"Clearly, not all of them," she said and gave me a little thunk on the head with her pen, twisting the corner of her mouth into the barest of smiles before redirecting her attention to Rider, who watched us curiously. "You are well aware that there are pranic vampires, the only type of vampire I can think of who would have this ability. In order to be a pranic vampire, one must have the psychic gift in one's bloodline, either through familial blood or through their vampire bloodline. While you do have a great deal of power, including telekinesis and other gifts not all vampires possess, yours comes with age."

"Maybe not entirely."

Nannette frowned. "What do you mean?"

"My father claimed to have visions."

Nannette blinked slowly. "Your father had visions? You didn't think to tell me this before?"

Rider lost the relaxed pose, his eyes glowing in warning.

"Not that I would ever demand personal information from you," she quickly said, dipping her head in a way that seemed foreign to the usually bold woman. "But for Danni, this information could be important. If there is psychic ability in your blood, it could have passed to her through her turning."

Rider drew in a breath, and the glow in his eyes receded before he spoke again. "I never mentioned it because I had no reason to believe it to be true. I didn't have the powers I have now when I first turned. I was like any other fledgling vampire. I've never had a vision. To my knowledge, neither has my brother. The only reason I know our father claimed to have the ability is because it was the excuse he gave my mother when he left her. He claimed he had to go on a journey because he'd had a vision. She never heard from him again. Frankly, it seemed like a made-up excuse to leave his wife and sons, especially when I was turned and showed no psychic abilities. Not to mention, I don't need permission to enter a private residence like pranic vampires do. However…"

"Reaching through a person's body to remove their organs the way you do isn't a common power," Nannette finished for him.

Rider nodded. "I'm aware. I recently fought alongside a vampire who could rival me in age and power, yet he could not do it. He seemed surprised that I could."

"It's an impressive ability, and psychic power in your DNA could be a factor in what allows you such an ability, even if it took time for that ability to develop. But for Danni, she could develop psychic ability sooner, especially if both you and Selander inherited the ability. Even if it was a recessive trait in you, one or both of you could have passed it along to Danni through your bites and it could be dominant in her, which would make its development at this stage a possibility. It makes more sense than her just randomly having this gift all of a sudden with no discernable cause."

"Whoa." I looked at both of them, my brain catching up to what they were saying. "So, are you saying Rider can just yank out hearts and spines effortlessly because of some psychic power he's given me and I'm going to be able to do that too?"

"After the way you tore that man apart in interrogation, I think it's safe to say you can rip out organs effortlessly already, just not with the whole reach right through them with the glowing hands bit that Rider has, and Rider's psychic ancestry isn't a concrete reason for his abilities. He's still very old and with age comes power. But if his father was psychic, that could definitely be where you got the ability. Or you could be wrong about your own DNA. You may want to ask your mother if there are any relatives who've claimed psychic abilities. So far you've shown strong gut instincts and now you're getting visions. Has anything else happened?"

"Like what?"

"Have you picked up on anyone's thoughts outside of when they've intentionally spoken to you through telepathy?"

"No. And outside of the few times I've followed women I saw at the bar because I knew something bad was going to happen to them, I haven't done anything remotely close to predicting the future," I told her. "Even then, I didn't know what exactly was going to happen to them and I didn't have anything resembling a vision. I just knew in my gut they were in danger."

Nannette stepped away, putting about a foot more distance between us, and held her pen out, allowing it to lie flat in her open palm. "Try to move this pen without using your hands."

I gave her what I was sure was a befuddled look before looking back at the pen. "What, am I supposed to try to kick it out of your hand or something?"

"Use your mind."

"Uh… I don't think my mind does that."

"Try."

Yeah, sure. I looked at the pen and promptly felt like an idiot. "I'm not sure what I'm supposed to be doing here."

"Focus on the pen and think where you want it to go," Rider said. "Then just let your power flow into it."

I looked at him. "Is that how you slam doors with your mind?"

He nodded.

I focused on the pen and thought about it rolling off Nannette's hand, figuring I'd start small. I wasn't sure how one pushed their power out. The only power I'd ever really felt coming out of me was what I could feel flowing around me when I called upon my succubus power, but I now knew that was a release of pheromones I'd felt. I didn't think releasing pheromones was going to do the trick. "I don't seem to have this particular party trick up my sleeve."

"You may develop it later," Nannette said, sliding the pen back into the pocket of her lab coat. "Or you may just stick to the visions and gut feelings. Both of your visions tonight were brought on by touch, so from now on, you should be careful about who you touch and when. Wearing gloves may help, but you touched the second guy through his clothing and triggered a vision, so we won't count on gloves muting the ability. They still may be worth a try if you don't want these visions happening randomly."

She looked at Rider. "Physically, she's fine. Psychic ability isn't something that shows up on a scan, so all we can do is observe and see what happens with her. I think once she gets used to the visions, she'll handle them much better. Until then, just make sure someone is with her at all times and they are aware of this new ability in case she has any more fainting spells. Now, let's discuss this prophet situation. From what Danni was able to get out of those sad sacks and from what she saw, it sounds like there's a vampire building a nest in your territory."

"I gathered as much," Rider said, his hard-edged tone implying what he thought of the situation. "Have you heard of any vampire going by the name Ramson?"

Nannette shook her head. "Danni, were you able to get any sense of this vamp's age or power level in your vision, or could you only see him?"

I thought about it, recalling what I'd seen. "It was such a quick flash. I saw him, and I could tell that he was listening to the heartbeats of the humans listening to him. I felt his hunger for the blood pumping through their veins, but I don't remember sensing his power like I sense yours. I only knew he was a vampire because I could sense his thirst for his listeners' blood, and it made sense when Cliff said he'd healed a woman of cancer."

"Show me what you saw," Rider said.

I recalled what I had seen, trying to remember everything as clearly, but the people listening to Ramson were a blur of faces now. Him, I remembered well enough to send Rider a clear image through our mental link before I reopened my eyes. "I'm sorry, but I was focused on him, not the people. I can't remember exactly how many there were or what they looked like."

"That's fine," Rider said, eyes closed, as he appeared to study the image now in his mind. "He's not anyone I've come across before, to the best of my knowledge. What about you?"

"No," Nannette said, and that was when I realized she, too, had closed her eyes, apparently having been sent the image from Rider. "I don't recognize that area either."

"That could be my fault," I said. "Had I sent you the image right after I had the vision, I'd probably remember all the details better, but it was a big tent in a wide open meadow. I assume it was somewhere in the country given the amount of trees edging it, but there were no landmarks to really tell where it could be."

"It wouldn't be too far away if this vampire is sending his followers here to hunt women. From what you saw before you killed Gary, I'm assuming they took quite a few women to him."

"Yes, but I couldn't tell where they were taken from," I told him. "My visions were just quick flashes of different women being… being…"

Nannette's hand rested on my shoulder, and my very blood recoiled, but her touch was enough to shock me back to my right mind. The succubus part of me was a killer of men who used sex to suck out their life force. Ironically, it also held an intense hatred of men who sexually harmed or abused women in any way. That part of me wanted to feel the warmth of male blood and the headiness of lust as I drained a man dry. It did not want the cooling touch of a woman simmering its rage.

Nannette drew her hand back, picking up on the way my body had stiffened. "Are you all right?"

I nodded, needing a moment before I could speak, pretty sure my words would come out as a deep growl if I spoke too soon. I waited until my fingers no longer held the edge of the examination table in a death grip and my heart no longer raced. "Sorry. Bringing those rape visions back up wakes up something in me that really wants to spill male blood. Thanks for the estrogen touch. I needed that."

"You're still feeling the urge to kill that strongly after what you did to that man tonight?"

"The visions were pretty powerful. I could feel the women's pain. I could feel how they—" I sucked air through my teeth as I turned my head away, my whole body braced as I used all my willpower to fight the replay of the visions stuck in my brain. "Let's move on past this, shall we? Those visions are seriously screwing with my impulse control."

"No more talk of those specific visions," Nannette said in agreement. "When did you last drink from your donor?"

"Last night."

Nannette rolled up her sleeve and held her wrist out in front of me. "Force yourself if you have to. Your succubus side should be sated after tonight's level of violence and the male blood you ingested in the process of tearing that man apart, but it sounds like it needs to chill."

I took her offered wrist in my hand and sucked in a breath, mostly to fight back the revulsion the thought of drinking from her caused, and forced my fangs to drop before I plunged them into her brown skin. I had to fight past my gag reflex, the succubus side of me not wanting female blood, but once it started going down my throat, it soothed my lust to kill.

"We still have the two other men from tonight's capture," Rider said as I drank. "The one you killed seemed to be the toughest nut to crack and the one they deferred to so now that he's out of the picture, we should be able to get the other two to spill their secrets, including where that meadow is. Or at least where they drop women off if they haven't been to that specific location you saw."

I drank until I feared one more swallow would bring it all back up and lifted my head. Nannette licked her own wound closed, knowing how much my succubus side would hate it if I did it for her.

"So we're going back to the interrogation room when we get back?" I asked.

"No, they're going to hang out there until you've had time to simmer down and get some sleep. If you go back in with those visions on replay in your head, you're going to kill the other two before we get enough information out of them."

"Sorry. I know we could have gotten more out of Gary if I hadn't killed him so soon."

"Maybe, maybe not. He was the most stubborn of the three and the most sucked-in by whatever that vampire did to make them believe in his bullshit so deeply. Besides, I would have killed him myself if you hadn't done it. The asshole called me a pretty boy. There was no way I was allowing him to breathe much longer after that."

"Ah, so that's why you didn't attempt to stop me."

"That and it served a purpose. After they've had a day to think about what they saw you do to their partner, the remaining two should be a lot more willing to answer your questions, regardless of whatever loyalty they may have to the vampire."

"I'm pretty sure Nannette beat Mike's loyalty right out of him," I said, chuckling. "He seemed to be coming around to logic before I accidentally pulled those visions out of him."

"Anything worth doing is worth doing well," Nannette said. "That includes whooping ass."

Rider straightened from his lean against the wall. "So she's all good for now? I can take her home and put her to bed?"

"Hey, I'm sitting right here." I waved my hand. "You don't have to talk about me like I'm not in the room. Or like I'm a child who needs to be tucked in."

I thought you liked the way I tuck you in, Rider said through our telepathic link, and I felt a blush warm my face.

"Danni should be fine. She's met her violence needs and then some," Nannette said with a grin. "And I just gave her some live female blood to act as a kind of sedative. Just keep her away from those men and don't let her touch anyone until she gets some rest and isn't as emotionally affected by the visions she had earlier."

"You heard her," Rider said, as he stepped closer and held out his hand to help me down from the examination table.

"Oh. I have some books and notes for you," Nannette said. "I'll email you some information too. You'll have it by the time you return to The Midnight Rider."

Rider had just helped me off the table and now frowned at me and Nannette. "What are you talking about?"

"I spoke to Nannette earlier about wanting to learn more about succubi so I can better understand the other half of me."

"And you thought this was a good idea, Nannette?" Rider sighed. "You know she wants to use her succubus side to interrogate men. You probably couldn't feel what happened tonight, but she just thought about using her succubus abilities and accidentally released pheromones. We're damned lucky things didn't go sideways in there."

Nannette looked at me. "Danni, were you aware you could release pheromones that way?"

"No," I answered. "I did something similar when we fought the krackling, but that was intentional and I mentally called out to that big ugly thing. I didn't know I could do something like that without meaning to."

"All the more reason to learn about her succubus side," Nannette said, meeting Rider's perturbed gaze. "You can keep her in the dark and allow her to keep having accidents and near-catastrophes, or you can allow her to actually learn about what she is so she is aware of all the things her body can do. Not only can she figure out how to use her abilities to her advantage, but she can learn to recognize when something has gone wrong before it gets out of her control. Perhaps if she'd known about the pheromones she can release, she would have been more careful earlier."

"I'm not banning her from learning about herself," Rider said, his tone just short of a growl before he narrowed his gaze on me. "It would be good for you to learn more about your other half, but you can't be reckless. Any ability you learn about and want to try needs to be attempted only under supervision. You must also keep in mind that you are a hybrid and your hybridness alters everything."

"I know, Rider. I just want to know more about what I am so I can stop being afraid of it. Yes, I think my succubus abilities could be an asset for interrogation, but only if I can harness them. You know very well I've never wanted to be some freaky sex demon, but these abilities are in me and they want out. Maybe if I can get in touch with my succubus half, I can figure out how to compromise with it instead of fighting it constantly while it keeps searching for a crack in my armor to take advantage of."

He stared at me long enough I was afraid he'd overrule Nannette, but he eventually nodded. "Fine, but be careful, and I think you need to work with Eliza on this. Especially now that you're having visions."

"I was going to recommend her as well," Nannette said. "Eliza is better with the metaphysical side of things than I am. She may know more about this new ability than I do."

Eliza hadn't been her usual cheery self since discovering her father's soul had been held prisoner inside the body of an archdemon. It was understandable given she'd helped us kill the archdemon in order to save her friends, losing her father all over again. Such an ordeal would have affected anyone, but Eliza was special. She was a lot softer than me, or pretty much any other vampire I'd yet met. We supposedly all had darkness inside us, but if darkness lurked somewhere inside Eliza, I sure hadn't been able to find it.

"I'll see if she's up to it," I said, and thought about Jon, the mysterious man who'd fed me prior to going up against that archdemon and somehow imbued me with his own power. I'd thought it had run out after I'd used it to teleport myself and several others out of the demon's realm, but… "Is it at all possible that these visions and gut feelings I'm having are related to what Jon shared with me when he fed me back in Pigeon Forge?"

"Nothing magical in nature showed up in your examination or scans," Nannette said. "From the way you described it, he passed his power to you through his blood, similar to a blood magic spell. Once his blood left your system, so should have all traces of his power."

"Sure would be nice if we could ask him."

"Seeing as how there's no way to contact him and one never knows when or if to expect a visit from Jon, you'll have greater success researching psychic abilities while digging into your succubus side," Rider said, taking my elbow.

A knock sounded at the door and I sensed Daniel a moment before he poked his head inside. His gaze roamed over me with concern before he turned it toward Rider. "Just got a call from the tech team. Pacitti just sent a message to that cell phone you gave them to monitor."

CHAPTER FIVE

We made it back to The Midnight Rider in record time and promptly took the stairs down to the area Rider referred to as The Bat Cave, where his team of techs could always be found glued to the computers in front of them. I didn't know a single one of them, but they consisted of males and females of various paranormal makeups. Some appeared human, none appeared to waste time fooling around. Every time I passed the area, I saw them tapping away at their keyboards or putting information up on the large plasma screen taking up nearly the whole wall in front of the rows of tables where they sat and worked.

"What do we have?" Rider asked as we reached their work area.

A short man with cropped dark hair, a wide nose, and rosy complexion standing in front of the big screen loaded with multiple windows of information turned toward Rider. He raised his hand and clicked the remote in it to enlarge one of the windows so we could clearly see the text messages sent to Jeff Brinley's cell phone.

"The text came from a burner phone but it appears to be from Pacitti based on the subject matter," the man, who I believed was some sort of shifter, said. "We're trying to trace it, but burners are difficult, even with our resources."

Rider nodded as we came to a stop next to the man. He folded his arms and read the screen.

I HIT THE MOTHERLOAD, J. VAMPIRES AND WEREWOLVES ARE REAL AND I FOUND THEM. BIG PAY DAY COMING. THESE FREAKS WILL WANT THEIR SECRET KEPT. OTHERS WILL PAY BIG FOR THEIR LOCATION. LAYING LOW WHILE WORKING OUT THE DETAILS. STAND BY. N.P.

"Has a ransom request come in?" Rider asked.

"Not yet," the shifter answered. "Nothing out of the ordinary has come through Miss Keller's mail and you've received all the mail we've received so far for The Midnight Rider if this guy's figured out your connection. We have someone in place monitoring her family's mail as well. Nothing suspicious so far. Pacitti hasn't reached out to Miss Keller's mother or grandmother by phone either."

"He's up to something if he's expecting a big payday," Rider said. "The others will pay big comment is a concern."

"Yes, sir. We've been monitoring chat all over the dark web since Miss Keller received that letter from him. If he's speaking to anyone about vampires and werewolves, it's bound to be on a website devoted to such. The problem is, there are so many to root through, from valid hunter sites with heavy encryption and password protection to roleplay boards where serious conversation can get lost in all the fluff. We're running searches round the clock to detect any mention of Miss Keller or Pacitti. He's being careful, but we'll catch him. The good news is none of the security cam images he sent her appear to have been posted online in any public forums so far."

"And the footage itself? You're positive there is no longer any trace of it out there other than what that snake has in his possession?"

"Yes, sir. From what we've been able to piece together, Pacitti had to have found the unconscious bodies before they woke up and called the police. According to the police report, they spoke with residents near the scene of the reported attack but didn't find any security footage corroborating the story they got from the woman who'd reported the attack on her, her husband, and their two friends. However, one of those men who'd claimed to have been attacked was the one who owned the residence that footage was taken from and he discovered his house had been broken into and the security footage stolen while still unconscious."

"Pacitti," Rider said.

The shifter nodded. "Although they were given descriptions of Miss Keller and her security detail, the police have yet to follow up and I highly doubt they will, given the convenient loss of the security footage. Notes in the report indicate they believe the group was either drunk or high. All of them have been arrested before for incidents involving substances or domestic violence."

"How could Pacitti have stolen the footage without any trace of it?" I asked. "Wouldn't the security company still have access to it?"

"If it were the type of security footage most people use these days," the shifter said with a grin. "I'm not sure if the group you tussled with were poor or just really old school about their tech, but the security system used was ancient. It recorded straight to VHS. VHS," he said again, enunciating the letters for effect. His eyes bugged out a little before he seemed to realize something and narrowed them. "Do you know what that is?"

"Yes," I said dryly. "I'm young, but I'm not young enough to have never heard of VHS. I can't imagine why anyone in this day and age would use such an antiquated system though."

"I can," Rider said. "If they'd been arrested for

substances before, they probably dabbled with dealing. A security setup that allowed them to delete what they recorded makes sense."

"Wouldn't they want to stay off the police's radar altogether, then, if that were the case?" I asked. "Why would they even report the attack?"

"Because they were pissed you beat the shit out of them," Rider said, looking at the screen. "What's his play? Why warn you in advance that he had the footage if he still hasn't bothered to use it?"

"I guess those are the details he mentioned he's working out," I said, nodding toward the words on the screen. "I'm guessing he hasn't figured out Daniel's a dragon since he mentioned werewolves."

"All he would have seen on that footage was Daniel disappearing and reappearing," the shifter said. "I'm surprised he made any kind of shifter connection off of that, given the way Daniel shifted. He never took any other form, so all he knew was that a man was blinking in and out of existence. Even if he did release that footage to the public, what Daniel did could be passed off as a glitch."

"Except for his hand getting shot to bloody bits and magically regenerating," I pointed out.

"I suppose there's that," the shifter said. "Do you want us to text back, try to engage him?"

"Keep it simple," Rider said. "We don't want him to suspect his friend's been compromised."

I supposed compromised was one way of putting it. Jeff Brinley was dead. Beyond dead. I'd obliterated the man.

The shifter turned his head and nodded at a small-framed woman working on a computer behind us. She appeared to be human and whatever was in the mug personalized with the name Kirsty on it smelled herbal, not coppery, as she lifted it to take a swig. She nodded back at the shifter, typed rapidly on the keyboard and then nodded toward the screen. We looked to see WHERE R U BRO? WTF IS GOING ON? SHIT SOUNDS CRAZY showing sent from Brinley's cell phone.

"Is that the way he would respond?" I asked, wondering if Pacitti would notice any discrepancies.

"Kirsty is good at posing as other people online and through chat. She studies their social profiles and their messaging patterns," the shifter explained. "Pacitti won't detect anything off."

I GOT A REAL SEXY SLAB OF RIBEYE IF YOU WANT TO MEET UP AND TELL ME WTF IS GOING ON popped up on the screen and the shifter shot a scolding look the woman's way. "Carruthers."

"What?" she said. "The man was seriously weird about meat."

"She's not wrong," I said. "I saw enough of Brinley's Facebook profile to know it would actually be weird if he didn't mention meat in a perverse way."

He shook his head and sighed. "We'll inform you right away if he responds, but considering how long he took to send a message since his last contact with Brinley, I wouldn't expect anything soon."

"What about the other situation?" Rider asked. "Any updates on my donor?"

The shifter used his remote again and the window with the texts shrank down, replaced with multiple security cam feeds showing what looked like an apartment door, a street view of a building, and other street views I couldn't place. The name Julie Chavez showed in the upper right corner of each feed.

"This is the last footage we have of her," the shifter said before pressing another button and the videos started playing.

The first feed showed a dark-haired woman exiting an apartment. Her face was turned down, so I couldn't get a good look at her, and I wasn't entirely sure I wanted to. I knew the woman was one of Rider's donors and I didn't need the visual of his mouth on her, even if it was innocent. I couldn't tell much about her. Her hair was long and bangs hid a lot of her face. She wore blue jeans, athletic shoes, and a big puffy coat that hid any hint of her shape. A dark purse was slung over her shoulder and I watched her tuck her keys inside it as she left the apartment and walked off-screen. The moment she disappeared from the first feed, another started playing and I watched her walk down the street, passing a parking lot.

"Her car is still there in the lot," the shifter said. "This feed was from a week ago. She continues to walk down the street several blocks until she turns onto Shelby Street, and that's where we lose her. No one ever approaches her. She doesn't speak to anyone. Her cell phone was left in the apartment. We've watched the security footage from the month prior and from that moment until the present. No one ever visited her apartment except for you or the other donors. There are no texts on her phone and no unknown phone numbers."

"She didn't just disappear, Tobias."

Ah, so that was the shifter's name.

Tobias—I scrunched my nose up at the name and decided the shifter looked more like a Toby so that was what I would call him—pressed a button on the remote to fast-forward to the point where Julie Chavez turned down Shelby Street. "No, she didn't disappear, but we lost her here. There are no traffic cams there we could access. We've searched all around, but we never pick her up again. We could trace license plates from all the vehicles we can see turning onto Shelby Street, but there are a lot of small side roads that intersect the length of that street. If she got in someone's vehicle, there's really no telling at which point they entered or exited the street. If they did. She could still be there somewhere, but we've gone through her phone. She doesn't appear to know anyone who resides there."

"Yet she turned down that street for a reason," Rider said, "and she chose to leave her apartment without her phone. She knows we can track the phone and the car. She wasn't abducted. This was an escape, and it was with help. She wouldn't have had cash. Dig deeper. You're missing something. I want her found now."

Rider's voice had steadily deepened until the last command came out as a menacing growl that caused Toby to swallow hard before nodding. I'd seen the way Rider handled his employees who betrayed him, and I knew all in his nest had a healthy fear of displeasing him, but I hadn't imagined him being as ruthless with the members of his tech team. But judging by the way the short shifter suddenly became overwhelmed with nerves, it appeared Rider could be just as hard on them.

"Of course, sir. We are still searching for any possible security or traffic cam feeds we may have missed, going back weeks, months if we have to. If Julie Chavez was in contact with anyone, we will find it. We can report her missing if you like, get the public's help in finding her. We, of course, wanted to get your approval before going that route, but if you wish to go that way, we have her information all ready to blast all over the 'net. We can also have her face on every telephone pole in the city within an hour." He clicked a button and a missing persons flyer appeared on the screen, filled out with Julie Chavez's name, description, a contact number, and a steep reward for information leading to her whereabouts. Above all that was her picture.

Dark eyes peered out from under a curtain of thick, dark, straight hair. Julie Chavez had a long oval-shaped face, a straight nose and full lips. She wore less makeup than I would have thought a former prostitute would wear, and I was surprised to see she appeared to be somewhere in the vicinity of her late thirties to mid-forties. For some reason, I'd always imagined Rider's donors to be young, voluptuous twenty-somethings with skimpy clothes and heavily made-up faces.

I looked deeper into those dark eyes and suddenly Julie Chavez came to life before me. I saw her amid several other faces in a rapt crowd as the man she saw as her salvation spoke before her, lulling her into a false sense of security as she hung on his every word, never knowing he was a snake and she was his prey.

"Danni!"

The scene that had been so real to me it had felt as though I were there standing under that tent in the meadow disappeared, replaced with Rider and Toby's concerned faces as they peered down at me.

"Did I faint again?"

Rider nodded, then settled me onto my feet, having caught me before I'd had the chance to hit the floor. "What did you see?"

I pointed at the screen where Julie Chavez's face still stared back at me. "I know where Julie Chavez is. He has her. Ramson. I saw her in that tent when I had the vision earlier. I just didn't know she was one of his followers until I saw her face just now."

I sent the image to Rider through our mind-link and watched as storm clouds entered his eyes, storm clouds that quickly gave way to the roar of thunder as he began barking orders at the people around us, all of whom quickly averted their gazes and started tapping ferociously on their keyboards, hastily jumping on the new task they'd just been given: Find Ramson before heads started to roll.

***

The fury rolling off Rider as we took the stairs up to the ground floor was palpable. Once through the door leading to the small room behind the public area of The Midnight Rider, we were greeted by Daniel's curious gaze as he leaned against the wall next to the garage entrance. Kutya stood next to him, his wagging tail quickly coming to a halt as he sensed his master's mood.

"Hank dropped the dog off about twenty minutes ago. I told him I'd watch it so he could head home. He looked tired," Daniel said. "What's wrong now?"

"Ramson has Rider's donor," I said when Rider just stood there, grinding his teeth, fuming. "I didn't realize I'd seen her in my vision earlier, but once I saw her face on the tech team's screen, I knew she was one of the people I'd seen listening to him."

"Shit," Daniel muttered, his now understanding gaze sliding back over to Rider. "Are you thinking this is a personal attack against you?"

"If it is, the bastard is going to soon regret it," Rider growled, eliciting a whine out of Kutya. Noticing the dog's reaction, his gaze softened a fraction, but his body remained as tense as it had been since I'd revealed Julie Chavez's whereabouts to him. "It's nearly dawn. Danni is in for the day. You can go home and grab some rest now. Keep an eye on Rome and bring him with you when you report back in at nightfall."

Daniel's concerned gaze shifted back over to me, but he only nodded before straightening from the wall and turning for the door that would take him out to the bar area where Rome would be, watched by whoever Daniel had tagged in to babysit the big guy and keep him away from anything not on his diet. "See you then."

"Come on." Rider smacked the side of his thigh with his open hand, and I wasn't really sure if the command was for me or the dog. We both followed him up the stairs leading to the small living quarters where he slept. The single room with attached bath that I'd been staying in with him, however small and sparse it was. But hey, it had a bed and a television set. And who really needed a kitchen when you couldn't even eat anything worth eating? The only sustenance I needed could be found in Rider's vein or in dark glass bottles available in the bar downstairs.

Rider pushed right through the door, no time wasted

on unlocking it. The door was spelled to only allow those he wanted inside, so locks were an unnecessary security measure. Kutya immediately trotted over to the chaise and stretched out, his eyes still showing unease, unsure how to take his master's foul mood.

"You're going to sleep until sundown, and please don't argue with me about it," Rider said in a clipped tone, already sitting on the foot of the bed to take his shoes off. "You've had a long night and fainted twice. I don't give a shit if Nannette didn't find anything in her examination. You need to rest."

The urge to reply with an attitude-laced, "Yes, sir, master, sir!" was right on the tip of my tongue, but I didn't follow through on it. I was actively trying to be less of a pain in Rider's ass. Besides, he was clearly pissed off already, and I didn't think it was a good idea to poke the big snarly vampire with a stick.

"Are you going to help me with that?" I held my hands up, palms facing him, when he looked up at me with a heated glare that did nothing to relax the poor dog watching us from the chaise. "I'm just asking. You know I often wake up well before sundown when I don't get a little extra help from you in that department. I'm not asking so I can blast you for using your sire power over me. Honestly... it would be nice to be able to go to sleep without worrying the visions I saw earlier might pop back up into my nightmares, and I'm a little too wired now to really even think about sleeping."

"That'll change as soon as the sun finishes rising," he said softly before standing from the bed. He pulled his sweater over his head and tossed it to the floor before drawing me into his arms. "I'm sorry you had to see such things. I can only imagine how hard it is for a woman to see something like that and not be able to do anything to stop it."

I shuddered involuntarily and wrapped my arms around him, craving his body heat. "Not the best part of my evening," I said in agreement. "I can think of a lot of benefits to this new ability, but witnessing something like that, almost feeling as if I were experiencing it myself through those poor women... It was rough. I wouldn't mind you taking away my ability to dream today."

"You will rest assured that nothing will invade your mind while you sleep." He kissed the top of my head before letting me go to cross over to the closet, where he yanked a black long-sleeve shirt off of a hanger and pulled it on before grabbing a pair of shit-kickers from the floor.

"Wait. What are you doing? I thought we were going to bed."

"You're going to bed. I'm hunting that cult-leading bastard down and wiping him off the face of the earth before I drag that traitorous bitch back here to add her head to the breakroom décor."

I drew back, stunned by the vehemence in Rider's tone, not to mention the callous way he'd just spoken of the woman he'd been concerned for not even twenty-four hours earlier. "Where did that come from? Rider, you don't know what happened. She could have been snatched off the street and brought to him against her will. I just prevented that exact thing from happening to a woman tonight."

"You had the vision, Danni. If what you shared with me was accurate, she was enthralled by the man's every word. She wanted to be there. Not only did she betray me, but she betrayed me to follow another vampire. One who has decided to hunt in my territory. It seems a little coincidental he sends his goons after a woman who was drinking in my bar so soon after one of my own donors goes to him. I never shared secrets with any of my donors, but they know I operate this business. They know how to contact me, and they know that apartment building is mine. Now I have to relocate them all for their own safety because of a traitor who left the generous safety I gave her to sell me out to a fucking pranic vampire building a nest of blind followers who will do anything he commands of them."

"If I hadn't sensed something bad was going to happen to the woman in the bar tonight, you would have never known someone in your bar was being hunted by him and his doting idiots. It's not like he left a note saying 'Hey, Rider. I got your donor and now I'm hunting your customers. Come and get me.'"

"Maybe he would have had he gotten her. You prevented that from happening and you took his men. You foiled his plans."

"I'm pretty sure his only plan was to send those dumb-fucks out to grab a woman off the street, giving them just enough information to make their gullible asses believe the random woman they grabbed had come to him in a vision, making what they did to her seem... I don't know... predestined or sacred or something. It's not like they were sitting in your bar watching her. That van wasn't parked outside when we followed her out of here. Those men were just driving around downtown, saw the brunette they'd been told to find in the general area they'd been told she would be in, and they went for her. I don't believe Ramson was specifically going after your customers, and I don't think he intentionally grabbed your donor in an attempt to get to you. I think she was in the wrong place at the wrong time, just like the others they've grabbed."

"You said the woman you saved recognized the driver from her building," Rider reminded me. "Not just a wrong place at the wrong time deal."

I shrugged, remembering Mike may have had a hidden motive behind grabbing that exact woman. "Yeah, true, but I still don't see a connection between your donor and what happened tonight."

"If she's innocent in this, Danni, why did she leave her cell phone behind? Why did she just randomly head out for a walk on a cold-ass day? If she had somewhere to go, she would have driven, and mortals never leave their cell phones behind. They're practically attached to the damn things."

"I don't know why she left her phone behind," I said, admitting to myself that was pretty odd. I wasn't obsessed with social media, but even I felt naked if I didn't have my cell phone with me and who the hell knew how to get anywhere without GPS? I'd tried to read a map before. I'd have had better luck navigating by the stars. And phones were more than just a way to connect socially. They were protection. I couldn't imagine any woman walking alone in downtown Louisville without a way to call for help if they got into trouble, especially not a former prostitute who knew how dangerous men could be to women on their own. But still… "She's just a human woman. One who has seen the dark side of man and has undoubtedly been hurt before. You're speaking of this woman as if she's one of the monsters we hunt."

"Humans can be monsters too, Danni. In fact, they often are, especially the ones who have been hurt. They can be worse than any creature with fangs and venom. You know this already. Didn't you tear one apart just this night?"

"Yes." I sighed. "But I still don't believe your donor turned on you. For one, when could she have? Your tech team has pulled everything they have on her and they haven't found any messages between them. She's had no unknown visitors, and frankly… I just know she didn't turn on you."

"How would you know that?"

"I would have felt it," I said, sure in my gut that I would have known if a traitor had been in my vision. "I didn't even notice her when I first had that vision of Ramson because she didn't set off any kind of reaction in me. I didn't know who she was to recognize her, but still, if she'd been some sort of traitor giving Ramson information about you, I'm sure my gut would have picked up on it. I had that vision of Ramson because he is a threat. He is the reason I knew to follow Mandi Fittro out of here. You told me your donor was missing, and I didn't get a single odd feeling. Not one bell dinged in my head. Because Julie Chavez wasn't and I believe still isn't a threat."

"Then why did you see her? You saw her, Danni. The moment you saw her face, you didn't suddenly remember having seen her before in that tent. You were hit with another vision. A memory wouldn't have made you faint. You saw her. You had a vision. That says guilty to me."

I reached up and cupped his tightly clenched jaw. "If you start accusing everyone I see in a vision of being some sort of evil traitor, I'm going to have to start keeping them to myself."

"Danni."

"I won't be responsible for innocent people being hurt or worse because you misinterpret what I see. I could feel the evil in Ramson when I had the vision of him. I could feel that Mandi Fittro was in danger when I saw her downstairs at the bar. If Julie Chavez really was a traitor, if she was feeding Ramson information he could use to do whatever it is you seem to think he might do, don't you think I would have felt that? I'm not one hundred percent sure how this strange gift or ability, whatever this thing is that I have, works, but it seems to alert me to people I can save. I love you more than I have ever loved anyone in my entire life. You are the most important person in the world to me. If anyone was out to harm you, do you really think my gut would ignore *that* while sending me out to save people I don't have any sort of emotional attachment to?"

Rider swallowed, and some of the stiffness in his body eased. "You really don't think Julie turned on me?"

"The moment I saw her face on that screen downstairs I knew she was in trouble, and the moment I realized she was one of the many faces in that tent hanging on Ramson's every word, I knew she was in over her head, but I never felt she was there to bring harm to you." I allowed my hand to fall away from Rider's jaw and settle over his chest. "We need to find her and all those other people, and not to kill them. We need to save them. So you need to stay in today."

"Danni."

"You need to stay in today. You need to rest so you can think straight, otherwise you're going to let your anger guide you and do things you will regret."

Rider just stared at me for a moment, his mouth tight and eyes full of shifting emotions, as he seemed to have an internal debate with himself. Finally, he tossed the shit-kickers back toward the closet and scrubbed a hand down his face. "I miss the days when I was foolish enough to believe I was actually in charge here."

I grinned. "Eh, you were kind of a pain then."

He narrowed his eyes, but they held no heat. "Even if Julie just happened to be in the wrong place at the wrong time and was abducted, she is still a danger to us if Ramson is a pranic vampire. Pranic vampires gain access to the minds of those they feed from. One drink of her blood or energy and he'll know where I house my donors and what better way to attack a rival vampire than to take out his blood source? I need to make sure my other donors are safe."

"Your other donors who live in a building with several shifters and vampires who fight and kill for a living?" I asked. "And what do you mean by energy? How does a vampire drink energy?"

"Pranic vampires don't just feed off blood. Blood may sustain their bodies, giving them immortality, but they can feed off energies and emotions, all of which they draw power from, and yes, members of my security staff live in the same building where my donors live, but I feel responsible for them. I promised them protection, and I lost one. That's unacceptable."

"Julie Chavez wasn't abducted from her apartment. You promised her safety, and you gave it. For whatever reason, she chose to leave her cell phone and her vehicle and go out walking all by herself. You are not responsible for your donors every second of the day and can't be held responsible for something that happens when they make poor choices, so cut the guilt."

I folded my arms and met Rider's raised eyebrow with a stern look. "You will find her because for whatever reason, I'm having visions of the man we know she is with, so quit acting like you aren't doing enough. You're doing enough just by listening to me and once we've both rested, we can interrogate those two men further. The others are safe because you've already informed your tech team of Ramson and they've informed all members of your security staff, including those who live in the building with your donors. If anything were to happen, they could reach you even while you slept, so there is no reason for you not to rest and start clear-headed at sundown."

"Fine. I'll sleep, but first I—"

I placed my finger over his lips. "You just threatened to kill one of the same donors you're so upset over believing you haven't protected well enough. You are not thinking clearly, so there is no first anything. You're coming to bed, and don't you dare even think about waiting until I fall sleep so you can do whatever you please, because I promise there will be hell to pay when I wake up."

He sighed. "Danni, if Ramson is a pranic vampire, and I highly suspect he is, if he's able to manipulate so many humans into believing he's some sort of prophet, he is far more dangerous than your average vampire. He could have powers that make mine look like cheap magic tricks. I can't allow him any ground. We have to get him before he gets us."

"If he's that dangerous, you should call in help."

"I already thought of Seta, but she's kind of off-world."

I didn't pretend to know what that was supposed to mean. "I wasn't thinking of Seta."

Rider's face went stony. "No."

"Come on, Rider. If Ramson is a pranic vampire and you think he might be that big of a threat, who better to help locate and bring him down than someone genetically designed to do just that?"

The sound of grinding teeth reached my ears before he responded. "You wouldn't be suggesting this because you still have an infatuation with the jackass, would you?"

"I was never infatuated with him, only the character he happens to look like. To be honest, I think he's kind of a wiseass, but he is good at what he does." I stepped as close to Rider as was physically possible and wrapped my arms around his waist. "I want you to get his help because I've seen you angry and murdery many times, but I've never seen you so upset that you would even think of suggesting killing a human woman you once saved and making a display of her head. I'm not sure if it's rage over the betrayal you think she may have committed or fear over what you think this vampire may be, but I'm worried about you, and you know how my gut has been lately. If I'm worried about you, there's probably a good reason for it. Call Jake in or I will."

CHAPTER SIX

Rider kept his word and ensured I slept through the day with no bad dreams. I hadn't dreamed at all, but that didn't mean I woke up worry-free.

"How long have you been up and what all have you done?" I asked the moment I opened my eyes to see Rider standing over me, having just used his power to pull me out of the dreamless sleep.

He was dressed in black pants and a black T-shirt, standard attire for kicking ass. Or killing ass. His hair was tied back neatly at his nape and although he didn't sport any bruises or cuts, that didn't mean much with his healing abilities.

"I gave you my word I wouldn't kill anyone before you woke up," he said. "I almost think you didn't believe me. Kind of hurtful."

"Yeah, well, you didn't exactly come to that agreement easily," I reminded him, referring to the arguing we'd done well into sunrise before he finally agreed not only to contact Jake Porter but to refrain from killing anyone or actively hunting down Ramson without first waking me.

"Sure I did, once you said the magic word."

"It's more like I said the magic number." I narrowed

my eyes at him, but couldn't stop the corners of my mouth from twitching with the urge to grin. For all his supposed abhorrence of Jake Porter, Rider enjoyed the book the slayer had snuck onto his bookshelf before leaving after helping us kill a krackling, especially page thirty-three. If I'd known the sex manual full of twisty, bendy, creative positions would have come in so handy in getting my way, I would have bought the thing myself ages ago.

"That's what I meant." He grinned, although his eyes didn't hold much humor. "Are you getting up now so I can go kill something?"

I sat up immediately and reached for the shirt that had been discarded on the floor that morning. "Do I have to repeat my question again? You promised me you wouldn't do anything while I was asleep."

"I said I wouldn't physically hunt or kill anyone and I haven't," he said as he watched me pull the shirt over my head and get out of the bed. "But unlike you, there's no one with the power to make me sleep until nightfall when my mind is preoccupied, so I've been up for a while, reaching out to contacts, checking leads. So far, there's not much on this Ramson character, but prannies aren't known for networking with other vampires."

"Prannies?"

"Pranic vampires."

"Ah." I playfully smacked the hand creeping up the backside of the hem of my shirt. "Focus."

"Believe me, I am."

"Not on that. You said you were going to kill someone. Who?"

"I don't know yet. Probably Porter."

"You called him?"

"I made a promise, didn't I?" He shook his head, a look of disgust on his face. "I still can't figure out at what point exactly you gained enough power in this relationship to make me call that jackass."

"I think I got it on Christmas when we first cracked

open that book."

"Figures the sonofabitch would leave something in my office guaranteed to take away my power," he muttered before kissing me. "Did you sleep well?"

"Dream-free like you promised." I purposely recalled the visions I'd had after touching Mike the night before and was relieved to not find myself overcome with rage. "Thank you for that. I think I'm rested well enough that the visions I had last night aren't overpowering my emotions like they were."

"Good. Hopefully, you're well-rested enough to handle the effects of any new ones since we'll be talking to Ramson's goons again. We should do that before Porter gets here. I don't want that slayer to know any weaknesses you have, so fainting in front of him is something we want to avoid."

I fought the urge to roll my eyes. "The man disappeared me right out of here and slit my throat. He took me to some sort of safe room where no one could detect me, not even with magic or your own sire power. I'm pretty sure the man doesn't need to find a weakness in me to kill me, and frankly, if ever there was a time the slayer could have killed me, it was then, but he didn't. He saved me. He can be trusted."

Rider's eyes darkened. "Reminding me that he slit your throat isn't the best way to ensure he leaves here alive."

"You know he had to or else I would have died."

"Yeah, I know. That's why he's still breathing."

"That and the fact he can't really die," I reminded him with a smirk. "I guess you could kill him if you want. He'll just wake back up."

"I hate that jackass," Rider muttered, tugging my shirt over my head. "But I agree he can be useful, so I made the call despite the acid reflux it gave me to do it. He'll be here soon enough, so we'll have to make this quick."

"This what exactly?" I batted my lashes, playing coy as my fingers dipped inside his waistband.

"This proof that you desire me and not that life-sized Dean Winchester cardboard cutout."

"No contest," I said as my back hit the wall and Rider's pants hit the floor.

***

Once I'd reassured Rider that Jake Porter's Dean Winchester likeness had nothing on him, we'd showered and dressed. Rider redressed in the clothes he'd had on while I opted for black leggings, a crimson cable-knit tunic, and black boots. I slid my Christmas gift from Daniel onto my wrist, ignoring Rider's glance at the charms, and unhooked my cell phone from the charger on the nightstand.

"The techs still haven't found anything in Julie's phone records," Rider said, watching me as I sent a quick text to Angel, checking in with her. "I had her car checked and went through her apartment myself when I discovered her MIA yesterday evening. It makes no sense to me why she would leave her cell phone and car unless she didn't want to be tracked by me. I know you said you don't think she turned on me, but—"

I closed the distance between us and stopped him with a quick kiss. "Do you believe in me?"

"Yeah, I believe in you."

"There are other reasons why she wouldn't want to be tracked by you that don't involve betrayal. I don't know what her reasons are just yet, but we'll find her and we'll get to the bottom of everything. Now… where's the dog?"

"Apparently, there was an incident with a rat and an overflowing dumpster during his last walk. Juan and Hank were hosing him down in the locker room last I checked."

"Been there, done that," I muttered, much to Rider's amusement. "Don't you dare say one word about that disgusting wererat incident."

"You brought it up."

"I can bring it up. You're not allowed to mention it because you can't seem to do so without getting that twinkle of laughter in your eyes. Now, what are we doing until Jake gets here? Think those nuts we left in interrogation are ready to be cracked yet?"

"Judging by the smell of sweat and urine permeating out into the hallway when I passed there earlier, I'd say yes," he answered, all trace of amusement fleeing his eyes. "Maybe we should hold off on that until Porter arrives. He said he's bringing someone who knows a lot about how pranic vampires work. Best we make sure we're asking the right questions when we get in there. Especially since you seem to kill our detainees pretty fast when you get pissed off."

"You could always stop me," I reminded him as he led me out of the room.

"Not always fast enough," he said softly as we took the stairs down to the ground floor. He turned toward me at the bottom. "You may have given your loyalty to me, but when you draw on your succubus power, it's a lot harder for me to stop you from doing what that part of you wants to do."

"But I didn't draw on my succubus power when I killed Gary, did I?" I tried to remember what had happened in the interrogation room, but it was all a black hole of missing time. One moment I'd been kneeling by Mike, the next I was on my feet and Gary was ... all over the room. "Please tell me I didn't do anything sexual to the guy."

"You didn't. You just tore into him like a rabid animal, but I should always be able to immediately freeze you when I want. It doesn't always work out that way though. The only reason I can think of for you being able to resist my power while you're enraged is your succubus side."

"All the more reason for me to figure out more about that part of me, not to mention whichever part is causing me to have these visions."

"Yeah, I was thinking about that. How about we take a

trip to visit Auntie Mo when we get a chance?

I nearly slapped my forehead. "Why didn't I think of that? Here I've been thinking if only we could contact Jon and we've had another psychic we could speak to all along."

"You've no doubt been a little overwhelmed embracing the fact you can even get visions in the first place. I imagine they must have come as quite a shock." He kissed my forehead. "I'm going to check in with the tech team and handle a few other things not Ramson or Pacitti-related. The bar is covered tonight, so why don't you go take a crack at those books and notes you got from Nannette? They're in my office. You can look through anything I have in there too, but be careful. Some of my books are very old."

"And many of them are written in languages I can't even read," I reminded him and cast out my senses, searching for Daniel since Rider had told him to report in at nightfall and the sun had gone down when Rider had awakened me. I sensed him in the bar. "What is Daniel doing tonight?"

"He's on standby for now in case we go out and his bodyguard duties are needed." Rider frowned. "Why?"

"He's on the clock, right? Nannette gave me a lot of information and some very thick books. I may as well get some help combing through it all. Rome can help too, unless you have him posted on the entrance again. I assume Daniel is babysitting him again while waiting to be put to other use, unless you have him on security duty out there."

"Rome is posted on the door where *everyone* can watch him. As entertaining as it is for me to make Daniel watch him, even I'm not sadistic enough to not let the guy come up for a little air." He grinned. "Okay, maybe I am sadistic enough to make Daniel stick to him like white on rice twenty-four-seven just for my own amusement, but I don't want the dragon to snap and kill the guy. He's special to me."

"Uh-huh. You're just afraid Auntie Mo will rip your ear off if anything happens to her grandnephew."

"That too. Daniel's not watching the bar tonight. He's only on that detail when you are. Use his help with your research if you want, but do it out there. You can help keep an eye on Rome."

"I thought the point of him being posted at the entrance was so he was right out in front of everyone where he can't sneak food," I said, not voicing my suspicion that Rider just didn't want me alone in his office with Daniel or how I felt about it.

"Rome's crafty and even though everyone knows to watch him, they all have jobs to do that can distract them." He carefully kept emotion out of his voice. "And if you're out there, you can make sure he doesn't sneak off somewhere on his break."

"All right." I didn't buy his reasoning, but I didn't want to fight about it, so I kissed him goodbye and headed for his office while he departed in the opposite direction to head downstairs to the Bat Cave.

Rider's office was down the hall that ran between the back of The Midnight Rider and the back portion of the building that served as his residence and MidKnight Enterprises headquarters.

The walls were gray, the carpet darker gray, and the stocked bookshelves, desk, and other furniture, including the plush dog bed, were black.

I glanced at the books on Rider's shelves, many of which were leather bound, some hand-stitched, and decided I didn't want to be responsible should something happen to them in the bar.

I grabbed three thick books from the stack on Rider's desk and set them on top of the laptop I'd left to charge there the last time I'd been in the office working on it, picked them all up, and headed for the bar.

Music from the jukebox greeted me once I pushed

through the door leading to the bar, and not a note of it was Christmasy. Seeing the tiger shifter back to work tending the bar after a much-needed couple of days off, I grinned. Poor Tony had been driven to the ragged end of his very last nerve by Mariah Carey's number one Christmas song by the time Christmas finally arrived. He'd demanded the Christmas music be taken off the jukebox by the time he returned or else he wouldn't be responsible for the damage he'd have to do to it. Rider obliged without a fuss, but I was sure that was because everyone was pretty tired of hearing it, and frankly, Rider didn't care what played on the jukebox.

"Didn't you graduate already?" Daniel asked as I approached the corner booth where he sat with his back to the wall, the perfect position to watch Rome where the big guy stood by the entrance, while he worked on the beer and massive triple burger and mountain of onion rings in front of him. He was dressed in jeans and a black Pink Floyd T-shirt.

"Many years ago," I said, sliding into the opposite side of the booth.

"What's with the homework, then?"

"Knowledge is power and you're never too old to learn," I replied, settling in. I slid the stack of books toward him and opened my laptop. "You can get started on those while I go through the notes Nannette emailed over to me."

"Say what now?"

"I need your help." I tapped the stack of books with my index finger. "I want to know more about my succubus side so I can control it better. Nannette sent me over her notes and research and loaned me these books from the underworld ward's library. Since we're not actively doing anything right now and probably won't be until after Jake arrives, can you help me out? There's a lot to go through and two sets of eyes are better than one."

Daniel had just stuffed an onion ring into his mouth

and it fell out as his mouth dropped open. "Jake? Jake Porter?"

"Yes. He's coming to help with tracking down Ramson."

"Great. Another visit from Douchey the Vampire Slayer."

I sighed. "Between you and Rider, I don't know who needs to be smacked upside the back of the head more. Jake isn't that bad, and he saved my life, remember?"

"I remember," he said bitterly. "I also remember him being a major smartass with a huge attitude problem, and he joked around way too—what?"

I'd rolled my lips all the way in, trying my hardest not to laugh, but lost it the moment Daniel narrowed his eyes at me. "You know you just described him the same way Rider or Tony would describe you?"

"I'm nothing like that giant ass boil."

"Sure," I said. "So, are you going to help me or not?"

After an eye roll, he popped the dropped onion ring back into his mouth and grabbed a black book off the stack I'd slid toward him. "What exactly am I supposed to be looking for?"

"I'm really not sure, but I told Nannette I wanted to know more about succubi so I'd have a better understanding of this thing inside me and she suggested going through these books and gave me what she has found so far herself. Those should have information about succubi or similar demons in them. I guess take note of anything that might help me figure out what all I'm capable of or how I can, I don't know, control myself better."

Daniel raised an eyebrow and flipped the book open, making sure it didn't block his access to the food in front of him. "And how about the vision stuff? I haven't really spoken to you since last night's interrogation. Did Nannette have any ideas about how you're suddenly pulling an Allison Dubois?"

"A wha—oh, right. She was that psychic in *Medium*. Um, yeah, she thinks I could have some psychic lineage, either from my own ancestry or something that passed down from Rider or Selander when they turned me. Or maybe it passed from both of them."

This got a confused brow furrow. "I didn't think Rider was psychic."

"He's not, and he doesn't believe Selander is either. But a psychic in my lineage would explain this ability. I haven't heard of any psychics in my family, but Rider's father claimed to have visions. Rider isn't convinced he told the truth though, and he doesn't have the ability himself."

"Looks like you need to do some digging through your family tree."

I fought the grimace that thought caused. Rider and I had spent Christmas Eve with my mother, and it had been a surprisingly pleasant time. Once she'd drugged my grandmother into a coma, that was. But it would take more than one decent visit with her to stop the automatic cramp I got in my gut anytime I thought of having to speak with her. "Maybe. We're going to talk to Auntie Mo too. Who knows, maybe she'll see us coming and have all the info we need before we can even ask."

"Like it's ever that easy," Daniel said, wiping his greasy fingers on a napkin before he flipped the book's pages. "I'll look for anything having to do with visions or psychic abilities too. We need to know why they're hitting you out of nowhere and making you faint. That's not good."

"Nannette thinks they're just overpowering me because I'm not used to them. Hopefully, I'll handle them better once I've grown accustomed to the power surge that comes with them."

"Hopefully," he agreed. "We can't have you passing out during a fight."

"Maybe Auntie Mo will have some advice for me. She may have fainted a few times in the beginning herself."

"Maybe," he said, glancing in Rome's direction before

he got busy flipping through the book, searching for useful information while I logged on to my laptop and opened the docs Nannette had emailed to me.

I knew she'd been researching succubi since the moment I'd been turned. Rider had told me as much early on, but I still hadn't expected so many pages of notes. On closer inspection, I saw many were medical notes taken from my visits to the underworld ward, and a log of incidents I'd had. I saw a lengthy document detailing the two weeks I'd spent trying to kill Rider during the Bloom and skipped past it. Some things I was better off just knowing the condensed version of. I felt horrible enough about what I'd put Rider through during that time without reliving all the gory details through Nannette's written description of the events.

"Geez," I muttered, scrolling through the docs.

"Problem?"

"Headache." I rubbed the center of my forehead for emphasis as I continued scrolling, bypassing pages of medical-speak. "I think I might need a medical degree to make sense of some of this. How are you doing over there?"

"I need more food."

I shot him a perturbed look, but grinned. "Between you and Rome, I don't know how there's enough food left for the rest of the population."

"Moderation," he said, but as he held his hand up to catch Hazel's attention and gestured for a refill on his basket of onion rings, I wondered if he knew what that word actually meant. "I haven't found anything about succubi yet, but I've barely cracked this thing open. Patience, grasshopper."

Great. Now he was using words that *I* didn't know the meaning of. "Not my strong suit."

"No shit." He frowned, having noticed something in the book and peered closer, suddenly studious.

I left him alone in case he'd found something that

could prove useful and went back to Nannette's research notes. By the time Hazel arrived at our table with Daniel's refill of onion rings, I was starting to feel less hopeful about my whole get-to-know-myself-better idea.

"Big test coming up?" the fae asked in a monotone voice, displaying her dry sense of humor as she set Daniel's greasy grub on the table.

I inhaled the scent of hot, fried goodness and let the sadness of junk food deprivation wash over me before I responded. "Every day is a test for me. I figure a little education might help me stop failing so much."

"If the rumors around here are true, I think you're being a little hard on yourself," Hazel said. "Didn't you just kill some giant Santa-looking hitman from hell?"

Instead of waiting to see if I responded, she arched a thin eyebrow, having made her point, and left.

"You should listen to the woman," Daniel said, his eyes still glued to whatever he had found in the book. "Yeah, you're a bit of a wildcard, but when it comes down to it, you get the job done. If you're guilty of anything, it's overkill, impatience, and a lack of confidence, but I would never say you failed. Not at anything. Hell, you saved my life, remember?"

"That was because I had Jon's power in me," I said, uncomfortable with the praise and flooded with nausea at the memory. "If I hadn't…"

"You still would have found a way to save me."

"You don't know that. I mean, I would have tried, but—"

"You would have saved me. Just like I will always save you." He looked up from the book then, his gaze met mine, and all the air was sucked out of the room. The temperature rose several degrees past uncomfortable as Daniel held my gaze, his eyes simmering with emotions I didn't dare name.

"Daniel…"

He blinked. Swallowed. Blinked again, and gave his

head a barely perceptible shake before he lifted one of the books left on the stack, looking under it. "I'm going to go grab some paper and a pen from Jadyn. She usually has an overstuffed backpack with her when she comes in."

He exited the booth before I could respond, which was fortunate because I didn't know what to say. I loved Daniel, and I'd be lying if I said I didn't find him incredibly attractive. If Rider wasn't in the picture, I'd probably have given in to that attraction a long time ago.

Whereas Rider had the whole tall, dark, and powerful thing going on, Daniel was tall, strong, and charming in a lighter way, although he could certainly hold his own in a fight. There weren't many entities more powerful than a dragon. But when it came down to it, the one who had the power to take my breath away, the one I saw myself with when I envisioned my future, the one I would love even if he became horribly disfigured... was Rider. This was something I'd come to realize the day after Christmas, when I'd sat down and had a little heart-to-heart with myself. The succubus wanted Daniel and just about every other man in the world, but the part of me that was truly all me was in love with Rider. Period.

But that same part of me loved Daniel in its own way and would be destroyed if I lost my best friend or hurt him in any way. For that reason, I had to be considerate of his feelings until he got past them, which he eventually would have to do, because Rider and I were forever, and for our kind, forever was more than just a lifetime.

Daniel returned from the bar where he'd spoken to Jadyn quickly while she grabbed a tray of drinks to take out to a table and ducked down behind it, where I assumed he had rifled through her backpack, because when he'd straightened, he'd had a legal pad and a couple of pens in his hand.

I watched him curiously as he slid back into his side of the booth and clicked one of the pens, the instrument poised over the legal pad while his other hand rested on top of the book he'd left open. "You found something?"

"Maybe. I'm not sure if it's anything that will ever apply to you, given your vampire side, but it's something really interesting about succubi. Or sex demons, anyway, and succubi are a form of sex demon. Did you know they can reproduce?"

I blinked a few times, words escaping me while my brain scrambled to figure out what that could possibly mean for me. "Huh? What?"

"Sex demons are fertile," he said as he jotted down information from the book. "I thought succubi were only created the way you were, by having sweet blood and getting bitten by an incubus. But according to this, sex demons are one of the few of the demonic species that can actually reproduce in the normal way. Succubi are included under the umbrella of sex demons. According to this, they can reproduce with anything non-sterile, so they aren't limited to only mating with incubi and other sex demons."

I could still have children? For a moment, my mind flooded with images of chubby-cheeked mini-fanged bundles of cuteness, but I obviously pictured Rider standing at my side oohing and aahing over our little bundle of paranormal joy, and the image immediately burst into flames. Rider was a vampire. He might be immortal, but his sperm was long dead.

"Interesting," I said, "but I don't think the fertility thing applies to me."

"You're half succubus," he said, busily scribbling away. "Even if you're half vampire, you could still retain your fertility from your succubus side. It's definitely something to look deeper into, especially if you want to have children. All you would need is a partner who can give you viable sperm. The partner doesn't have to be an incubus or vampire. A vampire obviously wouldn't—"

"Rider is my partner," I snapped, cutting him off before he could finish implying what he'd been heading toward. "Why would I even consider creating a child with another man?"

Daniel looked up, and as he swallowed, a blush colored his face. His eyes were cold and for a moment, coated in pain before he blinked the hurt away. "I'm just saying, any woman who wants to have a child shouldn't be denied that opportunity just because of something that was done to her. Selander Ryan tried to rob you of your life, and even though Rider saved you, vampirism robbed you of your ability to have children. But maybe your succubus side can give that back to you. You should be able to have children if you want to. I'd think any man who truly loved you would agree to that."

Heat engulfed me and I clamped my jaw, keeping my mouth shut while I processed what Daniel had just said, what he'd meant by it, and tried to figure out at what point had I given him any indication that what he'd just said was remotely acceptable. Possibly when I'd cornered him in a pantry and nearly kissed him, I conceded. Fine, so I'd given him hope, possibly even an actual reason to think there was a chance for us, but I loved Rider and I wasn't about to let anyone, not even Daniel, hint that Rider would ever keep me from having something so important out of sheer selfishness. Not when the man knew how Daniel felt about me and allowed him to be my personal bodyguard anyway because I'd asked for it and because he knew the man's feelings for me would guarantee he'd keep me safe against any threat.

Before I could open my mouth to tell Daniel as much, a prickly energy washed over me, warning me a threat was near, and Daniel's hazel-eyed gaze shifted over to the front of the room. He groaned. "Ah, great. The jackass is here."

Although none of the humans in the bar would have picked up on anything strange, I could sense every paranormal in the room go on high alert as the slayer's energy signature filled the room. There was no need for me to tell Rider that Jake Porter had arrived. He would have felt it like the rest of us, even if he was in the sublevels.

I turned to watch the slayer approach, looking so much like Dean Winchester in the old jeans, T-shirt, flannel, and brown leather coat, it was freakishly uncanny, but this time I wasn't quite as gobsmacked as I had been the first time I'd seen him. He had many similarities to my favorite fictional character, whom I may have had an unhealthy crush on, but he wasn't Dean Winchester. And he wasn't Jensen Ackles, despite looking as if he'd been cloned from the guy.

He was an incredibly attractive, incredibly dangerous slayer, born to kill my kind. Fortunately, he'd fallen in love with a pantherian woman and realized no one was evil just because of what they were. So although his DNA effectively made him our version of the boogeyman, he was on our side. At least, those of us who didn't allow our own paranormal attributes to turn us into bloodthirsty, indiscriminate killing monsters. And it looked as if he'd brought a friend with him.

I cast out my senses, but couldn't detect what the man with him was, if he was anything other than your regular run-of-the-mill human. He was tall, around six feet, two inches, with wavy black hair that fell free around his shoulders, one side tucked behind his ear to show off his strong jawline. His skin was golden and flawless, his eyes a piercing dark blue, and he dressed in black pants, combat boots, and a black button-down shirt with a black leather duster jacket.

"Who's the Rider wannabe?" Daniel muttered as the two reached our booth.

Jake turned his head to look at the man with him and grinned before looking back at us. "My brother-in-law is pretty, but he's not that pretty."

No, he wasn't as beautiful as Rider, his features broader, but he was very easy to look at. "Brother-in-law? Marilee's husband?"

The man nodded as Jake made introductions. "Yep.

This is my sister's husband, Khiderian. An expert on pranic vampires. Khiderian, this is Danni Keller, the badass warrior princess I was telling you about, and this is her pet dragon."

"Bite me, Losechester," Daniel said.

"Whatever gives you that special tingle, Mushu."

"I'm not a warrior princess, but I appreciate the compliment," I said, jumping in to diffuse the situation before things got hostile. "This is my friend, Daniel."

"Friend and bodyguard," Daniel clarified, putting emphasis on the second title. He sized Khiderian up with a hefty dose of warning in his eyes.

"Why don't the two of you join us?" I slid over. "You know your presence makes the others antsy."

"Hard not to notice." Jake slid in next to me and Khiderian waited for Daniel to move over to allow him space on his side.

"Rider should be joining us soon," I said, not needing to confirm as much. Rider would have automatically started toward me the moment he sensed the slayer.

"Of course," Jake said with a mischievous grin. "It's not in that snarly vampire's nature to let you near me unguarded."

"She's guarded," Daniel nearly growled.

Jake only grinned in response, his eyes sparkling with amusement before his gaze shifted toward the back door a second before Rider emerged from it.

"Ah, Count Gucci has arrived," Jake said, his smile widening. "Let the fun begin."

CHAPTER SEVEN

"Do you have to call him Count Gucci?" I whispered, although I knew Rider could still hear me if he chose to use his vampiric ability to do so. "He called you because I asked him to, because I thought you could help us. Don't make me regret it by being a pain in his ass on purpose."

"But he makes it so easy," Jake replied. "Not to mention a ton of fun."

"Jake," Khiderian said, his tone full of admonishment.

"Of course my sister would marry someone as stuffy as Count Gucci." He sighed and winked at me. "For you, my little Mulan, I will be on my best behavior."

"As awesome as Mulan is, I'm afraid I'm not remotely similar to her."

"You're a whole lot of badass hidden in an unsuspecting, small package that men who only think they're big and bad severely underestimate," he said, and pointed at Daniel. "And if I call you Mulan, I get to call him Mushu, and that just tickles me to no end."

"I got something that'll really give you a tickle," Daniel said, producing a blade quicker than I could blink.

"I see these two are already competing to see who gets on my last damn nerve the fastest," Rider said, having just reached our booth. "Remind me again why I invited this smartass back here?"

"Actually, your dragon was just offering to give me a tickle. A much friendlier welcome than I've ever gotten from you, although I'll have to give him a hard pass. You might want to give the guy a night off, let him go get his rocks or scales off, whatever dragons do for fun and nookie," Jake said, ignoring the rapidly intensifying death glare Daniel was shooting his way. "And you invited me because you know I'm a damn good ally to have when you're fighting a big nasty and because Danni asked you to. I'm going to take a wild guess that you're also very thankful for the gift I left behind for you. In fact, I'm betting you've made good use of it and have been doing a lot of things she asks of you. Page thirty-three, am I right? Nyla learned that negotiation tactic a long time ago. Oh, the things I've said yes to because of page thirty-three."

Rider's expression had been steadily hardening, but the corners of his mouth twitched. "Knowing its power, you should have torn that page out."

"Why should I be the only man roped into doing whatever his woman wants because of the promises made on that cursed page?" Jake chuckled. "Ah, face it, Count Gucci. If ever there was someone for me to spread this torment to, it would be your prickly ass. And be honest, you're glad I left that in."

"What the hell is this idiot talking about?" Daniel asked.

"You don't want to know," I said, surprised my overheated cheeks hadn't gone up in flames yet. Rider and Jake just shared an amused look.

"I don't know what they're talking about either," Khiderian said.

"And you never will," Jake said, glancing at the man. "Not as long as you're married to my little sister."

"Little sister?" Rider's eyebrows rose as he looked at Khiderian, giving him a thorough inspection. "You're married to the slayer's sister?"

Khiderian nodded.

"And you're the expert on pranic vampires we were promised?"

"That I am."

Rider's eyes narrowed as he studied him. I knew he was doing what I'd already done and failed: trying to detect what exactly the man was. His energy signature said human, but we both knew there was a lot more to him than that.

"What else are you?" Rider asked, voice low.

"My wife and I work with Jake's brother. He's a private detective. We work cases with him, and sometimes I do more… physical work."

"We're all in the same line of work," Jake said. "I obviously vouch for him, and if you can reach Seta, she'll vouch for him too. If you're really dealing with a pranic vampire, he's the guy to answer all your questions."

"And what makes him such an expert on pranic vampires?" Rider asked.

"I used to be one," Khiderian said, holding Rider's gaze steady when it turned toward him.

"Used to be?" Recognition dawned in Rider's eyes. "You're Khiderian, the fallen angel who became mortal after giving his life to save the woman he loved."

"I see my reputation precedes me."

"Christian gave me the short version." Rider returned his attention to Jake, taking in his appearance. "You took two books from my office and I don't see them on you. That's a problem."

"Relax, Knight Rider. They're already back on your shelf."

"How could you—" Rider pinched the bridge of his nose. "Remind me again why I shouldn't kill him."

"Because he's useful," I said.

"Yeah, about as useful as a hemorrhoid sometimes." Rider glanced around the bar, likely noting all the paranormals sizing the slayer up, hackles raised. "Let's move this to my office. Where I better find my books."

"Whatever you say, Count—ow!"

I raised my eyebrows innocently as I withdrew my elbow from Jake's side. "After you."

The corner of Jake's mouth twitched, but he didn't say anything as he slid out of the booth to join Rider and Khiderian. Daniel and I quickly gathered our things, the dragon shifter insisting on carrying everything for me.

"What's with the study sesh?" Jake asked. "I have your walking encyclopedia of pranic vampires right here. I guarantee he knows more than you'll find in any book."

"We were actually researching my succubus side," I explained, not bothering to hide the fact that I was half succubus from Khiderian. If Jake vouched for him, that was good enough for me, and I'd briefly met Marilee. Although we hadn't spent much time together, she didn't strike me as the type to marry someone shady. Jake sure as hell wasn't the type to let some jerk near his sister.

"This way." Rider shot me a disapproving look that suggested he wasn't thrilled with my openness with Jake, but he wasn't going to stop me from revealing what I was working on. He said nothing more as he turned for the back door and walked toward it, leading the way to his office.

"Working on weaponizing your succubus powers more?" Jake asked as we followed Rider.

"No. I mean, yeah, if there's a safe way to do that. Mostly I'm just trying to figure out what I am exactly, and how to keep any surprises to a minimum."

Jake's brow furrowed as he looked at me, but if he had any thoughts about what I'd said, he kept them to himself.

Rider pushed through the back door, Khiderian behind him. Jake held the door open for me and slid in behind me, forcing Daniel to bring up the rear. I thought I heard a low growl come out of him, followed by a throaty chuckle from Jake that earned him another shot of my elbow to the ribcage.

He grunted. "Play nice."

"Behave."

Rider shot an annoyed look our way before pushing through the door to his office. By the time I entered, Rider was standing in front of his bookshelf, holding a book he'd just taken from the spot where I recalled him finding a Harry Potter book and the sex manual Jake had left before leaving right before Christmas Eve. He narrowed his gaze on Jake. "How did you get past security this time? Even if you'd used the vents like you did last time, you would have been sensed the moment you neared this building. You only got by with that last time because we already sensed your presence and ignored it."

"Now, now. I can't tell you all my secrets." Jake winked and took a seat in one of the chairs in front of Rider's desk, slouching down in a posture that suggested he didn't have a worry in the world.

Rider looked at the book in his hand, shook his head, and placed it back on the shelf, muttering under his breath before he moved over to his black leather desk chair and settled in, telling me with a look to join him.

I moved toward him, but instead of sitting on the arm of the chair or on his lap, I stood at his side with one hand resting on the back of the chair. It was one thing to allow him to make a show of our relationship when he felt threatened by Daniel, but we were speaking to a slayer and a man I didn't really know. Men I might find myself fighting alongside, depending on how things went. I refused to not look professional while doing so.

Khiderian took the seat next to Jake, and Daniel lowered himself down onto the couch along the back wall, a scowl on his face. He settled the stack of books and my laptop on the cushion next to him and folded his arms over his chest, nowhere near as relaxed as Jake.

"So, what's the situation?" Jake asked.

"Danni had one of her gut feelings about a woman in

my bar last night, followed her out, and witnessed three men pull up in a van and try to snatch her," Rider explained. "Obviously, Danni jumped into action. They were brought here for interrogation. Two are left."

Jake's gaze slid over to me as his mouth curled into a grin. "I'm guessing Danni dispatched the one no longer with us."

"You guess right. However, you might be surprised to know that his death was brought on by a vision she had when she touched one of the other men."

Jake's eyebrows rose. "You're having visions now?"

I nodded. "I've only had three. Two during last night's interrogation, and one later, a little before dawn. That one happened when I saw someone on a screen, though."

Jake nodded slowly, his lips pursed. "Interesting development, but I can't say that I'm surprised. So where does the prannie come in?"

"The men who were captured appear to be in a cult," Rider continued as I stood silent, wondering what Jake had meant by not being surprised I could have visions now. "They call themselves Disciples of Ramson, and Ramson is the vampire Danni saw in her vision when she first touched one of them. From the way he had those people enthralled, we're sure he's a pranic vampire. They claim he has visions, sends them to collect certain people to bring to him for saving, but from the sound of things, he sends them after random women."

"Except the last one didn't seem all that random," Daniel chimed in. "She recognized one man as living in her building."

Jake glanced at Daniel before returning his attention to Rider. "When you say these women are brought to him for saving…"

"He's building a nest," Rider said. "He's convinced these fools that he can perform miracles because he cured a woman of leukemia."

"By turning her into a vampire," Jake said, a heavy dose

of disgust in his tone. He turned his head toward Khiderian. "Well, pranic vampires are charismatic and love to be worshipped, so a vampire leading a cult sounds likely to be a prannie to me. What do you think?"

"Very likely," Khiderian agreed. "Like Jake says, pranic vampires are very charismatic. Whereas average vampires may set off a human's inherent inner alarm when they're being actively hunted, pranic vampires rarely do. Their charisma is one of their superpowers. People want to be near them. They seem trustworthy, warm, and inviting. They can also delve into the minds of anyone unguarded. Humans with no trace of paranormal energy are easy prey, but they can get into the minds of shifters and vampires too. Only some witches, slayers, and other psychics have immunity from their mind intrusion."

"Can they mind-control people?" Rider asked.

"No, except for their fledglings," Khiderian answered. "Although it may seem like they can. They are master manipulators, as should be expected of con artists with the ability to read other's desires and fears. They always know what to say to convince their prey to follow them blindly, and they use that devotion to strengthen their power. They feed on energies and emotions, so convincing a multitude of people to worship him was smart on this vampire's part. He's feeding off of them constantly, which keeps him in peak condition."

"Other than being able to get into a person's head and tell what they fear the most or how to convince them to do things they otherwise might not, what makes them so dangerous?" I asked. "Can they be taken out the same as any other vampire?"

"They can be killed the same way as any other vampire," Khiderian said, "but they're not as easy to kill for a multitude of reasons. Pranic vampires happen when someone with psychic ability is turned, and that psychic ability usually makes them gain powers sooner than other vampires. Many have telekinetic power and some have pyrokinetic power. There are pranic vampires with abilities that rival witches' powers. All of them can feed off emotions and energy, even while in battle. In fact, they feed off the battle itself. The rage, the anger, the pain and the fear. Their enemies fuel them the more they try to defeat them, and particularly skilled pranic vampires are good enough to stay in the minds of their opponents, predicting every move they make, blocking them easily."

"Geez," I said. "How do you beat someone like that?"

Jake raised his hand. "Hiya. Slayer, remember? Prannies can't see what's in my head."

"That's because there's nothing in there but sarcasm and idiocy," Daniel said.

Jake pointed at Daniel, but kept his gaze on me. "I'm gonna let him get by with that one because he's wearing a Pink Floyd T-shirt. I can't in good conscience get blood all over a Pink Floyd T-shirt."

I grinned and shook my head. The two were more alike than they'd ever admit, but I wouldn't waste my breath trying to convince them to stop ribbing each other and get along. Jake had rubbed Daniel the wrong way from the very start, and Jake... Well, Jake just enjoyed pushing people's buttons and Daniel made it easy for him.

"Did you get this prannie's location?" Jake asked, back to business.

"I saw a big tent filled with his followers," I told him. "It was in a meadow somewhere but there were no landmarks or signage so it could be anywhere, but it has to be close enough if he sent those guys out here to grab a woman, and the woman recognized one of them from her building. I intended to get the location out of them but kind of blacked out and killed one after getting a vision of what he'd done to many of the women he'd been sent after."

"That's my girl," he said, grinning as we all heard the low growl erupt from Rider's throat. "Easy there, Count Gucci. I'm happily married, remember? I like your girl in a completely platonic way."

"Enough with the Count Gucci."

"Yeah, I guess you're not all that Gucci tonight anyway," Jake replied, angling his head to the side as he studied Rider's attire. "Looks like you got your ass-kicking clothes on. Must be salivating to pounce on this prannie."

"Among others I'd like to tear apart with my bare hands," Rider said, his dark gaze locked onto Jake.

The slayer grinned, knowing the statement was meant as a threat, but not one Rider meant whole-heartedly. If he really wanted to tear the slayer apart, he wouldn't bother telling him first.

"Well, I can't fault you there," Jake said, "but I hate to be the one to tell you, you're sitting this one out, big guy."

"Excuse me?" Rider leaned forward. "This vampire is building a nest in my territory and from what we've seen in Danni's visions, he has one of my blood donors. I'm killing the bastard."

Jake suddenly became a lot more serious, sitting up straight in the chair. "Your blood donor? A willing blood donor?"

"Yes, a willing blood donor," Rider snapped.

"I had to ask." Jake held his hands up, palms out. "You didn't say anything about him having one of your blood donors. Are you thinking he intentionally sought someone close to you or was she another random grab off the street?"

"It's hard to say," I answered, figuring Rider needed a moment to simmer down. "All we know is she went missing about a week ago, but we didn't know that until she was a no-show for her appointment yesterday. The tech team tracked her as best they could with security cameras at the building where Rider's donors live and from traffic cameras, but she went down a side street where there were none and hasn't been seen since. Other than when I saw her picture on the tech's screen and it prompted a vision of her in that tent listening to Ramson."

"So she was likely a grab," Jake said, thinking out loud. "Was there any indication of where she'd been headed? Does she have a job, friends? Or is this one of those free room and board in exchange for your vein and all your freedom type of deals?"

"Don't make it sound so villainous," Rider said. "My donors were all former prostitutes, saved from abuse and, in some cases, addiction. In exchange for their blood and their silence about our community, they are given an apartment and more money than they ever made doing what they were doing before. Not to mention, they are all far safer. They were never held prisoner, which is why Julie was able to simply walk out of her apartment and walk off the grid, leaving her car and phone behind."

"She left her phone behind?" Jake rubbed his chin. "Maybe not just a grab after all. I assume your tech team has been in that phone's history and is tracking all her financials."

"My donors only have debit and credit cards issued through my company, and they are all tracked," Rider said. "They are not allowed to take out cash, and before you get any ideas about it being a way to control them, they are free to do as they please, but I can't have donors able to just go wherever they want in the country without notice, not when they know what I am and where I operate from. Not to mention the building they live in is also home to many of my employees. A slayer's wonderland if ever discovered."

"I can understand controlling their access to money and tracking it to ensure your people's safety," Jake said, nodding. "So, from what I'm gathering, the building is monitored twenty-four-seven with cameras as well as your employees who also live there, and all purchases are tracked. She left her vehicle, which I'll assume has a tracker on it too, and the same deal with the phone. I'm guessing she knew about being monitored so closely if she left both of those behind, especially the phone. I could understand going out for a walk, but I don't know a lot of humans who can survive five minutes without a phone in their hands."

"You think she's been compromised," Khiderian said, "and you're likely right. If this Ramson is a pranic vampire and he's tasted her, he would have access to everything she knows. The question is if he plans on doing anything with the information. Any idea how long he's been here? He could be passing through with no interest in other vampires, or…"

"He could be building his numbers in an attempt to take over my territory," Rider finished for him. "Something that will not happen. I'm finding the bastard and I'm killing him. He's not the only one with powers."

"Your powers are impressive," Jake said, "but he can still read every thought in your head and know every move you make before you know yourself. What good are your abilities when he's already dodging or countering them? And unless you have any idea how old he is, you have no idea how advanced his powers are. He could incinerate you with a thought."

"If he's that old, I'd be able to sense it once I was within range and know what to expect."

Jake sighed and leaned forward, placing one hand on Rider's desk as he looked him straight in the eyes, the usual glimmer of amusement in his hazel eyes gone. "I know how bad you want him, man, and I get it, but think about all the things you know. You're worried about your employees' residence being found or this guy knowing where you operate your business? Think about what I have to fear him finding out. What Seta has to fear him finding out. You are a far greater liability to us than your donor is to you, and if you think for a moment, you'll realize what I'm talking about and know I'm right."

Any clue what that's about? Daniel asked through our mind-link.

I started to shake my head, but caught myself. I didn't

want to clue the two men in to the fact Daniel and I were having a private conversation. I answered him through the mind-link. *No, but I'm sure it has to do with whatever Rider helped Seta with while we were in Pigeon Forge. He won't tell me anything about it.*

I was sure some of the frustration I felt over his withholding of information slipped through into my tone, but it diminished as I watched Rider and Jake, noticing the fear in their eyes. Fear was an emotion neither man showed often, if ever.

"Shit," Rider finally said, and slammed his fist down on the desktop, rattling everything on top of it.

"Yeah, I know it sucks," Jake said, leaning back in his chair. "But if I didn't have this layer of special slayer protection around my mind, I'd make myself sit this one out too. You can't go near the guy, and other than giving us information about prannies, Khiderian has to stay out of this fight too."

"I thought you were a pranic vampire before…" Rider sat back, realization dawning in his eyes. "Damn. You lost your psychic ability too, and all your protection."

"As far as we know," Khiderian said. "With what I know, I'm not willing to put my mind shield to the test."

"Understandable." Rider heaved out a frustrated sigh. "Slayer or not, you need some backup. I have some guards with limited access to the inner workings of my business that I can send with you."

"Don't need 'em," Jake said, and pointed at me. "I'll take her and the dragon."

"The hell you will," Rider said, his tone firm as steel. "Danni isn't going near that vampire."

"Why? Because she's fragile or something?" Jake rolled his eyes. "You don't give her enough credit."

"And you don't know what the hell you're talking about." Now Rider's tone had gone full growl. "Danni is a hybrid, and she's…"

"Not even a year turned," Jake finished for him,

understanding why he'd paused and looked at Khiderian. "Neither of us are currently vampires and honestly, that not revealing your age thing is dumb. I'm a slayer. I know the age of everyone in this room, and neither one of us has any intention, let alone reason, to attack Danni. That said... if you think her newbie status makes her easy prey, you don't know your girl."

Rider made a move that appeared very much like a lunge, so I slammed my hand down on his shoulder and squeezed until I got my point across and he settled back into the chair with a grunt of annoyance. I would not pull the two men apart like fighting toddlers. Once I was sure he intended to stay seated, I patted Rider's shoulder.

"There's no sense getting upset when I'm simply stating facts," Jake said, and I would have accused him of egging Rider on, except his trademark wiseass tone was absent. "And the fact is, as a slayer, I can always sense the most dangerous predator in any room I enter. You're a badass, Knight. I'll admit you're one of the most powerful vampires I've come across, right up there with Seta and Eron. And I understand why you have the dragon assigned to watch over Danni. He's packing some mighty badassery as well, as I imagine any dragon shifter would. But neither of you is the most dangerous predator in this room."

Rider and Daniel shifted their eyes over to Khiderian, who laughed and shook his head as if to say it definitely wasn't him.

"It's not him," Jake said, and settled his gaze on me. "The most dangerous predator in this room... is her."

Now it was my turn to laugh. I was the only one. Jake and Khiderian both almost looked bored. Daniel studied me curiously, not seeming all that surprised by Jake's statement, and as for Rider, I noticed his eyes had gone all murdery and felt him about to lunge, so I firmly planted my hand on his shoulder again and sobered. "Okay, Jake. As amusing as that was, let's get serious."

"I am serious. I automatically assess every area I enter

for the biggest threat. It's just something I do, part of my genetic makeup, like a radar for danger. The only time you haven't been the biggest threat in the room was when we were fighting the krackling, yet you were the one who killed him." He met Rider's dark gaze. "You love her so you fear for her safety and want to keep her protected. I completely get that, but I'm telling you she can handle herself. She's setting off bells she didn't even set off the last time I was here, which means she's only gotten more dangerous since then. That she's not even a year into turning doesn't mean anything. She's not a normal fledgling."

"No, she's not," Rider agreed, although his tone was argumentative. "Because she's half succubus. If this sense of danger you have detects the biggest threats to you, it wouldn't be too far-fetched to say she's only showing as the biggest threat because of her ability to lure. Yes, it's powerful and worked well for us when she used it on the krackling, but things could have gone really bad really fast if Ginger hadn't been there for her to shut her power down. I recall even you were affected by it, just like you were lured by sirens. Yeah, I heard about that."

Jake's jaw clenched before he spoke. "I may have been affected by the siren song, but they didn't have enough power to fully lure me. They didn't get what they wanted from me, just kept me from killing them by singing that damn song while they tortured me. And while I admit I got a nice tingle from Danni's lure, she could never fully seduce me using her power. I'm immune to it."

Rider narrowed his eyes and glared at the slayer for a stretch before speaking. "Good to know, but most aren't, and it sounds like this vampire is a major threat as well, a master of manipulation who can enter minds. What do you think he would do if he had access to Danni's mind? Her succubus side is volatile enough without a pranic vampire pulling her strings."

"If she's having visions now, she has psychic power.

There's a damn good chance he can't get in her head."

"A chance isn't a guarantee," Rider said.

"Nothing in this world comes with a guarantee," Jake replied, "but we already told you pranic vampires can't control minds. They can only read them. Yes, if this guy turns out to be a prannie, he'll be a damn good manipulator, but manipulation only works on those who allow the manipulation. Have some faith in your girl. Danni's strong enough to take this guy down."

Rider's body tensed under my hand, and I knew he was in the midst of an internal struggle. It went against his nature to allow me to run headlong into a dangerous situation, but he knew that saying no would not only mean he didn't believe in me, but it would throw us right back to where we'd begun. With him controlling me and me resenting him for it.

"As someone who knows something about psychic powers," Khiderian said, "she's having the visions for a reason. Rarely does anyone have the ability to have visions on demand or just because. If she's seeing Ramson in her mind, it's more than likely because she's meant to see him in the real world. To stop him."

Rider rubbed his temples and grumbled under his breath before he lifted his gaze to Jake's and reluctantly nodded. "All right, but you also take Tony."

Jake frowned for a moment, then smiled as his eyes lit up. "The big, grouchy kitty cat that gets enraged by Christmas music and joy in any form? I love that guy. He's friggin' hilarious."

"This is going to be a disaster," Rider muttered to me.

I patted his shoulder, not sure what I could say. I'd already figured I'd have my hands full refereeing Daniel and Jake, but Daniel, Jake, and Tony? Yikes. I might need a stun gun.

"Now that's all settled—" Jake clapped his hands and rubbed them together. "Let's go beat some information out of your remaining cultists, and Khiderian here came for more than just this."

"I hear I have a great, great"—He made a hand gesture as if to say many greats—"granddaughter. I thought I should probably meet her."

"We tried to call Christian and tell him we were coming, but he didn't answer his phone," Jake said.

"Christian's been staying pretty busy lately," Rider said. "He's just taken over as minister at a local church and he started a program for the homeless. With the cold temperatures, he's putting in a lot of hours taking care of those in need. Jadyn's here working tonight. If you didn't see her when you came in, she was probably in the kitchen or on a break. She likes to spend her breaks with my dog."

Khiderian smiled. "I can join you in interrogation, in case I pick up on anything the men say. I know how pranic vampires operate better than anyone. I spent enough centuries as one, but I definitely want to meet my descendant after."

"How about you meet her now, then meet us after for the interrogation? Danni and Daniel can introduce you. I need to have a moment with Jake."

"Oh boy." Jake rolled his eyes and slouched in the chair. "Here we go."

"Rider…"

Rider lifted my hand from his shoulder and kissed it. "Everything is fine. I just need to speak with Jake privately. I promise you no blood will be shed … until we get down to interrogation."

"Just don't interrogate *him*," I said in a near-whisper and sighed before gesturing for Khiderian to come with me. "Follow me, Khiderian. Let's introduce you to your great-great… there's got to be something we can call her that isn't so long."

Khiderian chuckled as we reached the door Daniel held open for us. "I think descendent will do. I'm not even certain of how many generations of descendants are between us to know how many greats to tack on."

"It must have come as a great surprise to you to know you had a great—a descendant," I said as we left Rider and Jake in the office, where I hoped they would play nice with each other, and headed down the hall toward the back door that would lead us back into The Midnight Rider. "I know enough to know that Jadyn has angel grace because it was passed down through her bloodline from a fallen angel who impregnated a mortal woman before getting turned." I felt heat flood my face as I realized what I'd just said. "I'm assuming you had no idea."

"None. I hadn't been fallen for long before I was encountered by a vampire and turned." Regret flitted through his eyes. "I'd had the barest taste of the mortal life I'd wanted so badly before it was taken from me along with the ability to have children. Had I known I'd made one, I would have been there to—" He released a bitter laugh. "No, No, I wouldn't have gone near the child. My sire would have killed it had she known of its existence."

"Well, she sounds wonderful," I said sarcastically as I stepped through the door leading to the bar, which Daniel held open for us.

Khiderian snorted. "Killing her was one of the best things I ever did."

An old Elton John song blared through the room as we entered, loud enough to be heard over the voices and clinking of bottles and glasses. The bar wasn't packed, but it was busier than it had been the night before. There were enough people to keep the servers busy, but not so much that we couldn't grab Jadyn for a few minutes. I saw her leaning over the bar, giving Tony a drink order, and smiled. "I'm sorry you never knew your son or daughter, but let's get you introduced to your great... you know who."

He grinned, his gaze already locked on to Jadyn. I wanted to believe it was some sort of mystical connection that family had even through so many generations of separation, but in reality knew that Christian was friends with Khiderian and Jake, and Khiderian was married to Jake's sister. Either Christian or Jake would have surely shown the guy a picture of his kin when he was told about her.

We made it across the room in quick strides, and Daniel took a seat at the bar near Jadyn while Khiderian and I stood behind her and waited for her to turn. Sensing our presence, she did, and her green eyes were bright and friendly once she saw it was me behind her.

"Oh, hi, Danni." Her gaze shifted to my side and up. Way up, given Khiderian's height, which she hadn't inherited. "Who's—"

"Hello, Jadyn," Khiderian greeted her when her mouth rounded in an O. "You are even more beautiful in person."

Yep, he'd seen her picture and clearly she'd seen his too because her eyes had gone all misty right about the time recognition entered them.

She took the hand he offered and shook it awkwardly. "You're just saying that because you're my great-great, uh…"

"You can just call me Khiderian," he said with a laugh, "and I assure you my words are true."

"Why don't you take a break so you two can get to know each other?" I suggested. "I'm sure the other servers can handle things. It's not that packed in here."

"Are you sure? I don't want to inconvenience anyone."

"Go." I gave her a light push, prodding her away from the bar and the tray Tony had just placed drinks on.

"You just sent my server off on a break before she could take this out," the tiger shifter grumbled. "Are you going to take them where they belong?"

"Sure," I said, placing my hand over the center of my chest and adopting a flattered expression. "It means so much to me that you would trust me to carry a tray of drinks all the way across the room without an accident."

"You're right. I don't know what the hell I was

thinking. My brain must still be off the clock." He glanced over my shoulder. "Hey, Hazel. Take these drinks out."

"Well, that's just insulting," I said as Hazel slid past me to grab the drinks, although I'd known a reminder of the possibility of an accident would have caused Tony to reconsider and gotten me off the hook for having to deliver them to a table of possibly inebriated men or women on what was supposed to be my night off from working in the bar in any capacity.

"Yeah, I can tell you're real broken up about it by the grin on your face."

I winked at him, a gesture that provoked an under-the-breath word guaranteed to redden one's cheeks and an eye roll from the cantankerous shifter before he turned away to get back to doing his job. Or just to get away from me. I was betting on both.

"He just adores me so much he doesn't know what to do about it," I said to Daniel.

"You have that effect." He lifted a brand new bottle of beer to his mouth and took a drink. Then promptly choked on it as his eyes grew wide and amber colored liquid dribbled down his chin.

I followed his gaze to the front of the door where Ginger had just walked in and was glad I hadn't been drinking anything because I was already choking on my own tongue.

CHAPTER EIGHT

"Holy smokes." The words came out of my mouth in a near-whispered sound of shock, and maybe a bit of awe.

"There's nothing holy about that," Daniel said, wiping a napkin down his chin.

Ginger stood just inside the entrance, next to where Rome was posted on door duty, and the big guy looked like he might have needed medical attention. His jaw hung open and his eyeballs had nearly popped out of his head.

"What?" Ginger snapped before delivering a backhanded smack to his abdomen, which seemed to do the trick and cause his mouth to snap closed while his eyes returned back to where they belonged. "What's everyone looking at? It's like you've never seen a woman in a dress before."

I did a slow blink as she approached, taking in the look. Her normally spiky hair had been slicked down into a more elegant style reminiscent of the hairstyles in the roaring twenties, and her tiny black dress barely covered her unmentionables, revealing long, thin legs anyone would mistake for a dancer's. They wouldn't mistake her for a dancer though, not when the heavily applied, bold makeup, black fishnet stockings and skyscraper stilettos combined with the faux fur coat gave off a completely different vibe.

"So, I take it you're going undercover?" I said as Ginger reached us.

"Is there any other reason I'd have my hoo-ha out swinging in the frigid night air like this?"

Daniel choked again, having chosen the wrong moment to attempt another drink, and more beer dribbled down his chin. "Dammit."

"Do you need a bib or something?" Tony tossed a towel at him. "Don't get my bar top all sticky."

Daniel flipped him off but dutifully wiped down the bar top once he'd wiped his face dry with a napkin.

"What's wrong with dragon-boy?" Ginger asked.

"I think it makes him uncomfortable knowing you have a hoo-ha."

"Can you two please stop talking about your hoo-has?" Daniel wadded up his discarded napkins and tossed them into the wastebasket behind the bar.

"My hoo-ha never came into the conversation," I said innocently and batted my eyes.

"You're a grown man." Ginger placed her hand on his shoulder, showing off her purple-lacquered fingernails as she took the seat next to him. "You shouldn't be afraid of a little hoo-ha."

"Geez." He picked up his beer and stood from the barstool he'd been perched on. "I'll be hanging out with Rome if you need me."

"Boss's orders and one for you too, Ginger." Tony dropped off two glass bottles that were so dark non-paranormals would never know they were filled with blood and swiftly moved to the other end of the bar where someone flagged him down for a shot of whiskey. Apparently, Rider had thought I'd needed a top-off before we hit the interrogation room again.

Ginger and I lifted our bottles and clinked them together in a toast. "Is that a new shade of polish from

The Ho Factory or whatever that place is called where you get all your makeup?"

"Yep," she said and took a swig from her bottle. "This shade is Gonorrhea Grape."

I'd been mid-swallow and quickly pinched my nose and pressed my lips together tight as I choked so I didn't spurt blood all over the place and freak the non-paranormals out.

"Are you all right?" Ginger smacked my back.

A towel landed on the bar in front of me, followed by Tony's gruff voice, so low only we could hear. "If you're going to spew blood, do it in that."

By the time I forced the remaining blood that had been trying its damnedest to find another way out of me down my throat and discreetly wiped my face just in case, Tony was back to work, several feet away from me. "That's a horrible name for a nail polish," I finally said, wiping my eyes with the towel before I leaned over the bar to toss it into the bin the dirty towels went into.

"What? It's cute, and it was from a charity collection. The money went to funding sex education programs in middle schools. I got Gonorrhea Grape, Abstinence Aqua, Syphilis Silver, Prophylactic Pink, Virgin Vanilla—"

"All terrible names." I shook my head and settled onto the barstool next to her. "Um, I'm not sure that going undercover this way is necessary anymore. Did Rider not tell you about Ramson yet?"

"Yeah, he told me. He left a message on my voicemail earlier while I was sleeping. So we know Julie's with that guy, but we don't know how she ended up there. I went through her calls, texts and emails with the techs yesterday and took a good look around her apartment."

"Rider already did all of that."

"Yes, and I'm not saying Rider isn't great at finding people, but he doesn't know how to go into an apartment and look at it from a woman's perspective or really get a sense of a person from their living space, which is one of the reasons he put me on this job. I do a lot of missing persons jobs for him. Usually it's a missing person who needs to be killed when found type of deal, but sometimes it's a regular missing persons case handed off to me instead of going through regular law enforcement because the missing person is of the paranormal persuasion."

"I always wondered what exactly you did on these solo missions you go off on," I said. "I always pictured something more special ops or spy-like."

"It can be." She took another drink.

"I still don't see why you're about to go freeze your hoo-ha off when we know she's with Ramson and not anywhere where they want the services she once peddled."

"This is above Julie now. While you and I were sleeping like good little vampires, your man was busy working off of a hunch. He apparently hasn't gotten around to telling you yet, but since I can sense the slayer's presence, I can guess why he's been too busy to. This Ramson creep is a fake prophet, right? He talks a bunch of crap about cleansing souls or some crap?"

"Yeah."

"And he has at least one former prostitute in his cult that we know of, so it makes sense to assume he likes to collect, shall we say, women of questionable morals?"

"Yes, that was pretty much what I'd gathered from the men we interrogated."

"Right, so Rider took a deeper look into missing persons reports over the last few months. There's been a spike in sex workers going missing this month. That normally doesn't draw a lot of attention because sadly, it's not uncommon for them to go missing, but they're usually found dead pretty quick. Not the case with the ones who've gone missing this month, which led Rider to believe that was because they weren't being killed and dumped. They were being sucked into this weirdo's cult."

"And now you're going undercover, posing as a hooker—"

"Sex worker."

"Sorry. You're posing as a sex worker to see if Ramson is behind these abductions?"

"Yes. I'm still working on the Julie thing, too, trying to figure out why she left her apartment without her phone. Obviously, she didn't want to be tracked, which makes it likely she planned on doing something or seeing someone Rider wouldn't approve of, and she didn't want it to get back to him."

"Yes, but how did she end up with Ramson?" I remembered I was supposed to be drinking the bottled blood sitting in front of me and took a big drink. It was always better before it congealed. "The techs couldn't find anything linking him to her. Could she have really just been randomly snatched off the street? Could her being a former prostitute just be a coincidence?"

"Maybe. Maybe not." Ginger shrugged. "Rider doesn't keep those women locked up. They had to let go of their previous connections, considering those connections were drug dealers, users, fellow sex workers or pimps, but they weren't banned from meeting new people. They knew each other, of course, since they all live on the same floor of that building, and some of them even went to school."

"Really? Rider pays for them to go to school?" I asked, surprised because he'd always acted as if my wanting Angel to go to school or travel meant I was too close to her.

"He pays them for their blood and they are free to spend that money on anything they want as long as it's not drugs," Ginger answered, then continued. "Anyway, just because the techs haven't found any communication between Julie and Ramson doesn't mean Julie never spoke with anyone who might know Ramson. I'm sure not all of his followers were abducted like what almost happened to the woman you saved last night. He probably has his female followers sweet-talk others into joining. Julie was taking art classes. What better place to meet a fellow tortured soul?"

"Not all artists are tortured souls."

"Enough of them are to make it a stereotype." She took a long pull from her bottle, finishing it, which reminded me I needed to do the same.

I turned my bottle up and guzzled until I drained it, then licked my lips as I set it down on the bar top, making sure I didn't leave any telltale evidence of being a creature of the night. "So you're saying she might have met someone in art class who told her about Ramson and she purposely disappeared to go join his cult?"

"That's one possibility. She could have run into an old acquaintance while out somewhere where she wasn't being monitored so heavily. The donors' vehicles and phones are tracked, but unless they're somewhere suspicious, the techs wouldn't be triggered to investigate. The techs haven't found anything suspicious, but she's had art class, doctor appointments, and of course she's bought groceries and filled up at gas stations. She could have run into an old acquaintance anywhere. Maybe she agreed to meet back up with that old acquaintance the day she disappeared. I found a notebook she wrote poetry in. I'm no expert on the stuff, but I definitely felt a lot of loneliness when I read her words."

"But she could meet new people."

Ginger tapped her purple-hued fingernails on the bar top as she stared off into the distance for a moment, then sighed and returned her gaze to me. "We all are, but how many normies do we meet and get close to? We can't. Not really. Not when we have this huge of a secret to keep. Those donors have to keep our existence a secret as much as we do. It makes it hard to really get close to anyone outside of each other, and even though they live in a building with shifters and other paranormals who they could have a relationship with, no one is going to want to be in a relationship with the boss's donor, and just because they agree to sell their blood to one vampire doesn't mean they want to get into a relationship, or even a friendship, with another."

I thought about what the donors had to live with. I initially only thought about them in jealousy, imagining the feeding process as intimate as it was when I fed from Rider, but once I took Rider's word that it wasn't, I thought they'd been given a pretty sweet deal. An apartment and money too, and all they had to do was feed a vampire. I didn't know they were tracked or even think about them possibly wanting to lead a normal life again. "And they can't leave if they want to? Retire from being a donor?"

"I try not to get my nose too deep into Rider's business lest I get it cut off, among other parts I've grown accustomed to having, but I know most vampires who take on personal donors do so with the understanding that this is a lifelong job."

"So Angel is stuck being my donor for the rest of her life?" I suddenly felt like throwing up. "That's not what she signed on for. I never told her she'd have to be with me forever and if she decides to go to school, enter a career that takes her somewhere else, or falls in love, I want her to have that."

"Hey." Ginger reached over and covered my hand with hers, and the instant chill I felt courtesy of my succubus side shocked me enough to stop the tears threatening to fall from my eyes. "You're taking good care of Angel, and I don't know if Rider lets his donors retire or not, but I know he's always fair in his dealings, even when he's ruthless. Don't get ahead of yourself and jump to conclusions. Ask him."

I nodded, but thought back to how angry Rider had gotten when he'd thought Julie Chavez had betrayed him, and the threat he'd made. "You've known Rider a long time. Do you think he'd be capable of killing a donor if she knowingly betrayed him?"

"I think Rider is capable of killing *anyone* who betrays him. Donor, employee, friend. Male, female. It doesn't matter. Traitors get death."

"Hey there, honey. You're looking mighty pretty to be without a man tonight."

Ginger's body stiffened as the man's alcohol-soaked breath rolled over her from where he stood pressed against her back. She turned her head to take in the intruder interrupting our private conversation.

The man was Caucasian, stood around five feet, ten inches, and had an athletic build except for the beer belly which seemed to threaten the buttons near the bottom of his green flannel shirt which had been left untucked to hang over the well-worn jeans. His hair, or what was left of it, was a dark brown ring encircling the shiny bald spot on top of his head. He probably would have been a halfway attractive guy if he'd shaved off the hair he appeared to be desperately clinging to and drank less, possibly giving the broken capillaries covering his nose and cheeks a chance to heal, but something in his tone clued me in that it would take more than an improvement to his outside appearance to make him an attractive man.

"Are you speaking to me?" Ginger asked, although it was obvious he had been from the way his body had been pressed so close to her and his lusty gaze hadn't left her.

What apparently wasn't so obvious to him was Ginger's tone, which said *Abort! Abort!* However, missing this warning signal, he took her acknowledgement of his existence as encouragement.

"I don't see anyone else here beautiful enough to catch my eye."

Geez. I didn't know whether to be relieved or insulted. Then the guy not-so-discreetly scratched his nuts, and the decision was very simple. I felt sorry for Ginger though, but she'd already narrowed her eyes and curled her hand into a fist, ready to be thrown. "I'm sure you'll find someone else. I'm not the woman for you."

"Aw, now, sugar, don't be like that. You certainly look like a girl who knows how to have a good time."

AULD FANG SYNE

"And you look like a man who doesn't know how to take a fucking hint." She pushed him back, moving him out of her personal space. "First of all, I'm not a girl. I'm a grown-ass woman. Second, even if I found you attractive, which, let's be honest, would probably take a large amount of drugs and alcohol to accomplish, maybe a lobotomy, I wouldn't be interested in you."

The man's overly eager flirtatious manner abruptly changed and his eyes narrowed as his gaze went down to her stilettoed feet and rolled back up to where her small breasts were pushed up pretty well with the use of sturdy bra engineering to overflow the neckline of her tiny black sheath. "Oh, yeah? I was being nice, honey. A girl with her goods on display like this shouldn't be so uppity when a nice guy pays her a compliment."

"And this is why I only date women," Ginger muttered, looking at me.

"You ever notice how these types always seem to think they're the nice guys?" I asked.

"Yep, I've noticed that. It's mind-boggling."

"Oh." The man's eyes rounded as he understood why he wouldn't interest Ginger, even if he'd actually been nice, attractive, and actually had some swagger. Unfortunately, he lacked the intelligence to realize that should have been his cue to back off instead of closing in on Ginger, forcing her to press her back against the bar. "Hey, if you want to include your girlfriend, we can, but you gotta have a little meat in the dish, honey. I'm guessing you just haven't had a skilled man. I'll go real easy, then make it rough when you're ready. Once you've had a man who knows what he's doing, you'll realize what you've been missing."

Ginger grabbed a handful of the man's shirt and I moved, ready to vacate my barstool and join in the human piñata party, but before either of us could do anything, the man was slammed back against the bar and Daniel pressed against his front while holding the man's twisted arms behind his back.

"What the fuck are you doing?" The man's face flushed red as fear and anger fought for dominance in his eyes. "Get off me, you fruitcake!"

"Shhh," Daniel said, pressing even closer against the man. "No need to be like that, honey. I'm doing you a favor. You see, you gotta have a little meat in the dish, and fortunately for you, I'm packing a lot."

"You fucking freak." The man fought against Daniel's hold, no idea he was trying to get out of the grip of a dragon and had no prayer of doing it. All the struggling only made him writhe against Daniel more.

"Oooh, see. You like this. Don't worry, honey. I'll go real easy, then make it rough when you're ready. Once you've had a man who knows what he's doing, you'll realize what you've been missing."

"Back off, Daniel."

The man's body relaxed in relief as Tony approached him from behind the bar, coming to his aid, or so he thought, before Tony wrapped his muscular arms around the man's shoulders and leaned in close to his ear. "This one's mine. I'm gonna lube him up and ride him like a bull. A big, horny *bull*."

The man sucked in a huge breath, his eyes watered, and he started to shriek while his limbs shook.

"Shut up." Daniel stepped back, releasing the man's arms, and slapped the man hard enough to stun him, then waited until the dazed look left the guy's eyes. "What's the problem, boo-boo? I thought everyone not interested in men just hadn't had the right one yet. That's what you were saying, right?"

"That's not what I meant. A woman is supposed to be with a man and a man is—"

Daniel slapped him again. "Ya know, everyone's entitled to their opinions, but the problem with that is everyone seems to think their opinion is law and that bullshit doesn't fly here. A woman can be with whoever the hell she wants to be with, and when she says she's not interested in you, you back the hell off. Especially when she tells you she's not interested in men. You understand that, you homophobic little prick?"

The man's lip curled, but with Tony's bulky arms still wrapped around his shoulders and Daniel within slapping distance, he knew better than to disagree. "Yeah, sure. I didn't mean nothin' by it."

"Yes, you did," Tony said, "and for the record, a woman can also wear whatever she wants and that doesn't give you the right to force yourself into her personal space when she makes her disinterest known. I don't care if she's completely ass-out naked. No means no, fuck-face."

"You got all that?" Daniel asked him.

"Yeah. Yeah, I got it." Red climbed the man's cheeks as his eyes darted around the room, and he realized everyone had stopped what they were doing to watch the free dinner show. He swallowed hard. "Can I go now?"

"Aw, do you have to?" Tony circled the rim of the man's ear with his finger.

Daniel grinned for a moment, then his expression grew very serious, and lethal, as he stepped in closer to the man and lowered his voice. "I'm usually on duty as security here, so listen and listen close. If I ever catch or even hear of you harassing any of the women in this bar again, if I hear of you harassing women *anywhere,* whatever you offer to do to them… I'm going to do to you. You feel me?"

The man's skin went pale green, and he swallowed hard. "Yeah. Yeah, I got it."

"Get the hell out of here." Daniel stepped back and Tony let the man go, which the man wasted no time doing, making his hasty exit to the chorus of whistles, rowdy cheer, and applause.

"Before you get mad, we know you could have handled that yourself," Daniel said, "but believe me, this will leave more of an impression on him than just kicking his—hey, are you all right?"

I'd been so focused on Daniel and Tony giving the guy what he deserved, I'd been too distracted to notice Ginger's eyes had been tearing up. She sniffed and swiped her hands under her eyes, showing the strength of her waterproof mascara and eyeliner as it stayed impeccable.

"That was… No one's…" She sniffed again and took a deep breath. "I've put up with a lot of crap like that for a lot of years and I could handle him, but it's nice not having to because someone else… No one's ever just stepped in like that for me and what you guys did… and you're not even … I just…" She lunged forward, throwing her arms around Daniel's shoulders as she pulled him into a tight hug that caused water to pool in my eyes. His expression was one of surprise, but a smile soon spread across his face and he hugged her back.

"That's my cue to get the hell away from here," Tony muttered and fled to the other side of the bar.

"You're a sweetheart too, Tony!" I yelled while trying not to laugh at his obvious discomfort.

"Bite me," he yelled back, gruffly. "I just wanted to see if I could make the guy piss himself. It's a hobby of mine."

I let loose the laughter I gave up on holding back, and Ginger and Daniel joined in as they parted.

"I could have handled that though," Ginger said, straightening her tiny dress, a blush creeping up her neck as she realized how much emotion she'd allowed herself to show. "I would have sent him packing with his nuts rearranged. I would have made Danni the Teste Slayer proud, but I have to admit, your way of handling that was fun to watch."

We're ready to head down to interrogation, Rider announced through our mind-link. *Bring Khiderian in case we need his input.*

"Oh. I guess I'm going with you for that," Ginger said, apparently having been included in the mind-link. She rubbed her hands together. "Yasss. I finally get to see the Teste Slayer in interrogation. Who's Khiderian?"

"Fallen angel turned vampire turned regular mortal man," I said as I pointed at Khiderian, where he sat at a small table with Jadyn at the back of the room. "Actually, he was a pranic vampire, so Jake brought him in case we needed his knowledge."

"And he happens to be the fallen angel Jadyn inherited her grace from," Daniel added, "which is what allows her to communicate with animals."

"Cool."

"I'll grab him," Daniel said, moving toward the table.

"Well, girlfriend. It's time to slay some testes." Ginger blew a kiss to Tony, earning a grunt from the shifter, and led the way.

We pushed through the back door and the door after that one, entering the small room that contained the staircase leading up to Rider's private room, and the doors leading to the garage and the stairwell to the sublevels. Rider stood in the center, waiting for us, and Jake crouched next to him, giving Kutya, who was spread out on his back with his tongue lolling out, a belly rub. Hank stood by the door that led to the garage, his enormous arms folded over his equally massive chest. The wererhino greeted us with a nod of his head, which left me puzzled how he could manage the movement when he didn't have much of a neck.

Seeing me, Kutya quickly rolled over and jumped to his paws then ran right into my legs, hitting me mid-thigh and nearly knocking me over, but I'd learned to brace for the big guy's overenthusiastic lovin'.

"Hey, big guy." I bent to give him a good scratch between his ears like he liked.

"Well, he sure forgot about me fast," Jake said, standing from his crouched position. He nodded at Ginger and smiled. "Hey. I like the purple lipstick."

"Thanks. It's called Orchid Orgasm."

The slayer's smile grew. Rider fought the tug of his.

A moment later, Daniel entered with Khiderian,

followed by Tony. The tiger shifter held the slayer in his sights as he stopped at my side and folded his arms.

"Why the sour face?" Rider asked. "I thought you'd enjoy getting out of the bar to do some hunting and possible killing."

"I'd enjoy it more if I got to kill whoever I wanted," Tony replied, his gaze still locked onto Jake, which only made the slayer grin.

"Well, I can't allow that, but if anything goes sideways, you'll be glad to have the slayer with you. As much as it gives me indigestion to admit it, Porter came in very handy during our last big battle. You saw that with your own eyes."

"Yeah, I also saw him lose his shit and get bloodthirsty for anything paranormal. Are we going to have Jadyn with us in case that happens again?"

"You won't need her," Jake said, sharing a look with Rider before they both looked at me, eying me in a way that made me fidgety.

"What? Why are you two looking at me like that?" I asked, noting the gleam in Jake's eye and the hesitancy in Rider's.

"You remember that thing you did with the krackling downstairs in the cells?" Jake said.

"Yeah."

"I'm immune enough to not start humping your leg if you do that, but it should give me something similar to a slap upside the head if I get out of control and start wanting to kill anyone paranormal who shouldn't be killed, enough to snap me out of it."

"And the others around her," Daniel said, his tone clearly showing his disapproval of the idea. "She'll lure every male in the area to her."

"Jake will have a syringe filled with the hawthorn oil mixture Nannette created to knock Danni unconscious should that happen," Rider said, not very enthusiastic about the idea, but Jake must have convinced him of the plan. "As will you and Tony."

"That will leave her vulnerable," Daniel stated the obvious. "Very dangerous if we're in the middle of a fight that's so bad the slayer starts going all serial killer on us."

"Seems a better idea to just take out the slayer," Tony said, narrowing his eyes.

"Easy, kitty," Jake said. "I'm on your side."

"Call me kitty one more time and you're going to be in the ground."

Hank chuckled appreciatively. The large shifter wasn't a slayer fan either. None of Rider's men were.

"He'll just resurrect and crawl back out," Rider said, shooting a warning look Hank's way before changing his tone to the one that said no more bullshit, it was time to get serious. "And you're under direct order not to lay a hand on him unless it's absolutely necessary. That goes for all of you. You're a team and your enemy is Ramson and anyone he throws at you, not each other. Am I understood?"

"Yeah," Daniel muttered.

Tony answered with a grunt that must have been affirmative because Rider didn't press him.

"I know you're all very protective of Danni," Jake said, "and you have a valid reason to be concerned about me. I am what I am, but I am on your side. I would never intentionally hurt Danni and I wouldn't suggest for her to use her lure to pull me out of the bloodlust if I didn't believe it would work without any harm coming to her. Also, I had just fought through a shitload of shifters and vampires, been killed by an angel, and came back to jump out on a battlefield full of vamps and shifters trying to kill me again when I went into a bloodlust the last time. That's not something that happens every time I'm in a fight. I may not even need her to use her lure."

Tony's shoulders relaxed a little, but his expression didn't soften. "But what if you do and you have to inject her to stop her from signaling every male in proximity to go for her? She'll be unconscious, unable to defend herself, which will complicate things for us dramatically, not to mention that the lure is going to affect Daniel and me too. What good is it for us to have the syringes if we'll be under the influence of her lure?"

"He's right," Daniel said. "The last time I used a syringe on her, it was because of her going into the Bloom. I was fine as long as she didn't get her fangs in me, so I was able to use the syringe. If she actually lures Jake and it affects us too, we're not going to want to inject her. And frankly, two shifters aren't the type of men you want around her when she's doing that. It's not safe."

"You'll have the syringes in case the succubus part of her takes over unexpectedly and she wants to inject you with venom through her bite," Jake explained. "That's just a precaution since Rider won't be with us to stop her himself. As for the lure, it's not as strong as her actual bite. It'll entrance anything male, but without venom, it won't be as bad as you're imagining."

"If it wasn't a bad situation, we wouldn't need syringes at all," Daniel said.

"Danni may be able to stop the lure herself. If not, and it looks like her succubus side may overpower her and cause her to bite, I will inject her before anyone gets to her. Once she's unconscious, the lure is cut off and the succubus is shut down. The signal stops, no one's all hopped up horny balls, and we just kill the bastards while protecting her. Between a dragon, a tiger, and a slayer, that should be a piece of cake."

"Ginger may also be there," Rider added. "We're going to try to get her brought into the cult should a hunch we've been working on pan out."

"I'm guessing that's where the new wardrobe comes in," Daniel said as he and Tony looked at her.

"Ramson has my donor, a former prostitute," Rider said. "I checked and there has been an increase in missing sex workers in the area, but no bodies found. From what we've already learned from the dumbasses downstairs, Ramson likes to *cleanse* his followers. The missing women fit the profile of exactly the type of women he'd think would need cleansing. Ginger's going undercover to see if anyone's out scouting sex workers or just abducting them. If we're lucky, she'll find a way in."

"Isn't that dangerous for her?" I asked. "You said pranic vampires can read minds. He'll know she's a vampire immediately and once he reads her mind, he'll know all about you and that she was sent in to infiltrate the cult."

"She's not going to be sent in to infiltrate the cult. She's going to find out where it is so we can find it, unless we can find it another way. The tech team has a tracker for her to wear and we'll be able to get Rihanna to flash you right to her if necessary."

"We're not going to waste any time asking questions," Jake said. "Any time you can give a prannie is time that makes them more powerful. If Ginger finds a way inside, she'll send the signal and we'll be there. Once we're there, it's time to slay Ramson and anyone stupid enough to fight to protect him."

"Even Julie?" I looked at Rider.

"If she's been compromised," Rider said, his tone stern, eyes unreadable. "Any hold Ramson has over her should die with him, but you can't worry about saving her if she's trying to kill you."

"Yeah, it sucks," Jake said, probably reading my expression, "but that's war."

"War sucks," I muttered.

"That's the consensus." Jake smiled, then clapped his hands together, the sound echoing through the room before he rubbed his hands together briskly. "Who's ready to smack some jackasses around and get some answers?"

"Me! Me!" Ginger raised her hand, and I grabbed the hem of her dress before she flashed everyone.

"You might not want to raise your arms in this dress,"

I warned her.

"Oops."

Rider shook his head while Jake chuckled. Daniel stood awkwardly, looking anywhere but at Ginger. Hank and Khiderian seemed to study their own shoes, and Tony continued eyeing Jake like he wanted to tear into his carcass, which was something Tony was actually capable of and likely to do if allowed to. Kutya sat at my feet, obliviously enjoying the head scratching.

"We need you out there blending in, trying to draw the cult's attention in case we can't get Ramson's location from the men Danni brought in last night," Rider told her. "Juan is waiting for you out back. He'll be your backup should you get into trouble… or start to feel frostbite."

Ginger rolled her eyes and looked down at herself. "If I start to feel frostbite, it'll probably be somewhere he won't want me toasting in front of the heating vent in his SUV."

I choked on a laugh and wiped my eyes as Jake's hearty laugh filled the room and the other men just shook their heads.

Rider reached into his pants pocket and pulled out a bracelet, a simple brass chain with a heart charm that didn't look expensive enough for anyone to try to steal while Ginger was out playing her role.

Ginger sighed and walked over to him, her arm stretched out in front of her so he could fasten it on her wrist. "I never get to see Danni go all Teste Slayer in interrogation"

"No, but you've seen her go Teste Slayer out in the wild many times," Rider said, fastening the bracelet. He held the bracelet so that Ginger could see the underside of the rectangle-shaped clasp. "The tracking device is in the charm, so don't damage it. If you get taken to where Ramson is or otherwise get in a situation where you need us to come rushing in immediately, all you have to do is press this little button on the clasp and help will be sent to the location transmitting from the tracker. Press hard. It's designed not to be accidentally triggered if you get into a fight you can manage yourself or hit it some other way."

"Got it." She sighed and looked back at me. "Try to get the weirdo cult leader's location before I sprout icicles from my nether region, sweet cheeks, or too many men try to pick me up. There's only so big of a pile of unconscious men I can build before things get complicated."

I grinned. "I will. Be careful."

"Later, guys." She waved and left through the garage door.

"I like her," Jake said. "She's fun."

Rider ignored him. "You can go back to the bar for now, Tony. If we find out anything you would need to know during interrogation, we can fill you in later. Be ready to leave immediately if we get the location. Greg can handle things alone, and Macon is on standby if needed."

Who the heck was Macon? There were so many people in Rider's organization, I doubted I'd ever meet them all. I wasn't sure how he could keep up with them all himself, but I guess centuries of living taught you how to remember a lot of names and faces.

Tony gave one of his multi-purpose grunts and left. The man didn't waste time on words when he didn't have to.

"I don't think he's thrilled about doing this with us," I said.

"He'll be happy once he gets to beat the hell out of someone," Rider said.

"Or eat someone," Daniel added.

Kutya barked and started whining.

"I swear this dog knows what we're saying," Daniel muttered. "We're not talking about food, and I'm sure you've had enough to eat, you gluttonous mutt."

"You should talk," I said and heard the trace of attitude in my tone. Apparently I hadn't yet fully gotten over Daniel's earlier comments while researching succubi, and it was coming out in my tone.

The guys must have picked up on it too, because Jake and Rider both looked at me quizzically and I felt the gazes of Daniel, Khiderian, and Hank on me. Even Kutya let out a whine, sensing the tension. I didn't know which made me feel more like squirming— the confusion I felt coming from Daniel or the suspicious curiosity coming from Rider, but I knew both would be questioning me.

"So," I said. "Are we doing this thing or what?"

CHAPTER NINE

Hank was left in charge of Kutya since the sublevel was no place for a dog that picked up on emotions while an interrogation was occurring, even if he wasn't in the room.

What was that? Rider asked through our mind-link as we headed down the stairs.

What was what?

The tone you just had with Daniel.

I didn't have a tone.

He gave me a look that said *bullshit*.

I sighed mentally, since that was the way we were conversing. *I don't know. I didn't mean to have a tone. I'm probably just stressed since Ginger's going undercover. I don't want her to get hurt.*

Ginger can handle herself. We'll talk about this later.

Oh yay, I thought as Rider placed his palm over the panel next to the door, allowing entrance to the sublevel we wanted access to. Of course we would, and if he didn't get a satisfactory explanation out of me, he'd grill Daniel, and I didn't want that to happen. Both men held a healthy amount of respect for one another, but there was also a competitiveness that I feared could turn violent in any situation that involved me.

Rider pushed through the door, holding it open for the rest of us, then led us down the hall to where the men waited in the interrogation room.

"Daniel, Khiderian, you'll be with me in observation," Rider said.

"You're really sending her in there with just the slayer?" Daniel said.

Rider directed a dark look his way. "Are you questioning me?"

"If that's what you're doing, then yes. I'm her bodyguard. I should be with her anytime she's in the presence of a slayer. That's my primary job, right?"

Oh shit, I thought as Rider's eyes went cold and he stepped into Daniel's personal space, putting them face to face.

"When needed," Rider said, voice low, yet carrying more threat of danger than a roar. "And it's never needed when she's in my presence. If you think a wall between us is going to stop me from gutting that slayer before he could hurt her, you're more stupid than that rainbow mop you call hair. If you think I'd put her in danger, you're out of your fucking mind."

"Hey, no disrespect meant while on your own property and all that," Jake said, none of his usual joviality in his tone, "and I don't know what the hell is up with the pissing contest, but if you two brawl, I'm going to smack the bullshit out of both of you. We don't have time for this right now."

Rider slowly turned his gaze toward Jake and allowed a hint of his power to set it aglow before he growled low in his throat.

"I said no disrespect."

That glowing gaze turned back toward Daniel and as the two glared at each other in silence, I knew they were saying whatever was left to say between them through their own private mental link.

"Shit," Jake said, tossing a glance Khiderian's way. The

tall former vampire nodded, and they flanked the two men.

I didn't know if saying anything at the moment would diffuse the situation or make it worse, so I bit my lip and prayed Rider would calm down and Daniel wouldn't say anything smart-assed to provoke him further. From the look on the shifter's face, he wasn't just listening to what Rider had to say. He was speaking his piece too.

Finally, the thick smog of tension in the air lessened and the glow in Rider's eyes receded. Both sets of shoulders lowered half an inch, and the men stepped back from one another. Daniel turned toward Khiderian. "Observation is this room."

He led the way into the room, his gaze directly ahead of him as he did, and Rider wrapped his hand around the back of my neck before pulling me toward him to lower his head, covering my mouth with his. He kissed me long and hard, the action seeming to be more a display of what I was to him than a gesture of affection, but it curled my toes just the same.

Once he finished and raised his head, leaving my lips swollen and my knees weak, he kept his hand right where it was and aimed his dark gaze at Jake. "You know what would happen if you ever so much as entertained the thought of harming her."

"I can tell you with all sincerity I would hate to find out, but you don't have to worry about her with me. You knew that before the dragon got in your head."

Rider continued to stare at Jake for a moment, seeming to weigh the slayer's words, then softened his grip on my neck and caressed my cheek with his thumb before dropping a kiss on my forehead. "Try to get Ramson's location. Khiderian will observe, offering suggestions I'll relay through our mind-link. Jake, watch her eyes. If they turn red, the succubus has risen to the surface, and if she touches one of them and gets a vision, she could faint."

"If the succubus rises, I'll sense it before she shows the physical signs. And don't worry. I'll catch her if she falls."

Rider nodded after a moment of thought, gave my shoulder a light squeeze, and entered the observation room, where only a mortal man would be available to pull him and Daniel apart if the two gave into the hunger they both seemed to feel for a fight. I hoped Khiderian had enough former vampire or angel left in him to not get obliterated if the other two men in that room went for each other's throats.

"So, does that whatever-the-hell-that-was happen often between those two?" Jake asked.

"Far more than I'm comfortable with," I replied, "but even for them, that was really intense."

"Yeah. More and more, I'm thinking of sneaking you out of this building and going after this prannie by ourselves."

"You know I can hear you," Rider called out from behind the observation room's closed door a moment before he opened it and stuck his head out. "Try sneaking her anywhere again and we'll see how possible it is for you to resurrect without all your organs. Quit gossiping and get to work."

"I don't think he understands that I don't actually work for him," Jake said after Rider disappeared back into the observation room.

"If you're in this part of the building, you're either working for him or you're a blood buffet," I explained. "Be glad you're being treated like an employee and not a snack. Let's get this over with. Do you want me to ask the questions since I have the mind-link with Rider?"

"We'll wing it." He opened the door to the interrogation room and gestured for me to precede him. "After you, ma'am."

The smell of sweat and bleach hit me the moment the door had swung open, but as I walked through, I was relieved to not smell the overwhelming odor of urine. Having already been told the men had pissed themselves enough for the smell to permeate through the door and out into the hall, I'd been expecting something much worse. Cliff was seated at the table in the center of the room, and Mike busied himself pacing. Both had been given light blue scrubs to wear and their hair was still damp from the hosing down I imagined they'd gotten before the room had been mopped with bleach to cover up their recent bladder failures.

Cliff's hands shook as he balled them into fists on top of the table, or as close as he could get to fists given the broken digits. His posture didn't suggest him to be a threat. The fists appeared to be more a product of him trying to control himself so he didn't try to jump out of the chair and make a run for it. "Keep that demoness away from me."

Mike stopped pacing and backed into the corner to the right of the two-way mirror's edge, the same one he'd been huddled in the night before. His face looked better, but that wasn't saying a lot. Splotches of blue, purple, and near-black covered his smooshed nose and under his eyes. The gashes over his eye and in his cheek appeared to have stopped seeping blood, but he had no choice but to view us through a narrow squint because of the swelling of both eyes and the sound coming from his nose suggested he couldn't breathe properly through what was left of it.

"Damn. Did you do that to him?" Jake asked, studying the man who stood trembling in the corner while still trying to back farther away despite the wall at his back.

"No. That is Nannette's work."

"Nice. Not sure I've met her, but she does good work. Not as good as me," he added, his voice lower as it dipped into a tone that promised pain as he stepped toward Cliff and leaned down so that he was at eye level with the man. He braced himself with one hand on the table, stared directly into Cliff's wide, frightened eyes, and smiled with pure wickedness. "Hey there, buddy. So you don't like my friend Danni here, huh? A little too much woman for you? I hear you like to sing 'Kumbaya' with fake holy men while pretending to save chicks who don't need your kind of saving."

Cliff's face flushed red, but he swallowed down whatever words he might have said once he looked at me, and the trembling in his limbs grew more intense.

"Hey." Jake straightened and slapped him across the face. "Don't look at her when I'm talking to you. Answer me."

Cliff sucked on his newly split bottom lip before responding. "You didn't ask a question."

"I didn't ask a question?" Jake looked over at me. "He said I didn't ask a question. Didn't I ask a question?"

"I believe the question was implied," I said.

"That's right. It was implied." Jake slapped Cliff again, leaving a red welt on the man's cheek and drawing a sob out of Mike, who had slumped down to the floor and drawn his knees to his chest. "Answer the question."

Cliff glared at Jake until I thought for sure Jake would slap him again, but he finally responded before that happened.

"No, I don't like your friend," Cliff said, each word spoken slowly and enunciated clearly. "And I don't sing campfire songs with fake holy men. I follow the prophet Ramson. Ramson is the way. He is the beginning and the end, the alpha and the omega, the light that guides us to the world we must return to. He is the blood that springs eternal to save our souls and cleanse our impurities and weaknesses before blessing us with everlasting life in his vein where we will stand among kings."

Jake stood over Cliff with his arms folded, blinking at the man for several beats before turning his head in my direction, bemused. "What the fuck did he just say?"

"The same thing he said yesterday. I think it's something Ramson has them memorize. Like a mantra or prayer or something."

"Oh." He looked back down at Cliff. "All I heard was 'blah blah blah, I'm a big loser who can't get laid so I decided to snatch women for some Charles Manson wannabe with fangs, blah blah blah, I'm dumber than shit, blah blah, mommy issues, blah blah, probably daddy issues too, blah blah blah my dick is small and I cry into my pillow at night because no one loves me'."

"Charles Manson was insane," Cliff yelled, spittle flying out of his mouth as he lurched forward in his chair. "Charles Manson couldn't heal anyone. Ramson heals, and I don't care what parlor tricks you psychotic lunatics play on us. I know what Ramson is, and he's not a monster. He does the Lord's work, not the work of the devil." Cliff mustered enough courage to stand and point at me with his good index finger. "She's the devil! I saw it with my own eyes. She tore Gary apart with her hands and teeth, and she drank his blood. She's a demon."

"Did I tear into Gary with my teeth or my fangs, Cliff?" I moved in closer to him and Jake grabbed him by the shoulder when he tried to back away and slammed him down into the chair. "What did you actually see?"

"You know what you did."

"Yes, I do, and so do you, but the problem is you're trying to change what you saw. You didn't see a demon attack a holy man." Okay, maybe that wasn't completely true since I was technically half sex demon, but Cliff knowing that wouldn't help us any. "You saw a vampire kill a mortal man, something both of you thought was impossible. But you've seen what we are with your own eyes, and you know vampires exist. However, if you admit it, you have to admit that I told you the truth about Ramson being a vampire, and you can't bring yourself to admit that."

"Because admitting Ramson is a vampire," Jake joined in, "means admitting a lot about yourself. It means admitting you were gullible enough to allow the monster to convince you that you were doing holy work, and once you admit to that, you have to admit that what you've been doing is just kidnapping, rape, and murder."

"I haven't killed anyone!" The scent of fear filled the room, rancid and cloying, as Cliff's eyes bugged out of his head. "No one I brought to the—" He jerked, what he was about to say cut off, as if something unseen physically shut him up. "No one I brought to Ramson was ever killed. There is no murder and no rape, and we saved those women. There were no abductions. They wanted to be with Ramson. They just didn't know it yet."

I looked over at Mike, thinking again about how he'd obviously chosen a woman himself to take to Ramson, when Rider's voice entered my head. *Find out if the men drank from Ramson. Either from him directly or from anything that could have been spiked with his blood.*

I glanced at the mirror and nodded subtly before asking the question. "What did Ramson make you drink?"

Cliff rolled his eyes, or attempted to, before the pain caused by the action caused him to wince and decide against it. "First, Charles Manson, now Jim Jones. Who's next, David Koresh?"

"Interesting that you just named three men who fooled a bunch of easily manipulated pawns into believing they were their way to heaven," Jake said, probably not aware of why I'd asked the question because he didn't have a mind-link with us. "Sad that you can recognize those cults being led by killers, but can't recognize when you yourself are in one."

"True," I said, "but I wasn't thinking of Jim Jones when I asked the question. What do you and the followers drink, Cliff? Have you tasted Ramson's blood?"

"I told you he's not a vampire," Cliff shouted. "You will not convince us of this nonsense! After what you did to Gary, you will not convince me of anything except your evilness. You are wicked! Unclean! Unholy!"

Fire filled my veins a second before Jake punched Cliff in the throat hard enough to leave the man struggling for breath and held his hands up as one would do when trying to calm a very large, incredibly pissed off dog.

"Take it down, sweetheart." He spoke softly, gently, his voice calmer than the lull of an ocean wave. "Those were just words. Mean, nasty words, but just words, and they came from a man you know to be a complete fool. You are not wicked or unclean or anything he called you just now. You are not anything he will ever call you. You know who you are. Both of your sides. In case you don't, I do. Rider does too. You can ask him if you don't trust me, once we get you back where you need to be. Focus on my voice, honey."

I already was focused on Jake's soothing voice, but the testosterone in the gruff, husky deepness called to the part of me that wanted to come out to play. As tempting as that was, something inside me warned me that would be bad, so I breathed deeper and clenched my hands into fists, curling them so tight my short nails bit into flesh to draw blood.

"But you don't have to ask either of us. You don't have to ask anyone. You know who you are, Danni. You are in control of your own body and everything it holds within. That part of you trying to rise right now? We're not ready for it yet. We have to get answers from these men before we can even think of letting it out, so it needs to wait a while. I need you to do me a favor, sweetheart. I need you to stop breathing so hard. I know you think it's helping, but it's not giving you the control you think it is. Slow your breathing."

I took in a breath, but instead of pushing it right back out as I'd been doing, I held it in and forced myself to release it only a little at a time. As my breath slowly escaped me, the fire in my veins simmered, and I became very aware of the coldness creeping in. Coldness I knew would lead to a terrible outcome if I pounced on a warm, testosterone-filled male to gather heat.

"You don't need the heat, Danni. It is a want, not a need. Your eyes are looking a lot better already. I need you to close them now, and I'm going to quit talking."

Thank goodness, I thought, still able to hold on to rational thought, but not if he kept speaking to me in that deep, rough voice while my body yearned for a warm-blooded man.

"Don't listen to my voice anymore. Listen to your own voice, Danni. You are in control now. You have always had this power. Close your eyes, and don't open them until you've told yourself what to do. You got this."

The backs of my eyelids burned as they covered my eyes, which I knew without having looked in the mirror had to have gone red. I drew in a breath, took my time with it. It was scary. My body wanted to take air in fast and push it back out at the same speed, breathe faster than the fear in me screaming that I was about to lose control again, but I wasn't. I was in control of every breath, even if it almost felt like I was drowning. As long as I ignored the fear and slowly drew the air in, allowed it to slip back out just as slowly, I kept breathing.

But I would be fine even if I couldn't draw a breath, wouldn't I? I was part vampire. Vampires could live without air. Living without air might have meant living in a comatose state, but I would still be alive. The thought made it easier to breathe slowly, so I didn't have to put so much work into it. I had the freedom to think, to listen to my own voice.

Go back.

I don't want to. I want to make him pay.

I felt the grin curve my lips as I realized I was seriously having my own internal dialogue with me, myself, and I. Maybe Cliff wasn't the only crazy one in the room. That was all right. I'd take crazy. Crazy was better than stupid, and stupid would be killing our only two leads before getting anything useful out of them. I heard Cliff, who'd been struggling to breathe, start to gasp out an actual word only to be quickly muffled, and tuned him out along with Mike's soft crying. I tuned everything out but my voice.

We will make him pay, but we have to use him first.

I want his blood.

And you will have it.

I want it now.

Why? Because he called us names? Those names triggered you, didn't they? Unclean. Unholy. We feel that way sometimes, don't we? But are we being honest with ourselves? We have friends. We have a good, honorable man who loves us. Two, if we're being really honest. We've saved lives. We are not the monster. We kill the monsters. We will kill this monster, but first he has to lead us to the bigger monster.

Bigger monster. My other voice nearly purred. *More blood.*

More blood. We will have more than enough blood.

I want heat. There is heat here.

This heat makes us feel bad. Wait for me to get what we need from this man and we can find heat that doesn't leave us cold after.

And blood.

Yes, and blood.

I will wait, but do not take too long. I am hungry.

I sensed the shift in me as my succubus side withdrew, allowing me to take the reins, and opened my eyes to see Jake watching me curiously. He stood next to Cliff, his hand tightly wrapped around the back of the man's neck as he held the pointed tip of an open switchblade directly underneath the terrified man's eyeball. Well, that was one way to convince someone to be quiet and not move a muscle. Or an eyeball.

"Are you all good again, Teste Slayer?"

I nodded, too discombobulated by whatever the heck had just happened to answer with actual words.

Jake let loose a whoop of celebratory laughter and raised his hands in the air. "Holy shit, I gotta be completely honest with you," he said, appearing to address both me and the men we knew were watching from the observation room as he glanced at the mirror. "I had no idea if that was going to actually work."

My jaw dropped open as I watched him bend over and grip his knees, laughing heartily before he rose to his full height and wiped his eyes. "What do you mean you didn't know if that would work? You totally talked me down. Or you…" I frowned, trying to figure out what had really happened. "You told me to talk myself down."

"Yeah, I don't really know what the hell I was saying. I just opened my mouth, and that shit came out."

I'm going to kill him. Rider's very unamused voice came through the mind-link. *Are you all right?*

"Yeah, I'm good," I answered him out loud, pointing to my temple when Jake looked at me and raised his eyebrows in question. After just having a very strange, hard to explain conversation with my succubus side who was actually just a part of me so I'd basically been talking to myself but as if I were two separate people, I—ouch, my brain hurt just trying to understand it—I didn't really want to do the mind-talking thing. "Thanks for not jumping in, and allowing Jake to handle that."

"Who is she talking to?" Cliff asked, looking around the room. His gaze fell on the mirror. "Who's back there? Is it the men from last night? How many of you demons are there?"

Jake stood at Cliff's side again, one hand wrapped around the back of the panicking man's neck, the other holding the pointed end of his knife back underneath Cliff's eye. "I thought you understood I wanted you to stay quiet unless answering a direct question. Which reminds me…" He pressed the tip of the blade in, drawing a bubble of blood from under Cliff's eye as the man gasped in pain.

"What did Ramson give you to drink?" I asked again, knowing where Jake was going with the added pressure. "Jake here isn't all that patient so I wouldn't keep procrastinating. We're going to find out whether or not you answer, but if you don't answer, we're going to find out in a way that is far more painful for you."

"Go to hell, demon," Cliff said, glaring at me. "I serve Ramson and for that I will be delivered unto heaven. The blood of mine you shed will pave my way."

"This dumbass wants you to kill him," Jake said. "He thinks himself a martyr."

"Or he's just a chickenshit who thinks I'll kill him fast like I did his buddy," I said. "Then again, I think you're onto something with the dumbass thing. He's been talking about how serving *Ramson* is supposed to get him into heaven, but that whole concept breaks the very first of the Ten Commandments."

Cliff's nostrils flared as he clenched his teeth in anger. "You're lying. That's what devils do."

I rolled my eyes and waved my hand dismissively. "He's holding tight to his brainwashing. Keep him occupied while I chat with Mike over here. I have a feeling he'll be more talkative."

"Don't you say anyth—" Cliff screamed as Jake's blade went deeper into his face.

"Shhh." Jake released the man's neck so he could pet his head. "That's a good boy. Don't make a sound and the knife will stay right where it is. Do your thing, Danni."

I watched as tears spilled down Cliff's face while he struggled not to move an inch or release any of the sobs he held back and almost felt sorry for him. Almost. I couldn't forget that he'd willingly brought innocent women, and maybe even men, to a psychopath.

Why do you want to know if they drank Ramson's blood? I asked through my mind-link with Rider as I moved closer to where Mike sat huddled on the floor, his eyes peeking over his knees to watch me approach while he trembled.

Khiderian noticed the way Cliff started to say something, then stopped so suddenly it almost looked like he'd been physically stopped.

Yeah, I noticed that too. Ramson's blood has something to do with that?

A pranic vampire can control someone they haven't turned yet if they give them enough of their blood. These men might not be able to tell you anything, even if they want to.

Well, that's just great. I have an idea with this one though. Hold on.

I kneeled down in front of Mike and the man jerked back as if I'd struck him. His shoulders shook with the force of the fresh tears that had just been released from his body and I looked down cautiously, making sure the man wasn't wetting himself. Based on his reaction, I was willing to bet he'd been the main contributor to the room having to be bleached.

"Hey. It's okay, Mike. I'm not laying a hand on you. See?" I raised my hands to show him they were clear of his body. "I just want to talk."

Mike's eyes shifted over to where Cliff sat stone-still, Jake's knife a full inch in his face, and made a noise. I couldn't tell if it was caused by fear from what he saw, or pain from the way he'd moved his battered eyes to see.

"I'm not going to do that to you, and neither is Jake. Jake had to do that to Cliff because Cliff is being difficult, but you're not difficult, are you? You want to help us. You wanted to help those women. I saw it when I touched you last night. You didn't mean for bad things to happen to them." I almost gagged on the lie. Mike wasn't the worst of the trio, but he was just as guilty, and he had stalked Mandi Fittro. Although I felt genuine regret from him, it was too little too late for the women he'd helped to abduct, but I could pretend to think he was worth saving if it got him talking. "Tell me about Mandi."

His gaze snapped back to mine, a quick shift of color all I could see between the narrow slits.

"That's her name. The woman from last night. Did you know her name when you tried to save her, or had you only seen her?"

He shook his head. "I never spoke with her."

"Talking to pretty women can be scary, can't it?" I kept my voice soft, a little sympathetic.

He nodded.

"You liked her, didn't you?"

He nodded again, then stopped, frowned. "She was pretty, but she needed to be cleansed."

Oh geez. I fought the urge to roll my eyes or let my true thoughts show on my face in some other way. "Why did she need to be cleansed?"

"She had a lot of men friends. They spent the night. New ones every month."

And I bet you wouldn't think she needed cleansing at all if she'd brought you into her bed instead of them, I thought, but kept my expression blank.

"Ramson didn't send you out for her last night, did he? You'd been watching her long enough, figuring out her routine. You knew she would be at a bar and she would leave with a man, didn't you?"

Mike nodded. "Ramson heals the sick and cleanses the impure. I knew he could cleanse her, make her a good woman. Make her…"

"Make her yours?" I prompted when he seemed to struggle.

"He promised us wives, but only those who were not selected for himself," Mike said softly. "I knew he would cleanse her, even if she wasn't who he sent us for."

"And he would give her to you because he wouldn't select a wife that he didn't choose himself?"

Mike nodded, pink color spreading across his cheeks. I could just barely see it under the edges of all the other colors. "I wouldn't have let Gary… I wouldn't have let him do those things to her."

The things he'd let Gary do to the other women.

"I never liked the test. I thought we should just take them to Ramson and he would know if they needed cleansing or not. He was the one who sent us to get them, but we couldn't take them to the—" Mike abruptly stopped talking, staring at me with an unsettling intensity. I was sure if I could see more than just a sliver of his eyes, they would be full of confusion or frustration.

"You couldn't take them to where, Mike? Where were you going to take Mandi last night?"

He opened his mouth to tell me, but the only thing that

came out was a frustrated growl.

"They've drunk Ramson's blood," Jake said. "The bastard gave them enough to make sure they couldn't reveal his location to anyone."

"Were you in on our mind-link?"

"No, I just know how the bastards work and I figured Khiderian clued you in when you asked Cliff what Ramson gave them to drink."

"We don't drink blood," Cliff said, his words spoken slowly and carefully, knowing any movement could cost him his eye.

"Did you drink Ramson's blood?" I asked Mike.

He shook his head.

"What have you drunk while with Ramson?"

"Juice. It was part of the cleansing. The juice flushes out alcohol, drugs, and other impurities."

Jake and I shared a look before I sighed, wondering how in the world anyone could be that gullible. "Was this juice thick and red?"

"Thick, no, but it was red. It tasted like cranberry juice, but it was also… It had a strange flavor, like…"

"Kind of coppery?" I suggested.

Mike nodded.

"You drank his blood, Mike. You all drank his blood so he could own you without even turning you."

"Well, these guys are worthless to us if they can't tell us how to find Ramson. You want to kill them, or shall I?"

Mike sucked in a breath and went back to trembling, his gaze on Jake and the knife still below Cliff's eye.

"They can't tell us where to find him, but they told us enough for us to know he is definitely a pranic vampire and he's definitely building a nest. The only time they seem to be forced to shut up is when they're about to give us a location." I reached out to Mike but drew my hand back, remembering what had happened the last time I'd touched the guy. I wasn't quite ready to try that trick again, not if I could get some questions answered the old-fashioned way first.

"Mike," I said in what I hoped was a soothing tone. "You've been a big help. I can tell you're not like Gary or Cliff. You never wanted to hurt anybody."

He'd started crying again, and he blinked the tears away before shaking his head. "I didn't. I didn't want to hurt anyone or take anyone who didn't want to go. I wanted to help women. I wanted to help them be better people."

You wanted to get laid but weren't man enough to find a girlfriend the normal way, I thought, but kept that to myself. Insulting the guy wouldn't get us anywhere. I needed to play him, make him believe I could understand him and didn't blame him for what happened.

"Of course you did. You're a nice guy, and you're smart. You're smarter than Cliff and Gary, for sure. Gary wouldn't tell us anything about Ramson and Cliff is being just as stubborn, but you want to tell us about him, don't you?"

Mike nodded and his brow furrowed, just a little, before he grimaced and the pain forced him to let his brow smooth out. "I can't say it. I want to tell you, but I can't."

"That's because Ramson gave you his blood in that juice he had you drink. He's not allowing you to give his location to me, but so far, it seems like that's the only thing you can't say. What else can you tell me about him? How many people does he have?"

"She's using you," Cliff said, then screamed as Jake shoved his knife in deeper, which caused Mike to shrink back against the wall.

"Jake, I think you can stop doing that," I said, having to yell to be heard over Cliff's screaming. "Just knock him out or something if he speaks again."

Jake just looked at me for a moment and I could tell by his expression he was wondering when he'd started taking orders from me. I could tell because it was very similar to the expression on Rider's face when he thought the same thing. With a grunt, he extracted his blade from Cliff's face and slammed the guy head-first into the metal table, knocking him out cold and thankfully stopping the ear-splitting screaming.

"Ah, I love that sound," Jake said, opening his arms wide in a gesture indicating all the sudden silence before folding his arms and leaning back against the wall. Or what would have been silence if not for the weeping man before me.

"Sorry about that, Mike," I said, adding a little smile. "I know that was scary, but Cliff was trying to stop us from being friends. You want to be friends with us, don't you? Friends don't get treated like Cliff."

Mike sniffed and made a yelping sound. He reached for his nose but thought better of it. I imagined touching that swollen, mangled mess with a feather would have probably caused him pain, so I didn't blame him for steering clear. He gripped his knees, and I noticed his posture improve. He still trembled, but he straightened his back and when he spoke again, it sounded like he'd found some courage.

"You're right about me being smart. I know what you're saying is true. I saw what you did. You drank Gary's blood. You're a vampire."

"Yes," I said, silently hoping he didn't kick off a long spiel about how I needed cleansing too.

"Vampires kill people or drink from them. You don't want to be my friend. You just want to know what I know about Ramson."

Well, he had me there.

"You said he's a vampire too."

"He is."

"It makes sense. I wondered how he did it, how he healed that woman's cancer. I wanted to believe, and I did, but I knew there was more to it than him just blessing them." He leaned forward. "I will tell you whatever you want to know, whatever I can tell you, if you promise not to kill me. I will serve you instead of Ramson."

I wanted to tell him to go fuck himself. I wasn't

anything like Ramson. I wasn't running a cult and could never condone what he had done while serving the man he thought could give him eternal life. Instead, I smiled. "I knew you were the smart one. Smart enough to join the winning side. Now, tell me what you know, and if it's good enough, you have my word."

He started to smile, but grunted in pain and grinned instead. "And you have mine. I will serve you and whoever you are loyal to."

Then he started screaming.

CHAPTER TEN

"What's wrong with him?" I asked, jumping back.

Mike twisted and contorted on the floor, his hands clamped on either side of his head as his agonized screams bounced off the walls.

Jake had immediately straightened and rushed over once the screaming had begun and stood staring down at the man, who appeared to be being tortured in some way. "It happened the moment he said he would serve you," Jake said, voice raised to be heard above the screaming. "So this Ramson fucker, like most prannies, likes to play games, but covers his ass. He allows his followers to talk about him, give his name, and his little mission statement or whatever the hell that was that Cliff spouted off earlier, but they can't physically say the man's location and apparently if they ever attempt to switch their loyalty to someone else, this happens."

He gestured toward Mike just as Rider entered the interrogation room, Daniel and Khiderian right behind him.

"We're not going to get anything else from them," Rider said. "Ramson's too smart."

"Yeah, I'm sure this one's brain is completely

scrambled now," Jake said, looking down at Mike. "All we can do now is put him out of his misery."

He raised his foot, about to give Mike a kick guaranteed to be hard enough to end not just the horrible screaming but the man's life as well, but I jumped in front of him before he could.

"Wait! We don't know that his brain is scrambled. This could just be punishment for his disloyalty. Just pain. I can still get into his mind."

"Danni." Rider stepped closer to me. "We discussed this."

"Yes, and you said I could work on my abilities in a controlled environment. This is a controlled environment." I swung my arm out, showing the room. "I'm not going to try to lure him. I'm going to touch him and see if I can trigger a vision. Ramson might not be able to control his mind that way, and it's all we have."

"Danni, you fainted the first time you did that, and the second time you tore the guy to pieces."

"Tearing this one to pieces won't hurt anything," Jake said, speaking loud enough to be heard over Mike's noise. "He's just screaming anyway. It's a good idea and a lot better than waiting to see if Ginger lucks into being grabbed or told about Ramson, which could take days or weeks or never happen at all. I vote for this."

"Decide something because I have about two seconds left of listening to him scream like that before I just tear his head off," Daniel said, looking at Mike in clear annoyance.

"I vote for trying for the vision," Khiderian said, raising his hand. "I think it might just work, especially if he's given some of her blood first. Blood of another vampire can lessen the control a pranic vampire has on his pets."

"Pets?" If I wasn't already completely disgusted by Ramson, that name for his dumbass followers would have done it.

Rider looked at each man in the room, his gaze resting on Mike last, then returned it to me before releasing a defeated sigh. "Daniel, Khiderian, you can go back to the observation room."

Khiderian nodded and dutifully turned for the door without further comment. Daniel shot a disgruntled look Rider's way, opened his mouth as if ready to argue, but looked at me, seemed to think better of it, and left behind Khiderian.

Once the door closed, Rider turned toward Jake. "If she rips him apart, you will not step in to stop her by force."

"You think I give a shit if she kills these guys? I nearly scooped that one's eye out. You can do whatever you want with them once we get what we need from them. There's a difference between brainwashed and mind-controlled." He looked at Cliff and curled his lip. "These bastards didn't do anything they didn't really want to do anyway. Ramson just gave them the fortitude to do it."

"So I just pour my blood into his mouth?" I raised my wrist to slice with my fang, but Rider grabbed my forearm and shook his head.

"I'll do that. We don't want to risk you getting any venom anywhere near that guy. Just because he's screaming now doesn't mean he's safe."

Rider held my forearm as he walked me closer to Mike, then raised my wrist to his mouth. Instead of biting down to take a drink, he scored the flesh with a swipe of his fang, quick enough that I barely felt any pain, and just deep enough to bring blood to well above the surface. Then he grabbed hold of Mike's head.

While Rider yanked Mike's head back by his hair, I tilted my wrist over the screaming man's mouth, allowing my blood to spill into it. Given how quickly the thin blood of vampires poured, it didn't take that long for Mike to get a good mouthful.

"That's enough," Rider said, closing Mike's mouth,

forcing the man to swallow while I licked my wound, sealing the flesh before I lost too much blood. "How do you feel?"

"A lot better without all that screaming," I responded.

"You know what I mean."

"I feel fine. I'm not dizzy or anything."

"Yet." Rider glanced at Jake, who stood behind us, observing, before reaching for my hand and giving it a squeeze. "We'll be right here if anything goes wrong, and you're going to feed right after this. Good luck."

He removed the hand that had been muffling Mike's screams and backed away as I kneeled before Mike on the cool floor. Unlike the previous two times when I'd accidentally received a vision from touching, I was trying to do it intentionally. I had no idea what I was supposed to do to cause a vision to happen, but anything would be better than what we had so I reached out, took a deep breath, and focused on the image of Ramson I'd pulled from Cliff earlier as I grabbed Mike's head, touching my fingers to both of his temples.

Show me Ramson, I thought as Mike continued screaming, nothing immediately happening. I glanced over to where Rider stood a few feet away to my left and met his watchful gaze. I shook my head.

"What do you feel?" he asked.

"Nothing."

"Well, if you're able to carry on a conversation with him, you're not focused enough on the banshee in front of you, so that's not surprising," Jake said from where he stood behind me. "Clear your mind and focus on Mike. Maybe try focusing on your own blood inside him, see if that does the trick."

I wasn't sure what Jake knew about visions, but he was a slayer after all, and he'd been part of the paranormal world far longer than I had, so I took his advice. I took a deep breath, cleared my mind the best I could, which wasn't easy with a man screaming bloody murder in front of me and the warning energy Jake's nearness caused to prickle along the back of my neck, but I somehow cut through all of that to focus on Mike. Once I had all the outside noise and sensations compartmentalized so my focus was on the man in front of me, I closed my eyes and cast my senses out.

With intense focus, my vampiric abilities allowed me to sense blood. It was how vampires hunted prey. Once I cast my senses out, I picked up on all the blood sources in the room. I was a little surprised to discover that Jake's blood pumped slower than an average human's, but I had more pressing matters to give my attention to at the moment.

My sire's blood called to me, its strength a tempting offer after I'd poured some of my own into Mike, but I ignored it, focusing instead on that same signature inside Mike. Mike's heart beat erratically. The man was amped up on fear and probably pain. Whatever Ramson had done to him had to hurt. I lowered one of my hands from his temple to place on his chest, right over the spot his heart seemed to be attempting to burst through.

Calm, I thought, and felt his heart rate slow to a less anxious beat. I realized my blood was in his veins now and it was responding to me. I envisioned the blood flowing through him, powering every cell in his body as it traveled to his head and wrapped around his memories. I knew what I envisioned wasn't possible, but the visual helped me focus my energy.

"Show me Ramson," I said out loud, needing the weight of my voice to strengthen the command.

The vision I'd created of blood evaporated and I saw the pranic vampire again. He stood at the front of a room on a raised stage. Red curtains were closed behind him, setting off his all-white attire. He smiled as he stared at something in the distance. Or someone, I realized as it dawned on me I was seeing him through someone else's eyes. I was pulling Mike's memories, exactly how he'd seen them.

We walked down an aisle separating pews. A church. I caught glimpses of stained glass windows, but there was such little light in the room, I couldn't make out a lot. There didn't seem to be much by way of décor, as if Ramson didn't like such distraction. He wanted all eyes to be on him when he filled the room.

He walked down the stairs at the side of the stage and held out his hands in greeting. He took Mike's hand, and it was as if he'd taken my own. There was power in his touch. It zinged through my body, making me feel welcome, respected, even loved.

"You are home now," he said, and his voice gave the same feeling as his touch, but there was something else underneath it. An unspoken threat. He raised his other hand to Mike's temple, and whatever zing I'd felt before was nothing compared to the jolt that surged through my skull before everything went black and my stomach started doing flips.

"Danni."

I heard Rider's voice, quickly followed by a shushing noise, and I tightened my grip to keep from falling over. My eyes were still closed. I was still locked onto the thread of Mike's memories, and from the feel of things, I was locked onto his head, both of my hands pressed tight around either side of his skull. He'd stopped screaming and now only panted heavily, so I had no trouble hearing Rider and Jake arguing in hushed, semi-growled tones. Ignoring them, I focused on Mike, focused on my blood inside him, and I found myself in the church again.

We walked through a hallway. I was lightheaded. I was light-everythinged. I felt like I could fly if I just let myself, like I weighed nothing at all. The only thing with weight was the plastic bottle in my hand. It was a water bottle, but the label had been removed and there was no water in it. It contained a red beverage. I drank it, tasting the tart sweetness of cranberries and something coppery underneath. It tasted odd, but delicious. I continued to drink as the man, Ramson, told me about his church. Everything he said made perfect sense and sounded so good. All I had to do was go through a cleanse and he could save my soul, deliver me to heaven, even find someone to love me.

We passed a kitchen area where a group of women prepared food, smiling at me as we passed. They smiled at me like they liked me, like I didn't annoy them. Some were very beautiful, and they didn't look down at me, not even with the more attractive man with me.

A big man entered the room. He was built like the linebackers who used to stuff me into lockers in high school, and judging by the way he effortlessly carried two heavy sacks of potatoes over one shoulder, he wouldn't have any trouble knocking me around, but he didn't seem bothered by my presence or how close I was to the women.

"Welcome home," he said with a smile as he deposited the two large sacks on the floor near the kitchen island the women stood behind, chopping vegetables. He nodded toward them, then me, and left back out the door.

"This way," Ramson said, guiding me out another door, into another hall we traveled down until we reached what looked like a meadow complete with trees along the outer edge, if such a thing could be found inside a building.

The grass was green and lush, and the air was warm as we stepped out into it. I saw a big white tent in the center and there were women sitting cross-legged under its shade. I looked up, wondering what this area was, and saw the glass panes above us, covering the open area.

"What is this?" I heard Mike ask.

"The outside, inside," Ramson said. "I prefer this to the chapel. It feels more warm and inviting, especially during the day. The tent is for daily worship. This time of evening, however, I enjoy walking freely, feeling the grass under my feet."

AULD FANG SYNE

And so we did. We walked freely, and everyone I met was kind and unbothered. They drank the red juice from kegs in the front and gathered at the long wooden table near the back when it was time to dine. The women who'd been working in the kitchen brought out a delicious meal for us to enjoy, although Ramson did not partake. He simply stood over us, watching, with a smile, and I couldn't help feeling like a pig getting wonderfully fattened up for an upcoming holiday meal. I'd never felt so loved and appreciated.

Where is this? I asked, separating myself from Mike's memory enough to try to direct him to show me what I needed to see. *Show me where this place is.*

The vision faded, and suddenly I felt myself jostling. I was in a van, behind the wheel, navigating a narrow, bumpy dirt road. Cliff was in back with the bossy guy, Gary. There was something about Gary I didn't like, but disliking anyone wasn't allowed for the disciples. A true disciple of Ramson loved all, even our enemies. We saved people, cleansed them of their impurities. We did not judge them, even ones like Gary, who liked to bark orders and act like they were the most loyal disciple Ramson had ever had.

The woman in the back with them cried. I felt my chest ache. I didn't like it when they cried. The test was simple. They either submitted willingly or they fought to keep themselves soiled with unholiness. The ones who submitted were usually quiet, like they knew we were there to help. The ones who resisted were loud and had to be quieted immediately. This one hadn't fought that much, but she'd started crying after we'd made it halfway. I hoped Mandi didn't cry like that. I glanced in the rearview, saw Gary leaning over the woman we'd saved tonight. I would administer Mandi's test myself, make it easy for her so she didn't cry. Ramson would see what care I took with her and give her to me. I just had to wait for the right moment to switch her for whoever Ramson sent us out for.

We reached the giant oak tree with the two long, twisted branches that hung low, resembling arms reaching out to grab intruders, and turned right. The narrow dirt road seemed to stretch on forever, but eventually, the hulking shape of the old church could be seen over the hill.

The image snapped in half and I fell back, suddenly nauseous and overwhelmed with pain ricocheting through my skull, blinding me. I hit a hard yet soft surface and equally hard yet soft arms wrapped around me and pulled me into a cocoon. As the scent of midnight rain enveloped me, I knew I was safe in Rider's arms.

"Drink," he commanded.

Rich, powerful blood poured over my tongue to fill my mouth, and I drank reflexively, each gulp helping to diminish the pain filling my head and dissipate the dark cobwebs until slowly, I could see my gorgeous sire's worried eyes looking down at me as he fed me from his wrist.

I took a final drink and licked the wound to seal his flesh, giving him the signal I'd had my fill. I craned my neck as he lifted his wrist away and saw Mike slumped over in the corner, blood running out of his eyes and nostrils. "Holy crap. Did I do that?"

Jake was down on his haunches, inspecting Mike's damage. He looked at me and shook his head. "He just started bleeding and a few minutes later, slumped over right when you fell back. Not sure if the way you read him killed him or Ramson did this somehow."

"I just called Daniel and Khiderian in here," Rider said, cradling me in his lap as he sat on the floor with his back against the wall. "How do you feel now?"

"A little nauseous," I answered, "so don't jostle me. My head hurt really bad, but your blood did the trick to heal that."

"You overexerted yourself," Rider said as the door

opened and Daniel stepped in, Khiderian right behind him. "Some abilities take more energy than others. You must have burned through a lot of yours while reading him."

"Is she okay?" Daniel asked, his jaw popping as he took in the sight of Mike slumped in the corner, and I realized he wouldn't have been able to see what I had been doing from the observation room, not while Mike and I had been on the floor in the room's corner just below the two-way mirror.

"I'm fine," I said, resting my head against Rider's shoulder. "I just needed blood."

"You ever see anything like this?" Jake asked Khiderian as the tall man walked past me to crouch in front of Mike. "The bleeding started while she was still in there reading him, then he just ... I don't know. Sprung a leak or something."

"Yeah," Khiderian said, sounding pretty disgusted. "Pranic vampires can push too hard, trying to get past protective walls and cause their prey's brain to hemorrhage."

"Wait." My nausea intensified. "I was the one in his mind looking for something. Are you saying I did that to him?"

Khiderian looked at me over his shoulder. "Not necessarily. We suspect this vampire gave his blood to them. If he gave enough of his blood over a long enough period and had the ability to, he could have made them susceptible to long-term commands. We witnessed this when they both stopped abruptly when they seemed to be about to give us information about Ramson's location, and then this one started screaming right after he basically switched allegiances to you, a new vampire."

"So, what," Daniel said. "You're saying this Ramson guy programmed his followers to self-destruct if they ever turned on him?"

"Or were about to give too much information," Khiderian said, and stood. He grabbed a chair from the table and straddled it, facing me. "What were you trying to get to when Mike keeled over?"

"Ramson's location." I told them everything I'd seen and how it had felt like I had been the one to see and feel everything I'd experienced through Mike's memories.

"So the meadow you saw wasn't an actual meadow," Rider said after I finished. "It was an atrium in a church."

"A property like that shouldn't be too hard to find," Jake said. "It would most likely be an abandoned church."

"Unless Ramson got into the clergy's heads," Khiderian advised. "From the way you've described this, it's a big enough building to house a lot of people, and he could have just folded the clergy and parishioners into his own following."

"Or killed them," Jake said. "You killed many people in your day."

"Thank you for that reminder." Khiderian shot Jake an unappreciative look. "But yes, you're correct. Pranic vampires feed on energy and emotion to increase power, but blood is still what is needed to preserve life. Ramson and whoever among his followers that he actually turns all need a steady supply of blood."

"And new turns need to feed more often," Rider said, still sitting on the floor, holding me in his arms. He ran his fingertips down my arm absent-mindedly. "He would need to feed often too if he's supplying his own blood to his followers in that juice they all drink. I'm sure it's not a tiny amount he's giving them to have the effect it had on these two. Then there's the tent in the atrium. The glass would offer some protection from the direct rays, but he holds worship services under the tent in the daytime. He might be young himself, old enough to wake during the day, but still young enough to be extremely sensitive to the sun."

"Young or old, pranic vampires are often more sensitive to the sun," Khiderian stated. "I suppose it's just the way things balance out. For all the added power from the ability to feed off energy and emotion, heightened vulnerability to the sun is the drawback."

"And having to actually be invited into a private residence," Jake added.

"Yeah, that too." Khiderian turned as Cliff groaned behind him, regaining consciousness. "What are you going to do with this guy?"

"Danni's not going to read him," Rider said, his tone brooking no room for negotiation. "I doubt she'd get more from him than she got from this one, even if she gave him her blood, which she won't be doing either." He stood with me still in his arms, and lowered me to the floor once he was on his feet, but kept his arm around my waist, supporting me. I was still a little on the woozy side. "If forcing a vision out of someone who actually seemed to want to give her information made her so lightheaded and gave her a headache, she's not fighting to get anything out of that one. I'm not storing him any longer, either. He'll be blood for my vamps on duty."

Cliff raised his head, still groaning, and his gaze roamed over us before it fell to where Mike remained slumped in the corner. He took one look at the blood that had spilled out of Mike's eyes and nose and jerked back so forcefully he toppled the chair over and slammed onto the floor.

He opened his mouth, eyes fully bugged out, but before he could let loose the scream we all saw coming, Jake had quickly walked over and stomped the side of his head hard enough to send him back into unconscious oblivion. The slayer hefted the man up from the floor and deposited him on the metal table. "I assume your vamps will take care of the, uh, spigot situation for the blood buffet you intend to use him for."

"Yeah, we have built-in bottle openers for our drinks," Rider replied dryly, "but if you need a booster, you're welcome to cut into him."

"Yeah, thanks for the offer, but I'll stick with what you've already got bottled upstairs." He folded his arms and turned toward Khiderian. "So what do you think, K?

What's our best way to go after this guy?"

"I thought the super-duper slayer knew how to kill everything and always had a plan," Daniel said, not bothering to hide the animosity in his tone.

"I do know how to kill everything. Including you," Jake said in a warning tone. "But I hardly ever have a plan. I'm more of an instinct guy. That doesn't mean I don't see the benefit of a plan. Just because my way of doing things has gotten me this far doesn't mean an actual planned attack wouldn't be a good idea, especially if I'm working with someone else. I may be cocky, but I'm never arrogant. If there's someone available with expertise, I'm going to use their wisdom."

"Now that we've settled that," Khiderian said, looking between both men as they stared each other down and stewed, "I think we can all agree this is definitely a pranic vampire. From what you described, Danni, he must have gone deep into Mike's thoughts when he touched his temple in that chapel. That's why you blacked out for a bit and nearly fell over. With the amount of people you've seen so far in your visions and no idea how many others there are that you haven't seen, combined with the size of that place, be prepared to fight an army. If they're all drinking his blood steadily and they're the easily persuaded types, they'll do whatever he asks of them, even risk their lives fighting for him. He's probably only turning the ones who are resistant to his persuasion, and the ones who came to him for healing, just because they make a convincing demonstration to the others he wants to view him as a prophet."

"So even the ones who haven't been turned and maybe haven't done anything harmful to anyone would follow his command to kill us?" I asked, my stomach taking another nauseated dip at the thought.

"Yes, and they won't back down just because you ask them nicely," Khiderian warned me. "As hard as it may be, if you infiltrate that church and find yourself surrounded by them, you can't think of them as people. They're the enemy. Until the moment Ramson is killed and whatever's left of his blood in their bodies has dissipated, they are the enemy. But first, you have to find this place."

"That's where Daniel comes in," Rider said. "Daniel, you'll go up tonight and search for that church. You should be able to see the atrium from the sky. From Danni's visions, we know it's somewhere with dirt roads and a tree that looks like it's reaching out. It has to be close enough these jerks would hunt here. My techs have confirmed that both Mike and Cliff lived in Louisville with rent paid up until a few months ago. Gary was from Alabama, but if downtown Louisville is where they were hunting last night, the church has to be closer to here."

"And all three would have been living at the church, fully part of the cult, if they were trusted enough to be tasked with grabbing more women to build up the numbers," Jake said.

"The techs couldn't find any recent utility or rent payments for any of the guys. Cliff had a job working weekends at a factory in the south end, and Mike did some freelance web design. Gary had arrests for fights at casinos in his file, so he probably made money from poker." Rider glanced over at Mike before continuing. "I've known other vampires to allow members of their nests to work, only if all the money is brought back to them."

"Pranic vampires do the same thing," Khiderian said. "And if Ramson isn't automatically turning all his followers right away, but insists on them living on that property, he has to feed them and keep them comfortable. That costs money, money he's not going to go out and get himself if he has others willing to do it for him."

"Is that why he started the cult?" I asked. "For the money he can collect from the fools who believe in his garbage promises?"

"It could be." Khiderian shrugged. "But most pranic vampires are also very narcissistic. They live to be worshipped, so the money could just be a bonus. A pranic vampire could just walk into a bank and influence a weak-minded employee to open a vault for them and look the other way, if that's what they wanted."

"You were like that?" The question slipped out before I had time to think better of it. "I'm sorry. You just don't seem all that full of yourself."

He grinned. "I have my moments, but no. Maybe it was the grace still left in me as a fallen angel, but I fought against the worst of what I was. I did *convince* people to give me money, vehicles, shelter, and of course, blood, but once I'd freed myself of my sire, I only killed those who truly needed to die in order to save others. I never attempted to build anything resembling a nest and definitely not a cult."

"So your sire was a pranic vampire? That's how you became one?"

"No, she wasn't, and I became a pranic vampire because of my grace. Grace is similar enough to psychic power to cause vampires to be pranic when they turn."

"But Christian…"

"Christian was a pranic vampire. However, he rarely drank living blood and never attempted to use his abilities, so no one suspected him of being anything more than a regular garden variety vamp. If he had been a regular vampire and fed as poorly as he did for as many centuries as he did, he would have been extremely weak. It blows my mind how he nor anyone else around him ever caught on to what he really was." Khiderian gave Jake a pointed look.

"Hey, there was angel interference all around him," Jake said defensively. "Even *on* him, thanks to that tattoo. Those winged jackasses made sure nobody could figure out what he was."

"I figured out that Christian had been an angel within like a day of meeting him," Rider said.

"Bite me, Count Ponytail. Of course you did. You're

older than dirt. You were probably there to see him get pushed out of Heaven."

"Okay, you two," I jumped in before Jake and Rider could start bickering at each other. "Let Khiderian finish so Daniel can hopefully go find this place and we can take care of Ramson."

"Thank you." Khiderian continued. "Definitely find the church if you can, but your best bet for defeating him is to draw him away from his cult. Remember he feeds off energy and emotions. Those feed his psychic powers, which will allow him to hurt you without touching you, if that's what his abilities are. Be ready for anything and try to keep your emotions locked down. You don't want to feed his power while you're trying to fight him."

"Sure. That should be easy," I said before swallowing hard as nausea threatened to rise.

"It'll be hard, but you can do it. You will have Jake with you and the man is a vampire-killing machine—" Khiderian paused, seeming to realize who he was speaking to. "All right, so maybe that wasn't the best endorsement to give in present company, but you know what I mean. Jake is fast, strong, and immune to damn near everything. Focus on that if you start to feel afraid, and if you start to feel angry, remind yourself this is just another night or day of work for you. Focus on the job at hand, stay calm, and don't react to anything you see or hear because really skilled pranic vampires can make you see things."

I covered my stomach with my hand as its contents started sloshing around like a turbulent sea.

"Hey," Rider spoke softly as he held me closer to his side. "Are you all right?"

"Honestly… I think I'm going to throw up if I don't lie down soon. Forcing that vision made me all queasy and knowing I'm supposed to go up against Super-Vamp with all his special tricks and abilities isn't calming things down."

"You're strong enough to handle him, Danni. Get him

away from his people, away from power sources, and he's just a guy who more than likely can't even get into your head because you have psychic power."

I knew Khiderian thought those words were comforting, maybe even confidence-boosting, but they did nothing for my stomach.

"You are way too pale for having just drunk my blood," Rider said. "Let's get you into bed."

"Wait." I grabbed his arm before he could scoop me up again, blocking his attempt. "How do we separate Ramson from his people and once we do, how do we kill him? If he has all these psychic powers, what's our move when we get him where we want him?"

"If you can lure him out of the church with something he wants, that would do it," Khiderian answered. "But you'd need to know what that is. As to how you will fight him, he is just like any other vampire in that regard. He bleeds just the same. Cut him quickly and often. If you can't get a hit in, make him work for his safety. The more of his psychic power he uses to hold you off, the more he'll need to replenish, and if he can't get that, he's going to need blood even faster. Weaken him any way you can, then chop his head off. You have a dragon with you. Depending on his abilities, you may be able to set Ramson on fire, ending him that way. Try to see if he can call upon fire himself first or you might just be giving him a weapon to use against you. I would caution against bullets as he can redirect them right back at you if that's his ability, and keep a tight grip on any blades. Pranic vampires can't do mind-control in the sense you think mind-control is, but they can convince people to do things. Daniel and Tony should take care of fighting his followers, leaving Ramson to you and Jake to handle for the best outcome."

I nodded my head, not trusting myself to thank Khiderian verbally without throwing up, and wavered.

"All right. You need to take a break." Rider lifted me in his arms before addressing Daniel. "Danni's staying in tonight. You're on seek and find duty. I'll have the techs try to locate the church their way, but you're our eyes in the sky. Shift and call in every hour in case the techs find something. Return here after sunrise, whether you find the church or not. Rome will stay here after his shift is over so we can keep an eye on him. The two of you can bunk in one of the guest rooms. Jake, you can use the room you stayed in last time you were here, but if you even think of sneaking through the vents again, I swear I'll shoot you in the ass. Khiderian—"

"I'm headed home tonight. I'll be leaving after I talk to Jadyn again. With as much as I know about *things*, it's best I not be in the same city as a pranic vampire who may or may not be interested in taking over your territory. If that's his game, Ramson will use any information he has to get what he wants, especially blackmail."

Seriously, what was this top-secret thing that Rider, Seta, Christian, and Khiderian knew about but wouldn't speak of? Before I could think about it enough to get really perturbed, my stomach rumbled. "Put me down, put me down, put me down!"

Rider didn't hesitate to fulfill my panicked request and the moment my feet hit the floor I ran out of the interrogation room, into the women's bathroom across the hall, and dropped to my knees over the toilet in one of the stalls, not bothering to lock the door behind me before I threw up all the blood Rider had just given me. My body didn't seem to get the message that my stomach was empty, so I spent some more time clinging to the toilet while I dry-heaved.

"Fucking hell," I muttered once the stomach cramps and gagging stopped long enough I thought it was worth the risk to attempt getting back onto my feet.

I wiped my mouth with toilet tissue, tossed it into the bloody mess I'd made in the toilet bowl, and slowly got to my feet. Once I was sure I wasn't going to topple right over, I flushed the toilet and left the stall... to see Rider leaning against the wall next to the sinks, his arms folded as he waited for me. I yelped.

"What the hell? Why are you in here?" He raised his eyebrows, and I realized how rude I'd just sounded. I sighed as I made my way to the sinks. A glimpse in the mirror showed the pink blush of embarrassment under the otherwise green pallor of my skin. My eyes were watery, my hair was sweat-dampened along the edges, and I certainly wouldn't win any beauty contests. "I didn't mean that to sound so bitchy. I appreciate you making sure I'm okay, but I'd rather not have an audience while doing that. It's not exactly attractive."

"Do you really think I'd find you any less attractive just because you're sick?" Rider asked as I rinsed my mouth out with water from the tap. "I'm in love with you, dingbat."

I spit out the water and gripped the sink edges to brace myself until I had the strength to look up at him. Both of him. I had double-vision. "Did you just call me a dingbat?"

"Yes."

I stared at him, waited until there was just one of him before I spoke. "Did you call me that because you thought dingbat was punny?"

The corner of his mouth curved. "Yes."

I would have shaken my head, but it had started to hurt again. "How can you be so incredibly hot yet have such moments of utter corniness?"

"It's a gift. Can you make it upstairs on your own or do you need me to carry you?"

I thought about it and my eyes burned with the threat of tears. "Everyone will think I'm weak if you have to carry me to your room."

"Our room," he said, something in his tone I knew I should have paid attention to, but I felt too queasy to worry about it. "And no one in this building thinks the Teste Slayer is weak. Not when she keeps killing archdemons and kracklings."

Rider picked me up, being careful not to jostle me too much, and carried me out of the bathroom. Relieved to not find the other guys standing in the hall, waiting for us to emerge, I rested my head against his shoulder and closed my eyes. Rider could have zipped right past everyone in a blur of speed, but that probably wouldn't have gone over well with my stomach so he walked at a normal pace and I tried to ignore the fact that we'd be passing the tech team and various members of his security staff who were posted throughout the sublevels.

"Sir?"

I recognized Toby's voice and bit back a groan as Rider stopped to talk to the short shifter who'd grabbed his attention.

"I apologize if this is a bad time," Toby continued, obviously referring to the fact Rider was carrying me like a helpless child, which was just too awkward to keep pretending to ignore so I opened my eyes to see that yep, we'd stopped right by the tech team's area. I noticed Kirsty Carruthers, the woman who'd posed as Jeff Brinley in the text sent earlier, observing us with open interest, but she quickly averted her gaze when our eyes met. "But Pacitti just sent Brinley a text message you will want to see right away.

CHAPTER ELEVEN

"What the hell does that mean?" Rider muttered as the text message was brought up on the big screen.

"It appears to be some sort of code," Toby said.

No shit, I thought, looking at the oddly worded message.

372707767075   5K TOMORROW. NO PAIN NO TRIPLE GAIN. WILL MEET YOU FOR A SPIN IN THE PLACE WITH ED'S FAVORITE SWEET, THE ONE HE LOVED SO MUCH HE WOULD SELL OUT HIS BROTHER AND SISTERS FOR.
 NOON. BE THERE:
NW

"You're positive this is from Pacitti?" Rider sounded doubtful. "Did it come from the same phone as the previous message?"

"No, it's a different burner phone," Toby replied. "This guy is definitely paranoid. But we've been monitoring Brinley's phone since it was obtained, as well as his social media, and other than his mother and the company he worked for, no one has contacted him except Pacitti. He said he had something big and to stand by, so a coded message coming in from another burner phone is highly likely to be from him."

"He signed it NW. Is that a typo or more secret code?"

"Could be either," Toby replied. "We're searching his social media contacts to see if there are any Eds, Edwards, or Edmunds—"

"Edmund!" I snapped my fingers, the name triggering something in my memory.

"What?" Rider looked down at me. "Does that name mean something to you?"

I looked back at the screen and reread the message, growing annoyed as my neck cramped from reading it sideways. "Put me down."

Rider did as asked, but held on to my hips as I leaned back against his chest for support. I waited for the initial dizziness and nausea to pass and read the message again, right side up. "Ed's favorite sweet, the one he loved so much he would sell out his brother and sisters for. One brother. More than one sister. Edmund sold out his brother and sisters for sweets. He told the White Witch about them to get Turkish delight. It's from *The Lion, the Witch and the Wardrobe*."

Toby snapped his fingers and pointed at me, then looked back up at the screen. "That actually works. Good thinking, Miss Keller." He rubbed his chin, biting his lip as he reread the message. "That's the meeting place. So we're looking for a bakery or restaurant, maybe, someplace that has Turkish delight. That shouldn't be too hard to narrow down. Turkish delight isn't something you usually find within traveling distance of where he suspects Brinley to still be. He mentions a 5K."

The shifter turned toward his tech team. "Start searching for any 5Ks scheduled for tomorrow, anywhere within a half day's flight or driving distance from Brinley's residence. Hack in and check registers for Pacitti and Brinley's names."

"Do either of those men look like they'd ever run or even walk in a 5K?" I folded my arms and chewed my lip while I scanned the message, knowing we were missing something. "I don't think he's talking about that type of 5K. He must mean five thousand."

"Five thousand dollars," Rider said. "No pain, no triple gain. He mentioned a big payout in his previous message to Brinley. This is telling him to bring five thousand dollars to him tomorrow and he will make triple that amount."

Toby nodded his head. "Yes, that makes sense. Now we just need to know where. We're running the number sequence, trying to figure out what it could be. It contains too many numbers to be a phone number. We've plugged them into our decryption program to see if the numbers are replacing letters that may spell out the location of where we'll find this place that has the Turkish delight."

"Why is there a colon at the end of the message?" I asked, thinking out loud. "It should be a period after there, not a colon."

"Well, mortals these days aren't the best with punctuation," Toby said. "And the colon is right above the period when texting."

"No." I shook my head, my gut suggesting the colon wasn't the result of a simple fat thumb issue. "Pacitti is a moron, but he's crafty. Every single part of this message is a puzzle piece. He would have thoroughly looked it over to make sure it was perfect before sending it. That colon is deliberate, and so is the fact he used a return before typing that line. Noon. Be there. Colon. Be *there*. The NW after the colon doesn't have any periods. He used periods in his initials in the previous text. It's not his initials."

"It's directional," Rider said, catching on. "That's not a series of twelve numbers. I think he's hidden coordinates in the message. Try the first six numbers as the north coordinate and the last six as the west coordinate."

"Do it," Toby instructed Kirsty, and the woman went to work, her fingers rapidly gliding over her keyboard.

She looked up a moment later and a Google map appeared on the plasma. "Williamsburg, Virginia."

"Where in Williamsburg, Virginia?" Toby asked.

"It's just Williamsburg, Virginia," she said. "That's what comes up for those coordinates."

"It's Busch Gardens," I said. "He said he'd meet Brinley for a spin in the place with Ed's favorite treat. There's a ride at Busch Gardens in Williamsburg called Turkish Delight. I've been on it. It's a spinning teacups ride."

"She's right," Kirsty said, and the attractions page from the Busch Gardens website popped up on the plasma. She scrolled down to the Turkish Delight ride.

"So Pacitti is meeting Brinley at noon tomorrow on a spinning teacup ride at Busch Gardens in Williamsburg, Virginia," Toby said, then looked at me. "That was some good code cracking, Ms. Keller. If you ever get bored neutering and slaying monsters, you could be useful down here."

I grinned. "Nah, I just happened to have been on that ride before and I've read *The Chronicles of Narnia* at least ten times. There's no telling how many times I've watched the movies."

"Be still my nerd heart," he said, placing his hand over his heart, then he looked up above me where I didn't have to turn to know Rider was giving him a warning glare, and straightened his posture with a hard swallow. "Will you be picking up Pacitti yourself, sir, or would you like us to dispatch a team?"

"Send a team. He's just a human detective. A sneaky weasel of a human detective, but still not much of a threat as long as he doesn't use that video to draw hunters to us, so he should be easy to capture now that we know where he'll be."

"Yes, sir."

"Keep me informed if you get any leads on that church."

"We will, sir."

Rider let go of my hips and started to pick me up, but I stopped him with a hand to his chest. "I feel well enough to walk now."

He gave me a doubtful look. "All the way up the stairs?"

"Yes, Rider. All the way up the stairs, because I'm a vampire-succubus hybrid, not a wilting flower. Good grief, would you carry Daniel or Jake up the stairs just because they got a little dizzy and threw up?"

"You're not Daniel or Jake." He grinned. "And we all know the only way I would ever carry either of those two jackasses would be if it were to the edge of a cliff. And I would throw them over it."

I would have rolled my eyes, but I didn't want to risk the migraine right after proclaiming myself well enough to walk on my own. Still, my irritation must have shown, because Rider slid his arm around my back and prodded me toward the stairwell.

"Jake and Daniel don't get visions that leave them feeling drained after. Don't take my concern as an insult and don't risk your health trying to prove you're tough. We already know you are." He placed his hand over the panel and opened the door to the stairwell.

"I do feel well enough to walk instead of being carried," I said as we took the stairs up, "but I'm not up to any somersaults or bar fights."

"Good, because you're going to replenish the lost blood and rest in our room for the rest of the night."

"The rest of the night?"

Rider placed his hand over the panel next to the door on the ground floor and we stepped through it. "Yes."

"But—"

"No buts." He scooped me up effortlessly and took the stairs up to the bedroom.

"I'm a vampire. You can't send me to bed at night. It goes against everything that we are."

He lowered me onto the bed and chuckled. "You don't have to sleep, but you do have to rest. Vampires generally don't throw up unless we eat something that disagrees with us. Forcing that vision took too much out of you and you need to allow yourself time to recover or else you won't be any good to us once we find Ramson."

"So if Daniel locates that church tonight and calls it in, you're not going to try to keep me from going after him?"

"Not if you get some blood and rest so you're in good enough shape to go after him." He sighed as he sat on the bed behind me. "Not that I want you to go after this creep. I'd rather you stay here where I know you're safe, especially if I can't go with you, but Jake is right. I'm a liability in this case. And you won't be alone. If I'm not with you, Porter is the best partner for the job. He'll keep you safe."

I may have gawked as I turned to look at Rider. "Wow. That must have been some conversation the two of you had in your office if you trust him that much now."

"Yeah." He narrowed his eyes as he met my gaze, searching. "So you want to tell me what that was about with Daniel earlier? I don't think I've ever heard you use that tone with him before."

Crap. "I told you it was nothing."

"I know. Now tell me the truth. Did he say or do anything inappropriate?" His eyes darkened. "Did he cross a line?"

"No," I said quickly. Maybe too quickly.

"Danni, I know you. You wouldn't have had that tone with him for no reason."

No, I wouldn't have, because Daniel was my best friend and I was closer to him than I was to anyone else, except for Rider. He hadn't crossed a line earlier, at least not on purpose. It was pretty difficult not to cross a line when the line was too blurry to see and I only had myself to blame for that, which was probably why I'd gotten so upset. I wasn't mad at Daniel. I was mad at myself.

However, I couldn't tell Rider any of this because there was no way he'd be understanding about it. He knew how Daniel felt about me, but he didn't know about the times my succubus side had gone wonky and I'd felt very inappropriate feelings toward Daniel, the times I'd done things that would have encouraged Daniel. If he knew about those moments, Daniel wouldn't be in my life anymore. Daniel might not have a life anymore.

"What is it, Danni? What did he do that you're afraid to tell me?"

Sometimes having a partner who knew you so well had its drawbacks. I sighed and stayed as close to the truth as I could without getting Daniel maimed or killed. "Daniel didn't do or say anything wrong. As you've said yourself on more than one occasion, he is an honorable man. I don't know why I had a tone with him because he certainly didn't deserve to get snapped at. I probably owe him an apology."

Rider frowned, not convinced. "So you just snapped at him for no reason at all?"

"No, I had a reason. It just wasn't a very good one."

There was a scratching at the door and Rider opened it with his mind, allowing Kutya to enter. The oversized pup ran straight for us, jumping onto the bed, where he spun in circles, wagging his tail in excitement.

"Settle down," I told him with a laugh as I halted him long enough to scratch his back, which prompted him to plop down and roll over on his back for a belly rub. I looked at the door, which Rider had already closed. "Are you sure you're not a pranic vampire? You have some very impressive abilities."

"Not that impressive once you factor in my age," he said, "and don't think this distraction is going to get us off the subject."

Of course not. I sighed, wondering how I'd lucked into loving a man who could frustrate me so much. I might have been bitter about it if not for the fact I knew I frustrated him to no end as well. "Daniel and I were researching succubi in the bar and he came across something in one of the books, something that I guess you could say I didn't really want to hear. He didn't do anything wrong. He was just the bearer of news I didn't really want to hear."

The hardness in Rider's eyes softened, and he brushed my hair back from my face. "What was it?"

"Nothing I want to talk about now." I closed my eyes. "It really wasn't anything. I told you I'm just kind of stressed out with everything going on right now and I heard something I didn't like, and I got cranky. Can you please just not make a big deal out of it?"

"All right." I felt his lips on my forehead and a moment later, I was pulled back against his chest and his arm came around me, his wrist at mouth level. "You need to replenish some of that blood you lost. Take some of mine, then you're going to stay up here and take it easy. I'll have Tony run you some bottled blood up while I get some work done downstairs."

"What? You get to work and I have to stay up here?"

"Danni, you need to rest."

"I'm not arguing with you there, but I can rest and still do something useful. We left my laptop and the books Nannette loaned me in your office. I can at least do more research while resting."

"You did research with Daniel and found out something you didn't want to know and it put you in a bad mood," he reminded me.

"That doesn't mean I shouldn't keep researching. Come on, Rider. You wouldn't sideline anyone else like this. It's just research. You know I'll just go downstairs and find a bar fight if I get bored up here."

"I can lock you in this room with my mind."

"And I can guarantee you won't get laid for a month."

He snorted. "You drive a hard bargain. Fine, I'll have your stuff brought up along with another assistant, but only if you drink."

Ugh. I really didn't want to drink while my stomach was queasy, but blood was the elixir for damn near everything that ailed a vampire, so I bit into Rider's wrist and drank.

I felt his power as he used it to communicate with someone, I assumed whomever he was tasking with bringing my books and laptop upstairs and assigning to assist me in my research, which explained why he was feeding me how he was: from the wrist with my back to his chest. Feeding from the throat or, while closely entwined, usually led to something more physical with us. Of course, he was probably also avoiding such activity while concerned I wasn't well enough to handle it.

"For the record, that month of celibacy threat won't always work with me, so don't think you have a permanent ace up your sleeve. It was cute though."

I smiled, too busy drinking to reply. We both knew I wouldn't last a month myself.

"How do you feel now?" he asked when I stopped drinking and sealed his wrist with a lap of my tongue.

"The headache from throwing up is gone now. I don't feel nauseous right now, but I still feel a little off. More tired than I should be at this time of night, but I'm sure I'll feel better pretty soon. I'm going to brush my teeth."

I entered the attached bathroom and did a quick brushing before I rinsed with Listerine to get rid of the reminder I'd thrown up not that long ago. A look in the mirror showed my skin wasn't on the green spectrum anymore, but I was paler than usual and my hair was a limp mess. I ran my hairbrush through it before I emerged, surprised to see Jake coming through the door with my books and laptop. Rome was with him, and the big man carried a dark bottle of blood.

"You had Jake get my books and laptop out of your office?"

Rider straightened from the bed he'd just made after

Kutya vacated it for the chaise. "No, I had Rome get your books and laptop from my office with strict instructions to punch Porter in the balls if he tried to go in there without me present. I don't want Mr. Sticky Fingers anywhere near my bookshelves, but he should be all right up here researching with you while we wait to see if Daniel or the techs locate that church."

"Anything else you need, boss?" Rome looked around the room, his gaze locking onto the glass jar on top of the dresser where we kept Kutya's little bone-shaped beef, chicken, and cheese flavored dog treats. I thought I saw him drool a little. The poor man really missed his meat and dairy.

"No," Rider said, eyeing him in exasperation. "I'm going to walk you back to the bar and make sure you don't try to get any crumbs out of Kutya's dog bowl downstairs."

"Come on, boss. I'm not bad enough to stoop to that. I got my pride."

"Yeah, I think I see some of that pride dripping down your chin. No worries. We'll get you a nice bran muffin to cut your cravings."

Rome groaned, clearly more content to starve than to eat something that was actually good for him.

"You," Rider said, pointing at Jake. "Keep an eye on her. Make sure her stubborn ass actually rests and that she drinks enough blood. If she throws up again or seems off in any way, I want to know immediately. And as for you..." He snapped his fingers at me and pointed to the bed.

I rolled my eyes as I moved past him and made a show of getting on the bed, resting against the pillows he'd stacked along the headboard and plumped up for me.

"Good girl. Kutya, you're on guard dog duty. Don't let Danni get out of the bed, and bite Porter in the crotch if he touches anything."

Kutya responded with a very affirmative bark. I swore

the dog understood what we were saying, even without Jadyn doing her Dr. Dolittle thing.

"Nice try," Jake said, "but dogs are excellent judges of character." He handed the books and laptop to Rome and patted the side of his thigh. Kutya ran right over to him and rolled onto his back. "See?"

Rider watched the grinning slayer crouch down to give his dog a belly rub and shook his head. "Danni, this dog is broken."

I laughed, then noticed Rome had gone back to gazing longingly at the jar of dog treats. "He's not the only one."

Rider followed my gaze and shook his head. He took the books and laptop out of Rome's hands and placed them on the bed before grabbing the bottle of blood and handing that directly to me. "Drink it. Tony will send more up later until you're fully replenished. You threw up a lot."

"Thanks for the reminder."

"That's what I'm here for." He smiled and kissed the top of my head before turning toward Jake. "That and killing jackasses. I don't need to tell you to be on your best behavior, slayer."

"Nope, that's what my wife is for and she doesn't actually need to tell me either," Jake said, looking up from where he continued to rub Kutya's belly. "Danni's safe with me."

"She'd better be." Despite the clear warning in Rider's tone, he didn't threaten the slayer anymore, and much to my surprise, he actually pulled Rome away from the jar of dog treats and left me alone. In a bedroom. On a bed. With a slayer who looked just like Dean Winchester.

"Drink," Jake said as he stood, leaving Kutya very disappointed that the belly rub was over, and his tone was just bossy enough to make him very unattractive.

"You sound just like Rider." I lifted the bottle to my mouth and drank the liquid inside, glad it was warm. My stomach felt better than it had downstairs, but it still wasn't in good enough shape to handle cold, congealed blood. Vampire or not, congealed blood was just gross.

"That's possibly the meanest thing anyone's ever said about me." He grinned and picked up a book. "So you want to study up on your succubus side, get to know yourself a little better?"

"Yes. Almost as much as I want to know what in the world happened between you and Rider to make him actually just walk out of here and leave me all alone in a room with you."

"Not his usual behavior, huh?"

"I'm starting to question if he's been replaced with a shapeshifter."

Jake chuckled and sat on the chaise. "Nah. Rider and I just understand each other. He doesn't fully trust me and probably never will, just like some part of me will never fully trust him, but he knows my greatest weakness and I know his. I guess you could say we have each other by the short hairs."

I narrowed my eyes, studying him. "Does this have to do with the great big secret whatever-it-is that you two won't speak of in front of anyone else except Christian? Or the fact that Rider knows you have a wife you love more than anything, and you know about me?"

"Both, and no, I won't tell you anything about the great big secret whatever-it-is. I like you a lot, Danni Keller, and I'd trust you to have my back in a fight, but it's best for all that you not know anything about that. For starters, you wouldn't be going after Ramson if you knew about it."

"Even with this new psychic power protecting my mind?"

"We're not one hundred percent sure this new psychic power will completely protect your mind from him, but even if we were, no. And I don't really think your psychic power is new. People generally don't just wake up with psychic powers one day. The gut thing and the visions have probably been with you all along, or at least since you were turned. You just didn't know you had them, so they didn't kick in until you really needed them."

"You think so?"

"Makes sense. Makes more sense than you just randomly developing them out of the blue." He'd opened the book he'd taken from the pile and had been flipping through the pages, but he stopped and looked at me in a way that made me feel like a bug under a microscope.

"What is it?" I tried not to squirm under his laser-focused gaze. "Why are you looking at me like that?"

He continued staring for a moment, then blinked and shook his head. "I don't know. Something's different about you. You're way more… powerful or whatever than you were the last time I saw you. Maybe it's because you're discovering and honing your abilities."

"Maybe? You don't know? I thought you were supposed to know everything about everyone paranormal. I thought that was one of your slayer superpowers. Like how you sensed my succubus side rising in the interrogation room."

"I'm a slayer who didn't know the woman he was in love with was a pantherian-vampire hybrid until she was spitting out a chunk of flesh she'd bitten out of his neck." He grinned. "You hybrids are a hard bunch to get a good read on. Except for Seta. I knew she was a killer the moment I saw her. Of course, I had her pegged as just a really old and powerful vampire before I discovered she was actually a witch too. But I was still coming into my power then and there were other factors that probably went into me not sensing what Nyla was. I'm a lot better at sensing paranormal beings now, but you… You still throw me."

I frowned. "You knew I was a vampire and a succubus right away."

"Very true," he said, and went back to flipping through the book's pages.

I took a drink of blood and waited for him to continue, but he found something interesting in the book and kept reading silently. I finished the bottle and set it on the nightstand before reaching down for the stack of books and the laptop, pulling them all toward me. Kutya jumped up on the bed and turned in several circles before plopping down and yawning, his doggy breath making my eyes water before he rested his big head on my lap.

The legal pad and pens Daniel had retrieved from Jadyn's backpack earlier were with the pile and I reviewed Daniel's notes, my eyebrows shooting up as I realized sex demons had the gestational period of an elephant. I felt much better about my vampire side keeping pregnancy out of my future after learning that bit. Still, Jake didn't say anything to me. I tore a blank piece of paper from the legal pad, crumpled it into a ball, and hit Jake square in the face with it.

He jerked back, frowning, and looked at me. "What the hell was that for?"

"What aren't you telling me?"

"I don't know what you—"

"Uh-uh, don't play stupid with me. You said I still throw you, and in Rider's office earlier, you said I was the biggest threat in the room. What aren't you telling me?"

"I'm not keeping anything from you, Danni."

"Then what am I? Why am I the biggest threat and what do you mean by I still throw you?"

He just looked at me for so long I thought he wasn't going to answer, and when he finally did, he left me even more confused.

"I don't know. You are a vampire and a succubus, but you are also something much, much more powerful than just that. Whatever it is, I can't really see it exactly, but I know it's getting stronger. All I know for sure is that if I had to go against something big and bad, I'd want whatever it is you have in you backing me up."

CHAPTER TWELVE

I finished my third bottle of blood, one of the two Tony had hand-delivered to me while sending a warning glare Jake's way. The slayer hadn't left the chaise he'd settled on right after Rider had left, but he had stretched his long legs out and made himself comfortable. From the way Tony glared at him, one would think the slayer had crawled into the bed with me.

Fortunately, Tony never stayed long enough to distract us from our research and Jake didn't seem all that bothered by the hostility aimed his way. If anything, he'd seemed amused by it.

"Do you want a bottle of blood?" I asked. "I can have Tony bring you one the next time he comes up, or just give you what he brings me. I think I've had all the blood I can stomach for one night."

Jake grunted. "I don't think I'd take a bottle of blood Tony intended for me to drink, and you need to stay topped off. The visions are taking a lot out of you. I had some earlier, so I'm good. I don't need nearly as much as you guys do. I could honestly get what I need from a rare steak, but human blood is always better. I resurrect a lot faster without much of the dizziness or headache."

"What's that like anyway? Dying and coming back? Have you seen Heaven?"

Jake gave me a look. "I'm pretty sure I'm never stepping foot into Heaven, not even for a visit."

"Because you've killed? Jake, you save people."

"Yeah, but I've also pissed off at least one angel enough to get banned." He grinned. "No, I haven't been to Heaven. I don't go anywhere when I die. It's just blackness. At least, that's what I remember when I come back and I usually come back pretty fast."

"Usually?"

"A few minutes at most. Often the actual dying takes longer than the coming back, but if I haven't had enough blood in-between deaths, the resurrection takes longer. That's when I know I really need to get some of that gross stuff in me. It's usually not an issue unless I keep getting killed back to back."

I fought a grin, knowing that I shouldn't find humor when the man was talking about dying. Still, it was Jake, and he was just so cocky I couldn't help picking on him. "It seems like a better slayer wouldn't die so much. I thought you were a badass killing machine."

"I am, but we all have off days and I fight a lot of big, bad, and uglies. Sometimes I let myself get killed just so I can pop right up and get the jump on my opponent while they think they've won. Also, I was caught once. Those bitches killed the hell out of me. I have no idea how many times. That was actually when I met Khiderian and Marilee. They saved me."

"I'm glad they did. Please try not to die when we find Ramson. If you do and leave me alone to fight him myself, I'm going to kill you when you come back."

He chuckled. "If I do, it'll only be for a minute. I can't let you have all the fun. Speaking of fun... this ain't it." He flipped another page in the book he'd been reading.

He wasn't lying. While I needed to know more about my succubus side, with exception to a brief mention I'd found of succubi being able to erase memories after feeding from prey they wanted to keep around for multiple late night snacks, the books Nannette had loaned me were very clinical and boring. I nearly dozed off a couple times while reading and it took a lot of boredom to make a vampire fall asleep at night. I was starting to think that was the real reason Nannette hadn't yet discovered a way for me to rein in my succubus powers. She probably kept falling asleep while researching. If only there was a class or someone I could ask who really knew about…"Hey, wait."

"Hmm?" Jake looked up from the book.

"Why are we even reading these books? Don't you just know about all paranormal beings? Like, instinctually?"

"Yes, and no." He set the book aside, putting it next to him on the chaise, and leaned back, clasping his hands over his stomach. "I sense paranormal energy and can tell right away exactly what at least ninety-nine percent of paranormal beings are the moment I'm in proximity to them. I can even track many from a distance like I did the krackling that night we met. However, I wouldn't have looked at that thing and known it was a krackling if I hadn't come across it before while researching. I would have just known it was something big and bad. And I would have figured out it had to be kept in one form in order to be killed even if I hadn't read that before, but you were the one who figured out how to get it to take on one form and stay in it. Even slayers have to do a little research from time to time. I didn't take those books out of Rider's office just to mess with him, although that was a bonus. I did it because I wanted to know what was in them, to add to my knowledge."

"How did you get those books back into his office with no one detecting you?" I asked, now that he'd reminded me of them.

Jake grinned and wagged his finger at me. "I tell you and you'll tell him."

"No I won't."

"Is that his bed?"

"Yes."

"Are you in it?"

I sighed. "Yes."

"You'll tell him. I'm not mad at ya. I understand that's your man, so of course you'd tell him, but that's just not as fun for me as him wondering how I did it, so I have to keep this one a secret."

"Ugh, but that means I have to wonder how you did it too."

He laughed. "Added bonus."

"Jerk." I smiled, softening my insult. "Okay, so you knew I was a vampire and a succubus the moment you met me. So you already knew what succubi were to be able to recognize me."

"Yes." He nodded. "Those bitches I mentioned earlier, the ones who caught and killed me a bajillion times? Those were sirens. You heard Rider talking about that. They trap men in what is called a snare. They lure them in with their voice, project themselves as the man's ultimate fantasy woman, and they kill them. The bitches lured me. I'll give them that, but they never really snared me. They couldn't seduce me. For whatever reason, their singing broke through my immunity, but their seduction attempts didn't. It didn't matter that they were projecting themselves as Nyla. I saw the scaly ugly monsters they were underneath that. Anyway, I did a deep dive into research on them after I got out, trying to figure out why their voice worked on me the way it did."

"But you didn't find out?"

"No. Not for sure. I just learned what I already knew about them and my guess is that their singing voice is just the trap they set. Their actual power was in their ability to alter their appearance to a man's fantasy, and that was what I was immune to. When you released pheromones to lure the krackling, I felt it too, but it wasn't something I felt so strongly I couldn't resist it. If you bit me and injected me with venom, I'd more than likely be immune to it because that is your deadliest weapon, not your ability to lure."

"More than likely? So you really don't know if you would be or not."

"I'm ninety percent sure I would be, but we're going to try to never have to find out for certain. Anyway, you're not the first succubus I've come across. I researched them while looking deeper into sirens because sirens are a form of sex demon too. I learned how to recognize the signs that a harem is hunting in an area, so I was able to track one and kill all the succubi in it, and their incubus."

"You killed an entire group of succubi by yourself and not one managed to bite you and inject you with venom?"

"Not by myself. Don't let the girl next door look fool you. Marilee has my blood in her and she's one hell of a scrapper. Together, we took out the harem, and I took care of the incubus myself. But, even if I hadn't had that experience, I would have still sensed a demonic entity in you and I would have been able to deduce the type. However, since I'd had a run-in with succubi before, I could pinpoint exactly what type of sex demon made up your other half."

"Because you had already studied succubi enough. So, why are you up here reading a book if you already know about succubi? Why am I? You can just tell me what I am, what makes up this half of me that is always causing me problems."

"You think it's your succubus half causing all your problems?"

"Uh, duh. Yeah. I mean, if I was just a vampire, no one would be worried about venom and I wouldn't be accidentally luring men while trying to interrogate them. I wouldn't have had—" I stopped myself before I could reveal everything that had happened with the Bloom and how my sister now rested in a comatose state she would likely be stuck in for eternity because of it. "I wouldn't have been hunted by the Quimby family if not for my succubus side. The Quimbys had a pact with Rider not to hunt the vampires or shifters he vouched for, but they wouldn't even hear him when he said I was off-limits. A lot of his people died protecting me from them."

"That wasn't your fault. Barnaby Quimby was an asshole who never liked upholding the pact his family had made with Rider. He was looking for any excuse to get out of it. Rider's people aren't innocent civilians either. His people are fighters. They wake up every day, or night, depending on what they are, knowing it could be their last. That's the risk they take to be in his nest, and from the things I've heard, they're glad to risk their lives for the man who rescued them from horrible masters."

"They're glad to die for him?"

"Death is better than slavery. A lot of his people, especially the vamps, were enslaved for longer stretches of time than you and I could even fathom."

"Yeah, well, I still can't help but feel responsible when they die for him by fighting to protect me. And I can't be fully trusted around any of the men. They try not to show it, but I can feel the wariness when they're around me, afraid I'm going to turn them into rutting dogs."

Kutya barked, and the sound that came out of him actually sounded insulted.

"No offense, Kutya. You're a good boy." I reached down and scratched between his ears.

"The men who fight to protect me are actually afraid of me, or maybe even disgusted by me. Almost all the women in Rider's nest hate me. It's all because of this half of me they are all either afraid of or repulsed by. I probably can't do anything about the repulsion, but if I could learn enough about succubi to know how to control that part of what I am, maybe I can at least make the men stop being afraid of me."

"Call me crazy, but I think most are afraid of you because you're Danni the Teste Slayer. Men don't enjoy having their balls sliced, diced, or pulverized, and you've built up quite a reputation for doing that."

"Honestly, Ginger and Daniel have blown that way out of proportion. I don't just go around slicing testes all willy-nilly like they'd have you believe, and when I do take out someone's testicles, it's well deserved. In fact, I'm doing a favor for mankind." I sighed. "And that's not it. They joke about that. I think the men who work for Rider would rather I neuter them than seduce them and suck out their souls."

"Yeah, that's a hard choice," Jake said, grinning. "But in all seriousness, maybe the problem isn't your succubus side, but how you look at it. What if the men who work for Rider do fear you? So what?"

"So what?"

"So what. Rider Knight is one of the most feared and respected vampires in the states, but just because he is feared and respected so greatly doesn't mean he or anyone he protects is safe. There's always some big nasty out there salivating for the head of whoever the big dog is. The big dog is Rider. He's the vampire any vampire who wants to run shit is going to have to take out. He's the vampire any demonic, evil bastard wanting to spill blood all over this territory is going to have to erase. This territory is his kingdom. He is the king every enemy is gunning for, and you are his queen. Now, would you rather be the sniffling, dainty little queen that just sits there looking pretty while enemies surround your king just because you want to be liked, or would you rather be the co-ruler watching your king's back, keeping him protected because anyone who even thinks of attacking him knows they're going to have to get through his queen first and she's just as deadly as he is?"

I sat back as the weight of Jake's words hit me like a physical blow. "Well, gee, when you say it like that, the second option sounds a lot better. I'm not sure I could actually ever be considered a co-ruler, but—"

"If you don't realize what you've become, you're not paying attention," Jake said, cutting me off. "Rider may have made the call, but you're the one who requested my help. He wouldn't have done that if not for your insistence and all jokes aside, page thirty-three only goes so far. He did what you wanted because he values your opinion. He's not stopping you from going after Ramson with me, although he could. He is in love with you so he's always going to be protective of you, he's always going to try to dissuade you from running into danger, but when it comes down to it, from everything I've seen while observing him with you, you are his partner in every way. I'm not the only one who can see that."

The backs of my eyes burned and a heavy weight settled in my chest. It took a moment just to gather myself enough to speak. "I hope that's true because that would... that would mean a lot to me. I'm afraid of screwing up though, of letting this sex demon escape and ruin everything."

"The only problem I can see with your succubus side, Danni, is that you're more afraid of it than the men you seem so worried about scaring are. Sometimes it's better to be feared than to be well-liked. Embrace that shit and use it. Maybe then you'll figure out what other weapons you have in your arsenal because, although I can't see exactly what they are right now, I can feel them in there and I can tell they're badass."

"How can I use what I don't understand?" I flipped through the pages of one of the books. "That's why I'm reading all this, trying to figure out what I have in me so I can figure out how to use it."

"Do you think I had a manual for being a slayer? Or any kind of mentor?" Jake chuckled, shaking his head. "Hell, I'm still figuring out what the hell I am too. I can tell you this, though. Everything I've learned about slayers, I've learned by just being one. You can read as many books as you want, I'll help you do it, but at the end of the day, you're still going to have to figure out what does or doesn't apply to you. You can learn about succubi, but you will never find yourself in these books because the book about you hasn't been written. You are something that, to the best of my knowledge, has never been."

I tossed the book aside and threw my hands up in the air. "So this is all a waste of time!"

"Nah, I wouldn't say that. It kept you resting in bed until you drank enough blood to recoup what you lost."

My mouth slowly parted as I realized I'd been played. "You went along with helping me research just to make sure I stayed in this bed, resting. Rider had you, of all people, come up here to help because he knew I wouldn't suspect you of being just a babysitter."

"Hey, I do research in my downtime so this wasn't a waste, but yes, Rider and I agreed you needed to rest and drink and this was an easy way to make sure you did." He smiled as he stood, then rubbed his hands together. "But now your color is back and you've kept down those three bottles plus what you took directly from Rider's vein, so let's start class for real."

"Start class?" I sat up straighter and Kutya lifted his massive head, noticing the change of energy in the room. "You've been holding out on me."

"Yes, but I'm about to make it up to you. Welcome to Introduction to Succubiology. I am your professor, Dr. Badass. Pay attention and feel free to take notes."

"Sure thing, Dr. Badass." I tried not to roll my eyes.

Jake grinned but continued, pacing at the foot of the bed as he began his lecture. "Succubi are sex demons, which you already know. They can be born in two ways: through birth or through bite, but only a woman with what is called sweet blood can be turned through a bite."

"Can we skip to the advanced lesson instead of going over the basic stuff everyone already knows?" I asked as I sat with my pen poised above the legal pad Daniel had borrowed from Jadyn.

"Patience, grasshopper." He raised his index finger, but didn't look my way, continuing to pace and do what I assumed was his best impression of a college lecturer. "A group of succubi is called a harem and similar to vampire nests, harems have a master; the incubus. Succubi can service their master directly and often do, fulfilling the incubus's voracious sexual appetite and ensuring reproduction. Mating between an incubus and a succubus almost always results in an incubus of considerable strength. For this reason, many incubi would rather their harem mate with human men while fertile, lessening the chance of an incubus being born strong enough to overthrow them once it becomes of age."

"But succubi can still get pregnant by human men?" I asked, remembering what Daniel had said earlier.

"They can, but if an incubus is born of that union, it will not be as strong as one sired by another incubus. The odds of having a succubus will be greater as well, and I've found a few sources stating that a succubus mating with any entity other than an incubus could result in a lower level demon, especially if that other entity is a mere human."

"Interesting," I said, and genuinely meant it, "but not applicable to me. All the signs are there that my vampire side will ensure chubby little fanged babies are not in my future."

If there was an upside to what had happened to me, it was that I hadn't had a single period or even a menstrual cramp since I'd been turned. It was a much appreciated side effect, although I'd be willing to get the occasional period again in exchange for a cupcake. Or a doughnut. Anything chocolate.

"Are you all right with that?"

I looked up from the legal pad I'd been writing on, a little surprised to see such empathy in Jake's expression as he stood still at the foot of the bed, looking at me, and nodded. "I'm sure there will be many times I'll wonder what it would have been like to have children, and I may wonder what our child would have looked like if Rider and I could conceive, but when I think about all the danger I've been in since turning, I don't feel as bad about missing out on motherhood. Not to mention, what would I even have? It's been a constant struggle to come to terms with what I am now, and feeling like a freak even among other paranormals. I wouldn't want my child to go through that too."

"I get that, but you're not a freak. You're just… uniquely interesting. Now, what else?" He cleared his throat and went back to pacing. "The succubus can lure prey by releasing pheromones, something you know already because you did it when we fought the krackling."

"I didn't know I was releasing pheromones though. I kind of just called out to it mentally, and that did the trick. However, when I was in interrogation last night, I accidentally released pheromones just by thinking of luring Gary to see if that made him talk more."

"That's not too surprising. Succubi by nature are gluttonous. They don't deprive themselves of whatever they are lusting for, whether it be sex, violence, food, you name it, and they often use their ability to lure to get what they want."

"Great. So anytime I even think of something I really want, I'm going to automatically release pheromones?"

"I don't think so." He stopped pacing and leaned back against the dresser with his arms folded. "Succubi can control when and who they lure. You never lured anyone before you used it on the krackling, did you?"

I shook my head. "Not unless I did it unintentionally and wasn't aware of it, but I haven't been alone much since I was turned. Even when I thought I was alone, Rider had security watching me. I'm sure he would have told me if I'd done it before then."

"So you were turned and went months without using your luring ability, then discovered the ability not even a week ago. Imagine the luring ability is an animal that has been starving for months while locked away in a cage, completely neglected. Suddenly, it's let loose. It gets fed once and put away again, but it knows how to get out now."

"I see what you're saying. The nibble I gave it before Christmas wasn't enough for it. It got a taste, and it wants more."

"Exactly."

"So, how do I keep it from escaping whenever it gets the munchies? I can't keep luring men."

"Why not?" Jake held his hand up when I opened my mouth to protest. "Hear me out. This power you have just wants to be used. If you use it, you'll satisfy it for a while. If you use it regularly, it won't be so desperate to escape you because it knows the cage isn't going to stay closed for months."

"If I use it, I'll be luring men to me, increasing the chances of this succubus power escaping me and doing something that would … that would…"

"That would what? Why are you pushing back on this now, Danni? This is what you wanted, remember? You wanted to learn about your succubus side so you could learn to control and use your abilities. What's the problem?"

My chest rose and fell with far more force than was necessary for someone who didn't actually need to breathe in order to live. My palms sweat and the walls seemed to close in on me. Kutya whined and inched closer to me until he could rest his head on my lap again and I automatically wrapped my arms around him, hugging him close.

"Hey. Danni."

I blinked and realized Jake had moved away from the dresser to kneel next to me at the side of the bed. Concern filled his hazel eyes as he watched me carefully, and waited until my breath stopped coming in such quick, shallow bursts.

"That's it. That's good. In and out, nice and slow." He sighed and cautiously reached out, running his thumb over my cheek, and that was when I realized I'd shed a few tears. "I know you're afraid of losing control of your succubus side and cheating on Rider. That's why I had you talk to Nyla, but maybe I should have told you my side of our story."

He got up and sat on the edge of the bed, scratching Kutya under the chin before he continued. "Forgive me, but I'm going to be very blunt and crude because sometimes you have to be to really get your point across. My wife has fucked hundreds of men, maybe a thousand, and I don't give a shit because she's only ever made love with me. She told you what she is, so you're aware that she still goes into heat and she will do so as long as she lives."

I nodded, loosening my grip on Kutya. The big pup licked the underside of my face before resting his head on my lap again.

"When the heat hits her, it hits her hard, and she immediately calls me. No matter where I'm at or what I'm doing, or what bloody carnage I am knee deep in, I drop everything and I get to her as fast as I can. The entire time I'm on my way to her, my heart is racing, my palms are sweating, and my thoughts are moving too fast to process. All I can think of clearly are these three words: Get to her. Do you know why?"

I nodded and sniffed. "Because as hard as she tries not to give in to it, the heat could win and she could sleep with another man."

"And do you know why I'm so afraid of that happening while I'm racing to her side?"

"Because she's your wife," I answered. "Because you're supposed to be with each other and as much as you love her, something like that could destroy what you have."

"No, Danni. I get to her as fast as I can because something like that could destroy *her*. I know what she is, I know what could happen, and I won't sit here and tell you it wouldn't bother me if she had sex with another man. Of course it would. She's my wife. But I know it wouldn't mean she didn't love me. I know she would have fought her hardest against her very DNA because she'd rather suffer in pain than ever hurt me. I'd be upset, and I'd want to kill whoever she'd been with, but I wouldn't be angry with her. I wouldn't feel betrayed by her. I'd just... want to comfort her."

I felt fresh tears slide down my cheeks and wiped them away before shaking my head. "That's a beautiful thought, Jake, but you don't know what you'd do in that situation until it happens, and that kind of betrayal can't be easy to just shrug off."

"I know how I feel about my wife and how she feels about me, and I wouldn't just shrug it off. It would wound me, but as I stated, I know what my wife is. I also know who she is. If she had sex with someone else because the heat hit her and I didn't get to her in time, she would be devastated. Her pain and guilt would eat her alive and knowing she was going through that much suffering would hurt a hell of a lot worse than my jealousy so you better believe I would suck that shit up and do whatever it took to help her deal with the aftermath, and if Rider loves you the way it sure as hell seems like he loves you, he'd do the same. You're not going to lose him, Danni. Not over that."

I felt Rider's presence and swiped hastily at the remaining wetness on my face a second before he came through the door. He came to an abrupt stop, jaw clenched, nostrils flared, and dark eyes glittering as he took in the scene before him. I felt his power fill the room as Kutya whined and jumped out of the bed.

"You have three seconds to give me what better be a damn good reason for you to be sitting on that bed with her while she's obviously been crying."

CHAPTER THIRTEEN

"Oh good grief, Rider, when have I ever needed a reason to cry?" I asked before Jake could say something smartassed. He liked to poke the big snarly bear and there were times one should definitely not poke the bear. Judging by the look in Rider's eyes, poking him was a bad idea. "And it's not like there's many places to sit in here. This is a bedroom. And you!"

I pointed at Rider as I swung my legs over the edge of the bed and stood, and continued pointing at him as I marched toward him. "You sent him up here to make sure I stayed in bed and drank all the blood you had Tony bring up, not to actually help with research. If anyone should be mad at anyone about anything, I should be mad about being treated like a child in need of a sitter."

Rider looked down at the finger now firmly planted in the center of his chest, and angled his head to look around me at the slayer. "Really? You had to be obvious about watching her? And get the hell off our bed."

"Relax, dude. You had this giant mutant dog up here standing guard and Tony the Constipated Tiger coming up to glare at me at regular intervals."

"And yet you still found a way to make her cry." Rider

looked down at me. "And I'm not hearing a reason why."

"Don't blame Jake because I'm emotional." I took my finger out of his chest and smoothed his shirt. "I've been fainting and throwing up, haven't I? I'm a little wonky."

His eyes softened. "Are you feeling better now?"

"Yes. I drank all the blood and Jake can confirm I rested. In fact, I nearly fell asleep from boredom before he finally admitted to your ploy and actually started telling me what he knows about succubi."

"Did he now?" Rider's gaze shifted over to Jake as the slayer picked up the book he'd set aside on the chaise earlier and stacked it on top of the ones I'd left on the bed. "And what has he been telling you?"

"What she needs to hear," Jake answered for me. "That the best, fastest way to learn more about her succubus side is to use it."

"To use it?" Rider moved me aside and stepped toward the slayer.

Jake held his hands up in front of him. "In a safe, controlled way. Do you want her leaking pheromones all over the place without even realizing it like she did in that interrogation room before you called me in?"

Rider paused. "No."

"Because that could put her and anyone tasked with keeping her safe in a dangerous situation, correct?"

"Obviously. What are you getting at, Porter?"

"As I was telling Danni before you arrived and got all suspicious, she has been able to lure since she was turned, but she didn't know how to until she searched inside herself and figured it out when we went up against that krackling. Once she used her ability on it, she woke it up. It's hungry to be used, and it's not going to stay caged inside her now that it knows how to get out. She needs to feed it from time to time, enough to keep it content."

"That's what her blood cocktail is for," Rider said. "Nannette has her on a mixed diet of male and female blood, live and bagged, to keep her succubus side under control."

"A good idea, but not foolproof. Especially now that she's used her luring ability. She needs to use it consistently, and she needs to do so in an environment where she feels safe so she can get comfortable with it. Using it when a dangerous situation calls for it and she's already in fight-or-flight mode isn't the best way to learn how to draw it back in. She's too nervous when she does that."

"I agree that if she is going to learn how to use it safely, it needs to be in a safe, controlled way." Rider folded his arms. "I'm still working out the logistics of that."

"It's not that complicated. We put her in a room with a man and let her practice on him. Luring just makes the man desire her, want to get close to her or follow her command. He won't get all out of control unless she injects her venom into him. And she can learn to control the venom too, but first, we have to work on the luring."

"We?"

"You can withstand the lure. I might get a nice tingle from it, but I can withstand it enough to protect her, no matter what. She needs to feel safe, to know someone is with her to ensure things don't go too far. Then she can focus on drawing on her ability, and calming it once she's done using it. Once she can do that, we can bring in more men. Have her learn to really focus the lure on one target, no matter how many are in the room."

Jake heaved out a frustrated sigh when Rider just stared at him, jaw popped, clearly not enthusiastic. "It will make her a better fighter. Hell, if she gets good enough at it, she won't have to lay a finger on a man in a fight. She may even be able to dreamwalk. And think about it. Wouldn't you feel more comfortable training her here before sending her after Ramson with me? I can keep her safe if she has to use the lure to bring me back from a fit of bloodlust, but I think you'll breathe better knowing she's had some practice beforehand. Not to mention, I'm not going to always be here and you can't count on always being there or having Ginger handy when she needs to use the lure and pull it back in, either."

"What's dreamwalking?" I asked, recognizing the term from *Supernatural*, but I'd realized some time ago that familiar words and entities from television didn't always mean the same thing in the real world.

"Something far too dangerous to even consider," Rider said.

"Something that needs to be considered because if she has the ability to do it, she could do it by accident and I think you'll agree it would be better she know what it is so she can recognize herself doing it instead of just thinking she's in a dream, unable to be hurt or get somebody killed." Jake shifted his gaze over to me. "Dreamwalking is an ability incubi and succubi have. Incubi can only use it with females and succubi can only use it with males."

"It's how Ryan got into your co-worker's head and killed her," Rider said. "How he got to you in your dreams."

"And you didn't tell me this? I thought he could get inside my dreams because he was my sire, and the soul stitch thing was how he got into Gina's dreams, but he could have done that to any woman? My family was in danger? Could still be in danger if that's how he chooses to get to me if he comes back?"

"He would have had to have tasted their blood," Jake said. "Or made a connection through sex or saliva. I'm going to assume that never happened, so your family is safe. Also, he's dead, right?"

"-ish," Rider said. "Danni, he used the soul stitch attachment to get to you two then because he was dead, or... whatever he is. Also, that was what made it so he could possess you. I don't think he can dreamwalk into anyone's mind wherever he is now, not without a soul stitch attachment being involved. But yes, if he figures out how to get back into his body, he'll probably be able to dreamwalk into the mind of anyone who he has tasted or he has slept with. None of those things should apply to your family. They're safe from him."

I looked at Jake. "And you think I could do this?"

"It's possible. You're a hybrid so it's hard to say what traits you've adopted from either sire or what abilities have morphed into something completely unique inside you, but the more you actually use your succubus abilities, the more you can awaken and discover new ones. Dreamwalking would come in handy. For example, you drank from Gary and he drank from Ramson. Just that connection right there could possibly be enough to get inside Ramson's head and get his location."

"She is not going inside a pranic vampire's head," Rider growled.

"Obviously. She doesn't know how." Jake grinned when Rider growled again. "I'm just saying, if she learns how to do it carefully, there are benefits. Say any of your men get grabbed by the other side. If she has a connection, she can find them. Handy."

"That does sound handy." I refused to wilt under Rider's dark look. "Well, it does. But this lure thing, that seems like the most important thing to focus on now, especially if I might need to use it on Jake when we go after Ramson. I know he says he can keep me safe, and I believe him, but it's still an added complication we don't need. And it would be nice to not have to worry about accidentally releasing pheromones at bad times. I need to know how to give this part of me what it wants without losing control of it."

"All right," Rider said, "but you also have the visions to deal with. That's why I came up here to get you. Auntie Mo has agreed to see us. Actually, she called Rome and told him to bring you to her."

"Well, that doesn't sound ominous at all."

***

AULD FANG SYNE

Auntie Mo lived in the West End of Louisville, in an area known for its high crime rate, but she refused to leave it, even after Rome offered to buy her a new house in an area where you were less likely to be hit by a stray bullet. She said it was because she already had a perfectly suitable house and she was right where she was needed. Frankly, I thought it was because the woman would know if a bullet was headed her way before it ever left the gun, so why bother with packing until you absolutely had to?

Rider took the SUV so Jake could accompany us. He said it was to ensure we didn't come back to either a dead slayer or a dead tiger, but I knew he just didn't want Jake to pilfer anything else from his office so he wanted the slayer far away from The Midnight Rider when he wasn't there.

Rome rode in the SUV behind us, along with three other members of Rider's security staff. Hank drove the SUV in front of us. Jadyn had been handed dog-sitting duty until we got back.

"Do you always travel with an entourage just to visit a little old lady?" Jake asked from where he sat in the backseat, looking out the window.

"When added security is necessary," Rider answered. "We don't know if Ramson has fed from Julie yet. If he has, and he wants to try for my territory, he could wait to get to me away from the security of The Midnight Rider. Also, Danni was caught on security camera footage attacking a woman who shot Daniel's hand off. The security footage caught him shifting to heal the damage and grow the hand back. The greasy detective who got his hands on the footage already sent her one letter threatening to reveal us. We're waiting to see what he wants for his silence. For all we know, he could just want us dead. He could be watching us and waiting for his moment or he could have hired someone. Then there's Selander Ryan. The evil bastard hasn't given up on using

Danni to destroy me and so far death hasn't seemed to keep him from getting to her, so yeah, if we go visit a little old lady in the West End at night, we bring an entourage."

"Never a dull moment with you, Danni." Jake smiled. "So tell me about this greasy detective. Is he a hunter?"

"No, he's just an asshole," I said. "My mother hired him when…" I looked over at Rider, not sure if Jake knew about Shana's current condition. Christian knew, but he'd said he'd sensed her when he'd stayed in the sublevel. Jake had been in the sublevels and the man could sense anything paranormal. "My sister went missing and my mother thought I might have something to do with it, so he followed me. The jerk put a tracker on Kutya's collar right under our noses and used that to follow us to Tennessee where that incident happened. My mother has since ceased his services after the detective officially assigned to my sister's missing persons case found evidence of her being in Las Vegas."

"He used your own dog to track you? I hate him already."

"He tracked us to the property of a wolf pack we were staying with and left a letter with them before they strongly encouraged him to leave. It included stills he'd printed from the video and a message that basically said he knew what we were and we'd be hearing from him."

"Have you?"

"Not directly," Rider answered, taking over the conversation. "Remember the pedophile Danni eviscerated before the haint took her over?"

"Yeah, that's a scene one doesn't just scrub out of their brain."

Rider nodded. "That's the truth. That guy was an online poker buddy of the detective. We have his cell phone and Pacitti, the detective, has been sending him messages hinting that he has something big. The last message was in code, but Danni cracked it. He wants to meet Brinley at Busch Gardens in Virginia tomorrow at noon."

"Brinley is the pedophile?"

"Yes."

"The dead pedophile? So you've been posing as him and will be there at noon for the meeting to grab the detective."

"Not me personally," Rider answered. "I'm sending a team."

"If he's going to be at Busch Gardens by noon, I doubt he's here in Louisville tonight hunting Danni."

"If you wanted to be at Busch Gardens by noon, would you have any problem getting there by then?"

"No," Jake answered, his tone indicating he got Rider's point. "I was under the assumption this Pacitti probably doesn't know all of our methods of travel."

"Who knows what he has on us now that he's been made aware of our existence," I said, wishing I didn't feel such responsibility for the mess we were in with him. "The man's a snake."

"Speaking of snakes, where is Lana?" Jake asked. "I haven't seen her around."

"On a job," Rider answered.

"Figures," Jake muttered. "She'd be good to have around if we find the church. She could just slither through there and swallow everyone, make things a lot easier."

"You're going to have to do it without her," Rider said, glancing in the rearview mirror. "I don't expect her back until next week, and it shouldn't take us that long to find the church between Daniel and my tech team."

"Nothing yet though?" I asked.

Rider shook his head as we followed the SUV in front of us into the alley that ran behind Auntie Mo's house and parked. "But the techs are scouring the internet and Daniel is widening his radius. We'll find it."

"Maybe Auntie Mo already has." I reached for the door handle, but Jake was already there, holding it open, much to Rider's annoyance. Despite the years of bloodshed and carnage under his belt, Rider was still very much a gentleman at heart. He got annoyed when I opened my own door, and it appeared to annoy him even more when another man beat him to the punch.

Rider didn't respond until we were both out of the SUV and headed toward Auntie Mo's house, Rome taking the lead while the rest of Rider's security detail flanked out to cover us from all angles, except for Hank, who had been left behind to guard the vehicles. Expensive vehicles didn't last long on the streets or in the alleys of the neighborhood we were in, but one look at Hank, a giant muscular wall of a man who resembled a rhino even when he wasn't in his animal form, was a pretty good deterrent. If his sheer size wasn't enough to dissuade any would-be car thieves, he could handle himself.

"That would be convenient," Rider said, scanning the area as we walked, despite the protection of his men. "But she could have just passed the church's location on to Rome to give to us if that was what she wanted. She wanted to see you, so I'm thinking this is more personal, especially since you've developed your own psychic abilities recently."

Two large brown-skinned men stood outside Auntie Mo's house, one on either side of the back door. They eyed us cautiously as we opened the back gate and entered the yard. We stayed back a moment, allowing Rome to move forward and speak with the men. They exchanged a few words, did that complicated handshake-hug thing Rome always did with the men stationed outside his great-aunt's house, and he waved us forward.

"Not so fast." Rider clamped his hand on Rome's meaty shoulder as the big guy entered the house ahead of us. "I'm keeping my eye on you."

Rome made a frustrated noise in his throat and rolled his eyes, but otherwise kept his thoughts to himself.

"What's that about?" Jake asked, speaking low as we

stepped inside after the two men.

"Rome is on a strict diet after getting out of the hospital and he's not doing too well with the willpower thing."

"Oh yeah," Jake said, chuckling to himself as we all traveled down the stairs leading to the basement where Auntie Mo took visitors. "He had that giant, colossal chunk of shit surgically removed from his colon."

Men. I would never understand the things they thought were funny.

Auntie Mo sat at the little round table in her basement, wrapped in a light blue terry robe, waiting for us. Her thin, withered hands were clasped in front of her as she watched me from observant eyes that saw more than what was physically before her. Her long white and gray hair was divided into several box braids then gathered together into one thick braid that tumbled over a shoulder that appeared frail, but there was nothing frail about the older woman, evidenced by the way she quickly reached out to grab Rome's ear when he bent down to greet her, and pulled him close despite his size. "Why didn't I see you in church for Christmas Eve service?"

"Dang, Auntie Mo. I'd just got out of the hospital. I had surgery. I was resting."

"Resting? Resting?" Even Rider and Jake jumped a little as the woman's voice grew harsher. "You couldn't be bothered to join us in worship while we celebrated the birth of our Lord and Savior because you were resting? Just what did you need that much rest for that you couldn't sit your oversized behind in a pew and pray? You didn't have open heart surgery, you had a giant piece of poop taken out of your chute. Disgraceful."

Rider clenched his teeth tightly together and Jake rolled his lips in so far the surrounding skin went white while I just shook my head and watched as the elderly woman released Rome's ear with a shove that nearly caused him to lose his footing.

"Get on out of here and let me talk to your friend, and don't you even think about poking around in my kitchen like a pig. I told your mama she fed you too much. Never seen anything like it. Eat a person out of house and home but only if it's garbage. You're never going to get a good woman if you don't straighten up and fly right. Go to church. That's how you impress a good girl, not breaking records for monstrous turds. You—" She paused, straightened her glasses and squinted to take in Jake better. "Haven't I seen you on the TV?"

"No, ma'am," Jake replied, and opened his mouth to say more, but Auntie Mo cut him off.

"Don't you lie to me, boy. I saw you with demons and monsters and half-naked women on that blasphemous show. You can act however you want on the TV but when you're in my home, you better tell the truth or else get that smirk smacked off that pretty face."

Rider made a strangled noise and turned away, his eyes watering. He bit his lip to keep from laughing as Jake stood shell-shocked with his mouth hanging open. Rome grinned, amused to finally see someone other than him getting the brunt of Auntie Mo's no-nonsense attitude.

"Auntie Mo, this is Jake Porter," I said, saving him. "He looks just like Jensen Ackles, who is the actor you're thinking of, but he's not him. He's not an actor."

Auntie Mo leaned forward and squinted harder, studying Jake. "Come here, boy."

Jake looked at me and if I didn't feel so sorry for him in that moment, I would have laughed at the fear in the big, bad slayer's eyes. Instead, I placed my hand on his shoulder and gave him a push, prodding him toward the little old lady scrutinizing him. Rome chuckled softly until Auntie Mo quickly jerked her head in his direction, silencing him with only a look. She returned her curious gaze to Jake as he came to a stop in front of the table, and frowned. "I can't see you."

"Ma'am?"

She cocked her head to the side, staring at him, then pointed to her temple. "I can't see you. You got some kind of protection all around you. You a man of God, boy?"

Jake's jaw popped, and I imagined the *boy* was getting to him, but he didn't correct her. He was probably afraid she'd rip his ear off like she'd nearly done to Rome. "I believe in Him, ma'am, but I think this protection you're not able to penetrate is because of what I am. I'm a slayer. I kill evil things, and part of my protection is that psychics can't get inside my head or see too much about me."

Her lips pursed as she continued to study him. Then she nodded and sat back. "You're right. You're not that man on the TV. He's a lot better-looking."

I choked back a laugh and Jake slowly turned his head to give me a dark look before glaring at Rider, who rocked back on his heels with his hands stuffed into his pants pocket, smiling from ear to ear, clearly having enjoyed the entire exchange.

"Suddenly, it's very clear to me why I was invited on this trip," Jake muttered and walked over to where I stood.

"Mr. Knight."

"Auntie Mo." Rider nodded his head in greeting. "You wanted to see us?"

"I wanted to see Danni. You and your odd friend can wait outside with my great-nephew. Keep him out of my kitchen and in a church pew sometime."

"Yes, ma'am," Rider said, grabbing Rome by the shoulder and winking at me before they moved toward the stairs.

"I'm the odd one?" I heard Jake mutter as they took the stairs up. "This one practically gave cesarean birth to a giant lump of shit and you look like you came out of an Anne Rice novel. Join this century and get a haircut."

I took a step toward the table, but stopped, my attention caught by noise on the stairs. I turned to see Jake falling down them, but he caught himself on the railing.

"Sorry about that," he said with a bit of a growl while

glaring up the stairs. "I seem to have lost my footing." Then he launched himself up the stairs and something crashed above our heads.

"Boys," Auntie Mo said with an eye roll and a decent amount of disgust before yelling, "If anything gets broken up there, I'll paddle all your asses, whether you're my blood or not."

The noise immediately stopped, and Auntie Mo gestured toward the chair across from her. "Sit, Danni. We have much to discuss."

I did as told. I had a healthy respect for the sharp-tongued woman whose bone-thin hands could whip out like streaks of lightning to snatch an ear before you knew what was happening. I didn't ever want to know what that felt like.

"You have been waking up," she said, and I felt my eyebrows raise. "Your gifts are revealing themselves to you."

"Ah, so you didn't invite us here to tell us the location of the pranic vampire we're looking for."

Auntie Mo shook her head. "I dreamed of you, Danni. I see you're still having the same problem you had before when you were so lost."

I frowned. "What do you mean?"

"You need to face your demons. Until you do, you will never truly be free to embrace true happiness."

I blinked while I tried to decipher what the woman was talking about. Auntie Mo could be helpful, but she often spoke in riddles that just left me more confused than I'd been before entering her basement.

"I suppose you can't reword that into something I could understand a little better, could you? Or just tell me what I'm supposed to do?"

"Face your demons," she said again, and reached across the table to take my hands in hers. "Embrace the power within you and find your true joy. You have so much to be thankful for, so much love surrounds you, but you focus on the darkness so much, it eclipses all the light."

I sighed, wishing the woman spoke English. "Auntie Mo, don't get me wrong, I appreciate any time you spend helping me, but you're not really telling me anything I can understand right now. And what you've said so far could have been said over the phone or sent in an email."

"I don't toy with computers," she said. "They're just another portal for Satan's pornography."

Ohhkay. I didn't have a response for that.

She closed her eyes and rubbed her thumbs over the backs of my hands. Although she was a woman and my succubus side generally didn't like for me to have close contact with women, her touch was warm and didn't bother me. It kind of tingled, like her psychic power covered her hands to brush against mine, providing a barrier between our skin. "You awakened your power to defeat a great evil and now you are afraid of it taking over you."

I nodded. Although her eyes were still closed, I felt she would sense my agreement.

"Do not be afraid of what you hold inside you, Danni. It is part of you, part of what you were always meant to be."

"I was always meant to be a succubus?" I couldn't keep the disbelief out of my tone. "Of all the things I could have been, why was I meant to be something so far from anything I'd ever want to be?"

Auntie Mo opened her eyes and the brown depths were filled with compassion. "You shouldn't hate yourself, Danni."

"I don't hate myself. I hate this thing in me. I hate that I was stupid enough to walk out of The Midnight Rider with Selander Ryan, that I let him attack me. I hate that the man I love has to worry about me cheating on him because this thing inside me is always hungry, always prowling around inside me looking for a way out so it can eat what is not on the menu for it." I sighed and felt the tears forming. I sniffed and willed them to stay where they belonged. "I hate these surprises. I just want to know what I am and what I can do without having to discover it along the way, without having to risk so much. I'm a succubus, but I'm not. I'm a vampire, but I'm not. Now I'm having these gut feelings and visions which don't seem part of either entity. Why am I having visions now, Auntie Mo? What am I?"

"You keep asking that question of other people and seeking an answer from other people's discoveries, but only you can provide the answer to that question, Danni. You have the answer inside you now. You have always had it."

I fought the urge to roll my eyes as her spiel became painfully close to the one Jake had given me earlier. "Let me guess. You're going to tell me I need to let my succubus side out to play, because that is the only way I will discover what I am."

"You need to face your demons so you can come to a place of peace and agreement where you can harness your full potential without fear."

The urge to grab the old lady by her thin shoulders and shake her while screaming at her to speak English flowed through me but the fear of getting my ear snatched off kept me sitting well-behaved in my seat with my hands resting easily in hers.

She smiled knowingly, and I wondered if Auntie Mo was an actual mind-reader. "To answer your question, the abilities you've gained as a vampire are Rider's power passed on to you. Your succubus powers are your other sire's powers given through his bite. The visions are your power. I saw them in you the first time you appeared to me. Those who have lived many lives often develop psychic power. It's the natural accumulation of all the energy you have collected over your lives."

I blinked, processing. "But you said most of my lives were incredibly short. I was even killed in the womb in at least one of them."

"Yes." She nodded. "But all beings have energy and that energy never dies. You have carried the energy of all your previous lives with you, and in this life, it became a shield to protect you and a weapon to aid you. You've had this power in you from the moment you drew your first breath in this life. It has led you every step of the way to where you are now. It was that power that placed you in The Midnight Rider the night Selander Ryan found you. You have been looking at your turning all wrong, Danni."

I shook my head, trying to clear it. "I don't understand. If I had some sort of psychic energy protecting me, why would it put me in danger?"

"It didn't put you in danger. It led you to your soulmate and put you where you needed to be to become the weapon you had to become in order to end the evil that has hunted you for centuries."

"To end—you mean Selander Ryan? What do you mean by becoming a weapon to end him? Rider already killed him, and he's still out there terrorizing us."

"Rider can't end his brother's reign of terror," Auntie Mo said in a tone that implied that much should have been obvious. "You have to end it, Danni. You are the one with the power to do so. You just have to embrace it, know it, grow it, and use it."

I took a deep breath and raked my hand through my hair, processing this new revelation. "You almost make it sound like I'm, I don't know, destined or something."

"That's because you are."

My heart immediately started racing, sweat broke out on my upper lip, and nausea rolled in my stomach as I listed to the side.

"Danni." Auntie Mo called my name sharply as my hands slipped from hers.

I caught myself and took a deep breath as I wiped the sweat from my face with a clammy hand. "I'm all right. I just got a little woozy there."

"You're a little green. I didn't think your kind got green and woozy."

"Yeah, well, I'm all kinds of special." I wiped my palms on my pant legs. "I've been feeling kind of sick lately, ever since the visions started. I've had some blackouts and fainting spells, and after I made myself see a vision, I threw up. I was planning to come see you soon anyway because of that. My nurse thinks I might be feeling this way because the visions are overwhelming me. Does that seem right to you? Did you faint a lot when you first started having visions?"

Auntie Mo frowned as she shook her head. "I've always had this ability, so I can't quite recall my first visions. I've been having them since I could walk, maybe even before. Sometimes, after a strong one, I may need to rest for a while or I may have a headache, but I don't think I've ever blacked out or grown faint. I've definitely never thrown up. That said, I am a psychic. You are something else entirely. Receiving visions may affect you differently than mine affect me."

I sulked. "Damn. I was really hoping you could tell me that this was just some temporary thing, and I'd overcome it after a little time passes."

"I'm sorry, honey. I can't tell you why you're having such a hard time with the visions, but it could be temporary. Whether it is or not, you're a strong woman. I have no doubt you will grow accustomed to your powers and any side effects they may cause." She reached forward and patted my hand. The second time her fingers came down on my hand, she froze, her entire body going stiff, and her eyes grew very round as they stared straight ahead, looking right at me but seeming to see something much farther away.

"Auntie Mo?" I pulled my hand out from under hers and still, she did not move. "Auntie Mo."

I waved my hand in front of her face, and when that didn't get any reaction, I snapped my fingers three times right in front of her eyes. She didn't even blink. I clapped my hands in her face, and she remained a statue. Just as I thought she might have had a stroke and opened my mouth to yell for Rider, she spoke.

"You're all alone on the battlefield. Fear will bring pain and suffering, but love will not fail. A great change is upon you. When you find yourself in the darkness, keep going. Your blessing is on the other side."

Auntie Mo blinked and jerked back. She shook her head, frowning.

"What the hell was that?" I heard the shrill tone in my voice. I'd never seen Auntie Mo behave like that. "You were like a statue, and what was all that nonsense? Was that a vision? Is that how you get them?"

She blinked a few times, still frowning as confusion settled over her features, and nodded. "My visions come to me like that, yes, or in a dream. This one was strange. Pieces were missing."

"Pieces? What do you mean, pieces?" I replayed her words over in my mind and tried to envision what she must have seen, but couldn't. As usual, she'd spoken in a riddle, leaving me little to work with so I couldn't imagine what she'd been describing, let alone try to understand what pieces might have been missing. "Auntie Mo, I didn't understand any of what you said except for that bit about me being alone on a battlefield. Did you see me fighting alone? Rider would never let me go into a fight alone." My heart slammed to a complete stop. Rider, Daniel, or even Jake, for that matter, would never let me run into a fight by myself. The only way I could even imagine myself ending up alone against an enemy was if something happened to them.

"Auntie Mo, what did you see in that vision? Did I lose anyone?"

Her eyes were grave as she took my hands in hers and held them tight. "I could not see what is coming, only sense its power. You and your loved ones will suffer greatly, but you will only lose those you let go. Hold them tight, Danni. You need each other, even when everything is broken and the suffering tears you inside out. Hold on and focus on your blessing."

CHAPTER FOURTEEN

"Daniel found it."

I looked over to see Rider's head tilted to the side as he drove, able to maintain his focus and speak telepathically at the same time. Daniel must have checked in with the tech team or else returned to The Midnight Rider and reported the news to them. Had he reported directly to Rider, he probably would have used the phone. He wasn't big on unnecessary telepathic communication. We were both still adapting to the ability. Other people's voices inside your own head were hard to get used to.

"Where is it?" I asked.

"Someplace called Bitter Creek in Alabama."

"Alabama?" I felt my eyebrows shoot up. "And Ramson is there now?"

I waited a moment, feeling Rider's power as he continued to communicate telepathically. I knew the conversation was over when the thickness in the air dissipated.

"Daniel is still there, observing from a high point. He reported back that he could sense paranormal energy inside when he did a low flyover, but he's gone up to observe from a high point, hopefully high enough that

Ramson can't sense him. Daniel may be a big, fire-breathing dragon, but we don't know what powers Ramson possesses or if he's turned any other pranic vampires, so he's been ordered to keep his distance. He'll observe for a while, but I've ordered him to return by daybreak so he can rest before we go in tomorrow night."

"We?" Jake had been leaning forward since Rider had announced the news, and he now angled his head sideways to take in Rider fully.

"We as in us. Our side. Whatever. I know I'm sidelined on this one." Rider said the words, but everything in his tone told how badly he didn't want to mean them.

I reached over and squeezed his hand, opened my mouth to tell him I wished he could go with us, that we'd take down the cult leader and find his blood donor together, but Auntie Mo's cryptic words haunted me, filling me with dread. If I was going to be left alone on a battlefield, then I didn't want Rider anywhere near me when I went in to fight anyone. I didn't want to risk losing him. It was bad enough risking the loss of any of my friends and loved ones, but losing Rider? There was no coming back from that loss.

"Is he positive he found the right church?" I said instead. "Mike and Cliff were from here, and the three idiots were hunting here. I thought the church would have been in Kentucky or Indiana, somewhere close."

"Alabama isn't even a full day's drive," Jake said from the back seat and I looked back to see him fooling with his cell phone. "Man, this Bitter Creek is a serious boondocks. Rural, not very populated, and remote. A perfect location for a cult of crazies to hole up and not be bothered. According to Google Maps, it's a six-hour drive from Louisville, so it's not that strange that Ramson would send a team here to find women. Grab them, bind them, knock them unconscious, and it's an easy trip back."

"A rural area like that wouldn't have a lot of women to grab either, especially not sex workers, who Ramson seems to like snatching," Rider said, navigating the SUV closer to The Midnight Rider. "Daniel is sure it's the right location. According to my techs, he found the tree you saw in your vision. He said it was massive and looked like it was stretching its arms out to ward off intruders right at a fork in the road. The dirt road to the right of it led right to the church. He could see the atrium glass clearly from above and the white tent in the center."

"That's it then." I stared out the window, watching the buildings pass as we neared the bar. I'd been so ready to find the church and go in, guns blazing. Metaphorically speaking, of course. I hadn't been taught how to shoot yet. Rider kept mentioning needing to train me, but secretly, I thought he and Daniel were afraid to put a gun in my hands. I just wasn't sure if it was because they thought I'd end up accidentally shooting my own foot off or because they were afraid I'd shoot one of their testicles off. But now, I wasn't nearly as enthusiastic about kicking the church doors down and putting a stop to whatever Ramson was doing.

"Are you okay?" Rider asked as he navigated the SUV down the alley that ran behind The Midnight Rider and pressed the button on the remote clipped to his visor, opening the garage door as the SUV in front of us with Hank at the wheel continued on. The SUV behind us would wait until we were safely inside the garage with the door lowered behind us before they continued on as well, parking in a nearby garage that looked like it was available for public parking but Rider had reserved two levels for his employees. "I thought you'd be raising a fuss about having to wait until tomorrow night to go in."

I thought about my response as we pulled into the garage, the lights coming on automatically to light the way for Rider to park between his Ferrari and motorcycle, knowing I needed to choose my words carefully if I didn't want to set off alarm bells in Rider's mind. I might not have been as eager to go after Ramson, but that didn't mean I wasn't going to. If Rider knew what Auntie Mo had told me, though, if he knew there was a chance of me finding myself alone in the middle of a battle, he'd never let me leave the building, let alone go after a pranic vampire who needed to be taken down.

"Jake just said it was a six-hour drive to Bitter Creek. If we left now, it would be dawn when we got in place to attack. That might work for Jake and the other guys, but I'd be pretty useless. Even if dawn doesn't immediately take me under, it zaps enough of my energy to make the concept of attacking at sunrise pretty foolish on my part."

Rider opened his mouth to reply, probably about to remind me he could just have Rihanna flash us to the church now that it had been found, but closed it, seeming to think better of it.

"If we're not going in until tomorrow night after resting up and fueling, why don't we get in some practice on your luring ability," Jake suggested as we exited the vehicle. This time, he'd waited for Rider to come around and open my door.

I nodded. If I was going to eventually find myself alone on a battlefield, I would need to make the most of every weapon I had at my disposal. "Are we waiting for Ginger in case I need her, uh, assistance drawing the lure back in? I assume she's on her way back here now that Daniel has found the church. There's no reason for her to keep up the sex worker charade."

Rider opened the door for us to enter the back area of the building, and we stepped inside to be immediately greeted by Kutya. The big pup had been chowing down on kibble in the bowl we kept in the back of the room under the hook his leash hung from, but he put his appetite on pause to race over to us and start spinning in excited circles.

"That has got to be the perkiest scary-looking dog I've ever come across," Jake said as Rider and I gave Kutya pets and scratches, knowing the dog would never stop spinning if we didn't.

"He's still a baby," Jadyn said from where she stood at the side of the staircase leading up to Rider's private quarters. "He's all energy and youth right now. And he's not scary-looking. He's just big."

"Big is an understatement," Jake said. "When he's full grown, he'll probably be able to take out a hellhound on his own."

Kutya plopped down and rolled onto his back to have his belly rubbed.

"If he ever stops doing that," Jake added.

"He's a pet, not an attack dog," I told him.

"I noticed."

"Jadyn, can you watch him until Hank parks and comes in?" Rider asked, standing from the crouched position he'd been in. "Danni and I will be downstairs training and it's best he not follow us down there for this. Hank can take him for a walk once he finishes his kibble."

"Sure," Jadyn answered with a smile, undoubtedly imagining the look on Hank's face when he discovered he'd arrived back just in time to shovel Kutya's massive poop, which was inevitable after the big pup scarfed down a bowl of kibble.

I patted Kutya's belly and stood, signaling his belly rub was over and he needed to finish his meal. He looked up at me with pleading eyes, but after a moment of me shaking my head at him, he conceded belly rub time was over with a huff, rolled upright, and lifted himself to his paws to go back to his food bowl.

"Thanks, Jadyn." Rider placed his hand along the small of my back and led me into the stairwell, Jake following behind us.

"Ginger has been notified and is on her way back, but we won't be waiting on her," Rider said as we took the stairs down to the sublevels.

"You can't rely on having a woman around to grab and use to force your succubus power down," Jake said, sounding as if he was fighting the urge to laugh, "and I think Ginger is still insulted that you vomited after kissing her."

I ignored his obvious amusement as we reached the first sublevel and continued down. I'd assumed we would practice my ability to lure in the interrogation room or the training room, where I often sparred with Nannette or Daniel, but we'd passed that level. We were headed to the lower level and the only room I could think of on that level where we might practice would be the room with the cells. The dungeon, as I'd started thinking of it. Where we'd trapped and killed the krackling. Once we reached the lower level, Rider placed his hand over the panel and led us inside.

"So, how exactly is this going to go?" I asked as we headed toward the back of the level, passing the vampires and shifters posted throughout the space, protecting who knew what. I'd never been given a thorough tour of the lowest level of The Midnight Rider.

"You're going to lure your target and once you have him on the hook, you're going to let him go," Jake said, as if the answer were obvious.

"Okay, but how do I do that?"

"The same way you pulled your power back in the interrogation room when it was about to rise," the slayer answered. "You've done it already, Danni. You can do it again."

I sighed, wishing I had Jake's confidence in myself. Unfortunately, the fact that I'd done it once before meant nothing to me. Once wasn't enough. Once could always be a fluke.

Two burly vampires I didn't know but had seen around the building before stood guard on either side of the door leading into the dungeon area. They nodded at Rider in greeting and glared at Jake, clearly not fans of the slayer. It was a perfectly understandable reaction to the presence of a slayer, but by now, one would think Jake would get a free pass.

Despite the guards' presence outside the door, Rider still had to place his palm over the panel next to it to gain entrance, allowing us inside. We stepped into the large room that housed a group of cells to the left and a wide open space to the right, and I was surprised by just how clean it was. I'd known it had been cleaned after the carnage that had occurred the last time we'd been inside it, but given the sheer amount of blood and viscera that had coated the room, I still expected a stain or two at minimum. The krackling had eviscerated the radio DJ who had summoned it, leaving chunks of her along the walls, floor, and ceiling, and the scenery hadn't improved once it had gone after us.

I ran my fingertip over the wall. It came back spotless, not even a trace of dust. Even the inside of the cell that Danielle Muething had been gutted and torn apart in appeared squeaky clean with a polished floor and fresh sheets on the cot she'd tried in vain to hide under once her supernatural attack dog had come for her. "It's amazing how spotless this room is now after what happened here."

"Babe, you haven't seen half of what has happened in this space," Rider said. "And nothing gets a room spotless like a witch's cleaning spell."

"How much money have you paid out to Rihanna?" I asked, thinking of all the times I'd seen him forking over several large bills to the sassy witch who was always more than giddy to be called upon. I would be giddy too if getting called upon meant an easy thousand or more just for uttering a few words and flicking my wrist.

"I make it a habit to never think about the amount of money that goes from my pocket into hers," Rider answered. "I'm a strong man, but dwelling on that number could bring me to tears."

I rolled my eyes and grinned, knowing better than to take him seriously. This was the same man who'd offered to buy me a house and pay all my bills when I'd wanted to find a job. This was also the man who'd declared my blood donor a business expense that fell under my employment and refused to allow me to pay for my own apartment, since that was where she was living. I barely even got to spend any of the money he paid me to work security for him because he had the guards stationed at my apartment forward my bills directly to him and if we were together, there was no point trying to pay for something myself. I had no idea how much money Rider had, but he certainly didn't seem concerned with the thought of running out of it.

"So, you said Danni needs to feel safe so she can be comfortable enough to really focus on her ability," Rider said, turning toward Jake. "How about we have her in a cell where she can be assured no one can get to her no matter what, and the target can be out here outside the bars? Once she gets through that enough times that pulling her luring ability back in becomes easy, we can level up to having her do it with no bars between her and her targets."

Jake folded his arms and scanned the area before nodding his head. "Yeah, that sounds like a good way to start. You good with that, Danni?"

I looked over at the cells and wiped my clammy hands on my jeans before shoving them into my back pockets. "Um, yeah. As long as you guys don't leave me locked in there, and you're sure there are no chunks of Danielle Muething left in there."

"Who?" Jake asked.

"That woman who summoned the krackling."

"Oh yeah." He looked over at the cell. "Looks like she got all mopped up."

My stomach did a somersault, and I pulled my hands free of my pockets to cover it. Rider tracked the motion and frowned. "Are you still feeling nauseous? We don't have to do this now if you are."

"No, I'm fine," I assured him. "I think that imagery just icked me out a little."

"You're half vampire, half succubus," Jake reminded me. "Blood and violence are your thing. Nothing should gross you out anymore, except maybe kittens and rainbows. Possibly babies."

I thought back to my days working in an office environment, forced to endure the photographs of chubby, goofy-looking babies proud parents and grandparents used to force on anyone who couldn't get away quick enough or the stories that seemed to always involve spit-up, poop, or other disgusting liquids. "Yeah, babies can be pretty gross."

Jake grinned and gestured toward the open cell closest to us. "Go get comfortable and we can get started." To Rider, he said, "Who are we bringing in for her to lure?"

I'd started toward the cell, but stopped and turned. "I thought I was practicing on you two?"

"Your lure affects me to some degree, but not enough to really give you much of a challenge. Given the bond you and Rider have as sire and fledgling, and his partial immunity against your succubus powers, he's not the most challenging choice, either. While we have this cell handy and you have both of us here watching your back, ready to step in should there be any hiccups, let's put you up against someone you should be able to put the full whammy on and see how you do drawing that much power back in once it's been released."

My stomach did another topsy-turvy, and I looked at Rider. "Who am I supposed to be luring?"

Rider seemed to think about it for a moment before he said, "Tony."

"Tony?" The high-pitched squeak in my voice hurt my own ears, so I wasn't surprised when both men winced and looked at me. "You can't have me lure Tony."

"Why not?"

"Why not? Because it's Tony!"

Rider just stared at me, not getting what seemed so obvious to me.

"Tony is... *Tony*."

"Yes," he said, "and I am me and you are you. That's how that usually works."

I swallowed hard, fighting against nausea. My body warmed even as my skin grew chilled with tiny beads of sweat. The room spun.

"Hey Jake, can you step outside, give Danni and me a minute?"

"Sure," the slayer said, and moved toward the door.

I felt Rider's power pulse before he added, "and don't get any ideas about wandering. I've instructed the guards to shoot you if you step more than four feet away from the door or touch anything that doesn't belong to you."

Jake chuckled. "Got it."

Rider waited until the slayer was outside and the door closed behind him before he placed his hand along my lower back and walked me over to the closest cell. He lowered me to a sitting position on the cot and kneeled on the floor in front of me before taking my hands in his.

"Jake and I had some time to talk while you were with Auntie Mo. I know you're afraid that your succubus side is going to be too much for you to control one day, and it's going to get what it wants, what you may not want. I can understand that fear, but be honest with me. Which do you fear the most? What might happen if your succubus power causes you to do something you will regret later, or how you think I may react if that day ever comes?"

I lowered my gaze to my lap, unable to continue meeting his. "Does it matter when both things are so horrible?"

"Yes. It matters very much." Rider released one of my hands to tip my chin up, forcing me to meet his gaze again. "You've been wanting to know more about your succubus abilities, to learn how to use them as a weapon, so why are you hesitant to do it now?"

I took a deep breath, considering my answer. "Talking about doing something and actually doing it are two different things. I don't want to use my succubus abilities. Ever. I don't like them. I don't like anything about succubi. I hate the man who gave me these abilities, I hate that part of him is now part of me, and I hate that now that I'm in the best relationship of my life, with the man I love more than anyone on this earth, the man I will always love more than I can ever put into words, I have this thing inside me that can make me lose it all. I don't *want* to know how to use whatever abilities I have. I *need* to know how to use them. I need to use them so they don't use me and take away all that I love."

"That will never happen." Rider used his thumbs to wipe away the tears that had escaped my eyes and rose from the floor to sit next to me on the cot, one of my hands in his, our fingers intertwined. "I love you. That means I love every part of you, no matter what happens."

I gave him a look. "You don't have to lie to make me feel better. I know you would prefer I not be this sex-starved thing that can't be trusted to be around men unless they have syringes filled with something that can knock me out so I don't cheat on you."

"Let's clear something up right now," he said, his tone firm. "There is a difference between you cheating on me and you having sex with someone because your succubus side craves it and overpowers you. I won't lie to you and say that it won't bother me at all if that happens. I'm in love with you and we are together in a committed relationship. It's human nature to not want to share the one you love with others and despite our fangs and other gifts and curses, we have that much humanity left in us. Of course it would bother me, but it wouldn't make me stop loving you. It wouldn't destroy us. We would get past it and continue on as we are now. What we have is forever."

"You say that like it's so simple." I looked down at our joined hands and bit back my anger. It wasn't fair to Rider to lash out at him for lying, not when he was trying to make me feel better, and he might have even believed the words he'd said, but I knew better. "Every man who works for you is terrified of falling prey to my succubus side. Not just because they fear what I could do to them, that I could suck out their soul, but because they fear what you would do to them. You've told me yourself you would kill any man who touches me, and you make sure any man assigned to watch or work with me while not in your presence has a syringe to knock me out before I can jump them. You can't stand the thought of me being with another man, and I can't blame you one bit because I can't stand the thought of you being with another woman. I love you with everything I have, but if you were to have sex with another woman now, that would destroy us. Just like it would destroy us if I had sex with another man. That's just the way it is."

"Danni, if I had sex with another woman now, it would be because I chose to. Of course that would destroy us because I would be hurting you by going outside our union for my sexual needs. That is cheating. Yes, if you had sex with another man because you wanted him—not your succubus side, but you—that would be cheating. I couldn't forgive that no matter how much I love you, but I would never hold it against you if your succubus's thirst results in sex with another man, because that's all it would be. It would be a feeding. It would never be lovemaking. It would never be what we do. If something happens and you have to draw upon your power to stay alive and that power is too strong for you to draw back in, do you really think I would leave you because of an accident that saved your life? You have to know you mean more to me than that."

I swiped at the fresh batch of tears cascading down my cheeks, sniffing hard to keep from turning into a sobbing mess. I wanted to believe the words Rider said so adamantly, but no matter how badly he might want to mean them, it just wasn't logical for a man with Rider's temper and jealousy, or his controlling nature, to accept it so easily if I slipped and my succubus abilities got away from me. He'd never look at me the same way again, and I couldn't blame him for that.

"Danni, please believe me. I love you. The way I feel about you is far more powerful than however I would feel if there was an accident with your power. I swear it."

I took in another deep breath, mostly to hold back the threat of a choking sob, and forced myself to meet his gaze. "I know you believe that and you really want it to be true, but Rider, if you truly felt that way, you wouldn't be so on top of my blood diet. You wouldn't have Nannette studying me, searching for ways to help me control my succubus side. You wouldn't have had such fear in your eyes the first time I said I wanted to know more about my succubus powers. You wouldn't insist on being right there with me in interrogations when men are involved, or do the venom checks before I drink from a man. You wouldn't pass out syringes full of a knockout concoction to your employees like candy. You don't want me using my succubus power because you know what could happen if I lose control of it, and that's a risk you can't take. Because whether you can bring yourself to admit it or not, you know it would destroy us. You know you couldn't get past it. If you could, it wouldn't be such a huge source of your own fear."

"Is that what you think? That's why you think I'm so protective of you and why I didn't want you using your luring ability in interrogation? Because of my fear of how it would affect me?"

"Of course I do, and I'm not mad at you for feeling that way, Rider. I can't blame you for not wanting me to be with anyone else. I'm supposed to be yours."

"You are mine. This is mine." He placed his hand over my heart. "Everything in here is mine, and I am beyond thankful for that. As long as no one else has your heart, you haven't cheated on me. Your heart is mine, and only because you gave it to me. Your body is yours. I don't own it and I never will. When you share it with me, that means everything to me, because you choose to share it with me. To make something with me that is ours and ours alone. I wasn't with you during the Bloom. Not the real you. I know what it's like to be with you, Danni, and I know what it's like to be with your succubus's thirst. I also know how devastated you were to know what happened during that time, how awful you felt about what you'd done, and that was with me. It would be a million times worse for you to come out from under the succubus's control and know what you'd done with someone else."

"Rider."

"No. I need you to hear me." He held my face in both hands and looked directly into my eyes. "You are the most important thing in my life. In all my centuries, I have never cared more about or feared losing anything more than I have loved and feared losing you. Yes, I am extremely overprotective and controlling, and I have taken precautions to ensure your succubus's thirst doesn't escape you. I do fear you using your luring ability or biting into anyone without knowing if you have venom in your bite. I fear you losing control, Danni, but not because of how it would make me feel. No matter how bad it would feel for me, I'd get over it. It's you I worry won't because I still remember the night you found out about the Bloom. I remember the anguish in your eyes and what you called yourself."

I remembered too. I suppose whore was a harsh word, but that was what I'd felt like upon hearing I would go into a haze of lust, completely consumed by my need to fornicate with and suck the soul out of any man within my grasp.

"Don't think that my protecting you from a possible slip has anything to do with me keeping you from doing something I couldn't forgive you for. If an accident happens, I will forgive you. My biggest fear about that whole situation is that you wouldn't forgive yourself."

I tore myself away from him and stood, leaving the cell to get some distance, but when I turned, he was right there behind me. I shook my head, wanting to believe him, but knowing I couldn't. For one thing, it was just too hard to fathom him still loving me if my succubus side won. For another, it wasn't fair for him to be that wonderful. If I failed and hurt him in that way, I wouldn't deserve that much love. I wouldn't be worth it.

"If you still don't believe me, think about where we are and why. You're training to call upon your succubus power and use it. I know it can go wrong, but here we are, because you and Jake are right. It can be useful, and you do need to learn to control it so it won't control you. You have lived in fear of losing control ever since you were turned. If this gives you a sense of being in control, if it calms your fears even a little, I want that for you."

"I could fail."

"You could. I don't need to tell you to be careful when it comes to calling on your succubus power, because I know you'll be too scared of losing control not to be careful. I just need you to know that if you do lose control, you don't have to fear losing me. I'm not going anywhere."

He pulled me against his chest and wrapped his arms around me before resting his head on mine. "I wish I had succeeded in redirecting your turn or better yet, protected you from my brother altogether that night. I wish I could take the succubus's thirst out of you, but I can't. Sometimes I can't even force you to obey my command as your sire because that part of you fights my power. All I can do is help you deal with the hand you've been dealt and love you with enough ferocity to make up for when you don't love yourself enough."

He raised his head and pulled back enough to allow him to look me in the eye, not releasing me. "If you want me to help you fight your succubus power and keep it locked away, I'll do whatever I can to help you do that. If you want to learn how to use it and get better control over it, we'll bring Jake and Tony in here and train. It's your call. I'll do whatever you want. Just tell me what you need."

His offer projected an image of Tony approaching me, his eyes dilated in lust, and a wave of nausea rolled over me so hard I had to grip Rider's arms as my knees buckled.

"Whoa." Noticing my reaction, Rider's arms tightened around me. He peered down into my face, studying me, his eyes filled with concern. "If you're sick, you don't have to do any training tonight. You can just rest."

"No." I shook my head. I needed to learn how to control my succubus power and there was no better time to do that than when Jake was with us. As a slayer, the man could handle anything my succubus side might throw out there, and he'd already talked me down once. True, it may have just been a fluke, but there was only one way to find out. Rider was putting my needs and my feelings ahead of his own. I owed it to him to learn to control my succubus power, to do my best to avoid putting us in a situation where we had to find out if he could really do what he'd just promised and meant with his whole heart. But I couldn't do it with Tony.

"Danni, you don't have to do this if it's too much for you."

"It's not. I can do it." I took a breath, settled my nerves, which were not doing my stomach any favors, and stepped back out of Rider's hold, showing him I could stand on my own two feet. "I want to learn what my powers are and control them, not run from them, and I'm fine to train now."

"You're sure? Because you were green again for a moment there. You shouldn't push yourself too hard if you're still recovering from forcing that vision earlier."

"I'm sure, and I've recovered from that enough to train, but I can't practice luring Tony without turning green just thinking about it."

Rider's brow knit in a frown. "Why? I thought you'd be

comfortable with Tony. He's someone you know, someone you know doesn't desire you so you aren't screwing with his emotions, and someone you trust. You do trust him, don't you?"

I thought about it and realized I did trust Tony. He was cranky and growly, and acted as if I was a burr in his backside, but I knew that underneath all that, he gave a crap if I lived or died. He would have my back in a fight, even if he blamed me for causing the fight. That was just the kind of guy Tony was, and what he had done for Ginger in the bar showed how good his heart was even if he didn't care to broadcast his good guy status.

"I do trust him, and that's part of the problem. You're right that I know him," I continued as Rider frowned deeper, genuinely confused. "I know he is definitely not attracted to me, and I know I irritate him to death, but he'd still fight to protect me, risking his life if necessary. How can I repay him for that by screwing with his libido, luring him when I know damn well I'm the last woman he'd want to be with, even if I wasn't with you?"

"I'm sure you're not the last—"

"I've heard the man praying under his breath for the strength not to strangle me."

"In all fairness, you have that effect on me too, and I'm crazy about you." Rider smiled when I shot him my best unamused look, and kissed my forehead. "All right. I can bring in someone you don't know at all if you're actually more comfortable with that."

I thought about it for a moment and nodded. "I am."

"Okay then. And you're positive you feel up to this right now?"

"I'm sure."

He nodded, and I felt his power expand to fill the room, signaling that he was calling in my mystery prey, before he wiped away the last traces of wetness from my cheeks and called for Jake to rejoin us.

It was time to summon my succubus side and pray I

didn't give it too much power.

CHAPTER FIFTEEN

My prey for the training session turned out to be Macon, the new bartender I hadn't met yet. He'd been working out of state in one of the many bars Rider owned, and like Tony, he was versatile, meaning he could tend bar or crack heads, whatever the situation called for. Unlike Tony, I doubted he ate his foes. Macon was a vampire.

His skin was a deep brown with just enough crinkling around the eyes to show he'd been at least middle-aged when he'd been turned. It was hard to tell the exact age since physical features were often enhanced during the turning. For all I knew, he could have been wrinkled like a Shar-Pei before receiving the blood exchange that had given him immortality.

He stood around five feet, eight inches tall and, despite his overall slim build, his upper arms and shoulders held a great deal of muscle. Those muscles bunched under his black T-shirt as his entire body stiffened and his hands fisted at his sides. Head bowed, jaw clenched, he fought my control as he'd been instructed to do.

"You have him on the hook again," Jake said softly from where he and Rider stood just outside the cell they'd locked me in for my own safety and peace of mind. "Now try to focus on only him before you reel him in."

Yes, because the fish analogy would help me pretend the man standing twelve feet away from me wasn't some poor guy I was using for practice.

"I am focusing on only him."

"Your eyes might be focused on only him, but your lure is giving me a really happy tingle, hon. Dude, chill," Jake added after Rider emitted a low growl, then continued instructing me. "You need to focus all that energy on just Macon."

That's what I thought I was doing, so I wasn't sure how to proceed. My hands were sweating, my neck was stiff, and pain had spread between my temples about ten minutes earlier.

"Focus, Danni. Direct all your energy toward Macon and tune out everything else, especially us."

"That might be easier for her to do if you'd quit yapping at her," Rider said.

"I'm not yapping, I'm instructing. That's what one does when training someone. How about you focus on controlling all that growling?"

"Guys!" I snapped, silencing them before they could make my headache worse. "And he's got a point about the growling, Rider. I lose my focus every time you do it."

"Sorry," he muttered, and judging by the grunt that came right after, the apology had brought a smirk out of Jake, which earned him an elbow to the side or something worse. "You're doing great."

Sure I was. I'd baited the hook, so to speak, multiple times. That part was easy. Letting Macon off that hook was getting harder with each release, which was the opposite of what I'd expected. Luring and letting go did not get easier with practice. At least not yet. However, I had yet to affect only Macon, and until I could learn how to focus on only him, I couldn't consider myself remotely successful.

Apparently taking Rider's criticism to heart, Jake didn't

offer any more instruction as I stood staring at Macon, holding him in that tranced state. I didn't need him to tell me I was still affecting him, though. I could sense the desire of every man in the room, as well as the energy Jake and Rider put out while resisting the pull of my lure.

Thinking of that energy, I realized I'd overlooked something that should have been obvious. Power was energy. I picked up on the men's energies without even trying because they were different from mine. I didn't need to focus to feel them. My lure had its own distinct energy too. I only needed to focus on it.

I closed my eyes and sorted through the different energy signatures in the room until I found the one that came from me hidden among the male energies. Once I felt it, I could visualize it, and I did. Focusing on the energy itself instead of just staring at the man I wanted to control, I opened my eyes and visualized that energy contracting until it became a ribbon of smoky burgundy color, and I pushed that energy into Macon where I imagined it expanding to fill his body, placing him completely under my control.

"Good job, Danni." Jake's voice seemed lighter than it had at any point he'd been training me, and I knew it was because I'd focused all of my luring ability on Macon, relieving him of having to fight the pull of it himself. "Reel him in."

I focused on drawing Macon to me, much like crooking my finger, and his stiff body relaxed, no longer fighting against my hold. He moved forward and so did the front of his black pants, tenting over the erection straining to escape.

Go back, go back, I thought, stepping backward, although I was relatively safe and out-of-bounds inside the cell. I was just luring the man, bringing him to me. I'd done it five times already and all he'd done was move toward me in a daze. I hadn't intended to give the man an erection and make the situation so awkward my skin suddenly flamed with embarrassment. I hadn't even injected the man with venom.

"We told him what he was here for and he was okay with it, Danni. You're not doing anything wrong," Jake assured me and for a moment, I wondered if mind-reading was one of the slayer's superpowers. "Now focus on making him stand still."

I hadn't taken my eyes off Macon, but my focus was still divided between him, the jumble of thoughts racing in my head that bordered on panic, and the barely restrained possessive anger I sensed spilling out of Rider to fill the room like a dark, menacing cloud.

Macon reached the bars and tried to keep going, one hand reaching through to grab for me. Rider's power filled the room, there was a scuffle and deep-voiced words exchanged, then I became aware of Jake yelling at me to breathe and realized I'd been hyperventilating while staring like a deer in headlights at the zombie-like man baring his fangs while trying to pry apart the cell bars to get to me.

Breathe, Danni. Rider spoke directly into my mind. *Listen to Jake and breathe.*

His voice was strained, and I knew he was fighting to control himself from tearing into Macon, which did nothing to ease my panic, but I tried to focus on breathing, remembering how that had kept my succubus side from rising during interrogation. I may have let the succubus out of its cage to practice luring, but I needed to still keep it on its leash.

I focused on each breath, attempted to slow each inhale and exhale as I tensed, waiting for Rider to lose his grip on his own emotions and tear poor Macon to pieces. Or for Macon to find the strength to make it through those bars and pounce on me like he wanted to. How his pants hadn't burst open yet was beyond me.

"Slow your breathing," Jake said more firmly than before. "Tune out everything else and calm yourself. Take control."

I tried. I tried so hard a tear slipped from my eye. A moment later, the tension in the room eased as the dark, menacing energy that had been thickening faded away. I gasped in a mouthful of fresh air and savored it before expelling it slowly, visualized sending it into Macon, relaxing him, and just in the nick of time because he looked like he was about to start humping the bars and there was no way I was ever going to be able to face the man again if I made him do that.

Release, I thought, willing myself to let the man's mind and whatever else of his I held in the grip of my power go.

No, that voice that had argued with me in the interrogation room responded. *Enough teasing.*

Shit. I'd pissed off my succubus side. As if I needed that problem.

I let you out to play, I reminded it. *Now it's time to take a break. You won't be locked up forever.*

You expect me to believe you? You promised me blood.

I felt my face pull into a frown, wondering what it was walking about. I hadn't... Oh. In interrogation. I'd promised it blood when Jake talked me down. *I didn't break that promise. I told you we would get blood and we will. We did. We've been drinking blood.*

I want new blood. I want to spill blood.

All of this is preparation, practice. We need to rest for tomorrow night, and there will be blood. There will be rivers of blood.

Promise?

I promise, I assured the voice, fully aware of Jake watching me, sensing my internal struggle as my body shook under the pressure of containing the bloodthirsty, ferocious beast inside me. *But only if we let this man go now.*

The voice didn't respond, but as I concentrated on Macon, I sensed it slowly pulling back, loosening its grip on him as it drifted back into the cage inside of me and closed itself in, where it would wait to be fed.

I fell to my knees the moment the lure released Macon, and the vampire stumbled back. He looked down at himself, noticed the deflating erection and paled, his eyes bugged out as he scanned the room in terror.

"Relax, vamp," Jake said, a hint of amusement in his tone. "Count Snarly left before he could lose his shit. You're safe, but you might want to stay out of his way for a while. Definitely don't make eye contact with him."

Macon nodded his head, then looked at me and stilled, his cheeks flaming with red color before he ducked his head and turned away from me to make his escape.

Jake unlocked the cell door and stepped inside. "How are you doing, champ?"

"I don't feel like much of a champ." I muttered before I let my body topple over and stretch out on the hard floor. That lasted all of a second since my testosterone-deprived body had chilled into a frigid iceberg. I sat back up and wrapped my arms around the knees I'd pulled up to rest my chin on.

"I can hear your teeth chattering," Jake said, sitting next to me. He wrapped his arm around me, pulling me against his side.

"Jake, no!" Terror slammed into me and I tried to pull away, knowing why I was so cold and what my succubus side wanted to end that discomfort.

"Relax." Jake's arms tightened around me, tucking me in against him more firmly until my face was buried in the crook of his neck. The most dangerous place a succubus's mouth could be. "I'm about the only person you can practice this with safely. You can control your impulse to bite."

The hell I could, I thought as my fangs lowered on their own. "Jake…"

"Breathe, Danni. In and out, nice and slow. Just breathe, and focus on the warmth slowly spreading around you." As he spoke, he rubbed his hands down my back and arms, leaving his warmth everywhere he touched. "You don't have to kill for it. You just have to be patient and wait for it. You can have all my body heat you want without taking my soul. You can compromise with the beast inside you."

He continued rubbing his hands over me and I focused on the sensation of his heat following his touch until my heart rate slowed, and my breath with it. I relaxed my hands, not realizing until then that I'd been gripping the man's shoulders for dear life, and my fangs slowly went back into my gums.

"Feel better now?"

I nodded, my face still in the crook of his neck, but I didn't feel any panic, any fear of hurting someone I cared about. "It's not happy with me. It wants blood and thinks I've been teasing it, taunting it with a meal just to yank it away at the last minute."

"Sex demons are very insatiable, impatient creatures," Jake said, his breath tickling my ear. "But you are half vampire. While vampires can also be bloodthirsty, insatiable beasts, the mindset and value system of the person you were before turning goes a long way in determining your vampire side's temperament. And you are loyal to Rider, so despite having two sires, you're going to lean his way. The man can be a ruthless, cold-blooded killer, but from what I've heard and seen of him, it's never without good cause. Lean on your vampire side when the succubus side gets too demanding and you'll be fine. You come from very strong stock, Danni. And you are stronger than you realize. As long as you don't give in to fear, you can control your hunger. All of your hunger."

He released me and stood. "Speaking of hunger, let's get some blood into you. You just went through one hell of a workout."

His warmth had chased away the chill and the exhaustion that had sent me crashing to my knees after sending the succubus power back into its cage, and now I could focus on more than just my thirst and lethargy. "He left. I knew he couldn't take this. No matter what he says, how badly he wants to believe it, Rider can't handle me being able to lure men. He won't be able to handle it if I…"

Jake crouched in front of me. "That man wasn't growling at you, Danni. He was growling at Macon because he viewed him as a threat. If Nyla was the one in this cell and some other man was lusting after her, trying to get to her, I'd kill the bastard. That's just the need a man has to protect the woman he loves. He didn't touch him though. He fought against the animalistic desire to do so and he let you do what you needed to do, and yes, when he saw he was distracting you from learning what you needed to learn, he left. Don't take his leaving as something that it wasn't. He left to help you focus on protecting yourself instead of focusing on what you were picking up from him. He will always do what is best for you, no matter what happens. Now, get off your whiny little ass and come grab a drink with me."

***

I couldn't sense Rider anywhere in the building, which had me concerned, especially when Jake and I stepped through the back door leading out into the bar and I saw Hank talking to Tony as he guzzled a beer.

I walked over to him, Jake at my side, and didn't bother waiting for him to finish whatever he'd been saying to Tony before I interrupted. "Where is he?"

The two large men frowned at the intrusion, but didn't give me any grief. "Rider's taking Kutya for a walk," Hank answered. "Said he needed some air."

Tony directed a dark look Jake's way. "Can't blame him for that with all the pollution in here."

"Oh, enough of the attitude, Tony. This man hasn't done anything to you except make a few wisecracks and I can't say that I blame him given the shit you've been giving him since he got here."

Tony recoiled, just enough that it would have been

missed by anyone who blinked, but didn't argue back. Behind me, Jake chuckled under his breath.

"Once you recover from Miss Keller's scolding, grab her a drink, would ya? I'll take a beer too. In a bottle. Chilled."

Tony grumbled, but retrieved the drinks, setting a chilled beer bottle and a darker bottle, the opposite of chilled, on the bar top in front of us. "I'm still in charge when the boss isn't here, slayer. I'll kill you if you touch her, and I don't give a shit if it puts her in a pissy mood."

"I'd expect nothing less," Jake said, grabbing the bottles. "Let's grab a table, champ. Somewhere where the air is a little less tense and you don't have so many big brothers breathing directly down the back of my neck."

I smiled at Jake's word choice. I'd never had brothers, but I supposed in a way, Tony, Hank, and Rome were like brothers. Some older, irritable, and protective, some just a goofy mess, but they all cared about me in their own way and I'd definitely kill to keep them safe.

Speaking of Rome, the giant hunk of human muscle watched us from his post at the front of the room as Jake selected a booth and waited for me to slide in first before he lifted one of the bottles in greeting and winked at the man before sliding in opposite me. He'd chosen the side of the booth that gave him a view of the front door and most of the room.

"Do slayers have that cop thing too, where they always sit with their back to a wall, if possible, with a good view of the room?"

"Anyone used to getting jumped has that thing," Jake said, setting the bottles on the table. "If they have any survival instincts at all."

"But you don't always sit with your back to the wall. I'm surprised by how unbothered you appear sometimes, given the way every paranormal being in this building goes on alert around you."

"Just because I appear unbothered doesn't make it so,"

he replied, scanning the room. "But I see with more than just my eyes. When I was younger, before my slayer instincts really kicked in all the way, I always sat with my back to the wall. Now, it's not as necessary. It's pretty damn hard for anyone to sneak up on me."

"Because of your Spidey-senses?"

He grinned. "Something like that."

I thought about what Auntie Mo had told me. "Do you feel like these instincts of yours have developed more in recent years?"

"I suppose, but I guess that's natural. The older I get, the more I do what I do, my slayer power gets stronger."

"Rumor is you're the most powerful slayer there has ever been. There are others and they are all a threat, but you're the one whose name makes the big bads piss themselves." I took a drink of blood, eyeing him. "Do you ever think it's because you're leveling up each time you die and come back?"

The look he gave me was a perfect mix of confusion and amusement. "Say what now?"

"Did you know I have been reincarnated and killed young several times?"

He leaned back in the seat, appearing casual as he wrapped his big hand around the neck of his beer bottle, but I could tell his interest had been piqued. "I imagine most of us have been reincarnated. There's a lot of lore out there about old souls."

"So you know you carry the energy you had in your previous lives over into your newest one, that if you do it enough, it can develop into psychic abilities and powers?"

He nodded. "That's where you're thinking these visions are coming from? Makes sense if you've lived many past lives. Do you remember them?"

I shook my head. "Auntie Mo told me. It's all because of Selander Ryan, my evil sire. Rider and I are soul mates and we were together once in a previous life. I don't know what that life was or how we died, but he reincarnated and got turned. I reincarnated and got killed. A lot, according to Auntie Mo, and always at the hand of Selander Ryan or his minions."

"We really need to hunt that bastard down and kill him in a way that's a little more lethal and a whole lot more permanent."

"It's at the top of my To Do list. According to Auntie Mo, I'm the one who has to do it. It's my destiny or whatever." I took a drink of blood, swallowed a little too hard and almost choked when I noticed how Jake's face had grown pale and grim, but succeeded in getting the blood down without embarrassing myself. "What is it?"

"That word. Destiny. I know a little about that." He shook his head and took a big swig before setting his bottle back down on the table. "Destiny can bring you wonderful things, but damn, it's a hard road to walk."

I remembered the rest of what Auntie Mo had told me about what was coming. It sounded like there would be a blessing in the end, but yeah, from the way she'd made it sound, the path to get there was going to really suck. I forced down another drink and shoved those thoughts into the back of my mind, seeing no benefit in getting worked up about it before I had to. "Yeah, well, she also told me I've carried my spiritual energy over from every one of those lives and it has accumulated into whatever this is that I have now, whatever this is that makes me feel things in my gut and now see things when I touch people."

"Yeah, I knew she must have told you something pretty whammylicious. You were pretty damn quiet and distant after you left her. And, uh, I don't think the visions are hitting every time you touch someone. You were gripping me pretty tight downstairs for a minute there. You didn't see anything then, did you?"

I shook my head. "You have that protective slayer power, though, remember? Which reminds me of why I brought this up in the first place. I was thinking, do you think it's like a reincarnation every time you die and resurrect? I mean, you obviously come back in the same body, but does it do something to your psychic energy when you go through that?"

Jake's brow knitted as he thought about it. "So, you're saying you think I increase my psychic energy each time I get killed and come back?"

I nodded. "Why else would you be so much more powerful than any other slayer? Why would you be the only one who can fight through the urge to kill us all to actually get to know us and do what's right, not what's in your blood to do?"

He did that pale, grim thing again and finished his beer. "It's something to consider. A nice benefit from dying."

"Yeah, well, don't use it as an excuse to grow lax about protecting yourself. You're already far too blasé about the whole death and resurrection thing for my comfort. I mean, you've come back so far, but what if someone puts you in a woodchipper and scoops you into fifty different jars of mush or something? Could you come back from that?"

He did a slow blink. "Should I be concerned that you had that idea just stewing in your head?"

I gave him a look. "No. I have no desire to kill you."

"You, no, but I'm sure your mate fantasizes about it from time to time, so do me a big favor and don't give him any gruesome woodchipper ideas. And I'm never lax about dying. For one thing, it's not very fun," he said. "And I have too much in this world to protect. The few times I've purposely allowed myself to be killed were strategic. I knew I had enough of a blood booster to come back, that I wouldn't be killed in a way that would destroy my body, and it was truly the best way to beat my opponent. Slayers are pretty badass, but we're not invincible one hundred percent of the time. As strange as it may sound, death has saved my life a few times."

"Yeah, well, just make sure you do whatever it takes to keep death from claiming you permanently, and don't die around me. It'll freak me out. Grab some blood. I haven't seen you drink any since you've been back and I'm not trusting what you had before Christmas to be enough."

Jake grinned and snagged my bottle before turning it back, swallowing some of the warmed blood before placing it back in front of me.

"Ew. You put slayer cooties in my drink."

He laughed. "At least you're not calling them Dean Winchester cooties, but I guess you'd like those."

"I'm kind of more into Spike these days. You know, since I met a Dean Winchester lookalike and he turned out to be such a wiseass. It kind of killed the infatuation a little."

The wide smile that spread over Jake's face showed he was too amused to be insulted. "Spike from *Buffy*? Not too bad."

"Really? No smartass commentary? I distinctly remember you getting perturbed being compared to Buffy."

"That's Buffy. She was a dumbass. *'I can't love you because you don't have a soul'*. Stupid twit. Spike was twice the man Angel was, and he loved that moron before he had the soul. He—what?"

I lost the battle with my restrained laughter and let it rumble out of me until tears formed in my eyes. "You are such a geek for *Buffy*."

"Am not."

"Oh please. You're totally emotionally involved."

"I don't get emotionally involved with fictional characters on some dumbass television show with terrible CGI and crappy stunt doubles that don't even know how to hide their faces from the camera. I'm just saying… Spike's a pretty cool character. I mean, don't get me wrong, he's a complete idiot at times, but overall, he's—oh look." Jake's gaze shifted toward the entrance. "Speaking of complete idiots who don't have the worst taste in music and style, other than questionable hair color choices, here comes one now."

CHAPTER SIXTEEN

I turned to see Daniel standing next to Rome, talking with the big guy, but his gaze was fastened onto our booth and from the look in his eyes, he wasn't in the mood to deal with a wisecracking slayer. Oh joy.

"Behave yourself," I warned Jake. "I'm not in the mood to play referee between you two."

"Interesting that you should even have to. Rider's jealousy, I get. The dragon's seems a little misplaced. He knows about you two, right?"

I ignored Jake's knowing look and suppressed a groan. Was there anyone who didn't know how Daniel felt about me? I really needed to talk to him and put a stop to whatever this thing was between us before Rider lost his patience with him.

"He's my best friend," I said. "We're very close, but you can stop implying whatever you're implying. No lines have been crossed." None I was admitting to anyway.

"No shit," Jake said, flagging down a server. "If that dragon ever escapes the friend zone, Rider won't leave anything of him except blood, a few scales, and some glitter."

"Glitter? There are sparkles when he shifts form, but

he doesn't have any glitter in him."

"The dude has rainbow colored hair. There's got to be glitter in him somewhere."

I shook my head and fought an eye roll. "Behave."

"Party pooper." Jake's gaze went up as I felt Daniel's presence close to us and he sent me a look of warning as I slid over, making room for Daniel to join us, but he didn't need to. I was aware of Daniel's feelings and what Rider had been telling me had finally sunk in. Encouraging Daniel's feelings was playing with fire. Not a smart idea in any case, but exceptionally worse when the person whose feelings you were encouraging actually breathed fire.

Hazel reached our booth just as Daniel slid in next to me. "You guys need anything?"

"I'll take a triple cheeseburger basket with chili fries, a side of onion rings, and a slice of apple pie," Jake said, then pointed at me. "No comments about the pie. I'll take another beer too."

Hazel scribbled down his order. "How about you, Daniel? You want your usual?"

"Yeah, but double everything and add an order of spicy wedges, side of barbecue wings, fried pickles, tater tots, and I'll take a slice of that pie too."

"Beer to wash it all down?" Hazel asked, not even raising an eyebrow at the feast the two men had just ordered.

Daniel nodded, and the fae raised her eyes to look at me. "Another very bloody mary?"

"Sure. Thank you, Hazel." I waited until she left to address Daniel, noting the tiredness in his eyes. "Even for you, that's a lot of food for one sitting."

"I've been holed up in a tree for hours watching that church, not to mention I flew the equivalent of a six-hour car ride twice in one night. I could use the energy."

"You have the perfect opportunity to make an 'and boy are my arms tired' joke and you're not going to take it?" Jake asked.

"No, because I'm not that lame."

I bit my lip to keep from laughing at the annoyed look Jake sent Daniel's way and decided to get Daniel back on track before the two could start arguing. "It's been a while since I got any updates from Rider. Did you see Ramson or Julie?"

Daniel shook his head. "I saw some vans parked outside the church and two groups of men left in a couple of them. It would appear those clowns we captured were just one group Ramson deploys to go grab more women."

"That's what I was afraid of."

"Needless to say, those men who departed didn't make it out of Bitter Creek to snatch and hurt more women, so at least you don't have to worry about any women being hurt by them." Daniel paused as Hazel returned with two fresh, chilled bottles of beer and a warmed dark glass bottle of blood for me. He thanked her as she gathered the bottles Jake and I had already drained and left, then continued. "Thanks to my dragon vision, I could see down into the atrium, even from up high, but that tent blocked out a lot. There are a lot of trees in the atrium too, which made observing difficult."

"Did you get a sense of how many people were inside the church?" Jake asked.

"A lot. Easily hundreds, but the good news is that most of the energy signatures I picked up appeared to still be human. Well, good news as long as we can save them before any more get turned and we don't end up losing any of them when we go in to do that."

"But you did pick up on paranormal energy signatures?" I said.

Daniel nodded. "I don't have Jake's ability to pinpoint exact numbers or how many of whatever type are in a building from the distance I was at, but I sensed enough vampire energy to know there were more than a few. I also got the feeling a lot of that energy was below ground, so I'm thinking that church has a basement."

"That makes getting in and out without losing anyone a little trickier," Jake said, "but still doable. Tell me about the entry points."

The two fell into a discussion that eventually became a battle plan, only pausing long enough to dig into the obscene amount of food Hazel had brought out to them. I watched, growing more depressed by the minute as the two plowed through the mounds of food on their plates. The scents teased me and I stopped myself just short of reaching for one of Daniel's greasy tater tots, the desperation for real food so strong I'd nearly taken the risk of falling gravely ill just to have that delicious flavor in my mouth for a moment.

They were nearly finished with their small feasts when I felt Rider's presence in the building and looked at the clock that hung above the back door. He'd been gone quite a while for just taking a dog for a walk, even if Kutya was an energetic pup who enjoyed stretching his long legs and stopping to smell every interesting nook and cranny he passed.

"Hey, guys." Ginger appeared next to our booth, just in time to save me from going down a rabbit hole of *how badly did the luring training really bother Rider?*

"I see you're dressed more weather appropriate," Daniel said, noticing she'd changed back to her usual attire of jeans, dark T-shirt, and black leather jacket. She'd run her hands through her hair, mussing it until it was closer to her normal short, spiky look, but her makeup was the same, just as bold as ever.

"My hoo-ha is ever thankful," she said, grinning at Daniel's immediate obvious discomfort before looking over him to meet my gaze. "Hey, can we talk for a minute, girlfriend?"

Uh oh. My stomach took a dip and judging by the expression on Daniel's face when he turned to look at me, he thought the same thing I did: this probably wasn't good news if Ginger wanted privacy. Without saying a word,

Daniel slid out of the booth, allowing me an exit.

Once I left the booth and the overwhelming aroma of what little was left of the men's late meals, Ginger led me over to the bar, where we took corner seats. She tapped on the bar and a moment later, Macon, who had shown up to help Tony about fifteen minutes earlier, placed a bottle of blood in front of her.

"Did you need another?" he asked me, dropping his gaze.

"No, I'm fine. Thank you."

He nodded and quickly split, rushing over to the other side of the bar, although no one had been flagging him down for a drink.

"I think you make that guy nervous," Ginger said as she raised her bottle to her mouth. "The legend of Danni the Teste Slayer works again."

"Nah, his awkwardness and sheer desperation to get away from me is purely from me luring him and nearly making the poor guy hump the bars to the cell I was in."

Ginger choked and quickly pinched her nose closed to avoid a very gruesome scene. I apologized as I handed her a napkin for her to blot any blood that may have tried to shoot out of her nose.

"I'm going to need more details," she said as she finished and balled up the napkin before shooting it into the wastebasket behind the bar. "Starting with what the fuck?"

"Jake was training me to use my luring ability, helping me to know how to call upon it when I need it and then release it. I kind of had a little trouble releasing it sometimes."

Ginger sat staring at me for a while, processing. "So, Rider let a slayer put you in a cell in an area he lets very few enter so he could train you to actually summon the power you're afraid will take you over completely one day, and he was just cool with this?"

"He was with us for most of the time. He left after

Macon, uh, got a little…"

"Overly enthusiastic?"

"Yeah." I glanced at Macon, just a quick look. I didn't want the guy to feel any more awkward than he already did. "Poor guy."

"Oh please." She waved her hand in a dismissive gesture. "Men are pervs. They love that stuff. The freakier, the better."

"No, no one likes being manipulated like that, Ginger, and Rider was growling at the poor guy while he was unable to control what he felt."

"Yikes. That had to be scary for him, but kudos to him for not pissing his pants. He didn't piss his pants, did he?"

"No, he didn't piss his pants." He'd nearly burst through the zipper of them, but I wasn't going to tell her that. Macon was probably embarrassed enough.

"Well, see? That's not so bad. It could have been a lot worse."

"Yeah, I know. Rider wanted me to practice on Tony."

Fortunately, I'd got that out before Ginger could tip her bottle back again because the force of the laugh she emitted would have definitely sent blood spewing everywhere. We received several curious and some mildly annoyed looks as Ginger's laughter drowned out the music on the jukebox and she leaned back, the back of her head on my shoulder, before she nearly toppled right off the barstool.

I caught her and repositioned her narrow bottom on the barstool, shrugging my shoulders when Daniel and Jake shot us curious looks. I wasn't ready to tell Daniel about what I'd been doing while he'd been gone. Daniel was the only person to rival Rider in overprotective stubbornness, although he was usually fine with me fighting and working jobs. I knew, however, that was just because he was with me. Learning what I'd done without him there, and in the presence of a slayer, he'd be pissed.

A bemused Tony walked over to us and let out his

version of a sigh. It was barely audible, but knowing him well enough, I picked up on his hints of annoyance and exasperation easily. Seeing him, Ginger laughed harder, clapping her hands together as tears sprung from her heavily lined eyes.

"Two minutes sitting by you and she's gone goofy," Tony muttered, looking at me. "You ever notice the cloud of dumbfuckery that seems to float all around you?"

"You ever realize that if such a cloud floats around me, you must be stepping right in it too sometimes, making you part of that dumbfuckery?" I asked back with a sweet smile and flirtatious batting of my eyelashes. "Now go away and quit being so sweet to me before I lose all control and lay one on you, tongue and all."

Tony was at the other side of the bar before I could blink, which, combined with what I'd said, only made Ginger laugh harder. "Damn, he moved like a vampire."

"All right, Ginge." I grabbed her biceps and straightened her before she could take a tumble. "People are staring, which is going to make it a lot harder for you to drink a bottle of blood unnoticed. Calm down."

She wiped her eyes and tried to stop laughing, but only succeeded in laughing a little less loudly. "I'm sorry, girlfriend. The image that put in my head of his stuffy, snarly ass getting all hot and bothered for you just hit the spot. Whew, the teasing we could do with that, especially with how he acts so annoyed by you all the time… Oh, it would be hilarious."

"No, Ginger. It wouldn't be hilarious or even mildly funny. I would be treating him the same way that man treated you earlier, after he knew you weren't interested in him."

That sobered her. Ginger immediately stopped laughing and wiped what was left of the moisture under her eyes. "Ah, geez, Danni. I get what you're saying, but it wouldn't be the same thing. I just meant like, as a joke. Not all the way seduction. Under that touchy, gruff exterior, Tony likes you. And you're nothing like that jerk from earlier."

"No, I'm worse. That jerk could only force himself on someone. I can bend someone's will and use them for my own sexual gratification, whether they want it or not. I can take away a man's ability to fight back. I am a thousand times worse."

"No, girlfriend." She reached for my hand that was resting on the bar top, but stopped short, then patted it instead of holding it like she'd been meaning to do, respecting my succubus side's quirks. "You're a thousand times better because you have that ability and you don't use it. A lot of other women in your position would have been on the first plane to wherever Jensen Ackles is, ready to make him their love slave."

I grinned. "Yeah, based on what I've seen on Facebook alone, I believe that's true."

"No doubt." She took a drink of blood and sighed. "I'm sorry. I was just thinking of messing with Tony because the only time he shows any emotion at all, it's annoyance. I mean, even in the middle of a life or death fight, I've only ever seen him annoyed, like he's annoyed he has to be bothered to keep his own ass alive. But you're right. As fun as it would be to screw with him, it wouldn't be funny to do it that way, even if just for a moment. I was wrong for that."

"It's okay. I know you didn't mean anything by it, and weren't actually suggesting I force him to do something against his will. I may be a little overly prickly about it. I've spent a lot of time afraid of losing control of this power and hurting someone I love in a way I could never expect forgiveness for."

"I know, girlfriend, but you have good people watching your back."

I nodded, but Ginger's words weren't quite the reassurance she thought they were. The more people watching me, trying to protect me, the more people I could hurt if I lost control of my abilities. But I didn't want to dwell on that, especially not the night before I knew I had to go into a battle a psychic may have seen me standing alone in. A battle I couldn't back out of because too many innocent people's lives depended on us saving them and I was one of very few available who might have any kind of protection against having my mind invaded by the enemy. I was the only one available to keep Jake from going all super-murdery if the fighting got too much for him. Jadyn could calm him, but she wasn't a member of Rider's security staff. Therefore, not going in with us. I had to go.

"Hey, Ginge. You wanted to speak to me about something?"

"Yeah." I could tell by her tone, she didn't want to tell me whatever it was so much as she had something she thought I needed to know, no matter how much it sucked, so my stomach was in knots as I watched her drain the last of her very bloody mary and retrieve her cell phone from the inner pocket of her jacket. She opened up her photos app and set the phone in front of me on the bar. "Is that who I'm afraid it is?"

I picked up the phone and enlarged the picture, taking in the haggard features on the face that belonged on a much older woman. The woman in the picture with the long, brown hair should have been more youthful, full of life. Her dull, weary eyes had seen too much, and she'd done far too many drugs to regain any of her youthful glow. She'd aged herself with a hard life she'd brought on herself with her own poor choices, choices she'd tried to encourage her daughter to make too. "Yeah, that's definitely Nina Valdez. Angel's mother."

"Well, if her attire in the picture doesn't tell you all you need to know, you know what my undercover assignment was when I took that pic."

"Yeah, I know." I didn't need to see the tiny dress that didn't seem to have enough fabric to be a scarf, let alone a dress to know what Nina Valdez had been up to in the picture. "I already had a feeling this was a possibility once she came back to town. I kind of figured it out when she paid Pacitti for information on Angel. She didn't pay him with money and I know she doesn't pay for her drugs with money when she's in dire need of a fix and funds are low. She has a police file to back that up."

"Are you going to tell Angel?"

"That her mom came back to town and is selling her body in probably the same dark alleys Angel had to fight to not get raped in?" I shook my head. "I just wish she'd go away and stay gone. Stay out of Angel's life for good and let the girl heal from all the damage she's done to her."

"We could make that happen." Ginger raised her hands when I looked at her in what was probably my *hell fucking no, we aren't murdering anybody* face, because that was definitely the thought running through my mind. "I'm not suggesting we take her out of the picture in like a mafia way."

"In what way were you suggesting we take her out of the picture, then? The vampire way? I hate to break it to ya, but I think that's about the same as the mafia way. Probably just quicker and way gorier."

"You could buy her off. Give her enough money to leave town for good."

"That might work for no-good parents who are just bums. Nina Valdez is a no-good parent and an addict. An addict will just blow through the money and come right back, promising to do better."

"True. You could scare her off. Yes, she'll get hurt, but beating some fear into her will keep her away from Angel and it's not murder."

I shook my head. "No. I can't beat the crap out of Angel's mother, and neither can my friends," I quickly added, knowing Ginger was about to offer her services, ever helpful. "Angel still loves her mother. I know it because Nina left her a letter and although she hasn't told me what was in it, I know she kept it. She kept it because it's the only thing she has from her. I can't hurt someone she loves and pretend like that's helping her."

"All right then. You could take Angel somewhere else." Ginger shrugged when I looked at her. "Rider adores you, and he'll move on from here after he's been in the area too long anyway. That's what vampires do. I'm sure he wouldn't mind jumping ship sooner than planned if it was what you wanted. Angel's mother wouldn't have a clue where to look for her."

Although relocating was a far better solution than murder, especially from a moral standpoint, The Midnight Rider was Rider's headquarters. No matter how much money he had, it had to be a pain in the ass to uproot everything and relocate. I wouldn't ask that of him, and it wasn't the best way to handle the situation. It was just the easiest. "The thing is, Angel is an addict too. A recovering, sober addict, but addiction never really goes away. Helping her run from her triggers won't help her, not as much as being here for her, providing a support system while she continues to focus on taking care of herself and resisting her mother's influence."

"All right then." Ginger nodded. "We won't tell her what her mom's up to, and we'll keep an eye on her, be there for her when she needs us."

I couldn't hold back my grin. "I remember you once painting yourself as this total loner type, all about the solo jobs. No friends, just associates. Here you are caring about a human teenager as much as I do."

"Yeah, you assholes made me soft," she muttered, grinning when I laughed. "What can I say? The kid likes to bake, and she makes me cookies. I'm a slut for cookies."

"Ugh, I can't wait until I can be a slut for cookies again."

Tony had been wiping down the bar and had just reached the corner, placing him close enough to overhear what I'd said. He glanced at us, shook his head, and muttered something under his breath as he took off to the other side of the bar, abandoning the wiping down of our side. Ginger and I looked at each other and erupted into laughter. Tony didn't bother coming over to gripe at us for disturbing others sitting around the bar. Tony stayed where he was, and so did poor Macon. Fortunately for them, closing time was coming soon.

"I need to report in with Rider and head home before dawn," Ginger said, stretching over the bar to place her bottle in the bin kept on a shelf underneath since we'd probably scared Tony and Macon away for good and we never left blood bottles out where a regular human could accidentally grab one and discover the bar sold blood. "I am so crashing at sunup."

"I'll walk with you," I offered, sensing that Rider was in his office. It wasn't the most reassuring thing knowing that he'd returned and gone to his office before checking in with me. I couldn't go much longer without knowing where his head was after what he'd witnessed during the training session, so I was going to his office to see what was up. Ginger made a nice buffer if he was in a mood. "I was headed to his office anyway."

"Cool."

I glanced over at Jake and Daniel as we made our way toward the back, and noted that they seemed to be getting along fine enough. They were both leaning forward, talking animatedly. Plotting. Nothing like the promise of delivering death and dismemberment to a common foe to bring two snarling enemies together.

Ginger and I pushed through the back door and turned left. I sent my feelers out, trying to assess Rider's temperament before we entered the office, but he didn't emit any emotion strong enough for me to gauge. Kutya, however, was all excitement as we knocked on the office door and entered.

The big pup hastily left the comfort of his plush doggy bed to barrel into my legs. I grabbed his collar, a black leather one with metal dog bones adorning it, to keep him from jumping on me, and held him down while using my free hand to scratch between his ears and under his chin.

"Hey, boss," Ginger said as she promptly lowered herself into one of the two chairs in front of Rider's desk.

"How'd it go?" he asked her, although his eyes were taking in me and the dog. His face, expressionless, told me nothing, but at least I didn't sense any negative emotions rolling off of him.

"Well, despite all the odds working against me, I'm pleased to announce I managed to not lose my hoo-ha to frostbite out in that frigid, nipply wonderland."

Rider's gaze slowly swung from me to Ginger. "Good. I was beside myself with worry."

Ginger smiled at Rider's dry delivery. "I thought you would be. So, I asked around and there's good news and there's bad news. The bad news is I don't think Julie Chavez was a snatch and grab case. Word on the street is there's a woman recruiting prostitutes and escorts for some program that changes their life around, and that woman's name is Barb Staigerwald. You may recognize that name from the file the techs built on Julie. They used to work together, sort of a tag team operation they had back in the day before you rescued Julie in that alley and she left to become your blood donor. They were tight, like sisters, protected each other on the streets, often doing two-for-ones to ensure their safety."

"This Barb didn't protect Julie the night I found her. That man was close to killing her, and she had no one around to help."

I gave Kutya one last good pat on his flank, signaling petting time was over, and sent him back to his doggy bed before I took a seat in the chair next to Ginger's.

"When the money's good enough, they take the risks." Ginger shrugged. "Like I said before, when I started this case, there were a lot of places Julie could have run into an old friend. She worked with Barb long enough to trust the woman, and if she was already feeling like something was missing in her life and she wanted a fresh start, I could see her being tempted to meet up with Barb at a prearranged date and time, especially since word is Barb has cleaned up pretty nice. And she didn't have to become a blood donor to a vampire to do it. Which we know isn't entirely accurate, but Julie wouldn't have known that."

I sensed the regret within Rider and knew he was questioning what he'd done for Julie, if it hadn't been as good of a thing as he'd thought it was, but he didn't let any of that show in his expression or in his voice when he spoke. "So, what's the good news?"

"The sex worker I got all the deets from is fucking *hot*." She turned to me and smiled wickedly. "We're talking an ass you can bounce a quarter off of and thighs that could crack a walnut. I'm meeting her this weekend." Ginger sat back in her chair, a hopeful look on her face. "I'm gonna see if she can crack me."

"Good for you, but that has nothing to do with anything that matters," Rider said as I rolled my lips in, trying not to smile.

"Oops, my bad," Ginger said. "You're right. I guess there wasn't any business-related good news. You're just so much more approachable now since you've been getting that Teste Slayer lovin'. I come in here now and find I just want to gab and gab and gab—ooh, except now when you have that murder look in your eyes."

"Good work on the case. Now get out." Rider pointed to the door. "Get some rest and report in at sundown. You're going to go in with the team tomorrow evening."

"Hell yeah. Time to kick some prannie ass." Ginger high-fived me and moved to the door. "See ya tomorrow night, sweet cheeks."

"See what you've done to me?" Rider swung his hand out, gesturing toward Ginger as the door closed behind her. "My people used to fear me. Then you came along and now they want to tell me all about their sex lives and vagina temperature."

I snorted out a laugh. "I'm sorry. Do you regret saving me now?"

"Never." He rolled his chair back an inch and opened his arms. "Why are you all the way over there?"

"I wasn't sure where you wanted me," I answered as I stood from my chair and rounded the desk to sit on Rider's lap, leaning into him as his arms closed around me and his mouth found the sensitive spot on my neck below my ear. "You left during my training session. Are you upset?"

"No." He dropped a kiss on my neck before pulling away far enough so I could see his eyes when he spoke. "I was messing with your concentration, so I ducked out."

"You left the building, and you were gone a while. Too long for just a dog walk."

"I needed to think, and I visited a couple of my donors to tank up. I'll need to feed you well before you head out to that church tomorrow night. It takes a while to drink that much from a wrist."

The same regret I'd sensed in him earlier flitted through his eyes and the need I felt to console him outweighed the usual jealousy any talk of feeding from his donors usually caused. "You saved Julie's life and gave her an out from a situation that would have probably killed her eventually."

"She must not have been too happy with it if she wanted to escape to join a cult," he said, his voice soft, his eyes distant. "I don't know why she didn't just ask. If she was truly miserable, I could have made arrangements for her."

I sighed, and a little of it was from relief, remembering the discussion I'd had about donors with Ginger earlier. "You're a pretty intimidating person, Rider, even to me, and I feel safer with you than anyone. Going off of what you've told me about your contracts with your donors and the way you continually discourage me from growing any attachment to my own, I can understand why your donors would feel like they have no way out except for an escape, but now that you know this, maybe you can change things with them? Find a way to ensure them they're not going to be killed if they ask to leave?"

He was still as he considered this, but eventually nodded. "Yeah."

I waited to see if he would say anything else, but after several minutes passed, I realized he was going to remain bottled up tight unless I took action to uncork him. "So, what did you need to think about on that long walk?"

The ghost of a smile crossed his mouth as he looked into my eyes. "Nothing bad."

"If it's nothing bad, then it's something that can be shared?"

He shook his head. "No can do. That would ruin the surprise."

I felt my eyes narrow. "What surprise?"

"If I told you, it wouldn't be much of a surprise, would it?"

"*Lovas Lovag*," I growled, using the Hungarian name Rider had been given at birth and used before changing it to its current English translation. "What are you up to?"

"Be careful with that name. I don't want it getting around." He tapped my nose playfully. "You're going to have to be patient."

"Patience isn't a virtue I was blessed with, especially not when you're talking about some surprise that came about from a long walk you took after watching me lure a poor man you were growling at like you wanted to rip his head off or go for his jugular." I lowered my gaze, unable to meet his eyes. "I thought, maybe, you had to get away from me. That seeing me like that, what I can do to a man…"

"I love you. Nothing is going to change that, and I told you why I left. I left so you could focus better and learn what you needed to learn without me getting in the way."

He lifted my hand and threaded his fingers through mine. "You remember when I sent you to Pigeon Forge so I could help Seta with something?"

"Yes."

"It wasn't just Seta I helped. Her sire was there; an old, insufferable pain in the ass it took a great deal of self-control not to stake."

"Stake?"

"I like my vampire shtick. Shush and let me talk."

I chuckled as Rider continued.

"As much as I can't stand the guy, the more we talked, the more I observed, the more I couldn't help realizing we had a lot in common. We're both very old, very powerful vampires. We're also pretty big dumbasses when it comes to the stubborn women we love. I'm always going to be protective of you, Danni, because you are the one thing in this world I cannot survive losing. But when a slayer like Jake Porter tells me you're the biggest threat in a room that contains me and an Imortian dragon, I have to concede that you can take care of yourself."

He released my hand to brush a lock of hair back from my face, tucked it behind my ear, and looked deep into my eyes. "I don't have to be as afraid of some things as I've been, especially when that fear prevents me from giving you everything you deserve to have. I love you and I want you to know that without question. I want you to have everything you want."

I was more confused than I'd started out. "What—"

He placed his index finger over my mouth. "I'm a killer, not a poet. I don't get many ideas for grand romantic gestures, so just let me have this chance to hopefully give you a New Year's Eve you'll never forget. I know how much you still care about holidays and how rough of a time you've had since turning, so all I'm going to say is I think I can give you a good start to a new year, a new beginning where hopefully you don't ever feel the need again to question what I feel for you."

What in the world was he planning? The good news was if this surprise was going to be given to me on New Year's Eve, I didn't have too long to obsess over it. The bad news was... I needed to make sure we all survived the raid on Ramson's church first.

CHAPTER SEVENTEEN

I woke up and the next thing I knew, my head was in the toilet and everything I had drunk the night before was viciously ejected from my body. When it was over, I fell back onto the floor and stared up at the ceiling, taking only a moment to be thankful Rider had already been up and at 'em somewhere else when I'd awakened instead of in the room, available to witness what had just happened.

It didn't take long for me to realize it wasn't nightfall yet and Rider was in the building, close enough I could sense him on the move, and I knew right where he was headed and why. *Fuck.*

I scrambled to my feet, took a moment to wait for the bathroom to stop spinning, and flushed the toilet before swishing a mouthful of Listerine and stepped into the shower, no need to strip down since I'd woken up naked from the end of the night before when Rider and I had spent some quality time together right before the sun rose and immediately sucked me under into the dark abyss of day sleep.

I twisted the knobs, starting a steady downpour of warm water and tossed a Mountain Energy bath bomb I'd gotten in Pigeon Forge on the floor directly in the line of spray, hoping the vibrant, citrus scent would quickly fill the bathroom, overpowering the lingering scent of sickness that had remained despite being flushed down the toilet.

The day had come. I had a pranic vampire to kill and there was no way Rider would let me out to do that if he knew the need to vomit had pulled me out of day sleep. Vampires didn't get sick unless we were newly turned and dumb enough to eat food our stomachs couldn't handle. To my knowledge, succubi didn't get sick either, and I hadn't eaten anything despite how badly I'd longed for a taste of the food Daniel had been shoving into his gullet the night before.

So what the hell was wrong with me? I'd fed and slept after forcing that vision out of Mike. I should have recovered. Could it be the training? We'd thought the visions were the source of my nausea, but maybe calling upon my succubus power to lure caused it too?

Whatever the reason, I couldn't let Rider know I was sick. He was being pretty incredible about letting me go after Ramson without him being there, but old habits die hard and he would go into full overprotective mode if he thought I was impaired in any way. I had to be there. I recalled everything Khiderian and Auntie Mo said, and I knew I had to be there even if I ended up alone. I was the one who'd had the visions of the pranic vampire, who'd been guided by some mystical whatever to save Mandi Fittro from being abducted. I was meant to be there.

I quickly washed and turned the shower off. I opened the shower door and let the steam rush out before toweling off, fanning the air to disperse the fragrant steam. I grimaced as I sensed Rider's arrival in the bedroom and wrapped the towel around my body before using another to dry my hair, rubbing vigorously before discarding it, and quickly brushed my teeth.

My skin was pale and my eyes dull, but at least I didn't have any green tinge to my skin as I studied my reflection and spit out the toothpaste. I rinsed my mouth and my toothbrush, turned off the water and took a deep breath, searching for calm.

Once I got as close to calm as I could, I turned for the door and stepped out to find Rider standing at the foot of the bed, arms folded over his chest, feet firmly planted. Blue, searching eyes locked onto me. Kutya whined from where he rested on the chaise, and lowered his sizeable head onto his massive paws.

"Hey." I smiled and walked over to the dresser to grab clothes. "Is everything okay? You were already up and about when I woke up."

"I had to be. We had that meeting with Pacitti to infiltrate at noon," he said, reminding me of one of the other problems we had. "You were supposed to be resting, reserving your strength for tonight. Why are you awake so early?"

"It's not that early," I said, which was true. "I never have been a sleep all day vampire, remember? It's one of the things about me that bugs you."

"Only when it interferes with my own sleep unnecessarily," he muttered, "and you've been sleeping longer lately. You were sick last night, overexerted from the visions. You should get all the rest you can before going after Ramson."

"Well, I must have," I said, turning around with the underwear, jeans, and black long sleeve shirt I'd selected to wear. "Because I woke up on my own and here I am all bright eyed and bushy tailed."

"More like pale skinned and hiding something," he countered, his gaze shifting to the open bathroom door.

I inhaled, relieved to only smell citrus. "I'm not hiding anything. I just woke up before nightfall. Geez, Rider, what's with the third degree? It's not like I don't ever wake up before nightfall on my own." Hearing the defensiveness in my tone, I changed direction and set the clothes on the dresser before closing the distance between us and ran my hands up Rider's chest, letting them glide over the soft cashmere of his dark gray sweater before lacing my fingers around the back of his neck. "And I don't know why you're still going on about me being sick last night. You're very well aware I was feeling just fine when we went to bed together. I recall you were feeling pretty fine too."

"Yes, I was, up until day broke and you fell fast asleep while we were still having sex."

I blinked. "I did?"

"Well, I was still having sex. I gotta tell ya, babe, that wasn't a good moment for my self-esteem, especially since you clearly don't even remember tapping out before the finish."

Ouch. No wonder he seemed to be in a mood. I tried to remember the night before and although I clearly remembered being with him and enjoying it, he was right that I couldn't remember finishing. I must have been dead to the world the moment the sun rose.

I pulled away, feeling terrible. "I'm sorry. I must have been exhausted. I remember being very into what we were doing. I just... Geez, Rider. Do you realize how long last night was? Jake and Khiderian arrived, we interrogated those jerks, and I got sick after forcing that vision from Mike. You had Jake babysit me before visiting Auntie Mo. Then I practiced using my lure for a while before Daniel and Ginger came back. Then there were those briefings with them before we came upstairs just before dawn. You know I love you and love being with you. I was just so tired."

"I'm not upset." He wrapped his hand around the nape of my neck and pulled me closer before dropping a kiss on my forehead. "My ego can take a few hits. Hell, it's probably good for me, keeps me from getting too cocky, but I'm worried about you. You were out cold, Danni, like a brand new fledgling and with your hybridness, you've never been like that before."

"Again, it was a long night with a lot packed into a short amount of time."

"A lot including you being sick. Are you sure you're all right? You don't have to be part of this raid if you're not feeling well. We can devise another plan of action or wait a few nights."

"The more nights we wait, the more innocent people Ramson can abduct, indoctrinate, or turn, and seeing as how Daniel took out the two teams Ramson sent out to snatch and grab last night, and the one I stopped never returned either, Ramson is going to know someone's on to him. We have to go in before he runs and we have to search for him all over again." I forced a smile. "And besides, silly, vampires don't get sick unless they eat things they shouldn't."

"Yes, I know, but the normal rules have never applied to you."

"I'm fine, Rider. Really." I cozied up to him. "We can make up for the abrupt ending this morning right now if you want."

"Hell must have just frozen over." Rider groaned.

"What?"

He grinned. "I never thought I'd say no to you, especially with you this close to naked, but I'm going to have to do the right thing and pass. I want you fed, rested, and in peak condition before you go after Ramson tonight, especially with everything else going on."

"Everything else? What else is—ah!" I doubled over, one hand on my stomach and the other gripping Rider's arm as a sharp pain seared into my stomach.

"Danni?!" Rider's hands held tight to my hips, keeping me on my feet as he bent to see my face. "What is it?"

"I'm fine," I quickly said before he could get too worried, recognizing the sensation, although I'd never felt it quite that intensely before. "I'm just... I'm really hungry."

"Here." He sat on the foot of the bed and pulled me onto his lap, angling his head to the side as he gripped the back of my head and pressed my mouth into the side of his throat. "Take all you need. I tanked up."

I thanked him, the words muffled against his skin, and sank my fangs into his throat, but although his blood always packed a powerful punch and I needed what he gave me to replace what I'd lost after waking up, I hadn't been talking about blood when I said I was hungry. The need for blood was a thirst. I was *hungry*.

I drank from him, knowing the blood would give me strength, but my stomach continued to rumble as visions of salmon and soup and pot roasts danced through my head. Mmmm, pot roast with potatoes and warm, flavorful carrots that practically disintegrated once they hit the tongue, so moist from the hours spent in the crock pot... What the hell? Longing for cupcakes and doughnuts while nervous or stressed, I understood. But fantasizing about potatoes and carrots?

What in the world was wrong with me?

I didn't have the answer, so I continued to drink, not stopping until I was sure one more sip would make the rest come back up and the "seat" beneath me had grown too hard to be ignored. I licked the wounds I'd made in Rider's throat, eliciting a groan from him as I sealed his flesh, and grinned. "Are you sure you don't want to finish what we started before dawn?"

His fingers had been digging into my hips for several minutes and as I lifted my head from his neck to see him sitting with his eyes closed, jaw clenched, he pried them off of me and let himself fall back onto the bed before giving my hips a light push. "Go. Get dressed."

"Rider."

"Dammit, woman. For once, do as you're told. I'm trying to not let you expend any energy you might need for a fight, but you're killing me. Go. Now."

I chuckled as I got off of him, giving him the relief he needed, but couldn't help running a teasing finger over the hard length of him.

"Fuck!" His eyes popped open and his hips bucked off

the bed before he glared at me and pointed toward the bathroom, then growled. "Go. Get. Dressed."

I laughed as I grabbed my clothes and made my way to the bathroom, tempted to drop my towel before I reached it, but I could only tease him so much before it became mean. The teasing served its purpose though, distracting him enough that he didn't question why my stomach had been rumbling so freaking much during the first gulps of blood I'd taken or why I'd drunk more than I usually would have.

"Being a considerate, caring, good guy sucks," he called after me as I closed the door.

"Hey, you're the one saying no. I would have gladly ridden you until you saw stars."

"You're evil sometimes, you know that?"

I laughed and started getting dressed, but the laughter faded as the truth of his words sank in. Try as I might to be a good person, there was a darkness inside of me, one I might have to deliberately call upon. I met my gaze in the mirror and pleaded with the darkness inside me not to let me hurt anyone I loved.

***

By the time I emerged from the bathroom, Rider had made up the bed and his painful pants situation had deflated to something that wouldn't hinder his ability to walk. He stood by the door, waiting for me, and his expression was grim enough to stop me in my tracks.

"Uh oh. What's that face about?"

"Thanks, babe. You always know how to make a man feel good about himself."

"You know what I meant." I rolled my eyes before I crossed the room to stand on tiptoe and kiss him, just a quick peck given how adamant he was that we not enjoy each other's company too much before I helped take care of Ramson. "What's wrong?"

"Things didn't go well for the team I sent to grab Pacitti," he said, and opened the door, allowing Kutya to run out before us. "I was going to tell you that before, but got distracted."

"What happened?" My stomach took a dip as we descended the stairs and this time, I knew the cause. Freaking Pacitti. I hated that slimy bastard. "Did we get him?"

Rider shook his head. "The greasy piece of shit is smarter than he looks, or just paranoid, which can be just as effective for assholes like him."

We went through the door to the hallway that ran the back length of the bar and turned right, moving toward his office. "My techs are good at what they do, and Kirsty has pretended to be other people online or through text several times without fail, but Brinley was just too fucking weird of a person for anyone to impersonate well enough. Something tipped Pacitti off because when my team arrived at the teacup ride, they didn't find him."

"Maybe Kirsty didn't make enough lewd commentary about raw meat," I said as we entered the office and Kutya went straight for his doggy bed. "Or maybe I was wrong about the meeting place. Has he sent Brinley any other messages?"

Rider had dropped down into his desk chair and now sat staring back at me with that grim expression. My knees went a little jellified, and I felt nausea roll around in my belly again. "What?"

"He sent a message, but I'm not showing it to you until you come over here and sit because you already look like you might hit the floor."

"Yeah, well, that's what happens when you look at me with those grim eyes. It's scary." I rounded the desk and settled on his lap. "What was the message?"

Rider reached around me and unlocked his computer, then opened a file that had been saved to his desktop, revealing the gruesome image of a severed head in a box.

A head with a face that I had seen before, although I didn't know the werewolf's name.

"What the hell is that?" My question came out barely above a whisper, breath a very hard thing to find in the moment as my brain struggled to catch up to what my eyes were seeing.

"That's the message we received from Pacitti. The visual part anyway." Rider used the mouse to click on the arrow next to the image on the screen, switching over to a screenshot of the text that had accompanied the picture: NICE TRY. I WAS GOING FOR MONEY. NOW I THINK I NEED TO THINK BIGGER. BE IN TOUCH.

"How many did you send?"

"Four. All shifters, since it was daylight."

"How many came back?"

"None."

"How?" I scrambled off of Rider's lap, dislodging his hands when he tried to keep me in place, and rounded his desk so I could pace, unable to stand still. "How? They were shifters. He was just an out of shape, greasy detective. Even if he suspected Brinley had been compromised, how would he know how to kill a shifter? What to look for? How would he possibly know how to get the jump on what were basically trained soldiers?"

The office door opened, and Jake walked in, Rome right behind him. "He had help," the slayer said, plopping down into a chair across from Rider's desk. Rome took the one next to him.

I stopped pacing and turned toward Jake. "What kind of help?"

"I'd put my money on a hunter, maybe even an actual slayer," he said. "From the way you all described this guy, and the fact you're pretty sure he didn't know anything about vampires or shifters before he got his hands on that security camera footage, there's no way he's working alone. I might give a guy like that one lucky kill, but there's no way in hell he's going to pick off four shifters."

"And not in a public place like an amusement park," I said. "How the hell did four shifters get killed in an amusement park? Was there anything on the news?"

"We're not sure it happened at the amusement park," Rider said. "The team checked in when they arrived on the ground after their flight and when they arrived at the park. Sometime within an hour of that last check-in, their trackers went offline, and we were unable to contact them. A couple of hours ago, we received the message on Brinley's phone."

"Once again, I've caused good men to die."

"Don't go there, champ." Jake shook his head. "Shit happens and people die in this business. That's not on you."

"It is when they would have never been sent after that creep if—"

"If he hadn't threatened us," Rider said, cutting me off. "You didn't know there were security cameras around when you attacked that woman and you didn't know that sonofabitch was tracking you. Neither did Daniel, Rome or Ginger. You weren't alone in what happened. This isn't your fault."

"I'm the one who lost her cool and attacked that woman."

"You did what we all wanted to do when we saw our friend get his hand shot off," Rome said. "You just did it quicker, and for the record, baby girl, if I ever die going after someone who threatens you, I'm cool with it. We're family. That's what we do. You feel me?"

I gasped in a breath, his declaration hitting me like a solid punch right in the gut, and my eyes teared up, but before I could embarrass myself by blubbering something all emotional, Rome's stomach let out a thunderous gurgle and he grimaced as he shifted in his chair.

"Dammit to hell," Rider said, his gaze locked onto Jake. "You were supposed to be watching him while

Daniel got some sleep."

"Hey, I was. I did. I am." Jake looked over at Rome and frowned as the big guy gripped his stomach and tried to get comfortable. "Dude. You all right?"

"Does he look all right to you?" Rider asked.

"No, he looks like he's about to shit in your chair."

"I'm good," Rome said, the words coming out as more of a grunt. "Those peas I had for lunch are disagreeing with me."

"Peas, my ass," Rider said, still glaring at Jake. "What did you let him eat? And keep saying you didn't give him anything, you're going to see what it looks like when I do a cavity search to find out."

"Nah, boss. You don't gotta do that," Rome said, his eyes bulging out of his head as beads of sweat popped out on his forehead and upper lip. "I just had a candy bar."

Rider leaned forward. "And?"

Rome gripped his stomach harder as it made an ungodly sound. "Just a candy bar, boss. And a burger, but just a double one, not even a triple. Not even with bacon. And a milkshake, but it was just vanilla. I didn't—oh shit." Rome shot out of the chair and nearly tore the door off its hinges in his desperation to get out.

Rider's glare grew in ferocity and Jake shrank into the chair. "When. *The hell.* Did you get him all that? And why the fuck would you?"

"The candy bar was in my jacket and the dude could smell it." Jake shrugged. "He was like a werewolf sniffing meat, and then I got hungry and I couldn't just eat in front of the guy while he was salivating and damn near crying, watching me."

"You took him out where no one else could see you give him food."

"In my defense, I had no idea it would do that to him." Jake hooked a thumb over his shoulder in the direction Rome had run out. "I thought you all were just being all extra careful and screwing with him, having fun watching him suffer."

"I only have myself to blame for this one," Rider said, leaning back into his chair. "I should have known better than to trust you to keep a man from eating junk. This one's on me."

His power pulsed, and I knew he'd reached out telepathically to someone.

"I'm sure the big guy will be okay," Jake said, straightening back up in his chair. "He had one decent meal after all that health-nut crap you've been feeding him."

"Jake, his surgery was just last week," I said, genuinely worried about Rome. "No one was screwing with him. We were protecting him from himself. The man has no willpower."

Tony ducked his head into the office, not needing to open the already open door. "Yeah?"

Rider's pissed-off gaze shifted past Jake to Tony. "Escort Mr. Porter to whatever bathroom Rome is currently wrecking and make sure he has a plunger and whatever else is necessary to clean up the damages he's caused."

Tony's mouth slowly spread into a toothy smile. "Oh, it would be my pleasure to escort Mr. Porter and give him whatever he needs."

"Oh, come on," Jake protested.

"You've probably just put Rome back in a bed for at least a day or two. It's either this or I let my entire staff play piñata on your ass. With blades."

"And blowtorches," Tony said.

"Dude, you got anger issues," Jake said, but got to his feet. "Fine, but if Rome gives birth to his colon in there, I'm out. I don't know nothin' about birthin' no babies."

"I hate him," Rider muttered as the slayer left the office with an almost chipper Tony.

"Do you not realize we just witnessed a rare phenomenon? Tony actually smiled."

Rider just looked at me for a moment, then chuckled. "Well, if anything would make that tiger smile, the thought of Jake plunging Rome's toxic waste would do it. Come here."

I walked over to Rider and settled on his lap again, letting him wrap his arms around me.

"Those men didn't die because of you," he said, his voice soft in my ear. "They died because some asshole who can't just let people who are different live their lives killed them because he got caught trying to extort us. We're going to find him and we're going to make him pay. And then we're going to move on to the next threat because that's what we do. That's the price we pay to live as we are. It's not fair, but it is what it is. You're not going to spend another minute thinking about that piece of shit and you're not going to blame yourself for anything because you have another monster to take care of. You have innocent people to save. That's who you are. You are not a reason people die. You are a reason people live. Understand me?"

I wiped away the tears that had slid down my cheeks. "You really believe I can help take out someone like Ramson?"

"I believe you can do anything. Even if it's hard and dangerous and I want to lock you in my room to keep you from doing it." He kissed my temple. "Jake is a fucking idiot, but he knows paranormal power. You're a force to be reckoned with. You may not see it yet, but if you threaten a slayer more than I do, you are more than capable of taking out a prannie."

"I needed to hear that." I kissed him, putting all my love and thankfulness into it. "I needed to know you believed in me."

"I've always believed in you, Danni. I've just always wanted to protect you more, but I know I can't keep you sheltered from all the danger in the world. No matter how hard I try, it will find you eventually and it's best I let you learn and grow so you can protect yourself if a situation occurs where you find yourself alone and I can't get to you in time."

His words reminded me of Auntie Mo's vision, and a chill ran through me. "I'm going to come back to you after Ramson is dead."

"Damn right you are. We have a New Year's Eve to celebrate together." He nuzzled my neck for a moment before looking at the clock in the bottom right corner of his computer screen. "If you're sure you're rested enough not to need any more sleep, we'll wake Daniel once we find out how bad off Rome is and Jake finishes cleanup on whatever damage he causes, and go over the plan. We can have you in place not long after Ginger arrives tonight."

"Sounds good," I said, with only a slight tremor in my voice.

"Hey. You're going to be all right." He kissed my hand. "You'll have Jake, Daniel, Tony, and Ginger with you. Don't tell any of those idiots I said it, but they're the best of my best, and it goes without saying that taking a slayer into a fight at your side is practically cheating. If things get hairy, you can always castrate Ramson. That's never failed you."

I chuckled and looked deep into Rider's sapphire blue eyes, eyes that were filled to the brim with worry, but he was still letting me go and building up my confidence instead of voicing his concerns because he knew I needed to do it, and he believed in me. I was the luckiest woman in the world... as long as I didn't die or lose anyone I loved once we raided that church.

CHAPTER EIGHTEEN

Rider sighed as Tony left the office, having updated him on Rome's condition. "I probably should have put his ass in the underworld ward right after he was released from the hospital anyway, instead of relying on these idiots to keep food away from him, but I didn't want him taking up space they might need to treat those who need their services more."

"Rome does take up a lot of space." I grinned. "But he needs to be taken care of and the man would rather die eating a burger than doing what he needs to do to keep himself healthy. And I'm sure Nannette won't have any problem ordering him out of her way if they need space. She might even put him to work. I think he has a big crush on her."

"Nannette?" Rider laughed. "Good Lord, she'd eat him alive."

He looked at the clock on his computer screen. "I'm going to go light a fire under Jake's ass. Once he's done cleaning up the toxic dump Rome turned the men's bathroom into, we'll wake up Daniel and meet in the bar. Daniel's going to be hungry."

"I'll wake up Daniel while you get Jake," I offered,

getting up from Rider's lap. I needed to talk to him anyway, clear the air. "He's in one of those rooms in the sublevels, right?"

Rider's eyes narrowed for a moment, his jealous suspicions evidently still there. But he must have trusted me because he told me where to find Daniel, kissed my forehead, and left the office to find Jake, Kutya trotting along behind him.

I usually didn't go down to the sublevels without either Rider or Daniel, but my handprint worked just as well on the access panels next to the doors. The security guards on duty, posted at various points throughout the lower levels, nodded in greeting, but otherwise didn't acknowledge my presence. And none of them attempted to stop me as I made my way down the hall to Rider's version of guest rooms.

I knocked on the door I'd been told I would find Daniel in, and when there was no answer, I turned the knob to find it unlocked. I poked my head in and lost my breath.

Daniel was asleep in what looked like a hospital bed in the Spartan room that held only the bed, a couch, a small round table with chairs, and a counter area with a small microwave and refrigerator. His shaggy rainbow colored hair was a mussy mess over the white pillow, and the white bed sheets were bunched down around his waist. He didn't have a shirt on, so all I saw was golden, muscular flesh. My succubus side sat up and took notice. I even thought I heard the damn thing purr.

"Down, girl," I whispered. "You'll get all the sex you want later, but we're not touching that."

I crept over to the bed. "Daniel."

He must have been really sleep deprived when he crashed, because Daniel usually woke up pretty easily. Something about his dragon, he said. Dragons were always on high alert. That's why they were such excellent guardians of treasure.

"Daniel." His eyebrow twitched, but nothing else happened, so I reached for him, feeling as though I were reaching for some forbidden fruit. I decided a big, meaty shoulder was a better spot to lay my hand than his pecs. Definitely not those rock hard abs with the narrow dusting of honey colored hair disappearing into places definitely restricted.

I gripped his warm shoulder and shook him. In an instant, his eyes opened halfway. He murmured something unintelligible and pulled me down, his mouth aiming straight for mine.

"Daniel!" I pulled away, both hands now on his chest, pushing him while he gripped my biceps.

His eyes flew open. "Danni? Shit!"

He released me and recoiled as if I were a snake he'd picked up by mistake, and rubbed a hand over his eyes. "Shit. I thought you were her."

"Her? Who—oh." His beloved, the woman who had been killed in front of him right after accepting his marriage proposal. The one he'd told me I reminded him of after he'd become my bodyguard. Salia. "You were dreaming of Salia, weren't you? That's why you didn't wake up when I said your name."

"I was trying to hold on to her." He scrubbed his fingers through his messy hair and looked at me. "Sorry I grabbed you. I swear there are times you just favor her so much. Those damn eyes. The way you move. You could be sisters."

"Is that why you're so attracted to me?" I blurted before my brain had time to catch up to my mouth.

Daniel blushed and his gaze lowered, staring at his lap instead of me.

"I'm sorry to blurt it out like that. It's just… Everyone knows. And it's dangerous. I'm with Rider. I love Rider."

"I know," he whispered. "I'm sorry, Danni. I'm sorry for any trouble I've caused you two, and … I'm sorry for what I said earlier about the fertility. Salia died before she could have children. Before we could have a family. I just… I care about you. Maybe part is because you remind me of her. Lord knows you're the only woman I've looked at since losing her, the only woman I've… I'm sorry. I know you love him, and he loves you. Implying he would be selfish not to let you have another man's child was bullshit. Jealous, selfish bullshit. I had no right saying any of that. I have no right to you."

"I love you," I blurted, and smiled at the shock and confusion in his eyes. "When you almost died in Pigeon Forge, I felt like a part of my heart was being ripped out of my chest. I love you and I always will, but I'm *in love* with Rider. He and I have a connection that, it just can't be replaced, but if not for that, I would be head over heels for you. You're a good man, and quite frankly…" I gestured toward him. "Do you have to be this fucking hot?"

He barked out a laugh. "Now you're just trying to make me feel better about losing out to that uptight vampire."

"You respect that uptight vampire."

"I do," he admitted. "And he's good to you. Hell, I've tried to see things that weren't there, looked for any sign he's hurt you so I could sweep in and rescue you, but the fact is, he's a good man. So good he'd let a jerk like me creep all around his woman because he'd put up with anything to keep her safe, even at the cost of his ego. Man, I want to hate him sometimes, but he makes it impossible."

I laughed and wiped away the tears that sprang free. "You two are the loves of my life. You're my best friend, Daniel. I hope you'll always be my best friend. I need you."

"I need you too. I'm not going anywhere." He lifted my hand and kissed it. "I go where you go, remember?"

I looked at the hand he held, and at the bracelet on my wrist with the dragon-inspired charms. "Do you want your bracelet back?"

"Of course not. It's not mine, it's a gift for my best

friend. And I'm still going to take you to Imortia someday so you can see its real beauty. It's almost a match for yours. *Almost*." He squeezed my hand before letting go, and scratched his head again, mussing his hair even more. "Uh, you didn't wake me up to talk about this, did you?"

"No. It's almost nightfall. We're supposed to meet upstairs to go over the plan."

"Ah. It's showtime." He swung his legs over the side of the bed and fisted his hand around the sheets hiding his lower body.

"Whoa." I grabbed his wrist. "You're not naked under there, are you?"

He smirked as he raised an eyebrow and yanked the sheet back, revealing a little pair of black boxers that rode low on his hips, hips that didn't contain an ounce of fat. I looked down and saw muscular thighs that had clearly never missed a leg day, but hadn't reached that gross overly sized state, and wouldn't, because most of Daniel's muscle came from being a dragon, not some lunkhead with a Planet Fitness membership and something to prove.

"Seriously, why do you have to be so damn hot?"

***

Daniel was hungry, which came as a surprise to no one. What did come as a surprise was the way I reached over and grabbed one of his tater tots without even realizing it. I froze with my hand in the air, holding the tater tot in the center of the table, fully aware all eyes were on me.

We'd gathered at a table near the back of the bar, far enough away from the few customers who'd fought the cold to come out to drink the night before New Year's Eve. Daniel had ordered a small feast, and Jake had grabbed a very bloody mary, too disgusted to eat after what he'd had to clean up in the men's room, but aware he needed to prepare for the possibility of getting killed and ensure he could come back from it.

The two of them sat next to each other, managing not to bicker. Rider sat on Jake's left with me by his side, and Tony sat between Daniel and me. Ginger was on her way, having awakened at nightfall.

"I'm sorry," I said, putting the tater tot back into the basket I'd grabbed it out of, and reached for a napkin to wipe the grease from my fingers. "I don't know why I just did that."

"Was that hunger pain you had earlier for actual food?" Rider asked.

I shrugged. "I don't know. I mean, that would be weird, wouldn't it?"

"Not that weird if you've reached the point you can eat food without getting sick. Your body knows when it can."

"You mean, you think I can eat again? Anything I want?"

"Are you getting her the chocolate cupcakes or am I?" Daniel asked, grinning around a mouthful of whatever he'd just shoveled in.

"Screw the cupcakes. I want pot roast," I said, putting an abrupt end to Rider's chuckling.

"Pot roast?" The disbelief in his voice would have probably made me laugh if I wasn't so busy fantasizing about all the food I wanted to devour.

"Pot roast, meatloaf, green beans, chicken noodle soup, oooh, that deep dish chicken noodle dinner from Bob Evans, the one with the mashed potatoes and biscuits, and baked pasta with Italian sausage crumbles. And sauerkraut. And pinto beans with cornbread!"

I became aware of them all staring at me, jaws dropped, even Tony, and felt heat rise to my face in a blush. "What?"

"So let me get this straight," Rider said. "You don't want a cupcake?"

"Or anything chocolate?" Daniel added. "Like, at all?"

My nose scrunched on its own at the thought of sweet stuff. "No, I don't want anything sweet. Why? Is that bad?"

Rider shook his head slowly, but his eyes were saying it was. "No, no, that's all fine. Just a little surprising. You're usually very, uh, enthusiastic about wanting cupcakes."

"You usually cry like you just lost your dog because you can't have them," Daniel said.

I shrugged. "What can I say? I want food. Real food."

Daniel picked up his basket of tater tots and looked at Rider. "Can she?"

Rider was still looking at me strangely, so it took him a moment to realize Daniel was asking him if I could have the tots. "Um, yeah, it's probably safe if she's craving them, although vampires generally don't crave anything but blood. We know when we can eat food again and enjoy the taste of it, but it's never an actual craving."

"She's got the hybrid thing, though," Jake pointed out. "That always throws a twist in everything, but that said, we're about to take out a pranic vampire. It's not the best time to be experimenting with whether food is going to stay down or turn you into Linda Blair."

"That's true." I deflated into my chair with a sigh. "It's best I not risk it right now."

"You can eat when you come back," Rider said. "Are you sure you don't want me to have cupcakes waiting for you?"

"What the hell is up with you people wanting to feed the girl cupcakes?" Jake asked.

"Watching her eat them is like porn," they said in perfect synchronization.

Jake's eyebrows raised. "Give the girl a cupcake. Some things are worth the risk."

Rider growled low in his throat, and Jake winked at him. "Settle down, Fangzilla. It was a joke. You have to work on this simmering rage thing you got going on. Have you tried journaling?"

"I asked him that shortly after we met," Daniel said. "I don't think he's ever taken it into consideration. He's all growls and dismemberment and shit."

"That's sad," Jake said, and clapped a hand on Rider's shoulder. "You should get in touch with your feminine side."

"I'm going to get in touch with your feminine side when I tear your junk off and beat you with it if you don't stop being a pain in my ass," Rider said.

Jake angled his head to look at me. "You've clearly been a bad influence on him."

I laughed and kissed Rider's cheek, sensing his temper cool at the contact. "You can have cupcakes waiting for me if you want. It would take hours to make pinto beans correctly anyway, and I'm hoping to not take that long with Ramson."

Ginger arrived, dressed in black jeans and a black long sleeve shirt under her matching leather jacket. Even her lips were black as she squeezed in between Tony and me.

"And what lipstick color are you wearing tonight?" Jake asked, amusement already twinkling in his eyes.

"Midnight Blowjob," she answered. "So, what's our plan?"

***

"I know I don't have to tell you to be careful or give you any instruction, but I feel like I'll jinx you or something if I don't give you a million warnings to be careful and remind you to stay close to Porter, stay calm, and don't take any unnecessary risks."

I looked into deep blue nervous eyes and smiled. "You've come a long way, Rider Knight. The urge to toss me over your shoulder and dump me in a locked room must be killing you right now."

"You have no idea."

I chuckled and gave him yet another kiss goodbye. It was probably somewhere around the eighth one since everyone had armored up, grabbing blades, guns, and other goodies I didn't know how to use, but the others had been trained on. Of course, Jake was always prepared to fight and had kept weapons hidden on him the entire time he'd been with us. Rider hadn't bothered asking the man to give them up. For one thing, he trusted him, even if he acted like he didn't. For another, Jake would just tear up the bar, making weapons out of whatever he could find if something happened and he didn't have any on hand.

"You two are so sweet," Rihanna said, standing a few feet away from us, not even trying to look like she was giving us a moment of privacy. "But I feel like I should remind you time is money, although I do enjoy taking your dollars."

Rider rolled his eyes. "I need to find a cheaper witch."

"I heard that."

I chuckled despite the surge of nerves coursing through me. The time had arrived. We had to go. "We need to go. He has to know his men aren't coming back by now. We can't let him get too ready to defend himself from an attack."

Rider nodded, kissed me one last goodbye, and stepped back next to Kutya. "I'll have your cupcakes waiting, and we can get you real food too as soon as you get back."

"Can't wait."

I turned to the others who were all waiting next to the staircase that led to Rider's private quarters, all dressed in black, all ready to fight, and grabbed Daniel's outstretched hand. Then I took Jake's hand and turned to mouth, "I love you" to Rider as the group joined hands with Rihanna and she transported us to Bitter Creek, Alabama.

One moment I was holding hands with my team in The Midnight Rider, the next we were on the outer edge of the property Ramson had taken over.

"I don't fool with pranic vampires," Rihanna said, the first to let go, "so this is where I leave you. Reach out to Rider when you're done, and I'll be back for you."

"Damn, she left in a hurry," Daniel said as we all

released each other's hands, staring at the spot Rihanna had just vanished from. "It's a shame she didn't stick around to fight."

"A witch would have been handy, but we're a good team," Jake said. "Just stick to the plan."

The plan wasn't all that complicated. Daniel would take to the air, ensure Ramson and any other prannies he may have created didn't escape if they got past us inside, Tony would enter from the rear of the church with Ginger watching his back, and Jake and I would go right through the front door. Newly turned vampires would likely shit their pants and run from the slayer, heading toward the back right where a tiger waited to tear them apart. Or eat them. I'd seen Tony do both.

Jake would slice and shoot through whoever didn't, and I would pick off any he might miss, and be there in case all the killing overwhelmed his ability to keep a leash on his slayer power. I prayed he was right that I'd be able to calm him, otherwise I'd be the first of our group to die at his hand.

"Everyone in place," Jake said, no one questioning his leadership. As much as Daniel and Tony disliked Jake, there was no arguing it was best to let the slayer lead. "And keep your emotions neutral. Don't let that fucker feed off of you."

The men gave sharp nods, Ginger plopped a quick kiss on my cheek, told us to be careful, and they took off, Daniel taking a running leap into the air before disappearing in a cascade of rainbow sparkles, reemerging as a dark blue dragon with a silver underbelly, and Tony and Ginger sprinting away toward the back of the church.

"That's pretty damn awesome," Jake said, his voice full of awe as he watched Daniel fly higher and angled his head sideways, trying to get a better view. "His balls have to be like melons. Or bowling balls, maybe."

I snorted a laugh as we sprinted closer to the church, glad somebody else understood my curiosity. "I know, but

I can never see them. His back legs always block the view."

"Does Rider know you're trying to see your bodyguard's balls?"

"I'm not trying to see Daniel's balls, I'm trying to see the dragon's ba—oh, shut up. You want to see them too!"

"Yeah, I actually kind of do, and that's something I never thought I'd say."

"Look at you, all confident in your masculinity."

"Fuck yeah, I'm confident in my masculinity," he said as we saw the church ahead of us and ducked down behind a set of bushes to do a quick scan of the property. "My dick is huge."

I gave him a shove, nearly knocking him over. "Men. So obsessed with size. It doesn't matter as much as you think."

"Oh, so Rider's not packing much, huh?"

"Rider's packing more than enough, thank you very much, but it wouldn't matter to me if he wasn't because I love him."

"Yeah, but you'd love your vibrator more if he was lacking." Jake chuckled and dodged my next shove.

We're in place, Ginger's voice spoke into my head. We were all on the same telepathic frequency except for Jake. *Ready?*

"They're in place," I told the slayer. "We ready?"

"Go," he said.

Go, I repeated in my mind for the others, and we rushed forward.

I had my blade in my hand, a dagger because I preferred the length to that of a sword, and it was easier to sheathe in the sheath I had around my right thigh. Jake had a gun, one he said shot UV bullets. I wasn't entirely sure what those were, but I knew if sunlight weakened vampires, having straight UV pumped into one's body had to do a hundred times more damage.

The church was older, with signs that it needed repairs, but the massive doors looked sturdy. They didn't stand a chance against Jake Porter as he blew them open with one kick, and we moved inside.

The first room we entered was the vestibule, and it was empty. I knew from the vision I'd pulled from Mike that the next set of doors in front of us would be the nave and the sanctuary and the halls to our right and left would take us past those to the kitchen area and the atrium.

"There are vampires inside, and humans. Try not to kill the humans unless they're defending Ramson," Jake warned me. "That really pisses off the slayer in me."

Then he kicked through the doors to the nave, cracking the bolt that had been set in half before it went flying into the air, and we stepped inside. At least two dozen people were inside, trying to duck down and hide among the pews that stretched out toward the sanctuary, which was not in use by Ramson. I tried to sense him, but couldn't pinpoint his location among all the other energy surrounding me. My heightened nerves didn't help me either. Remembering what Jake had said about pranic vampires feeding off of emotion, I willed myself to calm down. I was with Jake Porter. I was safe. Daniel was in the sky, out of reach, and Tony and Ginger were practically trained mercenaries. Tony *ate* people, for crying out loud. We were going to be all right.

Even if this turned out to be the night Auntie Mo's vision came true and I found myself alone, I was going to be all right. I felt it in my bones. I was going to make it out of here alive. All of us were.

Jake immediately scanned the room once we entered, assessing threats, and before I could do the same, he aimed and fired, shooting a tall, thin man in the face. I watched in horror as flames erupted from the entry point and quickly swallowed the man whole, reducing him to nothing but a mass of char and goo.

Everyone in the room started screaming, and it took all my willpower not to join them. "What the hell was that?"

"UV bullet," Jake said, yelling to be heard over the

screaming people running away from us, exiting through the side door that would dump them into the hallway. "He was a brand new prannie. Come on."

"I thought you said prannies were hard to kill," I said as I followed him down the aisle toward the door the humans had escaped through.

"They are, but a newb's a newb. And I'm Jacob Fucking Porter."

I rolled my eyes but kept up with him as we reached the side door and entered the hallway, both doing a quick side-to-side scan as bodies ran in every direction, some of them smelling an awful lot like piss.

"Dumbasses," Jake muttered. "How fun is the cult now, you jackwads?"

He closed his eyes and took a deep breath before reopening them. "They're underground. It's just humans and regular vamps up here, nothing that Tony and Ginger can't handle on their own. We're going downstairs. Let them know."

We're going down below, I told the others through our mind-link as I followed Jake. *Jake says there are just humans and regular vamps up here. You got those?*

We got those, Ginger replied through the link, and it sounded like she was grunting. *Anyone have eyes on Julie yet?*

No, I replied.

No, Daniel said. *I've seen some humans run out, but not her. You guys be careful and let me know if you need me to dive in.*

We need you up there, I told him. *You're our containment. We'll be safe.*

I sensed his emotions through the link, and knew he was struggling with being so far away from us, so far away from me, but we'd all agreed this was the best plan. Most of the dumbass humans who'd joined the cult were only a danger to themselves, and the ones who were snatched didn't deserve what had happened to them. We couldn't let any of Ramson's minions out though, and that included the ones who were still human but were willing to kill for him. Any who stood against us were going down, but the humans who ran because they weren't rapists or killers could leave unharmed.

"Where the fuck are the stairs?" Jake growled as we dodged and swerved around the men and women screaming and running around us, looking for exits. In the distance, I heard a tiger roar and knew Tony was either snacking or slaying.

I grabbed the back of Jake's jacket and jerked him to a halt before raising a finger, gesturing for him to watch my back while giving me a moment, and closed my eyes. I may have never connected directly with Ramson, but I saw him in my visions. I was meant to see him. I was meant to find and kill him, so I had to have some sort of way to locate him.

I cast my senses out, remembering how I'd forced the vision out of Mike, and that I'd tasted the blood of Ramson's men, men who had tasted Ramson's blood. Even if I'd thrown it all up since, Ramson's blood had been in me and blood was power. There had to be something left, some bit of energy I could still lock onto.

There. I sensed him all around me. Everyone there had ingested his blood, either straight from his vein, or unknowingly mixed with the juice he'd given them. I locked onto that energy pulsing around me, focused on it until I could feel where it pulsed the strongest. "This way."

CHAPTER NINETEEN

"Sure you're not part slayer?" Jake asked as we made our way to the kitchen, killing two vamps and a human man who decided Ramson was worth stabbing a woman for along the way. I didn't get stabbed. I moved faster than the man. I also found the door to the stairwell leading down to the basement off the pantry. "I should have sensed this before you did."

"I don't need any more freaky bits thrown in with my cocktail of whatever-the-hell-I-am, thank you very much," I said. "I drank from men who drank from Ramson. With enough focus, I picked up his signature or whatever and was able to pinpoint where he was."

"Well, I sense him now, and he's got fangy friends," Jake said as we crept down the stairs, him in front because he had a little of Rider and Daniel's overprotectiveness in him.

Stairs to the basement are off the pantry in the kitchen, I told the others. *In case you want to join us when you run out of vamps to kill up here.*

Hook up with you later, Ginger said. *We found ourselves a little party. Having a*—grunt—*real good time.*

Be careful. I might need a woman to kiss if I have to use my lure and it doesn't go well.

Try to make the kiss hot this time, Daniel chimed in and I thought I might have actually heard Tony chuckle.

I'd tell you to bite me, Daniel, but I—grunt—*agree with you,* Ginger said. *Make it hot this time, Danni.*

I almost laughed, but we'd reached the bottom of the stairs and the air had shifted. Danger was near, and it came from more than one place. One of those places was right there in front of me and it had the hair along the nape of my neck standing on end.

"Did you just shift into super slayer mode or something?"

"Probably," Jake said, voice low, body tense. Head on a swivel and gun raised in front of him.

We'd entered a small room full of boxes, likely a storage area, and it looked like a hole had been blown out of the wall, and a tunnel stretched out beyond that. The thing seemed to be carved out of dirt and rock, and if not for my vampiric eyesight, I'd be blind in it.

"Are you going to be able to see in there?"

"What I can't see with my eyes, I'll feel," Jake answered.

I certainly hoped he'd feel it before it was on him.

I moved to the side of Jake a little as we entered and crept down the tunnel. From my new vantage point, I could see the intense focus in his eyes, the eyes of a hunter. His jaw was tight, his breath slow and controlled. Something powerful seemed to ooze out of his pores, and although it was a warning to all things paranormal that a deadly killer was within range, it was kind of a turn-on. No wonder the man was known as such an epic slayer. Female vampires probably saw him coming and offered to jump right on his *stake*.

Jake came to an abrupt stop and slowly turned his head toward me before raising an eyebrow, the killer look in his eyes replaced by one that was more of a mix between horror and amusement.

"What? Why are you looking at me like—oh shit, was I thinking out loud?"

"Yup."

Fucking hell. I looked down at the ground and wished for it to open up and swallow me whole, but of course it didn't, so I had to suck up what was left of my pride and self-esteem and look him in the eye. "We never speak of this again."

"Yeah, no problem. I'm not trying to start a fight with Rider Knight." He shook his head and started moving again, and I fell into step behind him.

"It's just because you look so much like Dean Winchester," I said as we continued down the passageway, and I stifled a cough. The musty earth was getting into my lungs.

"I thought you were hot for Spike now."

"Can't I be hot for both?"

"I think I like you better when you're just hot for Spike. Less chance of your man making good on his threat to tear off my junk. How's your succubus side doing?"

"Fine," I said, although I did feel a little ... *itchy*. "Why?"

"Because I can feel it creeping along the edge of its cage, which is probably why you're having horny thoughts about men you really don't even want to sleep with out loud without realizing it. Keep a leash on it or I'm going to have to use one of these hawthorn syringes on you and have to fight off these vamps with you hanging over my shoulder. Screws with my aim, you know? Remember what I said about breathing."

Shit. I'd been promising the damn thing blood and sex and its impatient ass was so ready for payout, I didn't even know it had started trying to crawl out. *Stay put*, I told it. *What you want is coming. Just wait.*

I won't wait long, it said back.

"Impatient, greedy bitch," I muttered.

Jake gave me another look.

"I'm not talking to you. We have to hurry up and kill Ramson and get out of here."

"No shit. You're halfway to Crazy Town."

I ignored the comment and coughed again. "What are we in, a cave system?"

"Underground tunnels. Vampires have been doing this for ages. They're strong enough to do it all themselves in a relatively short time. They carve out tunnels and entire rooms underneath a structure they use as their decoy. It's harder to sense them from aboveground, even for me, and they're safe from the sun in case someone kicks the doors down or tears the roof off to get to them."

"Except when you bring the sun with you in those nifty bullets."

"Exactly. Make sure you stay clear of these things."

"How about you just don't shoot me?"

"Gee, why didn't I think of that?" He shot me a perturbed look. "Shit happens in battle. Just watch where you're running and jumping if shit gets crazy, and try to stay behind me. That is, if you can stay behind me without getting lost fantasizing about my ass."

"Believe me, it wasn't your ass I was fantasizing about, flapjack."

Jake came to another abrupt stop, glared back at me, and for a moment I thought he might actually shoot me. "That was just mean."

He turned and continued on until we came to a wide open space. I sensed his body go on an even higher alert as we crept closer to the mouth at the end of the tunnel. The energy I'd sensed upstairs was stronger here, cluing me in that Ramson was nearby, but he wasn't alone.

We'd barely stepped into the wider space when vampires started pouring in from two tunnels on either side of the back of the room. Male and female, dark shadows all my age or younger in vampire years, from the feel of things, but some were a bit more powerful than others. *The pranic ones.*

Jake immediately opened fire, taking out as many as he could with his UV bullets before he'd be forced to switch to blades and hand-to-hand combat. As the bullets found purchase, the bodies lit up in flames, human-sized bonfires lighting up the room. There was nothing in it to run into or trip over other than a thick support column in the center, so they kept coming straight for us and Jake did his best to thin the herd.

Just when I'd begun to wonder how many bullets his gun held, I heard it click and he traded it out for a Bowie knife. "Keep your back to mine and don't let the fuckers get you."

Roger that, I thought, turning so my back was against Jake's. Between my dagger and his Bowie knife, we sliced and diced our way through at least a dozen vampires as we made our way to the center of the room, headed toward the tunnel on the left. That was the one where the energy was the strongest. That was where we would find Ramson.

I used my dagger to stake a brunette through the heart and kicked her aside in time to see a tall, wiry man with balding brown hair approaching me. He walked too slowly for someone engaged in battle and smiled like he held a really big secret. I found out what that secret was when he approached me and I swung my arm, only to have it frozen in place before my dagger could do any damage.

"Jake! This bastard is freezing me."

The pranic vampire's smile morphed into a vicious snarl, and he lunged for me. Half a second before his open maw could clamp around my throat and tear it out, a heavy weight pressed down on my head and I slammed into the ground ass-first just in time to see Jake's Bowie knife go through the vampire's throat then pull back out, showering me with blood.

"Gross!"

"It'll wash off," he said, yanking me back up onto my feet by my jacket collar. "Besides, you're half vampire. You love that shit."

"Not *on* me!" I yelled at him, then noticed a stocky vampire running straight for him. I reacted in an instant, sweeping Jake's legs out from under him and turning, dagger in hand. I drove it into the vampire's crotch and twisted while the man screamed in excruciating pain. I pulled my dagger free just as Jake rolled to his feet and stood behind the vampire, where he sliced its head clear off its neck.

The vampires kept coming, and we kept fighting, our only illumination coming from the still-burning remains of the vampires Jake had shot with the UV bullets. I was thankful to notice most of our opponents were regular vampires. I took care of those while Jake took out the pranic ones. Despite being pranic and therefore more powerful, they were young and dumb, most of them shocked completely stupid when they tried to get into Jake's head or mine and were met with what I assumed to be static or just a brick wall. I was thankful we lucked out for that because even with a slayer at my back, going up against so many, especially ones who could feed and gain power from the very thing we were doing to destroy them, was not easy by any means.

I was not thankful to find myself face to face with Julie Chavez. I recognized her instantly, took a quick assessment and realized she had been turned into a vampire, but she hadn't inherited the pranic ability of her sire.

"Julie, no!" I yelled as she rushed toward me, bringing her to a stop.

She cocked her head to the side, confusion or just plain curiosity outweighing her thirst for blood. "Who are you? How do you know my name?"

I jumped away from Jake before I ducked the blow of another vampire, making sure I didn't accidentally cause the slayer to get injured, and made quick work of the vamp. I wasn't very old myself, but I'd been training with Nannette and Daniel long enough to outfight the mostly clumsy opponents we'd been facing since entering the underground fight zone. These vampires just rushed us, mouths open, ready to sink their fangs into flesh. They didn't have any actual fighting skills.

"I'm Rider's girlfriend," I told her, kicking what was left of the vampire aside after I'd sliced him from his navel to his throat before getting my dagger into his heart and used it to pluck the organ out of his chest. "Rider Knight? The man who saved you from a life of nearly getting murdered and beaten to make ends meet? Remember him?"

I saw shame flit across her eyes before they hardened again. "He saved me, but I had no freedom. I just wanted to live life without restrictions."

"Well, you don't have much of a life now, given you've just been turned into a psycho's guard dog. Did he or his men rape you too? That's what they've been doing to others."

"No." She shook her head back and forth as she stepped backward. "No. I was given a home here. And power."

I sidestepped a vamp that had just run past Julie and launched herself at me, bringing my dagger up in time to split her open as she sailed past. She wasn't dead, but she was too busy writhing on the blood and body-littered ground to be much of a threat. "Rider would have let you go if you asked for your freedom. He would have done it without killing you first. You can still—Jake, no!"

I shoved the slayer back before he could swing his knife across Julie's throat, and held my hands up, shocked when he snarled at me. "Jake, we can save this one. She was Rider's donor. Jake?"

He went into overdrive, slicing and stabbing what was left of the vampires in a mad flurry of movement as I blocked Julie with my body and stared, my jaw hanging open as he obliterated over a dozen vampires, spraying blood and viscera everywhere. He was a man possessed.

"Jake?"

He sliced open the last vampire and ripped out its heart, turned toward me, and snarled again, his eyes completely crazed, and I nearly choked on a swallow, realizing this was what he'd been worried about. Slayer bloodlust. He came at me, his teeth clenched tight as if he were fighting himself, struggling internally, but losing. With a jerky yet fast movement, he swung at me, the blade arcing straight for my head.

I ducked and rolled, feeling the gust of air when the blade sailed over my head, narrowly missing its target. The moment I was on my back, my gaze locked onto Jake's, I held my hands up defensively and summoned my succubus power. "Stop."

He jerked to a stop, his hands wrapped around the gun he'd just reloaded with bullets guaranteed to turn me into a torch, one finger poised over the trigger, and the damn thing was pointed right at my chest. Where the hell were Ginger and Tony? Actually, come to think of it, I was glad they hadn't joined us yet. He'd kill them too if I didn't snap him back to himself.

"Come to me," I said, feeling my power surge out of me, filling the damp, musky air with something warm and humid. Intoxicating. "You don't want to kill me, Jake. You want to love me."

His eyes dilated, and then he shook his head, lowering the gun.

"That's a good boy. Put the gun down."

"All right, dammit. You snapped me out of it," he said, taking a few deep breaths. "Stop with the *hey there big boy* stuff before this gets even weirder." He ran a bloody hand through his hair and looked past me at Julie, who stood where I'd left her, completely dumbfounded. "That's the donor?"

"Yeah." I got to my feet, fighting through the succubus power still wafting all around me, and moved next to him so we could face her together.

"Breathe slowly, Danni. You have to reel that shit back in or else I'm hitting you with the hawthorn oil."

I nodded my understanding and started taking deep, slow breaths, but we didn't have a lot of time. We'd cut down his army, but Ramson was still down there somewhere, and we had to get Julie over to our side. I'd try to breathe slowly and talk at the same time. "I don't think you came here because you wanted to defend some man who's snatching women off the street, Julie. Rider knows you didn't come here seeking to be turned into a vampire. He'll help you."

Julie shook her head and opened her mouth to speak, and the back wall blew out, sending large chunks of rock and dirt hurling straight at us.

Jake shoved me to the ground just in time for the debris to fly over us and then yanked me back onto my feet. A wave of dizziness rolled over me, along with a shock of bitter cold as nervous energy filled me and my mind started racing with thoughts that were only half mine. I'd awakened the beast by using the lure, and it wanted to be fed.

It couldn't have picked a worse time, I realized as I saw the man stepping over the rubble of what was left behind after he'd used his power to blow out the wall. He wore a flowy white long sleeve shirt unbuttoned enough to show he had chest hair, and flowy white pants. His feet were bare, his chestnut hair curled around his shoulders. He looked exactly like I'd seen in my vision.

"Ah, look at all this tragedy. Who could have done such a thing?" He smiled as he looked at Jake, noticing how the slayer braced himself to fight, then scanned the carnage again before rolling his gaze over me and Julie before returning it to where Jake stood. "The moves, the kill count, the Dean Winchester copy and paste job... you must be the one I've heard so many stories about. Jake Porter, slayer of pranic vampires and all who go bump in the night. And who is your little girlfriend?"

"Danni Keller, slayer of testicles," Jake answered. "Fuck with her. I dare you."

No, no, don't fuck with me, I thought to myself as I struggled to focus on slow breathing while the big bad stood right in front of us, looking all kinds of good to my horny little friend trying to break free of her cage.

Stay in there, I growled internally.

You said I'd have blood and sex.

You will! Blood now, sex when we get back to the bar. Just let me do this alone. You'll get what you want!

Liar...

"Julie." Energy pulsated in the room as Ramson locked his gaze onto Julie's. "Kill them."

Her body snapped to attention, her eyes went dark and lifeless, and she sprang forward as if she were shot out of a gun, one thing in mind: kill.

"Kill that sonofabitch," I told Jake as I dropped to the ground and spun with my leg out, taking Julie's legs out from underneath her. I heard his gun go off not even a second later, but I couldn't take the time to see what he was doing because Julie was under Ramson's complete control now. She might not have been a trained fighter, but she was a scrapper, which made sense given her former profession. I imagined she'd had to fend off violent men more than just the one night when she'd nearly lost, but had been saved by Rider, only to end up in what had to be an even worse situation now because she'd trusted her old partner.

I didn't want to kill her. I wanted to take her back to The Midnight Rider and let Rider decide what to do with her. She couldn't have done much harm yet. She hadn't been turned long, and Rider wouldn't blame her for attacking us while under her sire's power. Unfortunately, I didn't think I was going to be able to save her.

I narrowly avoided getting my throat bit out and rolled Julie over, getting back on top where I had the upper hand. A quick glance showed Jake and Ramson fighting hand to hand. The pranic vampire apparently did have telekinetic power, judging by the way he'd blasted through the back wall and how Jake's gun was on the ground, broken in two. There was also the fact that he was hurling large chunks of rock at Jake without touching them. I grabbed a handful of Julie's long hair and slammed her head into the ground, hoping to knock her unconscious.

The whole time I fought her, our bodies so close together, my succubus side threw a fit, wanting away from the estrogen. It wanted the testosterone in the men fighting not that far away from me. I crawled over Julie to get to them, my mind screaming for me to slow my breathing, reminding me I'd sent the succubus power back before. I could do it again.

Now I feed, the succubus said.

"No!" I yelled out loud while steadily crawling toward the two men too busy fighting to notice me.

Something latched on to my thigh and my body was yanked backward, my knees scraping over the debris on the ground and sliding through blood and guts before I was roughly turned onto my back and Julie went for my throat, her fangs ready to tear into my flesh and rip out my jugular.

"No!" I raised my arms, grabbed her by the shoulders, and used all the strength I could summon to throw her over my head. I heard her hit something hard and turned just in time to see her slide down the dirt and stone column in the center of the room before it snapped in half and the ceiling crashed down over me.

I was on my back, but not flat. I was on my right hip, it having twisted as everything came down on me. Most of what fell was dirt, large chunks of it, but heavy rocks had been in the mix. It all weighed down on me, covering me. I felt wetness glide down my face as I struggled to move, to get an arm out or turn my upper body so I could get into a crawling position, but I didn't know if it was because I was crying or bleeding.

I opened my mouth to scream for help, but tasted dirt and immediately closed it. I tried reaching out with my mind, but there was too much panic inside me, too much fear. *Rider*. I needed Rider. I tried to reach out to him and only heard my succubus side laughing.

It's my time, it said as my body froze over and what little I could move was spent writhing in pain and need.

I was alone. Just as Auntie Mo predicted, I was alone on a battlefield, unable to reach anyone. I was wrapped in a silence so deafening I knew I had to be buried deep to not hear anything. Jake would have been yelling for me. Even if he wasn't, I would have heard him fighting. There was no way Jake lost to Ramson. No way. He would—Jake could have been buried too. I had no idea if the entire room had caved in or just the side I was on.

The thought of Jake being stuck under the rubble, unable to get free, dying repeatedly until he no longer had enough of a blood booster to come back gave me the strength I needed to put everything I had into rolling over. With a grunt and a near scream when pain sliced through me, I rolled my hip and back, dislodged enough rubble to get onto my hands and knees.

Yes, the succubus said. *Get to the man.*

"Fuck you," I said, spitting out dirt. "I'm saving him, not sucking out his soul."

The succubus only laughed, and I couldn't blame it. It knew it had me. My body was colder than ice, my loins aching, my breath escaping in desperate pants. I should have grabbed Julie Chavez and kissed her, used her like I'd used Ginger the last time this beast had gotten away from me, but I hadn't thought of it until it was too late, until I was buried under a ton of rubble, slowly crawling in the direction I remembered seeing the tunnel in the back of the room, barely making any progress because the rubble was all around me, cutting into my knees and palms, weighing me down.

"I have to get out of here." More wetness slid down

my face. It was definitely tears, although I knew blood covered me too. "I have to get out of here. I have to get out of here. I have to get out of here." The tears came faster, my aching body heaving with sobs as my desperation grew. I'd never been claustrophobic, but being buried alive was enough to drive anyone mad. "I have to get out of here. I have to get out of here." My voice grew louder, steadily rising along with my panic until I was screaming, my voice echoing around me, unable to escape the shield of rubble encasing me. "I have to get out of here, I have to get out of here, I HAVE TO GET OUT OF HERE!"

Something came out of me, a burst of power that momentarily obliterated the freezing cold that had taken over my body just as it obliterated the surrounding rubble, blowing an exit hole through the mess. I crawled through the rubble, climbing toward the opening, ignoring the pain, the chill freezing my body, and the aching between my legs.

Give in to it, the succubus coaxed me. *You'll have power unlike anything you've known before, and what you need now is power. You need to ease that ache and feed.*

"No!" I continued crawling, slipping on my own blood that came from my palms and knees, until I made it out of the heap of rubble and toppled over the edge, slamming down onto my back with enough force to knock the wind out of my lungs. I saw stars for a moment, the back of my head having hit the ground just as hard, but I knew where I was. I was at the mouth of the tunnel I'd seen at the back right of the room.

I looked for Jake, but could only see a giant wall of rubble blocking my view. He had to be somewhere in the room. I prayed he wasn't buried because I didn't think I could get to him. I didn't know what that was that had come out of me and blown a hole in the rubble so I could get out from under it, but I didn't think I had any of it left in me. I didn't have anything left in me but pain and yearning. I ignored the pain to writhe on the ground, on fire despite the freezing cold in my veins. I needed blood to soothe my thirst, and I needed a man to give me strength and warmth.

I couldn't go after Jake. Someone else had to find him. I had to… I had to push the succubus back down, put her back in her cage before I could face any of the men. I opened my mouth to order it back where it belonged, but I couldn't. I was in so much pain, so tired, so woozy from blood loss, blood I was still losing as it poured from the gashes in my knees and palms. So desperate for the taste of a man.

Tears spilled from my eyes, and even they were cold. Breathe, I thought. Breathe slowly. Put it back before—

"Danni! There you are."

No! I tried to slow my breathing, but it only increased, panic taking over as I heard his footsteps running toward me. Not him, not him, not him! I opened my mouth, tried to scream at him to stay away, but nothing came out but my quick, shallow breaths. I was hyperventilating. I was hyperventilating, and the succubus was laughing because it was finally going to get what it wanted. I had to fight it. I had to—

"Danni! Shit, there's so much blood. Hang on."

He fell to his knees and leaned over me, assessing the damage, his throat so close to my face as he checked my body for broken bones. So close to me. So much testosterone. So much heat. So much… blood.

My fangs punched through my gums and my succubus side gave me the strength I needed to grab his shoulders and pull him down far enough to plunge my fangs into his throat.

"Danni, ow… *Danni.*" He'd tensed, prepared to pull away and defend himself, but the tension evaporated as he covered me, one hand unzipping my pants as his blood poured into my mouth.

CHAPTER TWENTY

I came awake with a rapid heartbeat, sensing something was wrong. I sat up quickly to find myself in Rider's room, in the bed we shared, and I had a small audience.

"You're safe," Rider said, moving over to sit on the edge of the bed. His face was a blank mask, but I knew him well enough to know that was the face he wore when he didn't want to frighten or worry me. "We got all the blood and grime off of you, picked out all the debris in your cuts and sealed your wounds."

I'd been wounded. It came back to me. Rocks cutting into my palms and knees while mounds of rocks and boulders and dirt weighed me down, but I kept going. I kept going until...

"You're all right now," Eliza said, leaning over me from the other side of the bed, her pale cornflower blue eyes full of compassion. "You are safe now, with friends who love you. It's all right."

Why was she talking to me like this, like I was a trauma victim? Why was Nannette standing at the foot of the bed, observing me like I was some sort of specimen? "What happened?"

"It doesn't matter now, sweetheart. You just need to

drink some more blood, get some rest."

They weren't telling me something. I sat up and searched my mind. I'd gone with Jake to get Ramson. We took Ginger, Daniel, and Tony... I got lost. I was all alone, all alone in the rubble after everything came down on me. I was all alone... except for the succubus in me. It was thirsty, impatient. It was too strong for me. It wasn't now. It was well-behaved, locked in its cage... *sated.*

No. I shook my head as the memories came back. Crawling, aching, scared. I needed out. I needed to get to safety, I needed to get to help. I needed to stop the bleeding. I found a way out, a hole that had formed in the rubble. I crawled up and out, falling from the rubble once I'd cleared it. I was so weak and frightened, and that made the succubus so strong, so free to do what it wanted. And then he came to help me.

"No."

"Danni, he's safe too," Rider assured me. "You didn't kill hm. Ginger got to you in time."

"No." I remembered the sound of my zipper being pulled down, the feel of my pants as they were torn from my legs. I saw him looming over me... "The succubus won. I did it. I—"

"You did nothing," Rider said, voice firm. "Neither of you knew what you were doing, and you were too weak to stop it, too hurt. It took advantage."

"No." I shook my head, tears gliding down my face. "No. No. Nooooooo." And then I started screaming, realizing what I'd done, what I'd taken, and who I had hurt. I couldn't remember actually giving my body to another, couldn't remember what it felt like, but I knew it had happened, and I knew the dark part of me had loved it, had feasted on it, had... tried to take his soul.

I broke past the hands trying to hold me down and ran for the door, but it didn't open. I couldn't stop running. The room was small, but I ran anyway, dodging hands and arms as I screamed, unable to put the shame and rage and terror into anything else. My nightmare had come true. I had become the monster I'd so greatly feared becoming, and I'd hurt someone I cared about so much, took something from him I could never give back, caused him pain I could never heal. And I'd tried to kill him. And I'd hurt Rider. I'd betrayed the man I loved.

I started scratching at my skin. "I'm filthy, I'm filthy!"

"Danni, stop!"

I ignored Rider. He shouldn't care. I shouldn't let him care. I was filthy and disgusting, and horrible. I was unworthy. I fought against his hold, and made it into the bathroom where I ran into the shower, twisting the knobs until hot water rained down on me, and I tore off the T-shirt he'd covered me with after cleaning the aftermath of what I'd done, something he should have never had to have done. Because I should have been better, stronger. I should have been worthy. Instead, I was filthy and unclean, just like Ramson's men had said.

I grabbed the soap and slathered it all over me, trying to get the filth off of me, but it wasn't enough. My dirt was below the skin. I was the dirt. I was the filthy, vile thing that ruined everything it touched. I tore at my skin, sinking my fingernails in deep before I ripped at it, desperate to get rid of all my filth.

"Fuck! Danni, stop!" A towel was wrapped around me and I was pulled free of the shower, slammed onto the hard tile floor with bands of steel wrapped around me.

"Use your sire power and force her to stop," Nannette said. "She's going to kill herself."

"You think I haven't tried that?" Rider snapped as he held me tighter, wrestling with me on the floor, struggling to keep me in place as I bucked and writhed, trying to get free to scrub myself clean.

"You're not dirty, Danni," he growled against my ear as he held me against him, my back to his chest. "A bad thing happened, but you didn't want it to. You can't do this to yourself."

"Kill me."

"No."

"Kill me, please," I begged before dissolving into sobs. "Don't let me hurt anyone else. Don't let me hurt you again."

"The only way you hurt me is if you leave me. I love you."

"You can't!" I quit struggling, my energy depleted, my heart aching to the point I didn't understand how it didn't just crack in half and cease beating, doing me the favor of ending my torture. "No one can love me after what I've done. After I… I …" Nausea rolled in my stomach. "I raped Tony!"

I didn't even make it to the toilet before all the blood in me started coming back up.

***

I woke up in a new T-shirt, with Rider's arms wrapped around me. He'd dried off and changed into a new T-shirt and pants. We were alone this time, but he was prepared for me to run. I didn't feel like running though. I was strangely calm.

"It's New Year's Eve," he said softly. "You threw up until you passed out and then the day sleep took you under."

"Why am I calm?"

"Once you were asleep, I could get into your mind, give you a suggestion to remain calm. That's all I did, I promise. You've had your mind manipulated enough, but I can't let you hurt yourself."

"Why not? I hurt you."

"Only when you tried to hurt yourself and asked me to kill you."

"You should want to. After what I did, how can you even look at me?"

"Do you even remember what happened? I mean,

really? Was your mind even there?"

I thought back to what had happened and realized I couldn't. "It doesn't matter. I remember biting him, I remember him taking my pants off and I remember wanting it."

"You remember wanting it, or you remember your succubus side wanting it?"

A tear slid down my cheek. "Does it matter? It's my body that did it. My venom that made Tony…" I gasped out a sob as all of Rider's warnings flooded my mind. "Did you kill him?"

"No, I told you he was safe."

I turned my head to look at Rider, and it took every bit of willpower I had just to force myself to look him in his beautiful blue eyes. "You said if any man ever touched me, you'd kill him. It wasn't his fault, Rider."

"I know, and I didn't kill him. I'm not going to kill him, even though he's asked me to."

I blinked. "What?"

"Danni, the only person who feels as bad as you right now, is him. He thinks he raped you."

"I rape—" bile rose, and I had to force it down. "I raped him."

"No one raped anyone. What happened in that tunnel happened between your succubus and a venom-possessed man. Neither of you would have done that otherwise, and I'm not going to blame either of you. I'm not going to punish either of you for what you are already punishing yourselves for. Neither of you deserves it."

"I don't understand." I shook my head, trying to clear it enough to process what I was hearing and seeing. There was no rage in Rider. If anything, I only saw sadness, but it didn't even seem like it was for himself. "How can you not be angry? Hurt? Betrayed?"

"You didn't betray me. Neither of you did, and how can I be angry when the woman I love and a man I consider family are both so hurt they want to end their own lives all because they think they betrayed me?" He kissed my forehead. "There is nothing about this for me to be jealous of, nothing here for me to take as a betrayal. My only anger is with my brother for doing this to you."

"I should have been stronger. I should have been able to fight it."

"Danni, you haven't even been turned a year. The strength you've shown so far is amazing, but you're not invincible. I'm not letting you take the blame for this. I'm the one who let you go, and I'm the one who sent Tony with you. You could blame me for this. You could blame Jake for not knocking you out after you lured him." The way he said Jake's name was the only hint of anger he showed.

"None of this was your fault. You didn't know it would happen, and I thought I had the lure under control, but then Ramson was there. Knocking me out then would have endangered me. Everything happened so fast... Rider, what happened to Jake?"

"He's alive," Rider all but growled.

I sat up. "What happened after I got out of the rubble? I don't remember anything after biting Tony. How did I get back here? What happened to the others? Where are they?"

Rider sat up and stretched the kinks out of his neck before looking over at the nightstand, where a plastic container of chocolate cupcakes sat. "I had your cupcakes waiting. Did you want to try one?"

"No, I don't want a cupcake now. I need to know what happened to everyone." I could just imagine Daniel's reaction to discovering Tony and me in the situation someone must have found us in. He would blame himself for being so close, yet so far, for allowing what happened. "Where's Daniel? Did he hurt Tony? He has to be losing his mind."

"Daniel doesn't know about Tony," Rider said, "and it's best he never does. Ginger found you. She tried to pull

Tony off of you and she got pretty hurt doing it. Jake killed Ramson and Julie, and found you three. He subdued Tony while Ginger got the hawthorn oil syringe into you and contacted me. Rihanna brought you back first, then Tony. Ginger was taken to the underworld ward for care, but she's perfectly fine now. Day sleep and blood were all she really needed."

Thank goodness for that. It wasn't the first time Ginger had been hurt trying to protect me from myself, and the guilt weighed heavily on me. "How does Daniel not know? What was he told?"

"He was told that you were hurt when those tunnels caved in and you had to be transported back. He's been worried about you, but he hasn't been here yet. There was a lot of damage done in that church, so we had Daniel wait for the cleanup crew I sent in. He's overseeing that as well as staying to see if any snatch and grab teams Ramson sent out prior to him finding the church come back. If any do, we'll bring those men in for questioning and free whoever they grabbed. He's flying back when done. Tony is in a cell, chained with silver and with a silver blade in his leg. I can't let him shift and I can't let him escape. The man wants to die and I can't allow that."

I swallowed down more bile. "And Jake?"

"Jake was here. He came last, after insuring every vampire willing to kill for Ramson was taken care of, and he was upset, blamed himself. I blamed him too, so he didn't stay very long. He got a ride home with Malaika."

Malaika, a witch who could transport people like Rihanna could, and who hadn't been working for Rider at the time, so Jake would have called her in himself. Likely for a quick escape. "Did you kill him?"

"He's alive now," Rider said, avoiding a direct answer. "My concern is you and Tony. You need to get past this. Neither of you wanted it, neither of you were acting of your own free will. Neither of you hurt me."

"Rider."

"Neither of you hurt me. You're half succubus, Danni. I've known this might happen the entire time we've been together, and I love you anyway. The succubus is a part of you, and if this happens, it happens. It doesn't change how I feel about you."

He brushed a lock of hair back from my face. "I'll be honest with you. Had it been Daniel, I would have killed him. But Tony? Tony had no designs on you, and the man is crying and vomiting and trying to kill himself and begging me for forgiveness I've already given him. You're screaming and throwing up and trying to tear your own skin off. Who cares about me right now? I love you and I know you love me, and it kills me to see you so torn up over this. Baby, I don't blame you for a thing. I just want you to forgive yourself because I can't lose you to this."

"I can't lose you. I was so afraid." I fell against him, crying into the crook of his neck as he wrapped his arms around me and held me tight. "I don't deserve you."

"I'm no saint, Danni. I've done terrible things, and I honestly don't deserve you, but I need you, so I push all those horrible things I've done into the back of my mind and bury them, and I move on. That's what I need you to do. That's what I need you and Tony to do."

"Poor Tony." I sniffed as I raised my head and wiped away my tears. "Can I see him?"

"I was hoping you'd say that," Rider said, wiping a thumb over my cheek. "Because I think that might be the only thing to save him."

***

I kept Rider's T-shirt on, but pulled on a pair of jeans and Adidas. I fed first, even though I didn't feel like it, but Rider insisted I drink from him before we left his room. It felt strange, like I'd cheated on him and didn't deserve to be close to him anymore, but if he felt that way, he didn't show it.

He was remarkable, really. The only anger I'd seen in him was when he spoke of Jake, and although he didn't come out and admit it, I was sure he'd done something to the slayer, possibly even killed him. I didn't blame Jake for what happened. I felt sorry for him. After the discussion we'd had about him and Nyla, I knew he understood what Rider and I were going through with this succubus between us. I knew he would blame himself for what happened and feel sick about it because he'd assured us he would keep me safe. I also knew he was a man of honor, and if Rider had, in fact, killed him, it may have actually made both men feel better. And Jake could survive being killed.

Tony couldn't.

None of the guards looked at me strangely as we passed, and I knew they were unaware of what had happened. If any knew Tony was in a cell, they didn't know why. The few people who knew what had happened would never tell a soul, especially not Daniel. Rider might not give Tony his death wish, but Daniel wouldn't have even needed to have been asked. I thanked my lucky stars Ginger had been the one to find us, and Jake had been the one to stop what we were doing. Because Tony had done nothing wrong, and I wouldn't let him die because I'd failed to keep my succubus side in its cage.

My breath left my lungs and my stomach went hollow the moment I saw Tony in his cell. He'd been chained to the bars with thick ropes of silver and a silver knife penetrated his thigh. He was still dressed in what he'd worn in the fight, his clothes still covered in the blood. His arms were outstretched in a crucifix pose, his ankles and wrists bound to the bars so he couldn't move, and his eyes, when they looked up at me, tore a sob from my throat.

"No," he said, and quickly lowered his head, the only thing he could move other than his fingers. "I can't look at you. Not after what I did."

I turned toward Rider and saw moisture coat his eyes

before he turned his face away and sniffed. His body was ramrod straight, his hands shoved in his pants pockets, and I could tell they were tightly fisted.

"Can I go in the cell?"

Rider nodded and looked at the cell door. A second later, I heard the click, and it opened, unlocked by Rider's power.

"No," Tony repeated as I stepped inside the cell. "No, you can't be here. I can't look at you. I can't be around you."

I kept going until I stood in front of Tony and placed my hand over his heart. He sucked in a breath and then let it loose on an avalanche of sobs. "I'm sorry, Danni. I'm so sorry."

Seeing the big, tough guy who showed so little emotion that it was heavily joked about fall apart undid me. I cried with him for several minutes until I could suck it up well enough to speak. "I injected you with venom. The venom made you—it—the venom made it happen. You didn't do anything. You weren't in control."

Tony shook his head. "They pulled me off of you and I fought them. I fought to get back in you. I fought to… to do that to you. I deserve death."

I hated my succubus half. I hated my succubus half, and I hated Selander Ryan for putting it in me. I was going to hunt the bastard down and kill him until no black magic could keep him in existence. Screwing with me was one thing, but now this thing had destroyed an innocent bystander.

"You did nothing to me. It was the venom. I don't even remember it. Do you, Tony?"

He sucked in a breath and looked at me. "I don't have to remember it. I know I did it. I remember being pulled off of you." His face crumpled. "I'm so sorry. I'd never hurt a woman like—"

He couldn't finish what he wanted to say, his entire body shaking in sobs as his head hung low, his shame and guilt too much for him to bear. Too much for me to bear. I couldn't let him keep feeling the guilt of something I had done to him. I remembered Auntie Mo telling me I had to face my demons, and I remembered something I'd learned while reading about succubi.

All right, you greedy, selfish bitch. You want to come out of your cage to play, you're going to do it my way. I turned toward Rider, saw him wiping tears from his eyes as he stood outside the cell. "Do you trust me?"

His brow knitted in a frown, but he nodded. "Always."

"Take him down."

"Danni…"

"I'm not letting him die, but I will not let him live in this pain either. Take him down."

Rider sniffed and did another pass under his eyes before stepping into the cell. His power pulsed as he raised his hand, and the chains broke away from the bars. Tony fell onto his knees and looked up at Rider. He started crying before he crawled over to him and bowed at his feet.

"I'm so sorry, Rider. I'm so, so sorry. Give me death."

"Get up," Rider said, his voice harder than rock. "Get. Up."

Tony slowly rose to a stand, and the moment he straightened before him, Rider pulled him into a tight, one-armed hug. "You are more my brother than my own flesh and blood. You didn't do this to her. She didn't do this to you. This was something horrible that happened to both of you, and there is no blame to be found in either of you."

Tony sobbed against him, clinging onto him for support, and I stood quietly, letting them have their moment, and in that moment, my heart swelled painfully. I didn't deserve Rider, but I was thankful to be loved by him. Every doubt, every stupid jealous thought I'd ever had fled as I watched him console the friend who any other man would have killed in a frenzy of rage. I couldn't fully wrap my mind around how the person who should have been hurt the most was more concerned with easing the pain of the ones who'd caused all the pain. All because he loved that greatly. That purely.

"Sit him down on the cot," I said before I got too lost in emotion to do what I needed to do.

Rider maneuvered Tony over to the cot and stepped away, giving me room.

I crouched before Tony, grabbing his chin when he tried to turn away from me. "Do you think I should die for what happened?"

"What?" His eyes widened. "No. It wasn't your fault. I know you didn't want that. You love Rider. I had the hawthorn oil, but I saw all the blood and I didn't… I didn't…"

"You saw the blood and your only thought was stopping it, keeping me alive," I finished for him, finding it hard to talk through the pain of knowing how I'd rewarded him for trying to save me. "I know you didn't want it either, Tony. The venom made it happen. My venom. I already feel guilty and no matter what Rider says, I'm going to always feel that guilt, but if you try with me, we can get past it. If you end your life, you're ending mine. I've already hurt you. If you take your life, I will have killed you, and I can't live with that."

"What are you saying?"

"Kill yourself, you kill me. I can't go on living with your death on my conscience. Do you want to kill me, Tony?"

His lip quivered as he shook his head no. "I don't want to hurt you or Rider any more than I already have, Danni, but I can't live with knowing what I've done. I can't live with myself. I can't… live."

"You can." I pulled him in for a hug and his body recoiled, so I let him go. "The succubus part of me did this. It made you do what you did, but it has other tricks. What if I could make you forget what happened? Would that be okay with you, Tony, for me to take that memory out of you? Can I try that for you?"

Tony looked past me to where Rider stood. "You can make me forget what I did?"

"I think so. Succubi can do it. I think if I face this evil bitch inside me, I can get her to do it. But only if you want me to. I've violated you enough as it is. I won't violate your mind by taking your memory of what happened unless you give me permission. Do you want me to try?"

He stared at me for a moment, tears leaking from his eyes, and nodded. "Yes, please. Please try. I don't want this in my head."

I didn't want it in his head either. I didn't want it in my head, but it was a lesson I needed to remember. "All right. Just relax, and I'm going to try this."

I turned toward Rider. "I'm going to have a little face-to-face with my succubus, try to get her to do this. I'm not sure how it works. I might have to use the lure to coax him into the right state or even bite him. Just watch me, and if clothes start coming off, knock me the hell out, understand?"

Rider's jaw was tight, but he nodded. "Be careful."

I nodded my response, not sure what else to say, and turned toward Tony. I held his hands in mine as I sat cross-legged on the floor in front of him, closed my eyes, and summoned my succubus.

Hey, bitch. You've been a bad girl.

I've been a very bad girl, my succubus side purred. *And it felt so good... until your friends stopped me from getting a soul. His tasted good too. Good guys have delicious souls.*

He's my friend. You made me attack my friend. I could have killed him.

You kept teasing me.

I wasn't teasing you. You just had to be patient. I will give you all the sex you want, but it has to be with the man I love. I was trying to give you blood and violence. We were in the middle of a freaking battle. That should have been enough for you.

You keep taking me out and not letting me play.

You don't do what you're told. And as long as you don't, I'm leaving you in your cage.

You can't hold me forever.

Wanna bet? I will make it my life's work to keep you caged, bitch. After what you've done to my friend, after you could have destroyed my relationship with the man I love? Fuck you. I'll find a way to kill you, even if it kills me.

That's a little extreme. We can come to an agreement. I know what you want.

I sensed the fear in my succubus side and fought a smile. I couldn't let the bitch know I had her. *Is this another of those things you say I want but you really want, like sex with strangers and souls?*

No. I can make your friend forget what happened.

How can I trust you not to do the same thing to him? I won't let you hurt him again.

You don't have to trust me. Just trust I don't want you to kill yourself and kill me too.

Can you really do it?

Of course. I just need you to give me some room to work. I need to lure him so I can get in his mind.

No biting?

No biting. It may take some time. Memories are harder to manipulate than emotions. But I can do it.

I opened my eyes and took a deep breath. "Do it."

CHAPTER TWENTY-ONE

"Danni."

I opened my eyes to see Rider looming over me. I was cradled in his arms on the floor of the cell. Tony was on the cot, knocked out.

"I'm all right. What day is it?"

"It's still New Year's Eve, but whatever the hell you were doing, you were doing it for hours. I thought you were going to miss out on my New Year's Eve surprise I promised you."

He was still giving me a surprise after all that had happened? The man must really love me. I wasn't sure how I'd been so lucky to win the lottery with him, but I was thankful for it. And I was thankful the evil thing inside me had a few benefits.

"Get that knife out of Tony's leg."

Rider looked over at his friend. "If he can shift, he can hurt himself."

"When he wakes up, he's going to think he's in here because he saw Jake feeding me and he thought my succubus had risen and Jake was going to... you know. He attacked him. They fought and Jake nearly killed him, but brought him back here and you threw him in a cell when he wouldn't cool down."

Rider frowned down at me. "You altered his memory? I thought you were just going to remove it."

"That would have left an unexplainable black hole. The succubus made a whole new memory for him. All we have to do is make sure the others who were there know to go along with it and Tony will be fine. He'll never know what really happened."

"Damn, that's a relief." Rider took the blade out of Tony's leg and licked the wound left behind since Tony was unconscious, unable to shift shape to heal, and we wouldn't want to leave him bleeding out. "How long will he be out?"

"I'm not sure."

Rider wiped the blade on his pant leg and reached down to help me up. "Are you all right? You fainted and you're pale."

"What else is new?" I asked as I got to my feet with his help and waited for the room to stop spinning before we left the cell. "I'm fine though. I think I might have multiple personality disorder, but I'm fine."

Rider locked the cell door with his mind and placed the knife on the table outside it before pulling me into his arms. "We could try the same thing for you, you know. Your succubus side fights my power, but maybe while you sleep I can try to get in there and—"

"No. I need to remember this so I know what can happen. I need to remember this every time you try to warn me about something and my stubborn idiocy takes over. And I need the rage. I'm going to find Selander Ryan and I'm going to kill him. I'm not just going to kill him; I'm going to destroy every particle of him, every atom, every... whatever. I was never great in science or biology, but you know what I mean. I'm going to end him."

Rider pulled back and kissed my forehead. "I'm going to help you, and this time we're going to do it right."

Damn fucking straight we were, because I was going to

be the one to do it and I wasn't leaving anything of Selander Ryan behind to haunt us. My succubus side wanted blood? She wanted a soul? I'd give it to her.

"Shit," Rider muttered, and grabbed my hand. "Come on. It's almost midnight."

"And?" I said as he pulled me out of the room and sprinted through the hall, toward the stairwell.

"It's New Year's Eve. We have to be on the roof at midnight."

"We do?"

I had no idea what Rider was up to and he didn't say anything else as we entered the stairwell and made a mad dash for the top, but I knew whatever he had planned, I didn't deserve it.

The air was frigid as we stepped out onto the roof and neither of us wore coats, but I wouldn't complain. Already, there were fireworks in the sky for miles. It was customary in Louisville for obnoxious neighbors to light the damn things from June through September for the Fourth of July, so expecting them to wait until midnight on New Year's Eve was futile.

"Stand right here," Rider said, positioning me on the center of the flat rooftop, "and watch up there."

I looked where he pointed, into the inky night sky, and took in a breath of cold air as he backed away from me. I didn't have to wait very long before my vampiric hearing picked up the cheers from the bar below and the people in the surrounding buildings along with a sudden onslaught of fireworks and gunshots. It was midnight. Officially New Year's Day.

Fireworks of every color burst through the sky, but my gaze locked on to one set that seemed bolder, brighter. Fireworks that weren't fireworks, because they had clearly been created by magic.

Red and pink hearts lit up the sky before morphing into purple bats that made me giggle before they disintegrated in a shower of rainbow sparkles to be replaced by a question spelled out in magical white fireworks: *Danni Keller, will you marry me?*

I gasped, nearly choking on the frigid air that rushed into my lungs, burning my throat with its iciness, and turned to see Rider down on one knee, holding the most beautiful ring I'd ever seen out to me. It had a gold filigree band with a blood-red heart-shaped jewel the size of my pinky nail in the center, surrounded by smaller diamonds.

My legs gave out. They just turned to pudding and down I went, falling in a heap as tears spilled from my eyes. "Still? After everything that's happened?"

"Still," Rider said. "After everything that's happened and everything that will happen. No matter what."

I swiped away the tears freezing on my cheeks. "I thought you said we could never marry. Your enemies would know how you feel about me and use that against you."

"My enemies already know. Everyone knows because what I feel for you can't be hidden. I love you, Danni, and there's nothing or no one I won't fight for you, so if putting a ring on your finger brings out more enemies, let them come. We can take them together. I don't ever want you to question what I feel. This is what I feel. I love you for eternity and I want you to be my wife here and wherever we end up in the afterlife."

I lost it, dissolving into tears. The nightmare I'd been so afraid of happening, happened, and I hadn't lost him. Instead, I'd gained something I'd accepted I would never have.

Rider pulled me close, wrapping his arms around me, providing much needed body heat, and just held me while I cried. I didn't know how much time had passed, but when we started shivering from the cold, he pulled back to look into my eyes. "Danni?"

"Yes?"

He looked up at the sky where the magic fireworks had been and grinned before looking back at me. "I asked you a question."

"Yes." I laughed. "You already knew it would be a yes. It's always been yes."

***

"Fucking hell," I muttered, wiping my mouth before I flushed the toilet and grabbed the Listerine. I rinsed out my mouth and brushed my teeth, took a moment to stare at my reflection while I gripped the edge of the sink.

It made no damn sense. I kept craving food, but then I kept throwing it up. Either I could eat the stuff or I couldn't, but why the hell was I craving it if it kept making me sick? I took a breath, waited to make sure I wasn't going to hurl again, and exited the bathroom to see Rider standing outside.

"Get dressed. We're going to see Nannette."

"Rider, I'm fine."

"It's been a week, Danni. You haven't summoned your succubus power once in all this time. You haven't had any visions or tried to force them. You haven't interrogated anyone or trained hard. Yet you keep craving food just to throw it up, and you keep getting pulled under by the day sleep right at the crack of dawn and waking up sick. You're lightheaded, nauseous, and you're pale. This isn't normal and there's no logical reason for it, so you're going to the hospital. No discussion. Get dressed."

Everything Rider said was true. I'd thought it was my nerves that caused the nausea. Tony had awakened with the altered memory my succubus side had planted in his mind, and the secret of what had really happened had been kept from Daniel, but I knew what happened. Even though I had therapy sessions with Eliza to help me through it, I still felt the guilt and shame.

Rider and I were going to get married, but I was hesitating over the wedding date. I couldn't bring myself to sleep with him, not after what I'd done, no matter how many assurances he gave me that what happened was in the past and he loved me. I couldn't get what happened out of my mind, and that was surely why I was craving the comfort foods, even though I kept throwing them back up. As for the fatigue, I wasn't sure where that came from. Stress, maybe? Pacitti was still out there and I was worried about Angel and her mother on top of everything else. It had to be stress.

But Rider wasn't budging on the matter, so I dressed in leggings and a comfortable sweater and gave Kutya several pets and scratches before I could get out of the room. The big pup had seemed to sense what I was going through. He practically lived with his head in my lap. It was as if he were guarding me the way he refused to leave me, always with his head in my lap, keeping me safe.

We made it to the hospital without any trouble, the normal entourage along for the ride. Daniel had ridden along with Hank and Rome in the SUV behind us. He seemed worried about me too. I supposed it wasn't normal for a vampire to be so sick and lethargic, but really, they shouldn't have worried so much. I just needed to get a grip and come to terms with what had happened. Maybe quit avoiding Tony.

Nannette poked and prodded and asked a zillion questions. Then she put me in the big contraption that scanned me head to toe, looking for anything a normal exam may have missed. I noticed her expression seemed pinched when I got out of it, but she said nothing as she led me back to the exam room, Rider along with us.

"I'm going to have Marigold check her," she said, "but all seems fine so far. Nerves can make anyone queasy, even a vampire, and Danni's been through a lot. Excuse me for a moment."

Unease grew in my gut as Nannette ducked out of the exam room, leaving Rider and me alone inside it. Something was off with her.

"How do you feel now?" Rider asked.

Queasier than ever, I thought, my stomach doing flips. "All right. I'm telling you, it's probably just a case of me eating what I shouldn't."

"If you shouldn't be eating it, your body shouldn't be craving it," Rider said, not for the first time. "This is probably some weird hybrid thing. Nannette will figure it out. Hopefully soon. I hate seeing you feel so bad."

"You're too good to me." I forced a smile through the nerves consuming me. "Don't worry so much about me. You take good care of me and I'll survive a little nausea and tiredness. It's all going to be fine."

I felt Rider's power pulse as his head dipped a little to the side, and I knew someone was speaking to him telepathically.

He frowned before closing the distance between us and kissed my forehead. "I have to go check with the guys. We might have an issue in the parking garage. I'll be right back."

The door had barely closed behind him before Nannette and Marigold entered, walking fast.

"We have to make this quick," Nannette said. "Lie down, Danni."

Apparently, I didn't do so quick enough because she gently pushed me down, getting me flat on my back, and shushed me when I tried to ask what was going on.

Marigold, the older witch with the friendly features who'd examined me on previous visits, held her hands over my midsection and seemed to scan me with them as soft light came from her palms. Her hands stilled over me. She looked up at Nannette, and nodded.

"Oh, hell," Nannette said, her voice barely above a whisper, her eyes full of an emotion that scared the bajeezus out of me.

I sat up, not caring if they wanted me to or not. "What is it? What's wrong?"

"Oh, Danni."

The compassion in her tone was too much. Icy cold

fear snaked up my spine. "What is it, Nannette? Tell me."

She took a deep breath. "You're pregnant."

DANNI WILL RETURN IN 2024
Until then, look for the new HELLACIOUS series
debuting in June 2023

ABOUT THE AUTHOR

Crystal-Rain Love is a romance author specializing in paranormal, suspense, and contemporary subgenres. Her author career began by winning a contest to be one of Sapphire Blue Publishing's debut authors in 2008. She snagged a multi-book contract with Imajinn Books that same year, going on to be published by The Wild Rose Press and eventually venturing out into indie publishing. She resides in the South with her three children and enough pets to host a petting zoo. When she's not writing, she can usually be found creating unique 3D cakes, hiking, reading, or spending way too much time on Facebook. She also writes contemporary romance as Shylyn Ray. Find out more about her at www.crystalrainlove.com

Printed in Great Britain
by Amazon